From Pain To Love

My Heart Belongs to Him

KEA SIMONE

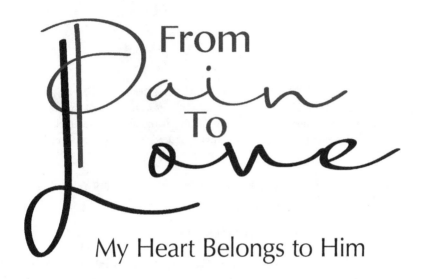

FROM PAIN TO LOVE: MY HEART BELONGS TO HIM
This book is a work of fiction. Names, characters, places, and incidents are the product of the author's imagination or are used fictitiously. Any resemblance to actual events, locales, or persons, living or dead, is strictly coincidental.

ISBN: 978-0-578-67023-2

Published by Kea Simone
Detroit, MI

Printed in the United States of America
First Edition June 2020

Cover Design by: Make Your Mark Publishing Solutions
Interior Layout by: Make Your Mark Publishing Solutions
Editing: Make Your Mark Publishing Solutions

Acknowledgments

I WOULD LIKE TO acknowledge Monique D. Mensah with Make Your Mark Publishing Solutions for talking me off the ledge. When I was ready to call it quits, you inspired me to keep going. Thanks for keeping me on track throughout the self-publishing process. Monique, I am forever thankful for all of your hard work.

I would like to also acknowledge De'dra Y. Armstrong for offering to work with me one on one. Although the process was long, you hung in there with me. De'dra, thanks for helping me bring my vision to life. You went over and beyond!

Dedication

To my favorite lady, Anna Ruth Shannon. I thank God for blessing me with you as my granny.

Chapter 1

Kismet

HER MOUTH WAS MOVING, but I couldn't hear a thing coming out of it. I think I went temporarily deaf. I was there but not really. As if the credits of a movie were rolling in front of me, I saw the names of all the guys I had been intimate with over the past twelve years. Chris. Tommy. The Dom. Ziek. The one-night stands with guys whose names I could no longer recall. And David, of course. *But which one?*

"Mrs. Falls," Dr. Parker called out, raising her voice seemingly an octave or two.

I looked up. I still could not muster the strength to speak. My jaws felt locked. A slow stream of tears cascaded down my cheeks, and a warm sensation escaped my ears. *Is this what they call an out-of-body experience?*

"Mrs. Falls, I know it's not the news you wanted to hear. But again, HIV isn't the death sentence it used to be. We've made a lot of advances in medicine, and people are leading normal lives today."

Nothing Dr. Parker said to me could soothe the pain I felt in that moment. The heaviness in my chest felt as though someone had loaded fifty bricks on top of me.

"Now, I know you have a lot of questions, and I'm prepared to answer them for you," she said as she tapped her pen on her desk.

"I need another minute," I managed to utter as I lifted my body and leaned back in the chair.

"Sure. Take all the time you need," Dr. Parker said as she closed my file and laid it on her desk.

Yes, I had a lot of questions, and although I just wanted to lament in my sorrow, I knew doing so wasn't going to provide me with the answers I needed, and neither were they going to do anything about the fact that a potentially deadly virus was now running through my veins. After I managed to compose myself somewhat, I straightened my posture in the chair. "So, what now?"

"Well, since I'm just your fertility specialist, you'll need to go see both your primary care physician and an infectious disease specialist who's specially trained to treat people with HIV and AIDS."

I shook my head, still in utter shock and disbelief. Again, those haunting thoughts of being dirty, damaged goods began to race through my mind. Destiny had chlamydia. Destiny is infertile. Destiny has HIV. Here I was, only thirty-five years old, childless, basically parentless, and had been going back and forth with a man who had more faces than a Rubik's Cube. *How am I going to recover from this? I just wanna die!*

"Destiny, listen. Having HIV doesn't mean you can't have a baby," Dr. Parker said.

"Can't HIV be transmitted to the baby during pregnancy?"

"Risk of transmission is typically low. But there are a lot of things to consider."

"Like what?" I said as I licked the salty savor from my lips.

"Well, we'll need to know what your numbers look—"

"Numbers? What do you mean, numbers?" I said, cutting her off.

"Your T-cell count and your viral load."

I raised my eyebrows. I wasn't familiar with any of the medical terminology Dr. Parker was using.

"I know they don't mean anything to you now, but in a

nutshell, they're just what the specialist looks at to monitor the disease progression. So again, conceptually speaking, it's very possible to get pregnant and have a baby. With HIV, although the risk for transmission is low, it still exists. So it's something you will need to consider."

"So, what is your best medical advice for me? To not have a baby?"

"I can't make that decision for you, Mrs. Falls. That's something you'll need to discuss with your husband and your infectious disease specialist."

Dr. Parker went into a whole different spiel about living with HIV, but my mind could no longer absorb the volume of information she was sharing. In my head, I started rehearsing the conversations I knew I had to have—with David, my best friend, Shonte, with my deceased grandmother, Honey, at her gravesite, and most importantly, with God, at home on my knees.

When Dr. Parker finished, she asked again, "Do you have any more questions?"

"Am I gonna die?"

She paused and then tapped her pen on her desk once again before answering. "It's probably unlikely, but it depends. It depends on how long you've had the virus, how much damage it's done to your body, and if we can keep it from wreaking havoc on your body. And it also depends on your lifestyle—the choices in food, exercise, and medication compliance. There's a whole lot of other factors to consider." She paused again. "Here. You'll probably need this," she said, handing me a business card she pulled from a box on her desk.

I took the card and tucked it into my purse without reading it.

"Call her office and set up an appointment. She offers one-on-one counseling, and she runs a very good support group."

I pulled the card out of my purse and skimmed it. The wording read: Dr. Angela Fleming, MD, Psychiatry. "I'm not crazy," I snapped. "I've got a disease, but I'm not crazy."

"Mrs. Falls, I understand that. No one said you were crazy. But I've been in practice long enough to have seen countless women sitting across from me just like you are today. These women leave my office refusing psychological care only to end up either committing suicide or living with severe depression. Don't let that be you."

I looked up at Dr. Parker. I could feel her genuine compassion. But it wasn't her compassion and empathy I was longing for at that moment. Sitting in Dr. Parker's office was that helpless little girl again, longing for the love, acceptance, and support from both her mother and her father.

"Don't hesitate to call her if you need to talk. She can also prescribe you medication to help you deal with this."

The remaining twenty minutes or so of the appointment was a complete blur. All I remember is making it to my car in the parking lot of the doctor's office, getting in, and slumping over the steering wheel.

My life, by far, was never picturesque. I can't even say I came from a broken home, because right out of the gate, my parents didn't want me. I ended up living with my grandmother, who I affectionately called Honey, as we all did in our family. I did some identity exploring in my days, but that's typical for a young woman who's just searching for the love of her absent father. But I found myself, on this day, at an all-time low. Finding my way through this maze would be one of the most difficult challenges I had to face.

Finding out how I landed here would require deep analysis, a willingness to be emotionally transparent, and the demonstration of courage under fire. Exploring the distant past is a must; it is where it all began.

Chapter 2

Roots

THE CRAWFORD FAMILY, THE maternal side of my family, has many secrets ... secrets most people would like to forget. The saying, "You don't know where you're going if you don't know where you've been" rings true for me. The woman I affectionately called Honey for most of my life, was actually my grandmother and the woman who raised me. Honey wasn't her real name, of course. It was the name she inherited from her brother Gerald after having her hair dyed blonde at the salon one day. Her brother gave her the nickname as a joke, but for some reason, the nickname stuck. I think I heard the story close to one hundred times. But it always fascinated me. And to tell the truth, I don't think I could ever grow bored of hearing it.

From what I've been told, my grandfather was a pedophile by the name of Albert Percy Crawford, Sr. Together, Honey and Albert had five children—Roz, Albert Jr., Shannon, Lynn, and Donitra. On the outside, they appeared to be a normal family. But inside the walls of their home, chaos of just about every kind took place. From sexual molestation that occurred at the hands of my grandfather, to the promiscuity of the Crawford girls, to the unveiling of a murderer, my uncle Albert Jr., the dysfunction in the Crawford family ran rampant.

I'm not sure if it was denial or embarrassment, but Honey's

mantra was "Keep family business inside these walls." And for the most part, it stayed there. I mean, at least that's the lie they all wanted to believe. The sexual trauma Roz and Shannon endured evidently caused them to live the promiscuous street life. Both Roz and Shannon had babies when they were in their teens. I was the product of Shannon's promiscuity. And keeping family business between the walls was not limited to the sexual abuse going on. Eavesdropping on one of Honey's conversations with her best friend, Cora, I learned the real reason why Albert Jr. "went away." He had killed the next-door neighbor during the course of a heated argument over something as mundane as the loud sound of Albert Jr.'s motorcycle muffler. I was too young to fully understand why the police had placed yellow tape around the Rileys' house that humid summer night. All I remember was being confined to the house for what seemed like an eternity. I remember Honey "going to see her baby" on various occasions. But it wasn't until I was a teenager that I really understood that it meant she would drive to Ionia, Michigan, stay overnight, then drive back to Detroit the next day. Albert Jr. being a murderer was never a topic of conversation … ever.

My mother, who I've always called by her first name, Shannon, got pregnant with me at the age of fifteen. By the time Honey figured out she was pregnant, Shannon was too far along for an abortion. You know, the back-in-the-day type. My father was a young man by the name of Ed Harrison. Shannon, they say, did not look her age. Her beauty was so captivating that she received her share of cat calls from men of all ages. I guess Ed, who I never called Dad but always by his first name, was no different than those cat-calling men who couldn't resist the temptation. Seduced by Shannon's beauty, he pursued her, seduced her, and she became pregnant. He was four years older than my mother, so Honey wanted to file statutory rape charges against him. But the damage had already been done—Shannon was pregnant and my scheduled arrival into the world was just under four months away.

Although Shannon was pregnant, there was no shotgun wedding planned. Instead, from what I was told, after Honey's threat, Ed moved on and started dating other girls in the same city. Yep, right under Shannon's nose. But when Shannon found out, which was byway of Roz's big mouth, Shannon showed up at a party and announced her pregnancy to Ed in front of his new love interest. Being the immature and irresponsible man he was, Ed's embarrassment and anger got the best of him. In uncontrollable anger and embarrassment, he dragged Shannon off the dancefloor into a nearby bathroom and beat her until she was unconscious.

The doctors didn't think I would live, initially; they were almost certain that Shannon would miscarry within twenty-four hours. I guess God had other plans because I lived. On September 26, 1976, Shannon gave birth to a five-pound, seven-ounce baby girl. She named her Destiny … Destiny Monique Crawford. But that was about all Shannon ever really did for me—gave me life. The spitting image of my father, Shannon wanted no parts of me, and she didn't try to conceal her hatred for him. Shannon never took the time to get to know me. Even as a child, when we both lived with Honey, Shannon always seemed a little standoff-ish. She never really demonstrated that warm, motherly love that most mothers show. And together, it all played out in my childhood and progressed well into my adulthood, manifesting itself in my behavior and especially in my choices in men. I remember the day she came home and told Honey she met the man of her dreams and was going to move in with him and get married. I think I was six years old when that happped. After an argument with Honey about it, Shannon had no choice but to pack her things and move out. It was the first time I heard Honey curse. Well … nearly curse.

"So, you gonna go shack up with some man you met two seconds ago?" Honey said with her hands on her hips, almost daring Shannon to say yes.

"Mama, I didn't meet him two seconds ago. I met him a couple of months ago."

"So why have you been hiding him?"

"Mama, I ain't been hiding him," Shannon said, puckering her lips to color them with hot pink lipstick.

"Well, he sure as heck ain't been around here. A man that won't come around your family got something to hide."

"It's not that he won't come around my family. I don't want him to."

"Why? You ashamed of your family or something?"

Shannon didn't say a word, but the expression on her face told it all.

Honey walked closer to Shannon. "What are you ashamed of, Shannon? We might not be rich, but this ain't no raggedy house. It's well-kept and clean. We got a sofa to sit on, there's a bed in every bedroom, there's a table and chairs in the kitchen, and there's a whole bunch of food in the fridge and pantry. So I wanna know what in the world you got to be ashamed of around here?"

Honey's entire face was beet red. Then it dawned on Honey. "Oh, don't tell me ... Don't tell me you're ashamed of your own baby? Please, Shannon, don't tell me you are ashamed of that beautiful baby!"

"I—" Shannon attempted to explain.

"I don't wanna hear it! You pack your stuff and get outta my house!"

That's how I was left behind with Honey. Unwilling to risk losing her man, Shannon packed her things and left that night. Whatever she couldn't fit into her little purple flowered suitcase that night, she fetched some time later. Honey would always make sure I was over someone's house or asleep when Shannon stopped by. She wasn't allowed to see me or speak to me for a good six months. Honey, bless her soul, thought she was protecting me. But just like the damage had already been done when Honey found out about Shannon being pregnant with me, the damage to my soul had already been done.

So as the story goes, Shannon rode off into the sunset with

Craig Vanderbilt, leaving her past, including me, behind. To this day, Craig is her world. The sun rises and sets on him.

Ebony toned, chiseled cheekbones, and jet-black, wavy hair, Craig was always a lady magnet, and he's even been known to stray a time or two. In her quest to prove that she can keep a man, Shannon has dealt with his indiscretions in her own way and stuck by her man, as they say. As a matter of fact, she'd almost invite you to the boxing ring if you tried to bad mouth "her man." That's what she called him—*my man*!

Shannon and Craig did eventually marry and have children, sons—Tyrell and Javon. I'm eight years older than Tyrell and eleven years older than Javon. I tried to have a close relationship with my siblings, but eventually the efforts to do so grew tiresome, so the relationship faded. It was difficult seeing Shannon openly adore and nearly obsess over my brothers but barely even acknowledge my presence. From their skin tone to their curly hair, Shannon often bragged on them. She would often play in their hair as they lay face down in her lap as infants.

Honey didn't like how Shannon treated me, so she tried her best to give me what she often referred to as "a life that was a lot better than any real life I've ever known." I never said anything, but to an emotionally damaged child, that rationale fell on deaf ears. I wasn't consumed with things; I just wanted to be loved and accepted by the two people who created me—Shannon Crawford and Ed Harrison.

I am a spitting image of my father, from skin complexion, especially the red undertones, to his eyes, nose, ears, and smile. I look like Ed Harrison. I even have fingers like my father. Shannon often reminded me how much she hated Ed.

"He was a coward! He didn't want me, and he certainly didn't want you!" she would say whenever she was frustrated or angry.

When I was fourteen, I had finally had enough of her dogging Ed out, and I snapped back one of those times.

"He's a coward. Only a coward gets on a train and goes back to Alabama, so he doesn't have to sign your birth certificate."

"Why are you always talking bad about my father?" I asked.

"I'm telling you the truth. He never even paid a dime of child support for you!"

"Shannon, stop filling that child's head with your hurt and anger. Destiny's a smart girl. She can decide for herself who Ed is and is not," Honey said, interjecting herself into the conversation.

"Mama, I'm tryna have a talk with my daughter. She's defending a man that doesn't even know or care if she ate breakfast this morning."

"You don't know or care what I eat for breakfast either!" I yelled back at Shannon.

Before I knew it, Shannon swung a left hook, and her fist landed square in my mouth. My immediate reaction was to look at Honey. I wanted her to give me the nonverbal cue to strike Shannon back. Somehow, I knew Honey wasn't going to do that. I didn't want Shannon to see me cry, so I brushed past her and ran to the half-bathroom just past the kitchen back door. I could still hear the two of them going back and forth. Leaning over the freestanding sink, I ran cool water and began to bathe my busted lip, listening in on the ensuing conversation.

"Why did you hit that girl?" Honey said.

"She got a smart mouth, that's why," Shannon retorted.

"Her mouth ain't no smarter than yours was at her age. You want that child to carry your hurt and anger, and it's too much. You already moved on with your life, so why you wanna keep dogging the poor man?"

Whenever Honey's tone changed, you'd better listen, and that's just what Shannon did. I didn't hear her go back and forth with Honey like she did on several other occasions. Honey was probably angrier at Shannon for striking me and drawing blood more than anything else.

"Shannon, that girl's gonna love her daddy no matter what,

just as she loves you. So, like I said, stop feeding that child your hurt and anger. If you hadn't been so fast—" Honey stopped in the middle of her sentence.

I managed to stop the bleeding and went back into the kitchen to retrieve some ice to help bring the swelling down some. I didn't even want to look at Shannon, but I had to pass her to get to the freezer.

"Don't let me get started," Honey said, swinging the dish towel she was using to dry the dishes over her right shoulder.

I knew where Honey was going with that statement. And even though Shannon treated me like an outcast, she was still my mother and I loved her. The same went for Ed. Even though he lied time after time, from promises to pick me up and take me to see a movie, to calls telling me to wait for the postman to come because he "supposedly" mailed my Christmas gifts, he was still my father and I loved him. Regardless of their shortcomings, they were still my parents. It's something about the blood that runs through your veins that connects you to your mother and father. That very same blood bonds you to them no matter what they do. I believe this is what they refer to as unconditional love. Regardless of how many times they messed up, I still loved them deep down.

Nevertheless, the absence of both my parents, especially my father, taught me to put up walls when I was growing up to try to protect my heart. The absence of my father, however, taught me that men do not stay. At a young age, I knew what abandonment looked like, felt like, and tasted like.

Living with Honey and my aunties was adventurous in more ways than one. I was treated like a younger sister, for the most part. Honey was very protective of me. If she even thought someone wasn't doing right by me, she went right into protective mode. She'd confront anybody and everybody.

Who lived with us depended on time and circumstances. My grandfather died when I was one year old. Albert Jr. moved to Lexington, Kentucky after he was released from jail. We didn't see much of him. Shannon was doing her own thing, living high on the horse with Craig in Southfield, Michigan.

I was very close to my auntie Donitra; she's only nine years older than I am. Out of all her siblings, she's the most educated and the most logical thinking. Breaking away from generational curses, Donitra escaped the possibility of being like her two older sisters or any of the other women in our family. She worked hard and put herself through college. She graduated from the University of California, Berkley at the top of her class with a Master of Journalism degree. My world crumbled when she announced she was not moving back home after she finished college. Besides Honey, Auntie Donitra was the person closest to being a mother to me.

"You can come and stay with me in the summer," she promised me on multiple occasions. And she made good on those promises a couple of times.

Auntie Lynn was the quiet one out of the bunch. Like Auntie Donitra, she didn't move back home after college either. Instead, she made her home in Atlanta, after graduating from Spellman College.

After losing their home to foreclosure, Roz and her husband, Cliff, moved into the basement of Honey's house. Cliff, as they say, was good with his hands. He finished the basement, putting up wood paneling, installing carpet, laying the plumbing, and a bunch of other stuff, turning it into a full two-bedroom apartment. He wasn't really Auntie Roz's type, if you asked me. He had a butterscotch complexion, his face was covered with moles, his eyes protruded from their sockets; he had a blunt nose, and he had soft, reddish-brown hair. Now Roz, on the other hand, was the epitome of beauty, with a mahogany skin tone, almond-shaped eyes, a jet-black, short pixie cut, and legs for days. Auntie Roz and Cliff's toxic relationship was poison to everyone living under the same roof. They were constantly arguing and fighting. Cliff loved to smoke weed and get all paranoid afterward, accusing Auntie Roz of cheating on him. He struck her a time or two, causing Honey, who was starting to slow down both physically and emotionally, to call the cops. He looked like a complete fool when the cops came to the house one night. While I was supposed to go to my room, I didn't. Instead, I crouched down in the darkness at the top of the stairs and listened in on the exchange between Auntie Roz, Cliff, Honey, and the police.

"Roz, I know you love him, but he gotta go," Honey declared. "I can't have nobody in my house threatening to burn it down."

"I didn't threaten to burn the house down, Ms. Honey," Cliff tried to explain.

"Don't call me Ms. Honey, either. Roz, he gotta go," Honey said.

"Mama, just give him one last chance. He's upset. He'll calm down in a minute, right, Cliff?"

"Look, we got a call that there was an arson threat made. We take those calls very seriously. I'm sorry, sir, but you're gonna have to come with us tonight," one of the police officers said. I could hear the clicking sound of the handcuffs being placed on Cliff's wrists.

I crawled into my room, and from my window, watched the police place Cliff in the back of their cruiser and drive off with blinking blue lights. Auntie Roz must have cried herself into oblivion that night. From my room, I could hear her wailing on and off throughout the night. She didn't get up until three o'clock in the afternoon the next day.

A few days after that incident, I got a call from Auntie Donitra. She told me she was sending for me to come visit her. I couldn't pack my suitcase fast enough. Getting away from all the chaos was just what I needed.

Chapter 3

Not Quite a Woman

WHILE I WAS AWAY visiting Auntie Donitra during the summer of 1993, Honey moved the family to our new house on Wayburn Street, near Outer Drive on the Eastside. We moved around a lot, never staying in one place too long. Honey's brother once joked, a person could never write our address in ink because we'd be sure to move before the ink on the lease could dry. Although it was a joke, it was the truth. Moving around with a lack of stability was our thing early on.

Chris was the first person I met on Wayburn Street. To make a long story short, Chris wasn't the most attractive young man. He kind of looked like the lead singer, K-Ci, from the R&B group Jodeci. I had my first sexual encounter with Chris. I was seventeen at the time. Our relationship didn't last long; it took a few unfortunate incidents for me to finally figure out he was not right for me. I should have walked away when I saw those little bugs moving around in my pubic hairs, but I didn't. I decided to confront Chris with what I saw.

"I need to talk to you," I said, walking up to him just as he was about to make a free throw. He was on the basketball court playing with a couple of guys in the neighborhood. That was their thing … their daytime thing. It was summertime, and the guys would hang out in the park during the day then do their thing in the evenings.

And doing their thing ranged from hanging out with girls to hanging out at Royal Skateland or Eastland Mall. I was getting a little older and Honey was giving me a little breathing room.

"Don't you see I'm in the middle of making a free throw?" Chris said, agitated that I had interrupted his concentration.

"But I need to talk to you," I said, refusing to move.

After realizing I wasn't going to move, he threw the ball to one of his boys. "Man, I'll be right back. Let me handle something right quick," he said, grabbing me by the hand and ushering me to the side of the court.

"I went to the clinic today."

"And?" he said, wiping the sweat from his forehead.

"They said I got crabs."

"Crabs?" he asked as though he'd never heard of the STD.

"Yeah, crabs. Those little things that crawl around in your pubic hairs."

"Man, I don't know what you're talking about 'cause I ain't got that mess."

"Chris, then tell me how I got it?"

"I don't know how you got it. Can't you get it from using public toilets?"

Although I knew he was lying, because I was a virgin when I met him, I started questioning myself for a moment. That is, questioning whether I should have confronted him in the first place.

"So what else did they say?" Chris said, now looking as though he actually cared.

"They gave me some special shampoo and cream for the itching."

"So you gone be good?"

"I guess," I said, foolishly falling for his game.

"All right. Let me finish up this game, and I'll stop by your house later."

And that's all it took. I was ready to go for another ride

on the merry-go-round with Chris. I was repeating Shannon's relationship pattern. I had a man, and I didn't want to lose him. At the same time, I was another victim of the Thomas generational curse. The Thomases were Honey's side of the family. All of the Thomas women had bad track records with men. In this regard, the women chose men who were liars, cheaters, rapists, etcetera, etcetera.

I left Chris on the basketball court with his boys and walked home. When I turned the corner at the top of our street, I could see Shannon's car in the driveway. I debated whether I should go home or make my way back to the court to watch the guys finish their game. I dreaded being in the same room with Shannon because the tension was always present. Even if she and I didn't engage in a verbal clash, our spirits didn't agree. But I was tired from all the stress and anxiety I had endured, so I decided to go on home. As far as Shannon was concerned, silence was the best defense. Honey really hated seeing us go at it, so to appease Honey, I bit my tongue on more occasions than I would like to remember.

Before I could get through the door good, Shannon approached me with a barrage of questions. "Where has your fast tail been? Do you know what time it is? You been with that little nasty boy down the road, ain'tcha?"

I rolled my eyes. "Where's Honey?" I asked as I walked briskly past Shannon.

"I know you hear me talking to you," Shannon said, trying to block me from going upstairs.

"I don't have to answer to you," I said, squeezing past her.

"Oh, yes you do. I'm still your mother," Shannon said, following me.

If I could have had it my way, I wouldn't have said another word to her that night. I reached for my doorknob and flung the door open. Shannon sounded like the teacher on Charlie Brown. I had totally tuned her out until I heard her say, "You ain't slick. I know your fast tail went to the doctor today."

How in the world does she know that?!

"Don't look shocked now. Yeah, your cousin Nicole called me and told me. She thinks you're pregnant."

"Nicole needs to mind her business," I said, taking off my jacket. Nicole was my auntie Roz's daughter, who was only two years older than me. I was fuming that she had the audacity to tell my business. I didn't realize I hadn't answered Shannon's question.

"So are you?"

"No, I'm not pregnant. But if I was, so what," I snapped.

"Then why did you need to go to the doctor?" she probed.

"Where is Honey?" I questioned for the second time.

"Okay, so you want to play with me. I'm about to call the doctor," Shannon threatened, storming past me and back downstairs.

Not only did the day not begin right by having to go to the doctor and find out I had a creepy STD, but it was going further south, with Shannon on the phone with the doctor's office screaming at the top of her lungs because they wouldn't release my medical information to her. The last thing I heard was her curse them out and threaten legal action before slamming the phone's receiver down. I closed my bedroom door and locked it.

At some point during the summer, usually at the end of July, all the grandchildren would spend time at Honey's house. The house was always packed, but we had so much fun. Although Craig's niece, Tamyah, was not blood related, Honey welcomed her. After all, Shannon was her aunt, albeit through marriage. Tamyah, who I often referred to as my twin from another mother, and I were very close. She had a golden-brown complexion with freckles and sandy brown hair. She went by the nickname Peanut Butter. We were like two peas in a pod. We got into so much mischief that summer. We smoked weed with the neighborhood weed man, and when we had some weed to spare, we would share with my brother, Tyrell, and my cousin, Marcus. We would all go behind the garage and smoke as we listened to Bone Thugs and Harmony.

Tamyah and I shared many secrets. Some secrets we shared, I wished we hadn't. When sneaking back into the house one night after being out with Chris, I found Tamyah lying across the bed crying uncontrollably. My first thought was that somebody had died.

"Tamyah, what's wrong?" I questioned, unlacing my tan wedge-heeled sandals.

Sitting up, a red-faced Tamyah managed to utter, "I can't believe he said that to me."

"Who? Said what? Who said what?" I repeated.

"Uncle Craig."

Confused, I asked, "Tamyah, what are you talking about?"

"I went out to smoke a cigarette earlier, and when I came back in, Uncle Craig said he wasn't gonna put up with me whoring under his watch."

"Why would he say that?" I asked.

I had always remained neutral when it came to Craig. He was Shannon's husband, and I didn't have anything against him. As a matter of fact, I didn't know if it was characteristic or uncharacteristic for him to make such a comment.

"I don't know, Destiny. Ever since I got pregnant and had that abortion, everyone thinks so low of me."

"Well, I don't," I assured her, reaching out to give her a quick hug.

"I know you don't. But it's hard knowing that everybody knows and holds that mistake against me."

Up until that point, I guess I was lucky to have not gotten pregnant. It wasn't because I was so careful and always used protection. God looks out for babies and fools. Isn't that what the Bible says? Well, the fool would be me.

"Look, girl. You gonna have to forgive yourself and let go of that guilt."

"It's hard, Destiny… It's hard."

"I know, I know," I said, rubbing my hands through her long, silky hair.

"You know what I don't understand?" she continued.

"What?" I said, flopping down on the bed next to her.

"You promise you won't tell?"

I had no idea what was coming out of her mouth next, but I promised anyway.

"He's the whore. He's the one that's been sleeping with my mom's friend, Christine, for over a year now."

My mouth flew open. "Christine?! You mean the one who makes the bomb banana pudding for Thanksgiving every year?"

Tamyah nodded. "I'm sorry, Destiny. I know Shannon is your mom and all, but you can't say anything. My mother will kill me."

"Hey, I know Shannon is my mom, but eventually, she's gonna have to come to her own truth about Craig. Don't worry, your secret is safe with me. But I bet I won't be eating no more of Christine's nasty banana pudding!" I joked.

"Girl, you just said she made a bomb banana pudding," Tamyah teased.

Even in our moment of disappointment, albeit for different reasons, we both shared a moment of laughter.

I went to bed that night with mixed feelings. On one end, I wanted Shannon to feel the hurt and betrayal I had been struggling with for years. The hurt that comes from wanting someone to love and respect you like you do them, only to discover that their love and respect is very much conditional. The truth of the matter was that Shannon was just as psychologically bruised and damaged as I was. In reality, she couldn't give me what she didn't even possess herself. Even though Shannon and Christine weren't true besties, because Christine was Aunt Veronica's bestie, the three of them ran in the same circles—you know, going on shopping sprees, having spa days, and going to wine tasting events together. The thought of it all made me want to punch Craig in his throat for betraying Shannon like that. Cheating was one thing, but with your wife's friend, or so-called friend, was altogether something different. And in my book, Craig didn't get a pass from me just because my relationship with Shannon was messy.

I remember lying in bed that night thinking of a way I could exact revenge on Craig. I knew enough thugs in the area, and if I told any of my cousins from the projects, they'd have Craig's tires slashed by morning and would finish the job by breaking a few of his bones as well. But Craig wasn't worth anyone having to serve time. And with that thought, I got up and retrieved the faded, gold Bible that sat on my makeshift bookcase, which was really a TV stand with double shelves underneath. I turned to Romans 12:19—"'Vengeance is mine. I will repay,' says the Lord." I took solace in that scripture. I sure hoped it was true because I had a few people I wanted God to put on His hit list for me, too.

Our family reunion was in Georgia the summer of 1994. I was still dating Chris, and our relationship had matured in many ways. We were no longer sneaking around. Everyone in our families knew and accepted the fact that we were an item. They might not have been too keen about it, but it was what it was.

I made a little money braiding hair that summer, so I went to the mall often to buy what I needed. I was hyped about the family reunion and wanted to buy my gear from the niche stores in the mall. Chris would often accompany me. He never had any money, so I always ended up buying him an outfit or two in addition to buying our food at the food court. I enjoyed his company, and I guess I was enthralled with having a boyfriend rather than not having one at all. So I chalked up his poverty as coming with the territory and rocked with it. On one occasion, a pretty girl named Kim walked up to me at the mall and tried to warn me about Chris.

"Excuse me, are you seeing Chris?" she said, having patiently waited for me outside the dressing room while I tried on outfits.

"Who wants to know?" I said, skeptical of whether she was accompanied by an entourage of girls waiting to jump me.

"I'm not trying to start no drama. I just want to warn you about him."

"Warn me about what?" I said defensively. I sounded like Shannon, defending my man, even in his wrong.

"He's a user."

I chuckled. "A what?" I heard what she had said. I just wanted her to qualify her statement.

"User. He's a user."

"Look, I don't know who you are and what you're tryna prove, but I don't get down like this. And how did you know we're seeing each other, anyway?" I added, wondering how she'd put us together. I had given Chris sixty dollars, and he had gone off to shop on his own. So it wasn't like we were walking around the mall holding hands or booed up.

"I work at Foot Locker, and I've seen you together in there a few times," she said. There was something earnest in her voice, but my pride wouldn't let me hear her out.

"Well, okay. But what's your point?" I said, growing more defensive.

"Like I said, I really don't want to start any drama. You just seem like a nice girl, so I just wanted to warn you."

"Who are you?" I asked, hanging the clothes I didn't want on the clothing rack next to the dressing room attendant.

"My name is Kim. Chris used to date my cousin, Trishe."

"Trishe, who?"

"Trish Sanders. If he says he doesn't know her, he's lying. He got her pregnant and left her."

"So, are you telling me he has a child he doesn't acknowledge?" In that instant, my defense of Chris began to wither a little, but I didn't want to show it. Denying a child hit close to home; I knew what that pain felt like, and I didn't want to be with a man who could deny his own flesh and blood.

"Well, she ended up having an abortion, and Chris didn't give any money to help. And not only that, he was always broke. He never has money. Trishe supported him throughout their relationship. And to make matters worse, he stole her ATM card and took eight hundred dollars out of her account. And that's not the worst thing. He's not faithful at all. He sees three and four girls at a time, so don't be surprised if you come down with something."

"I don't mean to cut you off, but I have to go," I said as I hung the last outfit on the rack. I had heard enough. It wasn't like Chris was my husband. And no, Chris didn't have a lot of money. But what twenty-year-old guy did?

"You look like a nice girl, and I just don't want you to get hurt," she continued.

"Well, thanks, but no thanks for your unsolicited advice," I said, snapping back at her before strutting off and leaving her standing there with a dumbfounded look on her face. If Shannon, Honey, and my aunties didn't teach me anything else, they sure taught me how to defend my man, guilty or not.

Chris and I rode the bus back to our side of town after we finished shopping at the mall that day. I decided to bring up the Trishe saga as we walked to our houses from the bus stop.

"Did you ever date a girl named Trishe?"

"Trishe, who?" Chris said, trying to recall the person.

"Sanders? Trishe Sanders?" I said, trying to jog his faded memory.

"Oh, that crazy chick?"

"Yeah, that crazy chick, Chris," I said, giving him the *you know what I'm talking about* look.

"Yeah, we dated for a hot minute," he finally confessed.

"Well, what happened?" I said, hoping he would engage me to expand the conversation.

"We broke up. I mean, that's what happens. You get together, and then you break up. It ain't nothing."

"You sure?" I probed.

"Yeah, I'm sure. You done heard some crap … Don't tell me, her cousin Kim, huh?"

I remained silent. Chris seemed like he could have been the type of guy that would hit a woman, and I didn't want one of the women he hit to be me.

"What did that heifer say?"

"She just asked me if we were going together," I lied.

"Bet she told you I stole money from Trishe, didn't she?"

"No. She didn't say that," I lied again.

"Well, that chick needs to mind her own business and find out why she can't keep a man."

Chris was defensive, no doubt about it. And one thing Honey always taught me was that a hit dog will bark, and Chris was barking ferociously.

"It's nothing. She just asked if we were dating, that's all."

"It ain't none of her business. And why you up there letting her fill your head with all this garbage?"

There was no rationalizing with Chis. He had a short fuse. We went to our separate houses without our usual smooching and kissing in his garage.

It wasn't too long after the encounter with Kim at the mall that

I would obtain firsthand knowledge of how conniving, dishonest, untrustworthy, and deceitful Chris truly was.

We had fun in Georgia at the family reunion. As with many other family reunions, ours was comprised of moments of love, laughter, arguments, full-fledged brawls, and then the makeup ceremonies at the end. But upon our arrival back home, we were met with grave disappointment—someone had broken into our home. After taking inventory, we realized all our valuables were gone. Most of the items were replaceable, but Honey was heartbroken when she realized her necklace from her mother was among the stolen valuables.

Including the travel time, I had been away for nine days, and I couldn't wait to get back to Chris. I had a calling card that I was only able to use once while I was in Georgia. Honey's sister, my great aunt, Liz, didn't like what she termed as "people tying up her line."

But Chris knew when I was coming back, and he met me outside of my house on the first night of my return. Luckily, his brother Dean was working overtime, so we had the basement to ourselves, at least for two and a half hours.

With Chris, the sex was always good because I didn't have anything to compare it to. To our surprise, Dean came home an hour and a half earlier than expected. Chris and I scrambled to get our clothes back on. We fixed up the pullout sofa as best we could, considering the limited amount of time we had between being stark naked to getting fully dressed upon hearing Dean's Chevy Nova pull into the driveway.

"I have to go to the bathroom," I said with the intent to fix my hair, my makeup, and my clothing.

I was in the bathroom when Dean came in. I couldn't make out the mumbled sound of their voices, but they sounded as though they were engaged in a spat of some sort. I stayed in the bathroom a little longer than I normally would, trying to give the brothers time to work out their little disagreement. After about ten minutes, I walked back into the sitting area. As I passed the sofa table, my eyes widened. Lying neatly on the sofa table was Honey's gold necklace with the diamond encrusted cross on it.

With one clean sweep, I grabbed the necklace and placed it in my bra. I immediately rehashed the conversation I'd had with Kim. She was right. Chris was a thief, a liar, and an unfaithful man, all the things Kim said he was.

I decided not to confront Chris. What good would it have done? Honey's necklace being in his home was all the proof I needed. I waited until Chris fell asleep that night, and I walked out of his house and his life—forever.

Chapter 4

Green Eyes and a Smile

HONEY WORKED AT THE J.L. Hudson department store located on Woodward Ave., until they closed their doors in 1983. The store held so many memories for Detroiters.

Not knowing what to do with my life after graduating from high school, I started working at my very first job at the Hudson's located inside of Eastland Mall the winter of 1994. Secretly, I wanted to walk in Honey's footsteps.

J.L. Hudson was where I met Mr. Green Eyes and a Smile, better known as Tommy Hutchison. Tommy was a tall, slim, high-yellow brother with mesmerizing green eyes, who was popular amongst all the girls in the mall. Even a couple of older women would become all googly eyed over him. He was just *that* good looking.

I was self-conscious about my looks, especially the huge gap between my two front teeth, and it caused me to lack confidence. My gap was so big that when I smiled, if you didn't know any better, you would have thought I was missing a tooth.

I was surprised when Tommy approached me. He wore a white short-sleeved shirt and had on a perfectly creased pair of light blue jeans that were nicely put together with a pair of brand-new white tennis shoes.

"Hey, gorgeous. I got two questions for you. What's your name, and can I get your number?" Tommy said with a warm smile.

Trying to keep from fainting, I managed to remember my name. Tommy had totally thrown me off my square. After pulling it together, I was able to spark up a conversation. "My name is Destiny."

"My sister's name is Destiny," he said, looking me over.

"What a coincidence," I said.

"Yeah, right. But now you gotta answer my other question. Can I get your number?"

I reached inside my purse and grabbed an old CVS receipt and wrote the house number and my pager number on it. "I'm giving you the house number and my pager number. I prefer that you page me."

"Why, you got a man and gotta sneak around?"

I snickered. Not only were his eyes mesmerizing, but he had a unique sense of humor, and he was flattering the socks off me.

"No, I don't have a man."

"Well, you got one now," he said, winking.

I froze. I preferred that he page me because I wanted to keep my dating life semi-private. Although Honey knew it was a different day and time in the dating world, she was still plain old fashioned when it came to certain things. If I was going out on a date, my date had to come in the house every time when he came to pick me up. She didn't like for guys to blow the horn and sit in the car and wait for me to come outside. With all that she and her daughters had gone through with men, Honey was just suspicious of the male species, period.

"You free this weekend?"

"Maybe," I answered, playing hard to get.

"I'mma page you. Let's hang out."

"Page me," I said.

As I walked away from Tommy, I blushed from ear to ear

because I couldn't believe the popular guy at work was interested in me. *Me! Me, of all people.*

For the remainder of the night, I could not focus on work. All I could think about was Tommy, wondering if he was really going to contact me. I was a nervous wreck. I kept hoping I would see him at least one more time before I went home, but I didn't.

Tommy didn't contact me the first night, nor did he contact me the second night. On day three, I thought I was going to go crazy when I looked at the schedule and noticed he would be off the following two days. I was just about to lose hope when Tommy's page came through around ten o'clock that night. We talked for about an hour or so before making plans to catch a movie at the Bel-Air Theater on 8 Mile and Van Dyke that weekend.

After enduring the hoopla with Chris, Tommy seemed like a breath of fresh air. He was a little older, and most importantly, he had a job and his own money. We met up in front of the theatre. We ended up watching some action flick, the name I can't even remember. We sat cozied up until the credits began to roll.

Even though there were plenty of conversations that took place in between our in-person dates, Tommy and I didn't have that important conversation about exclusivity until after we had gone out a few times. I can remember the conversation as if it just took place.

"You know the girls at Hudson's want to holler at your boy, right?"

"My boy? Who's that?" I said, trying to act oblivious.

"Me," Tommy joked, accompanied by a slight chuckle.

"Oh, and just so you know, the men at Hudson's wanna holler at your girl," I chimed back. My flirt game was on point.

"Oh, is that right?" Tommy said, rubbing his hands along the outer sides of my arms.

"That's right."

"Well, tell'em you're taken."

"Am I?"

"You daggone right, you're taken."

"By who?" I teased.

"By me," Tommy said with all manner of confidence.

And just like that, we became exclusive. But what exclusivity meant to a young, naïve Destiny did not mean the same thing to an experienced, older guy like Tommy. By our third date, sexual intercourse was on the agenda. We ended up having sex on an old, tattered, teal leather sofa in his grandparents' basement, which always seemed to carry a strange odor.

Well into our third month of dating, I received some troubling news about Tommy from my best friend, Shonte, who came over to personally deliver me the news. Coming by under the pretense of dropping off my romper that she'd borrowed for a hot date she had, we sat outside on the front porch, sipping on piña colada wine coolers.

"How's Tommy?" Shonte said in between sips of the wine cooler.

"He's good." And to the best of my knowledge, Tommy *was* doing good. But I had known Shonte for years, and the look on her face told me she wanted to say more. "What? You done heard some mess about him?"

"Umm … not exactly," Shonte said, taking a gulp of the drink.

"Come on, Shonte. Cut to the chase. What's the deal with Tommy? He up to no good, too?"

"Well, I heard he has a girl."

"*Has* a girl or is messing with a girl?"

"Does it matter? Isn't it the same thing?" Shonte argued.

"Not in my book."

"Are you falling for this 'guys are gonna be guys' crap, Destiny?"

"I'm not falling for anything. But I do know that I don't know a man alive that hasn't cheated on his girlfriend or wife."

"So what are you saying, Destiny?"

"Look, Shonte, I can't be around no man twenty-four-seven. So if he's gonna cheat, then that's what he's gonna do. He says we're exclusive, and that means a lot to me."

"Have you met his family or friends?"

"What's with all the questions, Shonte?" I said defensively.

"Nothing. I'm just tryna be your friend."

"Are you sure? 'Cause if I didn't know any better, I would think you were trying to be my shrink and not my friend."

"Look Destiny, I only came to bring your romper back and thought I'd at least mention what I heard through the grapevine."

"Stop listening through the grapevine. Until Tommy shows me something different, I'm just gonna keep kicking it with him. He makes me laugh, smile, and forget about the man who never loved me."

"I'm sorry, Destiny," Shonte said.

"I know you don't mean no harm and are only looking out for your girl. But after that incident with Chris, I'd rather just find out for myself if I'm being played or not."

And in less than twenty-four hours, I received a call on the house phone from a girl named Shawn, claiming to be Tommy's girlfriend and much, much more.

"Hello?" I answered after intercepting the phone's receiver from Nicole.

"Is this Destiny?"

"Yes, this is Destiny. Can I ask who's calling?"

"My name is Shawn."

"Well, who are you, Shawn?" I asked sarcastically.

"I'm Tommy's girlfriend."

"That's funny because Tommy asked me to be his girlfriend about three months ago," I shot back.

"Well, we've been together for a little over a year now," she countered, continuing our little verbal tug of war.

"Have you ever wondered where Tommy is on Friday and Saturday nights?" I said, hoping to really get under her skin. It was common "street knowledge" that guys spent their weekends with their main chick. "Have you?" I reiterated after she didn't respond. "Well, I'll tell you. He's with me, and we go every place from the River Mill Run to the cabins in Grand Rapids," I continued. This was what they called giving someone what they came for. Although she was prepared to burst my bubble with the news that she and Tommy had been dating for a longer period of time, I was prepared to let her know that I was his main chick. And that was just how it was gonna be as far as I was concerned. Plain and simple.

"And that's not all. I'm going on three months pregnant with our child."

I almost dropped the receiver. I wiped my forehead with the crumbled-up napkin that covered the bottom of the waffle cone I was eating. "You're pregnant?"

"No, I'm not pregnant; *we* are," she emphasized.

Exasperated and at a loss for words, I followed with, "Well, what do you want me to do about it?" I was trying to seem unbothered, but a ball of fire was rolling on the inside. All I could think of was getting my hands around Tommy's neck!

"I want you to leave us alone. We have a child on the way and we're gonna be a family."

"Well, that's kinda too bad, because I think I might be pregnant too," I lied. I had no real comeback for her. Although I didn't admit or exhibit any nonverbal cues, the tug of war game was over, and she had won.

"So I guess we can all live in his grandmama's basement because I promised myself that I would never bring a child in this world without both parents around to support them," the girl who introduced herself as Tommy's baby-mama-to-be said.

I moved the phone's receiver from my ear and looked at it. She was a bold one. But I had many more comebacks for her than she ever dreamed of having for me. "I don't think so," I said with added flair and arrogance.

"And I just have one more thing to tell you." She paused for a few seconds. "I think you should get tested for chlamydia. I got tested, and I have it. Where do you think I got it?"

I hung up in her face. Chlamydia? The last time I'd heard about chlamydia was in health class when I was a freshman in high school. I immediately paged Tommy. Being furious was an understatement. It took Tommy a few hours to call me back, but when he did, I confronted him about everything Shawn had conveyed to me. Quite naturally, he denied everything.

"Destiny, yes, I have known her for a while. I kicked it with her a few times, but I've never promised exclusivity with her. She really ain't my type."

I was silent. One thing about it was, if she was really three months pregnant, in six months, Tommy would be a father, and I didn't know how I felt about it. I mean, if I didn't want him to be anything remotely like Ed Harrison, my biological dad, then it meant he would have to be around Shawn and his child often. My mind rehearsed what Christmases and birthdays would be like. I didn't know whether I had the emotional stamina to stand by my man this time around.

"So she's lying?"

"She tryna trap me because I don't want her," Tommy said, using the age-old adage.

After sensing my obvious hurt surrounding the incident, Tommy begged me to come over his house, promising to cook shrimp scampi for me. He knew I loved shrimp scampi and he was good at making it. Although I was a bit reluctant, I drove Honey's faithful powder blue two-door Nissan over to Tommy's grandparents' house.

Tommy guided me into a very narrow driveway. When I

pulled in successfully, he signaled for me to roll down the driver side window. Leaning in, he planted a soft, wet kiss on my lips. "Hey baby, you still want that shrimp scampi?"

"Of course, I do," I said, preparing to roll the window back up and turn the ignition off. I was still numb, but I was desperately trying to mask it.

"We're out of shrimp. Let's just go eat out. I got you next time."

"Okay," I agreed. I was hungry, and I had developed a headache after hearing from that girl, Shawn.

"I'mma go lock up right quick, and I'll be right back," Tommy said as he planted another kiss on my lips.

The night ended with hot, steamy sex, but the next day, I was confronted with haunting demons. I kept hearing Shawn's words over and over. *We're pregnant. Chlamydia.* I mustered enough courage to call the women's clinic located on East 8 Mile Road near Gratiot and set up an appointment to get tested.

The next few days were equally as haunting, as I couldn't get an appointment for four days, and I had to wait an extra three days until the results became available.

Just as Shawn had cautioned, I tested positive for chlamydia. The antibiotic prescribed for the chlamydia was proof that Tommy was a lying, cheating boyfriend. And as crazy as it seemed, I still wanted to be with him. I couldn't let him go, not during that season in my life.

I was in sheer denial about the true status of my relationship with Tommy for a good while. The denial spilled over into my compliance with taking the medication for chlamydia. In fact, I didn't take the medication as soon as it was prescribed. Taking the Doxycycline pills twice a day for a week would be admitting to myself that I had a dirty girl's disease.

As Shawn had conveyed to me over the phone that night, she was indeed pregnant with Tommy's child, a son. Eventually, I had to come to the realization that no matter what Tommy said or did, he had an allegiance to Shawn. He would always be there for both her and their son, and Shawn held a piece of Tommy's heart that I just couldn't touch. With these odds stacked up against me, I decided to call it quits. Tommy and I had no formal conversation about breaking up; we just let fate have its way and drifted far apart.

Chapter 5

Don't Take It Personal

I LOVED MY JOB at Hudson's. Not only did I get a paycheck, I enjoyed the employee discount and the customers, especially repeat customers. They were the best.

I'll never forget my encounter with a frail looking Caucasian woman one day. While ringing her up, she struck up a conversation.

"... many years ago."

"Excuse me?" I said, not having really paid any attention to what the woman was saying to me. My attention was focused on getting through the day, so I could meet up with my girl, Shonte, later. All I heard was the tail end of her comment. The talkative older woman repeated her statement. But it seemed as though she added a sermonette to it.

"I prepared myself for this day many years ago. Trouble don't last always. Everything gets better with time. You'll look up one day, and the pain won't feel the same anymore. It means you're healing. One day, it will be completely gone. And baby, that's worth celebrating."

Now, she had caught my attention. Whether she knew it or not, she was speaking *to* my pain. I often felt hopeless when it came to Shannon and Ed. But because they were such vital figures in my life—at least they should have been—I had an extremely difficult time trying to make peace with the fact that neither of them wanted me. As young as I was at the time, I knew I was on the wrong track when it came to relationships. I always seemed to choose the guy who *needed* me, not necessarily wanted me. Even though I was on a relationship hiatus, if you will, I still had my share of admirers and guys asking me for my number. And I gave my number out to most of them. But as far as being in a committed relationship, I wasn't in one. I mean, after the hurt and betrayal I'd experienced in my previous relationships, especially with Tommy, I felt I needed to take a break from relationships … at least, that was my intention.

I decided to engage the older woman further. "Why do you say that?" I said, looking her squarely in the eye. It was more like I was staring into her soul. On the outside, I saw a wise old woman with curly silver hair, rosy cheeks, and a crooked nose. But I saw something else as well. I saw the pain of a woman who said, "I do," probably more than fifty years prior. A woman who had tried to honor her wedding vows, even though she cried many days and nights. A woman who now walked in the rewards of her labor and was adorned with wisdom to share with young women like me.

"Baby, there's so much in life to learn. You're just a youngin', but you'll see. This thing called life holds a lot of pain, and it's waiting for you … You can't escape it. It comes in all shapes and forms. People will lie on you, cheat on you, leave you, and do their best to see to it that you fail. But you have to hold your head up high and press on."

I picked up her final item to ring up. It was a package of children's toothbrushes. "For the grandkids?" I asked.

With her right index finger pointing to the toothbrush, she answered. "No, baby, this here toothbrush is for my husband. He's on his deathbed right now, suffering from prostate cancer. Now, I could make the last days of his life miserable, reminding him of all the awful things he did in the past, or I could do exactly what I'm doing now, living out love. This feeling right here is greater than any revenge I could have ever thought of exacting on my Jim."

"Oh, I'm sorry to hear about your husband. You have my sympathy," I said. I felt out of place telling her that she had my sympathy, but I didn't know what else to say.

"Oh, it's all right, honey. Although I know he's not dead yet, I know the day is coming. Thank you for your sentiment, though. I know what you mean."

"You're welcome. I—"

Before I could get the next word out, the tan telephone near my register rang. Whenever that telephone rang, it meant one of a few things—it was time for break, the manager was summoning me to the back, or Jeff, the security guard, was asking me to come verify that I rang up an item for a customer who had been suspected of shoplifting.

"Excuse me. I have to take this call," I said, holding my left index finger up.

It was Jeff's voice on the other end of the phone, summoning me to the security office. I finished ringing up the older customer, locked the register drawer, turned off my cashier light, and headed for the security office. I didn't pay the request any mind initially because it seemed like standard protocol. But I was shocked to see Monica, one of the store managers, sitting in Jeff's office when I got there.

"You can close the door behind you and have a seat," Jeff said.

Jeff was a dark-skinned guy in his late twenties or early thirties, who reminded me of Joe Torrey's character, Chicago, in the movie *Poetic Justice*. He tried to feel me out on a few occasions by trying to make small talk with me while in the breakroom. But I wasn't interested in him. He just wasn't my type. After I shot him down on a few occasions, he didn't seem to be feeling me at all. He always had something negative to say about Tommy when Tommy and I were dating. So I learned to stay my distance from Jeff, trying not to take his attitude toward me too personal.

I had no choice but to sit in the chair next to Monica because there were only two chairs besides Jeff's chair in the medium-sized office. Monica was a manly-looking black woman in her mid-thirties. Her complexion was the perfect match to a brown paper bag. I didn't have too much interaction with her, but she facilitated my new hire orientation. Outside of that, I didn't even see her often.

The vibe felt awkward the moment I walked into Jeff's office. Usually, when Jeff needed me to verify purchased items in a case of suspected shoplifting, Monica wasn't present.

"So ..." I said to Jeff, prompting him to tell me the reason for my summons to his office.

"We have reason to believe that you've violated provisions of the employee discount program, Miss Crawford."

Is he being formal now? Jeff had never called me Ms. Crawford. Initially, he called me "beautiful," "gorgeous," "smiles," or some other warm pleasantry. After he realized I wasn't interested in him, he just called me Destiny. But on this particular day, he addressed me in a formal manner.

"How?" I asked, trying to sound completely oblivious to what he was referencing.

"The employee discount program only permits purchase discounts for you and members of your immediate family."

I didn't say anything; I just gave him the dumb look.

"We've witnessed you giving discounts to people who are not your immediate family members," Jeff said with a smirk on his face.

"I apologize. I was unaware of this particular policy," I lied.

"We covered this during orientation. Plus, the information was part of your onboarding training materials. You should have been well aware of this policy," Monica chimed in.

"Well, I'm sorry. It won't happen again."

"We know it won't," Jeff said, holding up a folder that was lying on his desk.

"We're gonna need you to sign some papers in this folder,

and then grab your belongings from the backroom," Monica continued.

"So you're sending me home?" I asked.

"We're terminating your employment at J.L. Hudson," Monica confirmed.

"So you're *firing* me?" I felt a hot sensation creep up on both sides of my face. I'm sure that if it wasn't for my medium-toned complexion, I would have looked like a beet in the face.

Monica took the folder from Jeff and opened it. She retrieved a few forms from it that were already prefilled. "Read the form, fill in the empty fields, and sign at the bottom," she said matter-of-factly as she handed me the forms.

Too naïve to know my rights, I complied with Monica's directions, basically admitting that I knowingly conspired with others to steal merchandise from J.L. Hudson. And after a few moments of silence, I stood up to leave.

"Here's your copies," Monica said, handing me carbon copies of the forms I had signed. "Oh, and we're gonna need your employee badge, too," Monica continued, eyeing the badge pinned to my work smock.

How could they fire me after all the hard work I put in at that store? Close to nine months, I faithfully worked at that store day in and day out. Whenever they needed me to come in on one of my off days or whenever they needed me to close at night, I did and never complained.

The truth was I allowed myself to be put in the predicament. It was very much personal, no matter how you sliced it. This was really about me not giving Jeff the time of day and flirting with Tommy in his face. But I didn't give Jeff the pleasure of seeing the devastation on my face.

"I'll walk you to the door," Monica said.

"No, I'm good. I walked in here perfectly fine without an escort, and I can walk outta here without one."

"It's company policy," Jeff said with a sly grin.

As if to add insult to injury, I had to be escorted out of my place of employment, the place that allowed me to gain greater financial independence. All I could think about was what I was going to tell Honey. I walked toward the door and Monica followed me to the breakroom and watched as I dumped all my belongings out of locker number twenty-three into the linen gift bag that we were given on our first day of employment. I never even took it home. It came in handy, just not in the way I thought it would.

Monica followed me to the front of the store and watched as I walked out of the revolving door. I dared not turn around and give her the satisfaction of seeing the gloom in my eyes, now accompanied by salt-filled pebbles flowing down my cheeks. I would normally call Honey to pick me up at the end of my shift, but due to the circumstances, I decided to catch the bus home. It didn't hurt that it was fairly warm outside. Michigan's weather was very unpredictable. But on this particular spring day in 1995, the weather conditions were pleasant—it was seventy-three degrees, mostly sunny, and a soft breeze blew any loose-fit clothing people wore.

As I sat in the parking lot waiting for my bus, I had some time to think. The main thing was coming up with the lie I was going to concoct for Honey. Finally, after about forty-five minutes, my bus arrived. I stood up, gathered my bags, and stood in line to get on the bus. I felt as though I was in the middle of a nightmare for the past hour and a half. The squeaking breaks of the arriving bus, the sound of the doors opening, the muffled sound of those around me, and beeping car horns from the surrounding area made my head spin. It just didn't feel real. Sure, I knew I could find another job. But once again, I felt as though I had let myself down. Then I remembered the words of the stranger I had met only a couple of hours earlier—*Trouble don't last always. Everything gets better with time. One day, you'll look up, and it will be completely gone. And baby, that's worth celebrating.*

Roxbury Street is where I met Toya. From the day we met, we were destined to be friends. Once we discovered we were the same age and both our birthdays were in September, we became buddies. The only thing that separated us was a driveway, and at times, the jealousy Toya had of my real BFF, Shonte.

Honey should have been home from work on this day, which would have meant her car should have been in the garage. But it wasn't. I let out a deep sigh. *At least I don't have to confront her with the bad news today.*

I rushed inside and headed straight for my room. Frustrated, I closed my bedroom door behind me and rested my head against it, trying to think of my next move. While engaged in deep contemplation, my pager beeped. Toya's number flashed across the screen with the accompanying message, "911." That meant urgent. I grabbed the phone off the dresser and called her.

"Um, why are you home so early?"

I didn't respond right away.

"Girl, you know you heard me," Toya said between the crackling sounds of the gum she was chewing.

"I know I heard you. I just didn't know your name was Honey or Shannon, the two people who I am obligated to report my whereabouts to," I joked. But in a way, I was serious. There were positives and negatives with Toya living next door. One of the negatives was that she knew when I was coming and going. Apparently, she had seen me walking up the driveway to the house and realized it was earlier than usual for me to be returning home from work.

"Girl, I'm stopping by."

"Okay," I said, opening my blinds so I would be able to see when she approached. When I saw her heading up the driveway, I went downstairs and opened the door for her.

"Come on. Hurry," I said, grabbing her by the hand to escort her as I ran up the flight of stairs.

"Slow down," Toya said after nearly missing a step.

"Come on, slow poke," I teased.

I opened my bedroom door and quickly closed it behind us. My cousin Nicole was still living with us. She was very nosy, and the last thing I wanted was for her to learn about me getting fired.

"Shh, don't say anything."

"About what?" Toya said, seemingly confused.

"I got fired today," I said, holding my right index finger to my lips.

"You got what?"

"Yeah, girl, petty Jeff."

"The security guard?" Toya asked, puzzled.

"Yep, him. Petty ole Jeff."

"Well, he had to have some grounds to fire you. What did you do?" Toya said, wide eyed.

"They've been watching and saw me giving the employee discount to you and Shonte."

"Are you serious?"

"As a heart attack. But Jeff's been gunning for me ever since I kicked him to the curb for Tommy."

"So you can't appeal?"

"I dunno. They ain't mentioned nothing about appealing the decision. And besides, I don't know if I want to go through that anyway."

An awkward moment of silence befell. It was as if we were both contemplating my next move. Honey had some firm rules, and one of them was maintaining employment, since I didn't go off to college after graduation. College was in my plans, just not at the time. I wanted a break from books, studying, and writing papers.

"You know what you need?" Toya said, breaking the silence.

"What do I need, Toya?" I said, looking at her dead in the eye.

If I knew one thing about Toya, she was a free-spirited person. She never let anything get her down for too long. She could even bounce back from heartbreaks quicker than anyone I knew, including myself.

"You need to go out tonight and let some of that steam off."

"Girl, I got bigger fish to fry than to go partying tonight. Honey is not going to let me live here without a job. You know her rule ... school or a job, point blank."

"Well, you ain't gonna find a job tonight, so why don't you just get ready and let's go have some fun. Who knows? You might even meet a new beau tonight," Toya said, twirling around like a ballerina.

I didn't verbally commit, although Toya's proposal was tempting. Truth be told, my mind was still reeling from losing my job, my income, and my independence. To act as though my self-esteem hadn't taken a hit was not being truthful to myself.

"I don't know if I really feel up to it, Toya."

Toya brushed past me, walked over to my closet, and swung open its door. Like me, Toya was a fashionista. She had a knack for putting nice outfits together and stepping into the club to attract attention.

"What about this with some jeans or a mini-skirt," she said, holding up my white lace blouse.

I could almost hear the beat to my favorite jams. I gave her a half-smile, which meant I was at least contemplating the idea of going out.

"Come on, what's there to think about?" Toya instigated, dangling the blouse in front of my face.

"Okay, okay. Let me see if Shonte wants to go, too," I said, reaching for the phone on my dresser.

"Yeah, if she ain't knee deep into writing some paper, she'll be down," Toya joked as she handed me the blouse and retrieved her pager from her back pocket. "Let me know what y'all gonna do.

I gotta call this one back," Toya continued, pointing at the pager screen as a smile graced her face.

I knew the page Toya received had to have been from one of her male pursuits, just by the expression on her face. She was pretty and had her share of guys chasing her as well. To describe her, I'd say she was the brown-skinned version of the actress Cree Summer who played on the hit TV series *A Different World*. Her carefree personality spilled over into her sense of style, and it never kept her from exploring different fashions, dating people of different nationalities, or even eating different cuisines. Like me, Toya's mother wasn't really a central figure in her life. But unlike me, Toya's mother wasn't still walking the face of the earth. She had died in a tragic car accident when Toya was fourteen. Although Toya's life was spared, the accident left a physical mark as well as great emotional scarring. A large burn mark from the accident covered most of Toya's left forearm. But nothing really seemed to stop Toya from living her life to the fullest. She lived with her father and her great aunt and uncle.

As she often did, Toya let herself out. I grabbed the telephone receiver and called Shonte. As Toya and I had predicted, Shonte was indeed working on a paper. But after some convincing, she agreed, taking a needed break from her studies.

Trying to escape from some dilemma in our individual lives, the three of us—Toya, Shonte, and I—went out that night.

I spent most of the evening at the club thinking about how I was going to explain to Honey the reason why I lost my job. That is, between watching people on the dance floor getting their groove on, watching some men flirt with and pick up women, and others down drink after drink at the bar. I guess you can say most of the night was uneventful.

To avoid the parking lot chaos that usually occurred when

the club closed, we left a little early and headed home, making a pit stop at Denny's so Toya could pick up a burger and fries for her dad.

The lights in my house were off, including the front porch light, when we pulled up to it in Shonte's mother's car. Turning off all lights was Honey's way of letting me know she was aware I had missed my 2:30 a.m. curfew.

"Uh oh, all the lights are out," Toya said, also aware of what the sign meant.

"Yeah, I know. But I just can't tonight. It is what it is. I'll face Honey in the morning," I said, opening the front passenger door to let myself out.

"You know Aunt Ruthie couldn't care less about a curfew. You can stay over my house if you want," Toya said, attempting to get out of the car as well.

"Nah, I want to sleep in my own bed tonight. But thanks anyway," I said as I stepped out of the car. I waved bye at Shonte and watched her back out of the driveway. Toya walked to her house and I to mine.

I let myself in and headed straight for my room. I undressed in the dark and hopped into bed with nothing on but my bra and panties. Before I could doze off, I was startled by the buzzing sound of my pager. I was disappointed to see the number that flashed across the screen—it was Tommy's. I hadn't seen or heard from him in weeks; we were both avoiding one another at work. I slammed the pager upside down on the nightstand and rolled back over.

I was used to getting up early, even if I didn't have somewhere to be. I made my way into the kitchen, made a bowl of cereal, and went into the basement to watch TV.

I must have fallen off to sleep at some point, because before I realized it, I heard the sound of Honey's car passing the basement window as she pulled into the driveway. I sat up straight and waited to hear the back door open. I was sure the moment of truth was just moments away—getting a verbal lashing for staying out past my curfew, and the worst scenario, having to tell her I was jobless through fault of my own.

"Who's in the basement?" Honey called out, realizing the television was on.

"Me, Honey!" I yelled back.

"What are you doing at home? I thought you had to work today."

Knowing Honey hated it when we yelled back and forth, I headed upstairs to meet her in the kitchen. I didn't readily address her last question; I just started helping her put the groceries away she had just purchased.

"Girl, you still haven't answered my question," Honey snapped. Looking suspicious, she continued, "I'm waiting."

Honey, I had to quit. They keep putting me on the schedule to close, and it's hard for me to get a ride home from work when you can't pick me up," I lied.

"I never quit no job without already having another one lined up. That's just not the way things are done. But I'll tell you what, baby girl ... you have three months to get yourself together. By fall, you better have a job, or you better be enrolled in somebody's school. Pick one or both. I don't care, but you and your cousins are not going to drive me crazy," she said, referring to my auntie Roz's children, Nicole and Marcus, who were living with us as well.

I thought Honey's reaction was going to be far worse. Honey loved her grandchildren, but she was no foreigner to giving us tough love whenever she deemed it fit. She didn't hesitate to share the good, bad, and the ugly about her life, often regretting some things she'd done, which included having children at a very young age and staying with a man who was physically and sexually abusing their children.

Thinking I was free and clear, I headed back toward the basement.

"Oh, don't think I forgot about you breaking your curfew. I just got home from work, and I'm tired, but I'm gonna remember this. You're gonna wanna go somewhere or do something, and my answer's gonna be a resounding no."

Chapter 6

Changing Seasons

WEEKS AND MONTHS PASSED, and I spent the majority of the time searching for a job. As they often say, finding a job *is* a job in and of itself. And my case was no different. From time to time, Shonte came over and we'd bounce ideas off one another. I called it the, "What do you think about this?" game.

One particular day, while engaged in our new game, Shonte threw out a scenario that totally threw me for a loop.

"What do you think about me going into the military?"

"The what?" I said, totally taken aback.

"Yeah, the military. What do you think about me joining the Navy?"

"Why do you want to do that?" I said, unable to make the connection for what was driving her to join the military.

"There is nothing here for me. I'm in school, but it's getting expensive. If I join the Navy, I can have a career, *and* they'll help me with school."

I was silent. Truth be told, Shonte telling me she was contemplating going into the Navy felt like a break up of some sort.

Sensing my disappointment, Shonte added, "What if we joined together? I can put you in touch with my recruiter."

Knowing I wasn't interested in joining the Navy, I simply

responded, "Yeah, that is a thought." The reality was, I wasn't ready to be away from home. I didn't know what I wanted to do long term. An awkward moment of silence passed.

"Well, think about it," Shonte added before taking a sip of her Pepsi.

The conversation quickly switched to a more upbeat one—teasing one another about the physical appearances of past love interests. It was something we'd do from time to time, enjoying jokes and accompanying laughter between two great friends who were growing up and possibly apart.

Two and a half months later, Shonte enlisted into the Navy. Things seemed to be going good for her. We communicated by mail for the most part and by telephone whenever possible. Honey wasn't too keen on accepting collect calls, but she would allow them from Shonte occasionally.

I was still unemployed, so Honey decided to intervene. Although she didn't want me to get stuck working at a plant like she did, she knew I had to start somewhere. She brought home a job application for me to fill out one day.

"I spoke with Jim—that's Jim for me and Mr. Gladstone for you. I spoke to him about you possibly working at ABC Automotive."

ABC Automotive was an auto plant that made car parts for Ford, Chrysler, and General Motors. It was located at 11 Mile and Groesbeck in the city of Roseville. Honey had been working there for years in addition to working at Hudson's part-time before that location closed.

"Ooh, thanks, Honey," I said, nearly jumping into her arms.

"Now, I'mma tell you something. Don't you embarrass me. I am putting my reputation out there on the line trying to get you in. You do what you're supposed to and don't worry about trying to be among the popular folk or going out on dates with every man that says hello or tells you that you're pretty."

Although I knew Honey was serious, what she was saying was

funny to me. Honey and I both enjoyed a warm laugh, something we hadn't shared in quite some time.

Before I knew it, plant life was my life. Honey worked the day shift, and because I was new, I was assigned to the afternoon shift. My hours were from three o'clock in the afternoon until eleven o'clock at night. I didn't have a car at the time, so I had to catch the bus to work. But after my shift ended, Honey would pick me up. I felt bad about inconveniencing her, especially since she was getting up there in age. So, on occasion, I'd take a taxi home. I was determined to get a car. I worked relentlessly, even clocking overtime when I could get it, so I could save up for a car. When I had finally saved twenty-five hundred dollars, I started looking for a car. I was tired of bumming rides.

As a Christmas present to myself in 1995, I bought a used white 1986 Datsun. It had a small dent on the right bumper, but I was focused on it getting me to and from, not on its looks. Unfortunately, the car barely lasted six months before it broke down on me for the one hundredth time. The poor experience led me to consider financing a newer car that would be free from total breakdown.

Like most things in life, getting financed was no simple feat. It, too, came with its share of complexities. For the most part, not having any credit prevented banks from approving my application. After weeks and weeks of trying to obtain automobile financing, someone finally said yes. Although not my first choice, I settled on a 1996 burgundy Ford Escort. I felt as though my life was starting to come back together. Between the loss of my job at Hudson's, the loss of my girl, Shonte, who had joined the Navy, and my plummeting self-esteem, I was affected in ways I was unwilling to admit. But things were starting to look up for me. I was a fighter, and I knew it.

I kept my car immaculately clean, often visiting Lucky's Car Wash for a car wash and vacuum. Lucky's was owned by my high school classmate, Julius Davidson's, family. Tuesdays were known as Discount Tuesday, which meant you could get full service—exterior wash, wax, tire cleaning, and interior vacuum and cleaning—for half price, which was six dollars. And whenever Julius was working, he'd give me an extra five dollars off, leaving me only having to pay one dollar for a full-service cleaning. I couldn't beat that type of deal, so I took advantage of it often.

As I stood outside watching the attendants put the final touches on my car, I was startled by the revving sound of a motorcycle pulling up behind me. I turned around and watched the man as he tussled with his helmet, trying to pull it off.

"Hey, beautiful," he said, after finally freeing his head from the helmet.

I turned back to face the attendants, sure the man was talking to someone else in my vicinity. "Oh, so you gonna do me like that?" he said, after I didn't respond.

Turing to face him again, I answered. "Do you like what?" I said, trying to elevate my voice over the sound of the motorcycle's engine.

"Ignore me," he said, gliding forward and backward on his black Honda motorcycle.

"Well, I wasn't sure you were talking to me," I said, immediately taken aback by this man's stunning looks and his radio-sounding voice.

"Well, look around. Looks like you're the only beautiful thing standing in front of me."

I blushed.

"You got a minute?" he said as he turned his bike's engine off.

"I'm really on my way to work, and I'm kinda in a hurry," I said, trying to play hard to get.

"Must be someone on that job that got your attention, then."

He was flirting and digging for information at the same time, but I was loving it.

"Nah ... nah. It's not like that. Work is work. I keep it professional," I lied. I was going out with men on the job all the time, even though Honey had always warned, "You don't sleep and use the bathroom in the same place." I had broken this cardinal rule more times than I cared to admit.

"So, why don't you tell me your name?"

"Destiny," I said, moving backward a step or two in an attempt to get the sunlight out of my eyes.

"You look like a Destiny," he said, getting off the motorcycle.

"Thank you," I replied, sizing him up. A good six feet-two or three inches tall, with the whitest teeth I'd ever seen and a matching wide smile, he was good looking.

"Aren't you gonna ask me my name?" he said, walking up to me.

I chuckled. I hadn't realized I didn't ask him his name. "Oh, I'm sorry. What's your name?"

"Ziek. Ziek Wallace," he said, looking deep into my eyes.

Hmm ... Ziek. Very different, I thought.

"Do you have a number, so I can call you?" he said, cutting to the chase.

"You gonna call?" I said, flirting.

"Absolutely."

"And are you gonna teach me how to ride that?" I said, pointing at his motorcycle.

"I'll teach you how to ride anything you want," he said with a sly grin on his face.

I blushed again. After scrambling to find a blank piece of paper, I finally just retrieved a crumpled grocery store receipt and neatly wrote my name and phone number on the back of it, making sure the heart above the "i" in my name was fancy. I folded the receipt and slid it into his jacket pocket.

He smirked. "I'll definitely be calling you," he added, winking as he turned away and got back on his motorcycle.

I smiled and watched him as he restarted and revved the motorcycle's engine, backed up, pulled out of Lucky's premises, and sped off down the street.

Ziek and I played the cat and mouse game for a few weeks, as I refused to give in to his eagerness to go out on a date. Between work and going out with other male suitors, I had to find time for Ziek. And eventually, I did.

My first date with Ziek was very untraditional, to say the least. He arrived at my house around six o'clock that day. I heard him pull up, but he rang the doorbell before I could get downstairs, which meant Honey was going to answer the door. She judged every guy I dated. I knew she'd let me know her opinion of him with her nonverbal cues.

"Destiny," she called out.

"I'm coming," I yelled, which was something Honey really wasn't fond of. I looked in the mirror one last time, making sure I was pleased with my appearance. *I'm good*, I thought, grabbing my purse off the bed before walking out of my room.

Honey must've told Ziek to make himself at home because he was comfortably sitting on the sofa in the living room when I got downstairs.

"Hi," I said in a bashful tone. He was even more good looking than I remembered.

Honey was standing near the bookcase in the corner fumbling with the picture frames that had either fallen over or were leaning backwards. Some of the frames were old and worn, and the pictures inside were stuck to the glass. I waited for Honey to look at me, and when she did, I attempted to introduce the two of them to each other. "Honey, this is Ziek, and Ziek, this is my—"

"We done already introduced ourselves, right Ziek?" Honey said, looking at Ziek and then back at me. I could tell she wasn't too fond of Ziek. Honey didn't like "pretty boys." She said they thought the world owed them something because they were good looking. And because of it, she said she wouldn't give them the time of day. And I guess that's why she settled on Albert Crawford Sr. From the pictures plastered around the house as well as those in the countless number of picture albums, he definitely wasn't easy on the eyes. You didn't need to guess that my mother and her siblings got their looks from Honey, not their father.

"I'm ready when you are," I said, looking at Ziek and then at Honey through my peripheral vision. She had turned her attention back to organizing the picture frames. And that was good because I wasn't interested in hearing her opinion at that moment; I was captivated by the fact that a hot guy was interested in me. *Me.*

"Nice meeting you, Ms. Honey," Ziek said as he stood to leave.

"Uh, huh … you, too," Honey replied without turning to look at him.

"I picked up something to eat. I hope you don't mind," Ziek said as he opened the passenger door for me.

"What did you pick up?"

"Hold up," he said, closing the door and walking around to the driver side. "I bought sandwiches and some wine," he said when he got in the car.

"Meatball, huh? I can smell it," I said, turning to look at the bag from Mozoali's in the back seat.

"I remembered you said you liked their subs."

"Yes, I love them."

"I figured we could sit down at Botanical Gardens and enjoy a good meal while we get to know one another. I thought it would be better than sitting at some stuffy restaurant listening to music that we've never heard of before," he said, buckling his seatbelt.

His suggestion was out of the norm, but I was down to try it. And I was glad I did. I learned a lot about Ziek. He was honest about quite a few things. Whatever he wasn't honest about, I was sure I'd find out soon enough. We definitely vibed well. But I noticed he didn't ask a lot of personal questions about me, such as my occupation. I was smart enough to know why, so I started probing him myself.

"So what do you do for a living?"

"I'm gonna be honest with you, and you can decide what you want to do from there."

"Okay," I said, inhaling.

"I just got out of the pen about a year ago."

I nodded, giving him permission to continue.

"I sell."

Honey's intuition was always on point. But I wasn't going to judge him because he sold drugs. Drug dealers made the best boyfriends—they always kept money in your pocket, the most stylish clothes on your back, and the most expensive bling bling around your neck and fingers.

"So tell me more about your family," Ziek said, unaware he was requesting that I open a can of worms.

"Like I told you, I live with my grandmother and my two cousins. Well, they live with us on and off. Whenever their mom, my aunt, gets sick and tired of them, she ships them back to my grandmother."

"Hmmm," Ziek responded.

"What about yours?"

"Your family is angelic compared to mine," Ziek said, chuckling.

"I didn't think they got any worse than mine," I said, stuffing the last bit of my meatball sub into my mouth.

"Trust me. Y'all ain't got nothing on us. My mom's been an addict most of my life. Well, since I can remember."

Well, Shannon was no addict, but who was I to judge him based on his mother's status? Honey was a missionary, and I was turning out to be nothing like she hoped I would turn out. I didn't pursue college, I was engaged in premarital sex, and had it not been for God looking out for me, I could very well have been a single parent. "So what about your father?" I finally said.

"I know him. But he's always been too busy for his family. Too busy tryna be a renowned pastor, following in my grandfather's footsteps."

"Do you guys have a relationship?"

"He'd like to think we do. But I'm not interested in being all chummy chum with someone who doesn't practice what they preach. He's a hypocrite. He's a pastor, but I have a sister who's eight months younger than me. Such a hypocrite."

"I know the sentiment," I said, looking past Ziek at a couple dancing in the distance as if they had no care in the world.

"Guess we have some things in common, huh?" Ziek said, pouring wine in my glass.

"Yes," I said, lifting my filled glass to propose a toast.

"Here's to us. May we find love and happiness," he said, announcing the toast instead.

We clinked our glasses together before taking sips of the red wine. "This wine tastes so good," I said, taking another sip. "Where'd you get it from?"

"The winery. That's my kinda thing. I do wine tasting and the whole nine. You have to come with me some time," he said, winking. "Seems like it's your style," he added.

"My style?" I said, pointing my finger in my chest.

"Yes. Classy. I can tell you're not like a lot of these other girls out here."

"What do you mean?"

"You don't seem like you like a lot of attention drawn … a drama-free kinda lady."

"How can you be sure?" I said, raising my eyebrows.

"I'm a pretty good judge of character."

The compliment was flattering, but it was just the beginning. And guys will say anything in the beginning of a relationship. After all, they're trying to lure you with words and nice deeds. The devil never reveals who he is in the beginning. Plus, I knew myself all too well. I had the propensity of being dangerous—I fought hard to not fall in love; in my book, it was a weakness. I was notorious for recycling men if I needed to. Loyalty was a rarity in my life—I hadn't experienced much of it during my lifetime.

By night's end, I was up in the air on whether I would continue to see Ziek. I genuinely liked him, and I believed he genuinely liked me as well. Only time would tell.

Even though I had reservations about moving forward in a full-fledged relationship, I enjoyed my moments with Ziek. Being whisked around town in his black BMW convertible and sometimes on the back of his motorcycle made me feel like a queen. I think our commonality was the broken relationships with our parents. And I believed it was the glue that kept Ziek and I coming back to each another. We knew one another's vulnerabilities, we didn't judge each other, and we understood each other. It was as though in a perfect world, we were meant to be, but due to our own idiosyncrasies, a healthy, loving, and lasting relationship would never manifest. Neither one of us could fully or accurately articulate the phenomenon, but we both knew it existed.

And as the natural seasons were changing, so were the seasons in my life. The combination of my ensuing relationship with Ziek, the job at the plant, and having a car I was proud to own and drive, began to shift my perspective on life. I started feeling better about myself, even though I still had feelings of insecurity stemming from the rejection and abandonment of my parents. And because of it, I still battled my own demons, demons that arose with me in the morning and went to sleep with me at night, telling me I was unworthy of true love. Externally, I exuberated confidence, but on the inside, the confidence scale was on E, for empty.

Chapter 7

Games People Play

DESPITE THE FACT THAT it wasn't Honey's wish for me to get stuck working at a plant for the rest of my life, I became complacent. Steady money to buy pretty much anything I wanted, limited financial responsibility, other than the few dollars I had to give Honey, increasing independence, and a slew of male suitors made for an exciting life.

Terry was a tall, dark-skinned brother who resembled the singer Seal. Twelve years my senior, Terry was bald and had a thinly-shaven goatee. His looks might not have turned many women's heads, but they certainly turned mine. Terry had a wild sense of humor, always cracking jokes and finding the humor in almost anything. Our introduction in the breakroom one evening was by sheer happenstance.

"You know, it would help if you pressed the start button if you want to heat your food up," Terry joked after noticing I hadn't pressed the start button after placing my food in the microwave.

"Oops, I didn't even realize I didn't press start," I said, turning around to press the start button.

"I got it," Terry said, stepping in front of me to press it for me.

"Thank you," I said, gazing up at him. Terry was probably a good six-five or six-six. And that's when I realized he didn't have the smoothest skin. But I knew I could overlook skin texture if I was digging a man the right way.

"You're pretty new around here, aren't you?" he said.

"Kinda, sorta. But I've been here going on a year now."

"Has it been that long?"

"Yes."

"Hmm ..."

"What does that mean?" I asked, expecting him to interpret his "Hmm."

"Nothing. Just wondering why our paths haven't crossed all that much," Terry said, opening the microwave door after it buzzed, signaling that two minutes had elapsed.

"Have you always worked this shift?" I said as I retrieved my food from the microwave.

"Yes. But I recently transferred to this division."

"Well, then, that might be why."

"It doesn't have to stay that way," Terry said as he placed his container of food in the microwave.

"So what are you tryna say?" I said, flirting. I was well aware of what he was alluding to, but I enjoyed playing dumb.

"We don't have to stay strangers. We could get to know one another better. Are you open to that?"

"Sure," I said, grabbing a few napkins from the napkin holder on the counter.

"What's your name?" he asked as he tried to scan the writing on my badge.

"Destiny."

"And I'm Terry."

"Nice to meet you."

"So how about this weekend, Destiny? Can I take you out?"

"Hmm," I mumbled, giving Terry a little taste of his own medicine as I headed to my table in the breakroom.

"That must mean, yes!" he said with all manner of boldness.

"Is that right?" I said, feeding into his shenanigans.

"You like this bald head, don't you?" he said as he stroked his shiny bald head with both hands.

"I didn't say all that," I said, smiling. His sense of humor was tantalizing.

"Yes, you did."

"So now you're a mind reader, huh?"

"That's just the way the good Lord from up above made me," he joked.

"Is that right?"

He nodded. And that was our beginning.

That following Saturday, Terry and I went out for the first time. He picked me up at four o'clock that afternoon, and we went to a small pizza joint on his side of town. Although I was a church girl, I was smart enough to know what an early date signified—Terry, more than likely, had a girlfriend, and the evening was reserved for her. So I did to him the only thing I knew to do—placed him in the friend zone. Except, in his case, he had one added benefit—sex.

Terry was perfectly fine being in the "friends with benefits" zone because he didn't want a commitment himself. And since he didn't really want a commitment, only a good time between the sheets, that's pretty much what I gave him, initially. However, the time would come that no matter how much I tried to fool myself, having sex with Terry wasn't just about getting my rocks off. I started developing feelings for him. And all it took for me to become aware of my true feelings was to hear rumors that Terry was seeing other women at the plant. Things came to a head when I confronted him about it one evening.

With the intention on nipping it in the bud, I strutted over to his side of the building. I knew Terry worked in Corridor B, but I was unsure of the actual room. Luckily for me that evening, Mario, the guy who worked in the mailroom, was delivering the late mail, and I asked him if he knew which room Terry worked in.

"Tall Terry?"

"Yes, him."

"Oh, right over there," Mario said, pointing to room B2.

"Thanks, Mario," I said before nearly leaping over to the door of room B2.

I stood outside the door, peering through the small rectangular-shaped glass carved in the door. And there he was, all six-foot-five of him, flirting with a Spanish girl. I watched for a good five minutes before I decided to knock on the door.

"Can I see Terry Brothers for a minute? He has my keys," I lied to the shift manager who answered the door.

With a puzzled look, Terry came over to the door. "Your keys? I don't have your keys. Are you sure you're not getting me mixed up with your *other* man?"

Offended by his comment, I snapped. "Yeah, you're only saying that because you're in there fraternizing with your little Spanish girlfriend in there," I said, pointing.

"Excuse me?" Terry said, stepping out of the doorway, into the hallway, and closing the door behind him.

"You heard me! I see you in there getting pretty cozy with that Spanish chick."

"Savannah."

"Huh?" I questioned.

"Savannah. That's her name—Savannah, not 'chick.'"

I refused to say her name. "Yeah, her. I see you in there flirting with her."

"So," Terry said as if he didn't owe me any explanation.

"That's all you have to say?" I said, my lips curling.

"What else do you want me to say? We ain't no item. Remember, you were the one that said you just wanted to kick it for the time being. So that's what we're doing, right? We're kickin' it like you said, right?"

"That was in the beginning. Things have changed," I said, angry that he would throw those words back at me when he needed a defense. "Well, I changed my mind."

"Just like that, huh? You want to change your mind. How convenient of you, Destiny. You're selfish."

"Oh, I'm selfish when you want to stick your penis somewhere else, huh?" I said, now standing on my toes, trying to get up in his face.

"It's mine, and I can do whatever I want with it," he said, pushing the weight of his body against mine until I moved backward. Before I knew it, my right hand made contact with his left cheek.

He didn't even flinch. "I think you better leave before this gets ugly," Terry said in a stern voice. His eyes widened as if he dared me to talk back this time.

My anger and jealousy manifested themselves in the salty stream of tears that tumbled down my cheeks as I stormed off down the corridor.

Vowing to get Terry back for dissing me the way he did, I made it my business to flirt with other guys in his presence whenever the opportunity presented itself. And it didn't take long for the first victim of mine to appear—Dominic Chandler. I called him "The Dom" because his personality reminded me of an Italian mafia man. He was good looking as well—medium-tall, squinty eyes, and deep dimples that made me melt like vanilla ice cream on a hot slice of fresh baked apple pie.

The Dom had just finished his junior year at Michigan State University, where he was majoring in accounting. He took an internship at the plant that summer. I'd seen him around a few times, but our paths didn't cross until we were at one of our company outings. Like others, our introduction was a combination of back-and-forth flirting, name and phone number exchanges, and a promise to meet up for a bite to eat.

The Dom was the studious type. He took summer courses, which is why our time together was always limited. He'd sometimes bring his books with us when we went out on so-called dates. His being in school and only being an intern equated to him not having a lot of money to wine and dine me. Nevertheless, The Dom was the kind of guy Honey would have given her blessings. Deep down, though, I didn't believe The Dom would stay with a girl like me because I wasn't college educated or even pursuing a college education. I kept this in the back of my mind, telling myself I was only using him to make Terry jealous. And besides, The Dom would be going back to school within weeks, so there was really no need for me to get too serious with him. At least that was another thing I kept telling myself in my desperate attempt to avoid getting hurt—again.

"Do you know that guy over there?" The Dom asked one day while we were eating together in the breakroom.

"What guy?" I asked, turning to look in the direction he was pointing. It was Terry, looking, staring, smirking, and shaking his head as if he was in disbelief.

"Oh, yeah. His name is Terry."

"So I take it you *do* know him ... in more ways than one," The Dom said, putting his jealousy on display, whether he knew it or not.

"I mean, we dated for a hot minute, but that's it."

"Oh," The Dom replied as he stuffed another fork full of steamed broccoli in his mouth. "This broccoli is delicious," he said, complimenting my cooking skills. And that was another thing about The Dom; he didn't speak slang. His English was almost perfect. It was another reason I felt we were a mismatch.

My feeling was confirmed the day I met his mother and she automatically assumed The Dom and I met on campus. When The Dom didn't correct her assumption, I was sure that he, too, felt some way about me not being educated beyond high school. So I continued to see him for what it was worth. I had an agenda, and he was helping me achieve it.

"Thank you," I finally said, blushing. I was a pretty good cook, thanks to Honey.

Our last few weeks of seeing one another before he went back to school were filled with excitement, which was definitely out of the ordinary. We'd go to movies, amusement parks, and just hang out around the house. At times, I felt bad about using him. He seemed like a nice guy. And if he didn't suck in bed, I would have probably tried harder to make it work. Not only was he inexperienced, but his apparatus was on the small side, providing very little pleasure and any hope for skill improvement in the future. Luckily for me, I used his going-back-to-school departure as a way to "break up," if you will. And he bought it, hook, line, and sinker. This way, I didn't have a guilty conscience.

After The Dom went back to school in the middle of August, I mostly stayed to myself, as far as men were concerned. Yeah, there were some who admired me from afar, but they didn't approach me. And if I dared start a conversation with any of them, it was quick and very short lived.

So it was back to the drawing board for me. That was, until Mr. Boldness came up to my table while I was on break one evening.

"Do you mind if I join you?"

I recognized the voice and didn't even bother to look up. Instead, I just uttered a sarcastic response. "So now you care about if I mind your behavior?"

"I'll take that as a yes," he said as he dropped his tray on the table and sat down across from me.

"Well, I didn't exactly say that," I replied, now looking up at Terry.

"Look, I want to apologize for my actions."

"A month later, Terry? For real?"

"Better late than never," he said as he opened his can of Coca Cola.

"And you think that's okay?"

"You are one stubborn woman. You like to hold grudges, I see," Terry added, this time, winking.

"Terry, this is not the time or place for—"

"You won't answer my calls. You barely look at me around here," he said, cutting me off.

"Because I have better things to do than to be treated like the main thing one minute and then a side piece the next," I said as I stuffed my sandwich back into the Ziploc bag. I had lost my appetite.

"So you think I treated you like a side piece?"

I rolled my eyes, giving Terry his answer.

"Well, I'm sorry, Destiny. Can we start over? I miss you, sugar plum," Terry teased, reaching over to grab my hands. "Please?"

Even though I tried to prevent it, a warm smile formed on my lips. Whatever it was Terry had, it had lured me in once again. And before I knew it, Terry and I were once again doing our thing. And our thing meant anything from official dates to straight-up romps in the bedroom. And with no official labels or titles to this "thing" we had, it was only a matter of time before I would entertain the likes of another man looking my way. A man who would change my life ... *forever.*

Chapter 8

My Knight and Shining Armor

I USUALLY WORKED ON a press with a lady named Hattie. Hattie was an outspoken older woman. I was certain one of her hobbies had to be cosmetology because her makeup was flawless every day. Her hair was dark brown, about shoulder length, and she usually had blonde streaks on the ends. Even though I had never mentioned my "arrangement" with Terry, Hattie could sense there was something going on between the two of us. And although she didn't say anything, initially, Hattie observed. She was referred to as the eyes and ears of the plant. But she was a good person in my book.

"You know you have an admirer, don't you?" she said to me one evening at work.

"Puhleeze," I responded. The word "admirer" was starting to lose its flair. I had plenty of those, admiring my looks and body, but not wanting too much more outside of that.

"He comes by here often."

"Please don't tell me it's some eighty-five-year-old man who can half stand up," I joked.

"Don't shoot the messenger," Hattie said as she leaned her

head over to the right, gesturing that my so-called admirer was in the vicinity.

"Don't you think it's kind of stalkerish to just stop by and stare and never say anything," I said once I looked over and saw it was the same guy who'd come by several times a night over the past few weeks.

"He's new. I don't think he's being a stalker at all. He's watching you. Guys who observe you before they approach aren't just looking for one thing, you know. I'd give him the time of day, if I were you," Hattie said, removing her gloves to examine a broken fingernail.

"Yeah, I think he is new. Up until a couple of weeks ago, I hadn't seen him around here, either," I said, changing my tone and perspective.

"Well, don't be crazy. He's new and he's looking at you. So be open. Smile." That was all the advice Hattie gave me.

But several weeks passed before my admirer and I formally met and introduced ourselves.

"Excuse me," he said as he rolled down the driver side window of his hi-lo as I attempted to walk past him.

"Yes," I said, looking at him.

"Did you burn yourself or something?" he asked, pointing to the white gauze I had taped above my left breast to disguise the newly carved tattoo I had just gotten over the weekend. Even though it was a plant, it was still a place of business, and tattoos, nose piercings, tongue piercings, etcetera, etcetera were frowned upon, especially when worn by women.

"No, I didn't burn myself," I said, pulling up my smock to cover the gauze.

"Don't tell me … a tatt?" he said.

"Yes."

"So what did you get?" he said, as he propped his feet on the dashboard of his hi-lo.

"Excuse me?" I replied. The phrase "Excuse me?" is the default phrase a woman uses when she wants to play the cat and mouse game. I used it often, especially to gauge a man's true intent and interest.

"Your tattoo. What did you get?"

"Oh, I got a rose with my name on it."

Obviously flirting with me, he continued. "Can I see it?"

"Sure, if you're lucky enough," I said, flirting back.

"I like that," he said with a slight chuckle.

I could see that he was missing one of his incisors when he talked. He wasn't what I was normally attracted to, but it was his composure, if anything, that drew me. He didn't seem the least bit concerned about his looks. He beamed with self-confidence, which was alluring in and of itself.

"David. My name is David," he said, leaning nearly his entire torso outside of the truck.

"Nice to meet you, David. My name is Destiny."

"I know your name," he said, his smile widening as he saw the look of surprise on my face.

"How did you know my name?"

"Don't you worry your little pants about that. I have my ways."

"So you're not gonna tell me?"

"Maybe one day," he said, as he leaned back in and sat correctly in the driver seat of his hi-lo after spotting his manager approaching. "Take care, PYT. I'll be seeing you around," he said before quickly resuming his task.

And that's how I met the infamous David Sylvester Falls.

Our first date was spent consoling each other. It was September 13, 1996, the day Tupac died.

Coincidentally, Tupac was both our favorite rapper, and his death felt as though we had both lost a close family member. And this seemingly shared loss brought David and me close almost immediately.

Our relationship moved fast, even though a relationship was the farthest thing from my mind, initially. But my reservations didn't stop David from getting me a gift that October for Sweetest Day. I was totally caught off guard when he handed me a gift bag from Kay Jewelers, and I opened it to find a gold anklet.

"Thank you," I said, genuinely surprised and ecstatic about the unexpected gift. Other than my brief relationship with Ziek, I didn't get gifts from men. If anything, I was the gift giver and rarely the receiver.

"You're welcome," David said, motioning me to put my leg in his lap, so he could put the anklet on for me.

I placed my right leg in his lap, trying to make sure the sole of my foot did not rub against his private parts. But David just repositioned my leg between his crotch area, looking me square in the eye the entire time. He held his hand out for me to hand him the jewelry box, and I handed it to him. I watched David open the box, retrieve the anklet, and place it around my ankle.

"It's so beautiful," I said, rotating my ankle from left to right. I loved seeing the sparkles from the gold bouncing off the rays of the sun.

"You know I like you," David said, throwing me for a loop.

"I mean, I guess," I responded. I knew it sounded like a dumb reply, but I was at a loss for words.

"And this right here is proof of how I feel about you," he said, pointing to the anklet.

"Wait … wait. So what are you trying to say?" I replied, shifting my position and repositioning my leg once again.

"I'm saying this means I'm digging you, and I'm working toward us being exclusive."

"Whoa, wait. We never spoke about being exclusive," I said, now moving my leg off his lap entirely.

"Destiny, we spend hours on the phone talking. We hang out all the time. Don't you think that's the normal course of how this thing should go?"

I was stuck. I didn't have a response, at least not initially. I was a quick thinker and was sure I'd find the right words to say. But they just wouldn't form.

"That's normally how it's done, Destiny. I mean, what are you looking for?" David continued.

"Well, I have some concerns," I said. I had been in enough short-term relationships to pick up on certain behaviors.

"Concerns?" David asked, perplexed.

"Yeah, we hang out. But you've never invited me to your house. I don't know where you live, but you know where I live," I said, hoping he'd give me the answer I was looking for and satisfy my curiosity by saying he lived with his mama or something.

"What does that prove? My housing situation is complicated. All you need to focus on is that I'm here with you. I have not only told you how I feel about you, but I've demonstrated it as well."

"Complicated?" I responded, shaking my head.

"Yeah, complicated. Sometimes you meet people and you fall for them, but you can have other things going on in your life. You, of all people, should understand."

"Me?"

"Yes, you, Destiny. You don't think I've heard the rumors that you and that guy Terry have something going on?"

"Well, we don't," I lied. What Terry and I had was an understanding that we satisfy each other's sexual needs and keep it pushing from there. I didn't think we gave off the vibe that we had something going on around the plant.

"Are you sure?" David asked in a calmer tone, hoping to diffuse the mounting tension.

I didn't answer.

"I didn't mean to get upset. I actually wasn't going to even mention it to you, but it just kind of brought itself up."

"Well, it ain't true," I lied again.

"Okay. Okay."

An awkward moment of silence passed.

"So are we good now?" David asked.

I didn't respond. I was contemplating a way to keep my emotions out of it. I was beginning to like this David guy a little. But it seemed as though all my relationships were relatively short lived, and I just didn't want to give too much of an emotional investment anymore.

I looked at David in my peripheral vision; I felt pity for him.

If there was ever a woman who ran from love and commitment but claimed they were the very things she longed for, that woman would be me. As much as David's love for me was pulling me closer, my own destructive thoughts and behavior were pulling me away from him.

When David and I didn't spend Thanksgiving together that year, it was my cue to leave him alone. I liked him, so I knew I needed someone or something to distract me. That's when I started accepting phone calls from The Dom. From there, our five-minute conversations eventually turned into ten-minute conversations, then thirty-minute conversations, and finally, in-person meetups. I felt as though I had some sense of control when I was seeing guys like Terry, The Dom, and even Ziek, for that matter. Initially, I lied to David about my whereabouts. I was nobody's fool. I knew David was living with a woman, so my mentality was complementary—*What's good for the goose is good for the gander.*

Of course, hanging out with The Dom meant nothing more than romps in the bed. Again, he was in college, which translated into him being low on cash or altogether broke. The sex had gotten a little better this go around, and that was because he had gotten a hold of some Viagra from one of his college buddies, and we used sex toys and other things to make the sex fun and longer lasting. But outside of that, The Dom was still a very boring person. He rarely wanted to do things together or go places together, and eventually, I grew tired of being his sex buddy. It came to a head one night when I decided to call him out on it.

"Hey, you know what?" I said, trying to throw him off guard in a nonconfrontational tone. He didn't answer. We had just got finished having sex and he had dozed off into a deep sleep. "Hey, you ... wake up," I said, poking him with my right index finger.

"What, Destiny? I'm sleep. Can't you see that?"

"Well, excuse me. Do you know how many nights I'm sleeping, and you still wake me up to have sex with *you*?"

"Okay, what? What, Destiny?!" he said, sitting up briskly.

"How come we don't do things together anymore?"

"Destiny, we've been over this a thousand times."

"No, we haven't," I said, sitting up as well.

"Yes, we have. We don't go out because I don't have money like that. I'm a student, and I don't have a good job yet. That's why!" he said before lifting the flat bed sheet over his face.

"Well, I don't like it. All we do is have sex."

"Well, Destiny, it is what it is," he said, his voice muffled by the sheet covering his face.

And that was my cue to exit his bed and his life, for good this time. I jumped out of bed, threw my clothes on, and started gathering my other items to leave.

"So you gonna leave?" he asked as he snatched the sheet off his face.

"That's what it looks like," I said, forcing my feet into my Nike gym shoes. "And I can let myself out," I added as I stormed out of his bedroom, slamming his bedroom door behind me.

He jumped up and followed me. "You know, you really don't need to be leaving this time of the night, Destiny."

"I'm good. I got a car," I said as I reached to unlock the front door.

The Dom reached around me and opened the front door. I couldn't believe he wasn't going to fight harder for me to stay. I took in a deep breath, flung open the storm door, and bolted down the front steps.

It *was* dark out, nearly pitch black, but the glare from the porch light illuminated my front driver side tire, which was flat. "I think my tire is flat," I yelled at him as I pepped up my step to inspect the tire. The tire was indeed flat. I began to replay the drive over. *Did I hit anything? Run over anything?* I couldn't recall doing so. I walked around my car, only to discover that my front passenger side tire was flat as well. "Somebody did something to my tires!" I screamed.

"You must've run over something on your way over. Ain't nobody messed with your car," The Dom tried to assure me as he fastened his robe and ran down the front steps to survey the damage as well.

I wasn't a dummy, and no amount of convincing on The Dom's part would have made me believe that happenstance caused two tires on a nearly brand-new car to go flat without mechanical interference. I wasn't *that* naïve. I just looked at The Dom and rolled my eyes as hard as I could. "Just let me use your phone, will you?"

I followed The Dom back into the house and called AAA, and then we walked back outside and waited on the front steps for them to arrive. There was no chit chatting between us; we were like two strangers waiting at a bus stop. With only one spare in my car, there was no doubt they were going to have to tow the car back to my house.

When the tow truck arrived, the driver stepped out of the truck and called my name.

"Destiny?" he said, pointing. He was a short, stocky older guy.

"Yeah, that's me," I said, walking toward my car.

"What do we have going on here?" he said, inspecting the tires.

"Looks like she might have hit something in the road or ran over something," The Dom volunteered.

"Nah, this doesn't look like she ran over something in the road. Looks like you pissed somebody off, ma'am," the tow truck driver joked. We all knew what that meant—somebody had deliberately flattened my tires.

"That's what I thought," I said, turning to look at The Dom, who looked like a deer in headlights. So even The Dom must've been kickin' it with someone else. And whoever she was, she was definitely trying to give Dominic and me a warning.

"I take it you only have one spare, huh?"

"Yeah, just the spare in the trunk. And it's just a donut, anyway," I said, pointing to the trunk of my car.

"So you're gonna need a tow, right?"

"Yes," The Dom interjected.

"Will I be towing it to your mechanic or your house?"

"To my house, please," I responded as I fiddled through my purse for my driver's license. It was cold out, and I just wanted the night to be over.

"Do you have a ride, or are you riding with me?" the tow truck driver asked as he started sorting through the paperwork on the clipboard he was holding.

I waited for The Dom to answer, but he didn't mumble a word. After realizing he wasn't going to offer me a ride home, I answered the question. "I'll be riding with you."

"I know it's cold out, but just let me wrap up this paperwork and hitch up your car, and we'll be on our way."

"Okay," I responded.

"Hey, call me when you get home," The Dom said. I wanted to spit in his face, but I didn't. I just walked over to the passenger side of the tow truck and got in without responding. *You'll be one dead man if you hold your breath waiting for my phone call.*

The Dom never heard from me again.

David called me around two o'clock the next afternoon. He could sense I wasn't my normal self.

"What's wrong? You don't sound cheery like you do normally."

"Nothing. I'm just a little bored because I'm stuck in the house until Monday. I gotta get my car fixed."

"What's wrong with your car?"

"I got two flat tires, and the dealership isn't open until Monday."

"*Two* flat tires?" David said, trying to be sure he heard me correctly.

"Yeah, two," I embarrassingly replied. I was sure he was going to ask probing questions, but he didn't.

"I can stop by and see what I can do, if that's okay with you," he graciously offered.

"No, David, you don't have to. I'll be okay until Monday." I knew he genuinely wanted to help, but I was vulnerable and sad, which was always a dangerous combination for me.

"Destiny, just let me help. Trust me, it's not a problem."

I acquiesced. "Okay. Sure."

In no time, I heard Tupac's voice coming from David's truck. His music wasn't blasting, but it was loud enough to draw attention. Before I could reach the end of the driveway, David was making his way over to my car to inspect the tires.

"Dang!" he said as he shook his head. "You're gonna need two new tires."

"Can't I just get them plugged?" It wasn't a pay week for me, and two new tires were not in my budget.

"Nah. I wouldn't chance it. It's not safe. What if it snows?"

"Okay," I reluctantly agreed.

When it was all said and done, David had purchased two new tires for my car. Of course, a request to take me out on a date also accompanied the generous gesture. Quite naturally, I felt some sense of obligation to say yes. The situation, as unfortunate as it was, allowed me to see things for what they truly were. Perhaps I needed to go for something a little different when it came to men. I would have been trapped at home that weekend if David hadn't come to my rescue. With this single gesture, David had moved from a *maybe* kind of guy to my knight in shining armor.

There was no way, in good conscience, I could decline David's invitation to hang out that night, not after all he had done for me. So we ended up going out to a restaurant called Pizza Papalis, where I was introduced to seafood pizza for the first time.

Our night ended early, as we'd both had a full day, especially having to deal with the car ordeal. As he'd done previously, David walked me up the stairs to the front door of my house.

"I like you," he whispered in my ear as I positioned the key in the lock.

I liked him, too, but out of caution for developing premature emotions, I didn't exchange the same sentiment. Instead, I just said, "Really?"

"Yes. And I'm going to marry you one day."

I burst into laughter. I thought the comment was over the top.

"You're laughing, but I'm serious. You're gonna be my wife one day. Watch."

Before I could respond, David leaned closer, lifted my chin, and planted a wet, soft kiss on my lips. He gently slid his tongue in, and before I knew it, we were engaged in a deep, passionate kiss. I could have died and gone to heaven in that moment. It was the type of kiss that made your toes curl. Yeah, that kind of kiss. I could only imagine what he was like in bed.

As the saying goes, all good things must come to an end. And that's exactly what happened. I unlocked the front door and opened it. David reached for my left hand, which was free, and planted one last kiss.

"Sleep tight, sweetie," he whispered.

"I will. Thank you. Thank you for everything," I said as I blew him a kiss.

He smiled.

I watched David as he descended the front steps. As he opened the car door, I yelled out, "Call me and let me know you made it home all right."

He did the ole thumbs up, got in his car, and drove off. I closed the door behind me, rested my back against it, and closed my eyes tightly. *Feels like a dream.*

Chapter 9

Signs and Wonders

I HAD BEEN LOOKING forward to Valentine's Day weekend. David had invited me to be his guest at his cousin's thirtieth birthday bash in Grand Rapids. Even though it was just a little under a two-hour drive, we both took Friday off, so David could meet up with some of his kinfolk on his father's side of the family. Knowing that Honey would never go for me going on an overnight trip with a man, I lied and told her Shonte was going to be in town visiting her grandparents in Grand Rapids and David was driving me there to meet up with her, since he was already going there for the birthday party.

Honey never questioned me hanging around Shonte, so I felt I was safe with the lie. Now, Toya? She was a different story. Honey always said Toya was fast and to keep her away from any man I was dating. I never questioned Toya's loyalty, but since older women seemed to have an extra dose of intuition, I kept certain things about my love life private when it came to Toya. And besides, in this instance, I didn't want to get caught in a lie, especially with Toya living right next door, so I just left her out of it. I did give her a heads up, however, and told her that if Honey questioned why she didn't go as well, to just tell Honey she couldn't get off work.

Dressed, packed, and ready to go, I stood on the front steps with my luggage, waiting for David to pull up. When he did pull up, he didn't get out of the car right away. Instead, he sat and continued to puff on the cigarette he was smoking. That, if anything, was my only drawback about being around David—he was a chain smoker. When I realized he didn't seem to be in a rush to come get my suitcase, I proceeded down the porch steps with it. That's when he finally got out of the car, threw the cigarette butt on the sidewalk near the end of the driveway, and proceeded to meet me halfway.

"Honey said she's sick of seeing cigarette butts in front of her house," I said, pointing to cigarette butts lying on the sidewalk in front of the house.

"Key words are, *in front*. She doesn't own the sidewalk," David shot back.

"What is up with you?" I said, thrown off by the curt comment he had just made.

David didn't respond. He grabbed the suitcase out of my hand and turned away, headed back to his car without engaging me further. I walked back up the front steps to make sure I had indeed locked the front door. The thought of someone walking into our home and taking our hard-earned belongings once again was unfathomable to me. After making sure it was locked, I made my way over to the front passenger door and waited for David to open it for me. He opened the door and closed it after I got in without saying anything. That's something about David I was becoming accustomed to—he was very temperamental. I never knew which side of him was showing up, nice David or mean David.

I waited for him to get in and pull off before I addressed the obvious silent treatment he was giving me. "So are you going to tell me what's going on?"

"I think you might be in a better position to do that for me, Destiny," David said, looking at me intermittently as he continued to drive.

"I have no idea what you're talking about, David."

"You don't?" he said with a slight smirk.

"What's funny?"

"Nothing's funny, Destiny, trust me. But I have to find some type of humor in this mess before I go off."

"Go off? Is that a threat?"

"Take it however you want to take it. But I'm gonna tell you this one time, and one time only. I will not let you make a fool of me."

"What on God's green earth are you talking about, David?" I demanded. I could feel my temples pulsating.

Without warning, from the center lane, David swerved the car onto the right shoulder.

"What are you doing?!" I yelled, looking back to see if any imminent danger was approaching.

"You heard me, didn't you?" David said, slamming the gear into park.

"I don't know what you're talking about. So, no, I didn't hear you," I shot back. Being raised by Honey, I wasn't the timid type.

"What was one of the first things I asked you when we started dating?" David said as he lit up a cigarette.

"I dunno, David. You asked a bunch of questions. I can't remember."

"I specifically asked you if you were messing with Terry, didn't I?"

"You did. And I said no."

"And you lied to me," he said, taking a deep first drag of the cigarette.

"I didn't lie to you. I didn't have a relationship with Terry."

"But you were messing around with him."

I didn't respond. I just kept quiet as I tried to reminisce on what vibe I might have given off to cause David to further probe about my dealings with Terry. Our relationship was supposed to be a "friends with benefits" type of thing and nothing else. And it had been long over once David and I started dating seriously.

"Wanna know how I know?"

I nodded.

"Because he has a sex tape going around of the two of you." He took another deep drag. "Yeah, you and him."

"Have or had?" I snapped. I was embarrassed and angry at the same time but tried not to show it. I had no idea that our secret was out. But then again, that's just like a wimp—to brag about what and who he's doing. *A sex tape? Terry made a sex tape of the two of us without my knowledge or permission?* "So is it have or had?" I repeated defensively.

"Does it matter? He has one. Do you know how stupid I felt with dudes passing the tape around and patting him on the back while I'm standing over there looking like a fool? Had you told me this, it would have been a whole different ball game."

"Why would he do this to me?" I sobbed, finally reaching my breaking point. The lever broke.

"You mean, why did you do it to yourself? You know the saying, how people treat you is based on what you allow," he said matter-of-factly.

We sat on the side of the road for about another ten minutes, with neither one of us saying anything. But then, out of nowhere, David blurted, "Just forget it. I don't even want to go to Grand Rapids anymore. I'm taking you back home."

"Don't do that, David," I pleaded. "We had a nice weekend planned. And besides, your cousin has already paid for our plates. That's not right to RSVP and not show up."

"I'll give her the money for our plates. It ain't no big deal. I'm in a funky mood now, and the last thing I want to do is go parading around folk with fake smiles on my face."

I took a deep breath. What I was seeing now was a side of David that reminded me of what I'd heard about Albert Crawford Sr. My grandfather would have full-fledged plans with the family then back out at the last minute just because he was in a funky mood or because Honey made him mad. Anything would set him off, they said.

David put the gear in drive and made a wild U-turn, heading back toward my house. I could not believe what was transpiring. I really wanted to go to Grand Rapids, but I didn't want to seem as though I was begging, so I didn't plead with him any further. I turned my head slightly, facing the window, looking at the faces of other drivers and passengers as we drove past them.

When David pulled up in front of my house, I attempted to open the door, but it wouldn't open. "Can you unlock my door?" I asked, bluntly.

Without speaking, David unlocked the door and got out to retrieve my suitcase from the trunk. I didn't wait for him, I gathered my purse and the lunch bag that contained the food I had packed for our road trip, and I exited the car.

David left the suitcase in front of the front door. "I'll be talking to you," he mumbled as he walked past me and headed back to his car.

"Yeah," I mumbled back. I was angry at Terry for making the tape, angry at David for using it as a weapon, and angry at myself for allowing myself to be an easy target for both of these men to exert their power over me. I pulled the suitcase into the house and left it by the front door. I ran upstairs to my room, flung the lunch bag against the wall near my dresser, and flopped face down onto my bed, soaking my pillow with tears from my anger, sorrow, and regret.

Images of what I imagined would be on the sex tape bombarded my thoughts as I lay on the bed, languishing in my self-inflicted misery. Legs up. Legs down. Legs spread apart. Sitting on top. Lying flat on my back. Lying on my stomach. Bent over, doggy style … all for the eyes of strangers to see. I let out a loud wail. I was tired of losing at love. My relationships were all short lived. I was beginning to wonder whether I was deserving of a loving, healthy relationship. I yanked the pillow sham off my pillow and buried my face in it as I let out another loud scream, and another, and another.

I woke up to the sound of Honey's voice as she gently tapped me on my back. "What time are you leaving? You gonna be stuck in a lot of traffic if you don't hurry up and get outta here."

I turned over and sat up. "I'm not going," I said, rubbing my eyes.

"What happened?" Honey said in an affirmative tone. She was asking me, but she wasn't asking me. She knew something was wrong; my red, puffy eyes told it all.

Of course, I couldn't tell Honey what really went down, but I was looking for some answers to help me understand the madness I had experienced with David earlier. So I made up a different story. "I got into it with David."

"Figures," Honey said, followed by a loud sigh. "Well, what happened?"

"I don't know, Honey. We were on our way, and we just got into a huge argument."

"Over what?"

I didn't readily respond. I didn't want to put my foot in my mouth. But if there was a sex tape floating around the workplace, I was pretty sure she had gotten wind of it, too. "Terry around there telling lies on the job," I said, trying to fish for information. If Honey knew about the tape, she would definitely let the cat out of the bag. Since she didn't lead me to believe she had any knowledge of the tape, I let the lie stand.

"Do you see why I told you not to get involved with men on the job? It's a big mess. And it always makes the woman look bad. All men have to do is pull their pants back up and zip their zipper. Women? Not so easy. Now, you're involved with this David guy, and if you asked me, I think there's something wrong with him," she said as she sat on the bed beside me.

"No, Honey. He's different. He's not like any of the other guys I dated," I said.

Honey just raised her eyebrows, giving me that *"Oh, really?"* look.

"For real, Honey. He didn't pressure me into having sex with him right away like the other guys did."

"Is that what impressed you?"

"Well, it's one of the things that did," I said, defending my position and my man, as I'd been trained.

"Destiny, let me let you in on a secret. There ain't but two reasons why a guy doesn't pressure a woman about sex. Either he's homosexual or he's getting it somewhere else. *Your* job is to figure out which one it is."

Did she just tell me the guy I am in love with is either gay or has someone else?

"Don't be a fool for no man. Your grandmama married a fool, your mother got with a fool, had you, and then married a whole different fool. You're fortunate. You have the chance to look at our foolish ways and run in the opposite direction. There's something about this David guy that doesn't quite sit well with my spirit. I spend too much time in the Lord's presence for him not to show me things. And I'm just here to tell ya, that David guy ain't up to no good. And he ain't fooling nobody. I know he's out there running the streets."

Running the streets was the old folks' way of referencing "selling drugs."

"All it takes is for you to be with him when he gets busted, and you're going down with him. And you know how I feel about that. Just like I told my kids, don't call me from the jailhouse, 'cause I ain't coming to get'cha."

I nodded. Honey just didn't understand. I just knew I felt something different with David. The chemistry was different. He seemed genuinely happy to be out in public with me. He wasn't trying to hide me. Despite how disappointed I was with David for canceling our trip, I made up in my mind that day that I was going to stick by him, no matter what. I was going to prove to everyone, especially Shannon, that I was deserving of love from a man, too.

Chapter 10

Daddy Issues

THE NIGHT BEFORE ANN called, I dreamt I was being chased by a tall, masked man.

Gasping, I sat straight up in bed, forcing my eyes open. The familiar surroundings made me realize it was just a dream. I placed my right hand over the left side of my chest; the thumping sound of my heart sounded like cadets marching in a fierce marching band. My nightgown was drenched. *It's just a dream ... it's just a dream. I'm glad it was just a dream. Or was it a sign or warning of some sort?*

Ann Harrison-Matthews was one of Shannon's childhood friends. I never knew the whole story because every time I walked in on a conversation someone was having about her, it ended abruptly. Now that I was older, I had enough sense to know that nine times out of ten, when that happens, the conversation has something to do with you in some way, shape, or form. But from what I did gather, after eavesdropping on a conversation between Honey and her church friend, Leslie, Shannon and Ann had a falling out many years ago, after Shannon got pregnant by Ed and he dumped her. Growing up, I always thought Shannon was the other woman and Ann was Ed's main girl. Nevertheless, even though Ann and Shannon's friendship ended, Ann did keep in touch with Honey. I remember getting the mail out of the mailbox and seeing letters to Honey from Ann from time to time. Every year, Honey made sure we saved one of my school pictures for Ann. One year, I questioned Honey about it.

"Why do we always have to save that lady, Ann, one of my school pictures?"

"Because she's nice. Think of her like Auntie Donitra and Auntie Roz," Honey replied as she tucked one of my wallet-sized third grade pictures into an envelope and licked the flap. This was the extent of her explanation to me. I never asked again.

Life went on. But one particular day, when I had gone downstairs to pack my snack bag for work, I overheard Honey talking on the cordless phone.

"No, no ... Destiny drives. She can drive herself over there. But listen, Ann, I don't want no stuff." Honey didn't play no stuff. She said what she meant, and she meant what she said.

I'm not sure what Ann said on the other end of the receiver, but whatever it was, it was enough to assure Honey it was safe for me to go over to Ann's house. I could barely wait for Honey to hang up the phone before bombarding her with questions.

"Who was that? Was that the same Ms. Ann from before? What does she want with me? I mean—"

"Whoa, wait, chile! And slow your roll with me." Honey paused for a moment, sat down at the kitchen table, and took a sip of her sweet tea. "Okay, now. So, yes, that's the same Ms. Ann, and she wants to see you. Actually, Ms. Mae wants to see you, too."

"Who is Ms. Mae?" I asked, reaching into the refrigerator to grab a handful of grapes.

"That's Ms. Ann's oldest sister."

"Honey, who are these people?" I said, putting the grapes in a bowl.

Honey paused. She looked at me with that, *You sure you ready for this?* kind of look.

I nodded.

"They're your kinfolk."

"Who? And how?" I said, expecting her to elaborate. After rinsing the grapes and putting them in a container, I joined Honey at the kitchen table.

"They're your daddy's sisters. They ain't never done nothing to you or your mama, and they just want to see you."

Now it all made sense. Honey's church friends would always say, "Destiny sure looks like those Harrison girls." I paused for a moment before asking, "Are you coming, too?"

"No, Destiny. You're an adult now. I did my job. I shielded you from as much hurt and rejection as I could when you were younger. That's why I didn't let your mama take you back, either. She wanted to, but I told her I'd go to court and tell them that husband of hers was on all types of psychiatric medication. Of course, because she loves her man so much, she backed down and left you right here with me."

Honey and I both burst into laughter. I never knew that Shannon truly wanted me to live with her. I knew she would say it from time to time, but that was usually when she was in a bidding war with Honey about something trivial. In that moment, my animosity toward Shannon lessened. I still had major issues with her, but to know she was willing to have me live under her roof counted for something. What, I wasn't sure. Nevertheless, it counted for something, no matter how minute.

"And I have a feeling Ed is going to be there. Ann said he was gonna try to make it. They're having a big Sunday dinner over there in a few weeks. We're having our Women's Day at our church, so I wouldn't be able to come anyway."

I reached for one of the napkins in the napkin holder on the kitchen table and wiped my hands and the pebbles forming on my forehead.

"Baby, I knew this day was coming. Just put on your big girl panties and tell the man how you feel. Now, he couldn't come around Here, 'cause as far as I was concerned, he raped your mother. He was a grown man messing with a teenager. He got out of town, which was the best thing for him. I can't say he never thought about you all these years. I mean, why do you think I sent Ms. Ann a picture every year?"

I hunched my shoulders.

"Tell you what. When you go over there for that get-together, see if all those pictures are on display somewhere. Better yet, let me know if even a third of them are out on display. I can guarantee you they're not. I knew all along that Ann was sending the pictures to her brother."

My stomach felt queasy.

"Honey, I want to show him what he missed out on, but I'm so scared to even look at him."

"You'll be all right," Honey said, leaning over and placing my head in her bosom.

"What do you think Shannon is gonna say?" I asked.

"Let me worry about her. If you choose to see your father, I support your decision. Case closed."

Honey and I chatted a little while longer as she finished up her sweet tea. Without giving up too much information, she shed more light on what happened between Shannon, Ed, and Ann, for that matter. I wasn't sure how I was going to handle it all, because on one end, although Shannon and I obviously had issues for many years, I felt a loyalty toward her and felt as though meeting with Ed was somehow a stab in her back. I knew Shannon would feel betrayed by me meeting with him, but I was confident that, as she said, Honey would handle any impending dilemma between Shannon and me. But if I had to tell the truth, I was nervous about meeting with Ed—with all the built-up anger on the inside, there was no telling what would actually come out of my mouth.

I left Honey downstairs washing her cup at the kitchen sink

and went to my room. I *needed* David. I called him, and he picked up on the first ring.

"Hey, I'm on my way to you," he said.

"To me?" I questioned, peering through the blinds in my bedroom.

"Yeah, I'm about ten minutes away. Figured we'd go grab something to eat before work tonight."

"I'll ride with you, but I'm not hungry."

"What? You're not hungry? Let me write this one down," David teased. I was never not down for going to grab something to eat. But with Ed on my mind, I didn't have an appetite. "I'll blow the horn when I pull up. Just come on out."

"Okay," I said, reaching for my makeup case. Even though David had seen me on some not-so-good days, waking up with no makeup or messing up my makeup during one of our make-out sessions, I didn't want to get comfortable with him seeing me that way. I still wanted to look as though we were going on that first date.

After I reapplied my makeup, I changed my clothes, putting on my work gear, which was always some brand of denim jeans and a plain long-sleeved shirt. I slipped on my comfortable Air Jordan's, did one last glance in the mirror, and ran down the stairs and out the house to meet David.

Honey didn't particularly care for David for a myriad of reasons. The number one reason was that she thought he looked sneaky. And because Honey was never one to hide her feelings, both David and I agreed that I'd meet him outside whenever he came over in the attempt to avoid an eventual clash between the two.

When David pulled up, I jumped right in on the passenger side and we sped off.

"I told you Honey doesn't like people screeching off in front of her house," I reminded him.

"And I told you I don't go by Honey's rules, didn't I?" David shot back. "I'm a grown man, and I give your grandmother respect by not coming in her house because I know she's not really feeling me—not feeling *us*, for that matter. But what I won't do is walk on egg shells around her. And I know you love your grandmother and all, but it's about time you become your own woman."

"What are you tryna say?"

"I think you know what I'm saying," David said as he looked cautiously in his rearview mirror.

"David, not today. I already know I gotta get out of Honey's house, but I don't want to leave just to have to come crawling back because I can't handle being out on my own. So, for right now, I live under Honey's roof, and I have to respect her rules."

"You have a choice," David said, still looking in his rearview mirror intermittently.

"What are you looking at? I asked, trying to peer through the sideview mirror to see what was diverting David's attention.

"Nothing … nothing," he said hesitantly.

"So you think I have a choice, huh?"

"Of course, you do, Destiny."

"David, I can't," I said, shaking my head.

"Can't what, Destiny? I'm tryna be in your corner. What—"

"That's not it. I didn't mean for it to come out that way," I said, cutting David off.

"So what's wrong?"

I didn't readily answer. Instead, I let a few moments of silence pass and offer a possible explanation.

"Destiny?" David asked with an austere curiosity.

"He's coming."

"Who?"

"My sperm donor."

"Who?"

"My sperm donor," I repeated, now looking out the passenger window.

"Your father?"

I nodded. Somehow, David knew I needed a moment. My mind reflected on those moments in my childhood when my fragile innocence allowed me to believe what my father uttered from his lips—that he was coming to pick me up to take me "somewhere." Somewhere could have been the mall, the carnival or local country fair, or something as common as the park. As a young girl, maybe around five or six years of age, I loved going to the park because I loved getting on the swing. I would often imagine that if I could swing high enough, I could magically land in some unknown world fashioned far different than my reality. A world in which I lived behind the doors of a modest brick home with loving parents who cared more about the trajectory of my life than they did their own fragile egos. I was probably somewhere around ten or twelve years old when I finally realized my imagined world would never come to pass. And reflecting on the imagined world was the reason I was struggling with whether I should meet with the man who had abandoned and disappointed me ten times over.

"Did you hear anything I just said?" David said, pulling over to the side of the road.

I was so caught up in the moment, wrestling with haunting emotions from my past, that I didn't realize I had completely zoned out on David. I looked over at him. I will venture to say I saw something in David's eyes that I hadn't seen before, something I had never seen in the eyes of any of the men I had dated. Was it love? Only David could have vouched whether it was love, and I was too emotionally fragile to inquire, just in case it wasn't. So I answered David's question instead.

"I didn't hear you. I'm sorry."

"Is he here now?"

"No, he'll be in town at his sister's house in a couple of weeks. I'm supposed to meet him there."

"You said the word 'supposed.' Does that mean you don't have any intentions on going?"

"I don't know," I confessed.

"Well, I'm going to tell you this. My father wasn't the best man in the world, either. But he was my dad. And I miss him ... a lot. You don't know how many times I wish I could just walk into a room and hear my father's voice. Heck, I'd settle for him cursing me out for something dumb I did, just to hear his voice again."

What David said struck a cord. At least Ed was still alive. If ever I had the opportunity to get some answers to long-held questions, now was the time. The opportunity I had been longing for most of my life was right before me—Ed wanted something from me. That's when it hit me. I was in a unique position, not to reject him, but to show him the opposite of what he showed me—to extend myself to him, to be the adult daughter who doesn't abandon *him*. Yes, this was the moment I had longed for. And that's when I made up my mind that I was going to meet Ed.

"I'll go," I said, nodding.

I felt light, free the moment my feet hit the floor that morning. The day had finally arrived. I was going to meet Ed and other members of my family.

I stood in front of the dresser mirror staring at myself. I had gone to Sophies the day before and got my hair done in box braids. Sophie's was an African hair braiding shop on the other side of town. Normally, I would have a headache the following day after getting my hair done. But on this day, I didn't.

Still examining my appearance, I wondered what would be going through the minds of the people whom I did not know but still shared the same bloodline. From what Honey said, Ed's coming into town was going to be more like a mini-reunion for the Harrison family. Quite a few of the family members were going to be at Ann's celebrating this dual occasion—Ed's visit and my introduction.

As I stood in front of the mirror, I couldn't help but wonder what they would think of me. I found myself questioning, *Am I pretty enough? Who do I look like? Who do I act like? Do they see Shannon through me? Will they reject me because of Shannon?* The truth was, I really didn't know what I was walking into. The unexpected could always happen.

I reached for the little torn-off piece of brown paper bag where Honey had written Ann's address down for me—*1423 Speckled Circle, Grosse Ile Township. House is Cape-Cod style with blue shutters.* Honey had beautiful penmanship. People always told her she should go into business for herself doing calligraphy for specialized invitations and greeting cards. Like many of us, Honey just followed the system, not believing in her own gifts and talents.

As I stared at the torn-off piece of brown paper bag, reality set in. In just a little while, I would be inside of a house with relatives who were strangers just hours beforehand. It was one of the strangest concepts for me to wrap my head around.

The drive to Ann's house was just a little more than thirty minutes, as she lived in Grosse Ille Township, a suburb in the outskirts of Detroit. Although most of the ride was on the local roads, I did have to drive on the expressway for a short distance. Speckled Circle was literally a circle with houses on both the inner and outer sides. Finally, there it was—1423 Speckled Circle, a big white Cape-Cod style house with blue shutters.

Several cars were parked in the driveway as well as in front of the house. I parked just a little further up on the outer side, where I was more in front of the next-door neighbor's house than I was Ann's. I watched a group of children come running from the left side of the house. It seemed as though they were playing some sort of chasing game. I gulped down the last of the Fiji water I had been sipping on during the drive over. I adjusted the rearview mirror to get one last glimpse before getting out of the car. *Well, if they don't like what they see, then too bad.* I remember thinking this, but I didn't believe it in my heart of hearts.

The moment of truth had arrived, and either I was going to restart the engine and pull off or open the car door and confront my past and embrace my destiny all at the same time. As I walked up the driveway, I approached a group of men, maybe eight of them, playing dominos.

"Hey, darling, just go on up and open the door. It's open," one of the men directed. He had salt and pepper hair and his facial features resembled those of Ed, at least from what I could last remember.

I tried to turn the doorknob, but my palms were too wet. Noticing my obvious difficulty in opening the door, one of the little boys playing the chasing game stopped running and opened the door for me.

"Thank you," I said to him.

"You welcome," he said in a choppy southern accent right before he jumped down the small set of steps and onto the ground.

Unbeknownst to me, the back door led to the kitchen area. I was welcomed by a group of women who were in the kitchen. One stood in front of the stove, stirring something in a large pot. She was light skinned and had a beauty mark under her left eye. Honey said Ms. Ann had a mark under one of her eyes, but she couldn't remember which one. The light-skinned woman was Ms. Ann.

"Hey, baby," she said, taking the spoon out of the pot and placing it on the utensil holder in the center of the stove. She stretched out her arms to greet me. I wrapped my arms completely around her thin frame. "You don't have to call me Auntie, but I'm your auntie Ann, your dad's youngest sister."

By this time, the other women in the kitchen had ceased their activities and conversation and gathered around my aunt Ann and me, each one waiting to be introduced.

"Hey, sweetie. I'm your auntie Mae. I'm your daddy's oldest sister. I'm not like your auntie Ann, who's giving you a choice to call her aunt. I'm your aunt, and I prefer you call me Aunt Mae. Your daddy was wrong for keeping you from us all these years."

"Mae, she doesn't wanna hear all that the first time she meets you," one of the other women chimed in. She looked slightly older than Mae. "Hey, baby, I'm Cousin Donna from Alabama. We couldn't wait to see you," she continued, adjusting the checkerboard headwrap she was wearing.

"This is Ms. Fran. She's a good friend of the family," Ann said.

I got a quick whiff of Ms. Fran's cigarette breath when she hugged me and kissed me on my right cheek. "She looks just like you and Ed, Ann."

All the women agreed, uttering, "She sure does," in unison.

"She sure does look like Cousin Ed," the youngest woman said. She was actually Cousin Donna's daughter, Shalisa. Shalisa looked to be in her mid-twenties. She gave me a quick hug before hurriedly taking her seat, which was when I noticed she was pregnant, very pregnant.

"I can't stand too long," she said, pointing at her stomach as she sat back down.

"When are you due?" I said, trying to make small talk.

"I got two and a half months left. But I'm hoping they come early," she said, as she gently caressed her stomach.

"Twins?" I asked, already expecting her answer to be yes.

"Yes. It's a boy and a girl."

"Are you excited?" I asked, taking a seat at the kitchen table beside her.

"Yes. We can't wait. My husband is head over heels about these babies already."

Shalisa and I clicked right away. We sat at the kitchen table and got intimately acquainted, all while the other women finished preparing the food for the festivity. Shalisa was twenty-nine years old and married to a guy name Roderick, who was in the U.S. Marines. He was currently deployed but was scheduled to return home just a week before Shalisa's due date. Shalisa was a school teacher, but she was taking a few years off to take care of the babies.

Although her mother lived in Alabama, Shalisa lived in nearby Dearborn, Michigan, a twenty-minute drive away from me.

"Sweetie, I think I hear your daddy's voice in the living room. He must be up from his nap," the lady who introduced herself as my Aunt Mae said to me.

I stood up and adjusted my skirt. I felt light pebbles of sweat pop out on my forehead.

"Don't be nervous. Ed ain't nobody to be nervous about. Go on out there and speak with your daddy," Aunt Ann encouraged.

"My father," I said nonchalantly, correcting her. I didn't like that it seemed no one was considering my feelings. They all seemed to be more concerned about how Ed would feel.

I could tell that my aunt Ann was taken aback by my correction because her facial expression changed. "Well, when you're ready, Destiny. He's in the front room."

"It's to your right," Aunt Mae added.

I didn't say anything. Instead, I just started walking toward the front room.

There were three men sitting in the front room arguing over something involving sports. One of the men appeared to be older than the other two, sporting a full head of gray hair. The men stopped talking, acknowledging my presence.

"That's my baby," one of the men said as he smiled, revealing a gap between his two front teeth, just like me. He wore a pair of dark blue jeans paired with a black, Tupac T-shirt. It had to be Ed. I resembled him so much. At his age, I wasn't expecting to see him in a Tupac T-shirt, but I felt a sense of relief that we may have had something in common—music, if not anything else. And although his hair was cut into a small Afro, it wasn't difficult to see its coarseness. I finally understood why my hair was so thick and coarse.

"Excuse me," I responded as my eyes rolled into the back of my head. I wanted to play hard and tough. I certainly didn't want him to think I was going to come running into his arms. I still had a lot to be angry about. And the man sitting less than three feet in front of me owed me a lot of answers. And apologies.

"Wanna sit down?" he invited.

"Nah, I'm good," I said, folding my arms as I stood in the archway of the room.

"Let me introduce everyone. I'm Ed, and—"

"I know who you are," I said, cutting him off.

"Okay. Okay," he replied, trying to diffuse the mounting tension. "And this is my brother-in-law, Melvin. And this is my other brother-in-law, Duncan. My brother Ron is out back playing cards or dominos," Ed continued.

I said hello and shook the hands of the two other men.

"I'm your aunt Mae's husband. Nice to meet you, young lady," the man who was introduced as Melvin said before excusing himself.

Speaking in a Caribbean accent, the other gentleman said hello as well. And he, too, excused himself, leaving me and this stranger who I knew to be my father in the same room together.

"You sure you don't want to sit down?" Ed asked again.

I didn't answer, but I did take a seat at the far end of the sofa, sitting diagonally from Ed, who was sitting on a gray suede reclining chair.

"Destiny, I know you have a lot of questions. And I have a lot of answers for you."

"Really?" I snapped.

"Yes."

"So how about we start with, where have you been?"

"In Alabama. I went back to Alabama when your grandmother threatened to send me to jail."

"I know you came back to Detroit since then to visit. You have family here. Why didn't you come through like you promised you would?"

"You must don't really know your mother, do you?"

"Shannon?" I replied, making sure he was indeed referencing

Shannon and not Honey. I also wanted to make it clear to him that I didn't call Shannon mom, just like I didn't call him dad.

"Yes, Shannon. Shannon kept a lot of mess going on. Look, we were young when she got pregnant with you. I was just a boy, really. I didn't know anything about being a man or a father, for that matter."

"But you knew how to get a girl pregnant and then walk off and leave her." I had no filter. I wanted my words to sting and pierce his belly like daggers, just like his lies and abandonment had done to me.

"There was more to the story, Destiny."

"Really?" I answered sarcastically. "So why don't you help me understand because I've never understood it."

"I liked your mother. I really did."

"Stop calling her my mother. Her name is Shannon, and that's what I call her," I said matter-of-factly.

"Okay. Shannon. Well, Shannon was bossy and manipulative. When she got pregnant, neither one of us had anything. I told her I would go into the service, so I could earn money to help take care of you. But that wasn't good enough for Shannon. Shannon wanted me to stay right here, but with nothing to offer. So how long do you think our relationship would have lasted? Our parents were equally ashamed and upset with us. It was like a no-win situation. So I told Shannon I was going into the service, and she took it to mean I was deserting her."

"What about the fight at the party?" I inquired, referencing the long-held story that Ed had beat Shannon up at a party because she caught him there dancing with another girl while she was at home barefoot and pregnant.

"We did have a disagreement at the party," Ed acknowledged.

"Ed, you beat Shannon up so bad that she almost lost me, and *that's* why Honey threatened to call the police."

"Okay ... I know things got out of control at the party. But the only thing I can say is that I lost it. Shannon confronted me and told me I would never see you, and I snapped," he said, shaking his head.

His eyes looked glossy as he tried to fight back tears. I saw the human side to Ed, a side I didn't think even existed. There I was sitting just feet away from a man who essentially said he'd temporarily lost his mind the moment he thought he lost rights to his own child—me. But something on the inside still wanted to be mad, to hold onto anger and hostility, which were opposite traits of those that the church and Honey had both instilled in me.

"So now what? I'm an adult. You've missed out on virtually twenty-plus years of my life. How do you fix this?"

Ed didn't readily respond. Instead, he peered inside his shirt and pulled out a plastic cord and placed the prongs on the opposite end into his nostrils. He adjusted a small black box that sat on the coffee table.

"What's that?" I asked.

"Oxygen," he said, leaning back in the chair into a more comfortable position.

"What's it for?" I asked inquisitively.

"My oxygen level is compromised."

"Why?" I asked matter-of-factly. I could tell Ed was holding something back, and I wanted him to be forthright with me.

"My doctors tell me I got that smoking disease. What they call it?"

"COPD?"

"Yeah, that's it. COPD. Doctors say I'm in stage two."

"I don't know what that means. Does that mean you're dying?" I said, almost anticipating a forthcoming sad sob story from him.

"Eventually, yes. I'll die eventually … that's if the good Lord don't heal your daddy."

This time, the word "daddy" rang differently in my ears and my heart. I had every right to curse him out, but in that moment, strangely, I felt compassion. Death or impending death has a way of stopping you in your tracks and forcing you to examine things in a different light. I could use the remaining time Ed had left to keep harboring on his absence and shortcomings, or I could use it to form a new relationship, one that could make Ed's last days happier and erase the hate in my heart I had for him. It wasn't a decision I was ready to make in that instant, but one that I needed to ponder.

"So who's taking care of you in Alabama?"

"Been staying at your aunt Mae's house and at my mama's, your grandmother's, house. Your aunt Ann wants me to come back to Detroit. She says I can get better medical treatment here. What do you think?"

I wanted to ask, *Is this why you're here*? But I didn't want to add insult to injury, so I didn't say anything. In the back of my mind, however, I wondered whether meeting with me was Ed's way of trying to get me to help take care of him. Truth be told, I wasn't the Susie Homemaker type of person. I'd spent so much time in church growing up that, now, since I was an adult, I liked to hit the streets. I loved the direction my life was going. I loved spending time with David, and I certainly never imagined being confined to the house to take care of a sickly man who was never there for me.

Ed's dilemma changed my entire mood. I spent the remaining time at Aunt Ann's house, pretending to be enjoying the company of the strangers-slash-relatives who surrounded me. But the entire time, I was wrestling with doing what was hard but right. There just were no guarantees—no guarantee that Ed would even make it back to Detroit that next spring as he planned, no guarantee that I wouldn't be married to David and having a family of my own, no guarantee I would even feel the same compassion I felt in that moment. On top of it, I had a lot of questions, not just for Ed but for the entire Harrison family. I wanted to know why none of them came looking for me or even tried to have a relationship with me, especially those who lived right there in Michigan. But I realized I wasn't going to get the answers that day. Besides, that day was about me—celebrating *me*. I realized it was in my best interest to just let the day play out and ask the tough questions some other day.

Finally, although not as I had imagined time and time again, I was in the same house, under the same roof, between the same walls as the man whose blood ran warm through my veins. It was the strangest yet most comforting feeling I had ever felt.

Before I closed my eyes to go to sleep that night, I thought about Honey's words. I didn't recall seeing any of my school pictures on display at Aunt Ann's house. Honey was right. Aunt Ann was sending my school pictures to Ed all along. A warm smile swept across my face. I slept like a newborn baby that night.

Chapter 11

Trouble in Paradise

"GO AHEAD, DESTINY. YOU know you want to know what's in here," David said as he dangled an aqua green fluorescent gift bag in front of my face before placing it in my lap.

I waited a few seconds before I removed the white tissue paper and pulled out our favorite tape, *The Day*, by Babyface. That was *our* album. On several occasions, we would go to Meijer after work and listen to "Every Time I Close My Eyes" on their music kiosk. I immediately opened the tape, so we could listen to it in the car.

"Slow down, girl. Don't you want to see what else is in the bag?" David said, reaching over to prevent me from putting the gift bag on the floor of the car.

I pulled the remaining items out of the bag one by one—a cucumber melon scented shower gel, body spray, and lotion gift set.

"I'm proud of you," David said, staring at me then back at the road.

I knew he was referring to me meeting Ed and the entire Harrison gang a few weeks back. Ann … Aunt Ann had called and invited me to Duncan's fiftieth birthday party she was hosting at some big shindig restaurant. She mailed me an invitation, but I hadn't RSVP'd. Honey emphatically told me she wasn't interested in attending the celebration. The only other person I felt comfortable asking was David, but he was going to be out of town visiting his half-sister, Dawn. Well, that's the story he told me. It was no secret that David dealt drugs, and out of town could have simply been a pickup for him. And tagging along with him to make a drug run or pickup was out of the question, as far as David was concerned.

"Thank you," I finally responded, planting a soft kiss on his cheek.

"So you gonna listen to your tape?"

"I will," I said as I carefully began to unravel the plastic covering.

Sensing I wasn't beaming with excitement, he asked, "What's wrong, boo?"

I leaned my head back on the headrest and closed my eyes. I didn't feel up to going to work. I wanted us both to just call out and get a hotel room, so I could spend the entire night in his arms. But since I had already called out one day the previous week, it was just wishful thinking. David and I had been going pretty strong for more than a year by this time, and rumor still had it that he had a live-in girlfriend, a woman that David only vaguely mentioned once or twice. And when he did, he referred to her as his ex. Although it wasn't the best time to bring the subject up because we were en route to work, there really wasn't another opportune time to bring it up. I opened my eyes and sat up straight.

"What's her name?"

"Whose name?" David asked, totally caught off guard.

"Your ex? The woman you live with."

"Destiny, why are you going there? Just why?"

"Why not, David?"

"She's not important, and her name is not important, either. So why does it matter?"

"Because she lives with you," I said, throwing the tape back inside the gift bag. I no longer wanted to listen to "our" song.

"So what? She lives with me until she can get up on her feet."

"David, you're not being rational. What if I lived with my ex? How would you feel about that?"

"Destiny, the day started off great. I don't like going to work in this type of mood!" David screamed, simultaneously hitting his fist on the steering wheel.

"All I asked is, what's her name. And you're right. Her name isn't important. What's important is why does she live with you?" I said in a tone that David had never heard come out of my mouth. It was bad enough that he had another woman who was not a relative of his living with him. And I was fooling myself to believe that the anonymity of this woman wouldn't bother me. The closer David and I became, the more it bothered me.

David swerved off to the side of the road and put the gear in park. "All right, Destiny. You want the truth?"

I widened my eyes as if to say, *Heck yeah, I want the truth*!

Correctly interpreting my nonverbal cue, David responded. "Well, then here's the truth, Destiny. Her name is Nettie. Yes, she lives in the house with me. She is my ex. She had a miscarriage with our son, and because of it, she had a mental breakdown. That's why she's still at my house. Now, do you want me to be a heartless jerk and put her out, so she can really fall apart and end up in some institution just so you can sleep better at night knowing I ain't screwing another woman?! Is that the kind of man you want?!"

I could see the veins popping out of David's neck. I had never seen him *this* angry and snap at me in such a manner, not even the time he went off when we were supposed to go to Grand Rapids to his cousin's birthday bash. I shifted my body toward the passenger door, just in case his fist came flying toward me. I was prepared to open the door and jump out of the car if I had to. I didn't respond to David. In fact, I was trying to decide whether I believed him and decide whether I wanted to be a part of a weird triangle relationship. I had never seen the inside of David's place, but some other woman had—on a daily basis. That's when I decided, *Two can play that game.*

David and I worked our entire shift that evening without communicating. At the end of our shift, I didn't see him standing by the time clock to punch out, which was where we would normally meet up. I waited until 11:30 P.M., but David was still nowhere to be found, so I clocked out. I hitched a ride with Hattie, able to flag her down before she pulled out of the parking lot. The minute I got into her car, she knew something was wrong.

"David, huh?"

"Yeah," I confessed.

"What's going on?"

"We had an argument before work today. He picked me up, so we could grab something to eat before work, and we got into it."

"About what, if you don't mind?" Hattie said as she lit the cigarette she was holding between her lips.

"Just the usual," I lied.

"Destiny, any other day, people can barely separate the two of you up there on the job. So whatever you guys argued about today or tonight is not the usual."

I chuckled. That was one thing about Hattie; she was very observant and discerning. I should have known I couldn't get away with lying to her. "Okay, okay. I guess I'm just really stressed about a lot of things, like …" I paused.

"Like?" Hattie said, rolling down the driver side window to exhale the cigarette smoke. I was glad she didn't let it out without rolling down the window. I hated cigarette smoke.

"Rumor has it that David lives with someone." I was embarrassed to admit this to Hattie, but I knew she would give me sound advice.

"So?" Hattie said as she rolled the window back up.

"What do you mean?" I said, a little taken aback by her nonchalant response.

"What did you say or do?"

"I confronted him about it. Actually, I asked him to tell me who she was."

"What does that matter?" Hattie said, taking a light pull on her cigarette.

"Hattie, I'm just tired of being played and played with," I said, fighting back tears.

"Is this the part where you want me to tell you to kick him to the curb? You're sadly mistaken if you think so."

"Huh?" I said, not quite following her line or reasoning.

"Let me just give you some good ole sound advice. Most men, and people, for that matter, come with some form of baggage. Don't you let the next woman out here tell you what she will and won't take from a man, because most of them out here are just blowing hot smoke. Let me tell you what my granny told me. She said, 'Hattie, darling …' You see, she always called me darling. But she said, 'Hattie, darling, when it comes to dealing with the man you want, don't you worry about girlfriends; you worry about wives.'"

"What does that mean?" I asked, seeking more clarity.

"It means, unless the man has a wife at home with a ring on her finger and papers filed at the courthouse, you have just as much right to that man as she does. And if she really had him, she'd have the ring, the papers, and his last name."

"Wow. I've always been told that a woman should never play second."

"You know the Bible well, don't you?" Hattie asked, rolling down the driver side window once again to exhale.

"Of course. I lived in church with my grandmother when I was growing up," I said, turning my head so I wouldn't get a strong whiff of the cigarette smoke.

"Remember David in the Bible?"

Now, why did she have to use that particular biblical character as a reference? But I nodded, nonetheless.

"Well, remember when Samuel came to Jesse's house looking for the next king of Israel?"

"Yes," I said with a little excitement in my voice. If I didn't know anything else, I knew a lot about the Bible. Years of going to church nearly every day of the week paid off in some of the most unexpected ways.

"Remember, David wasn't brought into the house for Samuel to even consider. But you know the story. It was the outcast, the little dusty looking brotha out in the field who was the chosen one."

I lifted my smock from my lap and began to wipe my face; the tears had escaped the ducts and slowly traveled down both sides of my cheeks. In that moment, I no longer felt vulnerable. I decided to tell her about Ed.

"There's something else."

"You ain't pregnant, are you?"

"Oh, God, no," I said, imagining how devastated I would be if I were.

"Go 'head," Hattie said.

"You know I don't talk about my family life that much because it's all messed up. But you know my story. Now, after all these years, my dad recently visited."

"Did he?" Hattie asked, shocked.

"Yeah, he came into town recently."

"So you saw him?"

"Yes. I met a few of them ... from his side of the family."

"So what did you think of it all?"

"Hattie, I dunno. On one end, it makes me feel good that my dad wants to see me and wants to have a relationship with me. But a part of me questions his motives."

"Why?" Hattie asked, taking another deep pull on the cigarette.

"Because he has COPD."

"Lots of folk do that, Destiny. Don't fault the man for trying to clean up his wrongdoings. Let him clean up his wrongdoings, so that if he dies, his conscience is clear. That man knows he ain't done right by you, and he has no other motive but to try to make it up to you and ask for your forgiveness. He's gonna need it if he ever wants to rest in peace in his grave."

I thought about what Hattie said, and it made sense. But I knew it wasn't going to be easy letting my guard down when it came to Ed. And I couldn't promise myself that I was never going to bring up the live-in woman situation with David again. But I didn't feel as powerless in either of the situations as I had previously, before speaking with Hattie. As far as David was concerned, in the worst-case scenario, I would just leave David and put myself on the market for someone who was ready for the type of relationship I truly desired.

I did my usual stop by Honey's room when I got home that night. Most of the time, I was stopping in to take her glasses off her face, as she would regularly fall asleep with them on because she was "supposedly" reading the Bible. I'd turn her radio down a little then turn off the lamp light on her nightstand.

This night, I stood by the side of Honey's bed, watching her sleep. Honey was aging for sure. Although she was very strict during my upbringing, I knew she meant well. And even though I didn't always see eye to eye with Honey as an adult, I loved her and couldn't begin to imagine my life without her.

I leaned over and gently kissed Honey on her cheek. She cracked open her left eye and gave me a half smile. I smiled back.

"Love you, Honey," I said as I walked toward the bedroom door.

"Love you, too, sweetheart," she said in a groggy tone.

I closed my eyes as the warm water washed the white suds from my body. I wished the water had the power to wash the cares of the world away as well. Midway through my shower, I could hear the faint sound of my telephone ringing. I jumped out of the shower, grabbed my towel and threw it around my naked body, and made a mad dash for my bedroom.

"Hello," I answered.

"Hey. It's ... me," David replied, panting between words.

"What happened to you tonight?" I said as I leaned against my dresser.

"Long story, Destiny ... long story."

"So you just left me out there stranded? Luckily I was able to hitch a ride with Hattie."

"I'm sorry. I had every intention on coming back, but things got out of hand."

"Out of hand? How?" I felt my ears getting hot.

"I left early and got caught up in something. I'm in a little trouble right now, and I need you."

"Need me? David, what's going on?" I wanted to be sure his life wasn't in any danger. Yes, I was pissed with him for leaving me stranded, but I didn't wish any harm on him.

"You busy?"

I chuckled. "David, it's after midnight. Of course, I'm busy, trying to take my shower and get in the bed."

"Can you do me a favor and pick me up from the gas station on Harper and Cadieux?"

"Why? Where's your truck?" I asked as I sat on my bed.

"No questions, please. Not now. I'll tell you everything when you get here." I could hear the mounting agitation in his voice. I didn't press David any further—he was easily agitated, and his mood swings were unpredictable.

"Okay, give me twenty minutes; I need to throw on some clothes."

I hurriedly dried myself off and got dressed. Although David didn't provide any details other than saying that he needed me to come, I was down for the cause. It's what they called being a ride-or-die chick. I had been bitten by the bug and was gonna be there for David, putting all other matters aside, including Nettie.

When I pulled up to the gas station, I spotted David standing next to what was left of his truck. The entire passenger side was caved in. Next to his truck was a motorcycle lying on the ground. I was unable to determine who the driver of the motorcycle was because there were several people at the scene. Actually, I wasn't all that concerned about who the driver was; I just wanted to make sure David was all right.

"What happened?" I said, running up to him.

"I need you to go to my house and get my insurance information. It's not in my truck. Mitch should be there. He'll know where it is," David said as he wiped blood from his bottom lip.

Although I had been to David's house plenty of times to pick him up or drop him off, I had never gotten out of the car because of the Nettie situation. But the moment of truth had finally presented itself less than twenty-four hours after I had confronted David about her. Hattie told me to basically ignore her, and it was just the bold pill I needed that night.

Before I got out of the car, I remembered I was wearing an old, tired headscarf. I quickly snatched it off my head and combed my hair with my fingers. *Oh well, my man needs me, but she won't catch me looking busted.* I don't remember walking up to the door, but with my heart pounding, I took three deep breaths and knocked. I waited for a few seconds before knocking once again. I knocked a few more times and waited for someone to come to the door, but no one ever did, so I got back into my car and headed back to the gas station.

David's truck was being loaded onto a flatbed tow truck by the time I arrived back on the scene. I parked and headed over to where he was standing as he wrapped up logistics with the on-scene police officers.

"No one was there," I said.

"What's today?" David said, trying to recall the day of the week.

"Tuesday," I said, wondering whether David had suffered a head injury that was impacting his memory.

"Oh, yeah. I forgot, Mitch is on the westside. Can you take me home?"

"Yeah. No problem," I said, patting him on the back, my way of consoling him.

"Dang, my truck is messed up," he said as the tow truck driver slowly backed up and pulled off with David's banged-up truck.

"You can always get another truck," I said, trying to console him once again.

It was quiet during the short ride to David's house. That is until he blurted out a strange confession. "I guess that's what I get, huh?"

"What do you mean, that's what you get?" I asked as I came to a stop at a red light.

"I was gonna get Terry tonight," he said, leaning his head back onto the passenger side headrest.

"Terry?" I asked.

"Yeah, that sucka."

"Why, David? That tape mess is water under the bridge."

"You think so?"

"David, let it go. I told you that anything Terry and I had going on was before your time. So you out here trying to seek revenge on him is a waste of your time and energy. Look at you. Now your truck is all crashed up."

"That dude is real lucky. This ain't just about no tape of you and him. He's been up there popping off at the mouth. I swear, if I had ran up on him tonight, he would've been one dead cat."

I didn't readily respond. This was yet another side of David

I didn't know existed—being angry or jealous enough to kill someone. I just let the silence run its course, and before we knew it, I was pulling back up to David's house.

"Thank you for coming to my rescue," David said as he reluctantly reached for the door handle.

"You're welcome," I said, still uneasy about what he had just confessed.

"I want to apologize about what happened earlier tonight, too."

I nodded. I was trying to adhere to the words of wisdom Hattie had shared with me earlier that night. I didn't want to say the wrong thing, so I just didn't say anything.

"What's on your mind?" David asked, still holding onto the door handle.

"Nothing. I'm just tired. It's going on three o'clock. My body is tired, that's all," I said.

"Stay with me tonight. Don't drive back home."

My eyes widened. "Here?"

"Yes, here. I want you in my arms tonight."

"You know I have a curfew."

"Destiny, you're grown. You work and support yourself."

"But I live under Honey's roof."

"You don't have to," David said, looking me dead in the eye.

What was he saying? He couldn't be inviting me to come live with him and his ex. How crazy would that look?

"So are you going to stay with me or what?" David said with his sad puppy dog look.

"You just don't know Honey," I said. Yes, I was an adult. But I wanted to respect Honey's rules. I would rather move out on good terms than be kicked out on bad terms.

"I got you if Honey kicks you out. I promise, I got you."

I took that chance and stayed at David's house that night. There was no Nettie; at least she didn't appear to be there that particular night.

After engaging in passionate lovemaking, I fell asleep in David's arms, just as he desired. I was willing to suffer the consequences of staying out all night, or "laying up" with David, as Honey called it. In that moment, my physical and emotional pallets were satisfied. Nothing else really mattered.

Chapter 12

Strike Three

I AGREED TO LET David use my car to do some "running around" the next day, since he had crashed his truck. For David, "running around" meant many things, from picking up his clothes at the cleaners to running some drug deals. Under normal circumstances, I wouldn't have let him use my car, but bailing out on him when he needed me wouldn't have been fair, since he came through for me when I had two flat tires. Not being that ride-or-die chick would have certainly made him think twice about choosing me over the next woman. No man wants a woman in his life that he can't depend on when he needs her.

We grabbed something quick to eat that morning at Park Street Diner and then headed straight to my house. During the entire ride, I couldn't help but think about what the consequences of having stayed out all night with David would be. I tried to engage in small talk, but David knew my mind was preoccupied with having to eventually face the music with Honey.

"If she puts you out, just come stay with me."

Even though I didn't say it, I was thinking, *So you gonna have both of your women living with you, huh? How do you suppose things are gonna turn out?"* But instead, I just gave him "that look."

"I told you, I got you."

"And her?" I finally got the courage to ask.

"Don't worry about that. You won't be out on the streets, that's for sure."

"So where will I be, David?"

"I'll tell you what, Destiny. I had a pretty messed up night last night until you came and got me. I really wanted to be with you last night. I wanted you, not Nettie—you. I wanted you by my side last night. Let's don't mess up what we shared last night."

I wanted to devour his words. He chose me over Nettie. I had to remember what Hattie told me: *Don't worry about girlfriends; worry about wives.* Either I was going to let it be my motto or leave David alone once and for all.

"Okay," I said in a low voice.

Honey's car wasn't in the driveway when we drove up to the house. I was relieved.

"Let me know what's up," David said as he leaned over to kiss me goodbye.

"I will," I said, opening the car door to get out.

"We'll grab dinner again tonight before work. I'll call you when I'm on my way."

I nodded as I exited the car and closed the door behind me. I watched David drive down the street until he disappeared out of sight.

When I opened the front door, I could hear the faint sound of gospel music coming from Honey's radio. Honey never left the radio on when she left the house, so she had to have left it on by mistake.

As I headed in the direction of her room, I could hear movement in the kitchen. I turned to head for the kitchen instead. Honey was pouring hot water from the tea kettle in her cup to make some green tea, which was pretty much the only thing she drank in the morning. She was just as startled to see me as I was to see her. But she quickly regained her composure and continued pouring the water in the cup.

"You know last night was strike three, don't you?"

"Honey, let me explain."

"Destiny, you don't have to explain. I've not only been very clear about my rules and expectations, but I've been lenient as well. I know you feel you're grown and all, and that's okay. But like my mama told me, 'Grown folks need to live on their own. Two queens can't rule in the same castle. One of them has to go.'"

"So can I get till the weekend to move out?"

"No, you need to get your stuff out within twenty-four hours. I'm not gonna make it easy for you. You didn't even have the decency to call and let me know you were all right," she said, placing the kettle back down on the stove.

There was no sense in trying to get Honey to change her mind. I wasn't mad at her for enforcing her rule, but I did feel as though she could have given me a little more time. I wanted to head straight for my room to begin the daunting task of packing my belongings, at least what I could manageably take with me in the first wave, but I knew Honey wasn't finished verbally reprimanding me.

"I don't know what it is about that David boy, but he's not good for you, Destiny," Honey continued, as she opened a tea bag and dropped it in the steaming hot water in her cup.

I knew enough to know that what David and I had going on was not normal, but there was something about him that was alluring, that didn't want me to leave him or release him, whichever it was. I had my share of guys, and most of my relationships were like passing ships in the night—short and fleeting. I had no problem attracting men. That was the easy part. But keeping them or maintaining a relationship was the issue. David and I had the same type of personality, and together, we were toxic. But neediness kept us coming back to one another. Just as I had made up my mind about how I was going to deal with Ed and Shannon, I had made up my mind about how I was going to deal with David. And for the time being, he was a keeper.

"I love him, Honey," I confessed.

"You love a guy that sells drugs, has another girlfriend, can't come in the house and sit down at the table with you and have a decent meal with your family, or invite you to his house to have one?"

"Yes, I love him, Honey. I can't explain why, but I love him."

"And he's worth you gettin' put out, too, huh?" Honey said, taking the first sip of her tea.

I didn't have an answer for Honey. Had David not told me I could move in with him earlier that day, I would have been in a frenzy. Strangely, though, I was not; I was very calm. The only thing I might have been a little frantic about was figuring out how I was going to move my belongings out of Honey's house.

"Well, is he?" Honey asked again.

Before I could answer Honey, my pager went off. I reached into my purse and looked at it. It was Auntie Donitra.

"Excuse me, Honey, it's Auntie Donitra. I need to call her back," I said, exiting the kitchen as I spoke.

As soon as I got to my room, I called Auntie Donitra. It had been nearly three weeks since we last spoke. I certainly had a lot to tell her, especially the latest drama—getting kicked out.

"Hello," Auntie Donitra answered, sounding cheerful.

"Hey, Auntie Don," I said, trying to disguise the hurt in my voice. Every once in a while, I'd call her Auntie Don instead of Auntie Donitra.

"How's it going, niecey?" Niecey. It was Auntie Donitra's nickname for me.

"I'm good," I lied.

"No, you're not. I can hear it in your voice. What's going on?"

"Honey just put me out," I said, breaking down.

"Wait? Put you out, like you have to take your stuff and get out?"

I couldn't form a coherent response. I loved David, but the truth of the matter was, moving in with him was something I probably wasn't ready for. He had already showed me several sides of him—the loving side, which was always fleeting, and the explosive, angry side of him that made me question my safety.

"Destiny!"

"Uh huh," was the only response I could utter between sobs.

"Okay. I need you to get yourself together. Now, focus. Honey put you out, so what's next?"

"I gotta start packing my stuff," I replied, gathering a little composure.

"Where are you going?"

"With David."

Auntie Donitra didn't reply right away. I could tell she didn't really cosign the move. But my back was against the wall, and she was hundreds of miles away. So living with her was out of the question.

"Guess you ain't really feeling that, either?" I said, hoping she'd lend some support.

"Well, I mean, I can't judge your relationship with David. I know Honey doesn't like him, but then again, who does Honey like? No guy is good enough for Honey's girls."

Auntie Donitra was right. Come to think of it, Honey didn't like any of the guys her daughters chose. What made me think it would be different with me?

"I ain't even gonna ask when you have to be out because we all know that Honey's golden put-you-out rule is enforced after twenty-four hours."

We both chuckled.

"Well, I know now is not the time you want to hear a lecture, but I'm just gonna throw this out there. If it doesn't work out with David, and I hope it does, but if it doesn't, go stay with Roz," Auntie Donitra said.

"Roz?" I shrieked. Was she out of her mind? I had lived with Auntie Roz growing up. Roz's children, Nicole and Marcus, were like Bey-Bey's kids. Although Nicole was two years older than me, Honey always made me look after Nicole. Honey said Nicole was naïve and couldn't tell a watch from a wrist. When Roz first married her husband, Cliff, they didn't have a pot to pee in, so they moved in with Honey until they got up on their feet. So it seemed only logical that they would return the favor and let me stay with them if push came to shove, especially given the many times I babysat Nicole's snotty-nosed son, Brenden, and tutored Roz's son, Marcus, in math. But I wasn't going to place any bets on it because I knew people didn't always play fair.

"I mean, she owes you for all the stuff you've done for Nicole and Marcus over the years," Auntie Donitra said, giving credence to what I was thinking.

"If push comes to shove, that's what I'll do," I said, leaving it at that. I was beginning to feel just a tad bit better talking to Auntie Donitra. We both knew staying with Shannon was never going to happen, so neither one of us even mentioned the idiotic idea.

"Well, moving in with a man is a big thing, Destiny. I mean, you never truly know a person until you live with them. But I understand that you have to do what you have to do, so I'mma support you."

"Thanks," I said, having gained her understanding and support.

"Now, what's David's address? I'mma send you some money," Auntie Donitra volunteered.

Before I could even respond, she changed her mind. "Never mind. I'll wire it to you through Western Union. I'll page you and let you know when you can pick it up."

"Okay. Thanks, auntie," I said.

After I hung up with Auntie Donitra, I paged David with our emergency code, 9-1-1, to tell him the bad but good news—Honey was kicking me out, and I needed to take him up on his offer. I looked around my room, trying to gauge how long it would take me to pack up my belongings. I figured I might as well start packing while I waited for David to call.

Honey always brought empty boxes home from the job, so

I just went into the storage area in the basement and grabbed a few. Since David had my car, I couldn't put the packed boxes in my car, so I just brought the ones I was able to lift downstairs and placed them by the front door. On one of my trips down, I saw Honey, most likely on her second cup of green tea, inspecting the packed boxes.

"You can come back for the heavy stuff and take just what you need for the next couple of days."

"Thanks," I said, placing the box with my cosmetics on the floor by the door as well.

"Why didn't you put this stuff in the kitchen near the back door where your car is parked?" Honey asked.

"Cause my car is not out there."

"Where's your car, Destiny?" Honey asked.

"I let David use it," I said, trying not to make eye contact with her.

"He keeps you out all night and takes off with your car, huh? How do you know he ain't driving another woman around?" Honey said, shaking her head.

"Honey, it's not like that. Why do you keep making comments about him like that?"

"Like what, Destiny?"

"Like he's using me or something. It's not like that," I said defensively.

"Then tell me, what's it like, Destiny?" Honey challenged.

"He had an accident last night. That's why I went out, so I could go pick him up."

"He done tore up his car and ready to tear up yours. Don't you be one of these dumb women out here. Protect your assets. And you know I don't really mean the word 'assets.'"

"I know, Honey. I know," I said.

"All right, I don't have much else to say, 'cause you just gonna follow your own mind, so ain't no sense in me using up the last of my breath."

Our eyes connected. I could see the hurt in Honey's eyes. There's something about giving tough love; it's nearly as painful to the giver as it is the receiver.

"You know I didn't want to do this, but I had to," Honey added.

"Yeah, I know," I said. Although the suddenness about what was going on was scary, moving in with David wasn't such a bad thing—it was the chance to bring our relationship to the next level … or so I thought.

I was lucky if I got three hours of sleep before it was time to get up for work. Since we had to pack the car with boxes, David came an hour early. We packed as much as we could reasonably fit into my car and headed off to work. I didn't have an appetite, so we didn't go to eat as we normally would have. David arranged for his brothers to help him pick up what I'd left behind that weekend.

Other than being abnormally exhausted, work was typical. I decided not to tell Hattie I was moving in with David because, truth be told, I didn't know how temporary or permanent the move was going to be. So, to save face, I didn't mention it to her. And that's when I remembered I hadn't told Toya either. I called her while on break, and she agreed to meet me at my job when I got off.

Spotting her as soon as I exited the building, I walked over to her car and hopped in on the passenger side. "Girl, I'm tired," I said, letting the seat back.

"So what's this juicy news you gotta tell me?" Toya said between licks on the lollipop she was sucking.

"You know Honey put me out, right?"

"I knew it was coming sooner or later. That dude done turned your world upside down," Toya joked.

I didn't readily respond; it took me a minute to process her statement.

"So what are you gonna do?" she continued.

"I'm moving in with David."

When she didn't show any interest, I inquired. "You don't think that's a good idea?"

"Well, you could have always moved in with us," Toya said as she bit down on the lollipop.

"It just happened so fast, and David volunteered."

"Well, then, I mean, if that's what you feel comfortable doing, then go for it. I'm just not so keen on David."

"You barely know the guy, Toya."

"Humph," Toya responded.

"What does 'humph' mean?"

"Nothing. Never mind me and my opinion. You like him, and it don't matter if I do or don't."

I wasn't sure where Toya's apprehension about David stemmed from, because one thing I didn't do was tell Toya about my man issues. Shonte, maybe, but not Toya. She was my girl and all, but she was the girlfriend I'd never leave around my man. And Honey taught me that.

Does Toya know Nettie? I wasn't sure, but the question stayed in the back of my mind as Toya and I engaged in other small talk while I waited to meet up with David when he got off, forcing Toya and me to part ways.

David and I met outside in the parking lot, not near the exit door where we clocked out. I wanted to remain as inconspicuous as possible. Terry was still working at the plant, and no telling what tricks he had up his sleeve. As it was, he'd tried to corner me in the breakroom on two occasions, trying to see if we could hook up for a rendezvous. The first time, I just tried to ignore him, but the second time, he earned a hard slap in the face. It was bad enough I had to recover from the whole sex tape fiasco, but having the boldness to step to me, knowing I was involved with another man, took the cake. They just didn't come more narcissistic than Terry did.

I was quiet on the ride to the house, not because I had second thoughts about moving in with David; I just didn't know what to expect. Bringing up Nettie's name always caused a fight between us, so I left it alone. But just because I didn't talk about it didn't mean not knowing their true status didn't bother me. Quite the contrary. And it made me question David's and my status all the time. But this wasn't the night to worry about Nettie, so I just erased her from my mind, for the time being, that is.

The house was dark when we pulled into the driveway; I didn't even see so much as a nightlight on in the house. David put the car in park and turned the volume on the radio up. One of his favorite classics was playing. I just focused my attention on the modest brick ranch. But we were both startled by a knock on the driver side window. I locked the car doors when I saw the heavyset white guy standing outside the car.

"Girl, that's Chuck. He ain't gonna hurt nobody," David said, chuckling.

"What does he want?" I said, leaning over to get a good look at the guy.

"He's cool. He's one of my guys. Why don't you go let yourself in. I need to chat with him for a minute. I'll bring your stuff in," David said as he reached into his back pocket and handed me the keys to the house.

With some trepidation, I unlocked the car doors and got out. David directed me to go around to the back to let myself in. There was a set of five to six steps in the back that I had to walk up to get to the back door. I put the key in the lock and turned it to the left. When I heard it click, I turned the doorknob and pushed the brown wooden door open. Reaching over to the left, as David had directed, I turned the lights on. I was standing in the kitchen area. I could hear the humming sound of an air conditioner in an adjacent room. I performed a quick visual inventory of my surroundings, taking the liberty to tour the remaining downstairs area. Although David dressed lavishly and drove an expensive car, his house didn't reflect the same lavish lifestyle. In fact, David's interior design was closer to country living than contemporary style.

After twenty to thirty minutes passed, I retreated to the living room area and turned on the television. I found *I Love Lucy* as I was flicking through channels. Tired from the drama that had occurred over the past twenty-four to thirty-six hours, I dozed off right on David's sofa.

I woke up to the purring sound of an overweight goldish-orange cat that had crouched up next to me. David had never mentioned he had a cat, which led me to believe it was something Nettie had probably left behind, most likely on purpose, so she'd have an excuse to come back to fetch it.

"Get down, Rusty!" David yelled.

I jumped. "Dang, I didn't even know you were in the house."

"Yes, you were sleep, so I just brought all your stuff in."

"Where is it?" I said, looking around.

"It's upstairs in our room."

Did he just say, "our room"? Did I really move out of Honey's house into this man's house? Everything seemed perfect in that moment, and even after we had both taken our showers and gotten ready for bed. But then he received a page.

"Gotta go handle something right quick," he said before exiting the bedroom and going into one of the adjoining bedrooms to return the call.

I was too tired to even inquire about the who, what, where, why, and how. I just nodded, pulled the comforter and covers back, and crawled into bed, acting as though I wasn't bothered. On the inside, I was fuming.

The sunlight crept through the blinds in the room early that morning. I had dozed off somewhere between three o'clock and four o'clock, but I was still tired. I sat up. David was nowhere to be found. I reached for my pager that I had placed on the nightstand next to the bed. It was 7:23 a.m. I was beginning to think moving in with David was not going to be anything remotely close to what I had imagined.

I made my way to the kitchen to see what I could make for breakfast. Nothing. The refrigerator was empty. The cupboards were empty, and the pantry was empty. Before I could head back to the bedroom, David walked in.

"Good morning," he said as if he had done nothing wrong the night before.

"Good morning?" I repeated sarcastically.

"Yeah, it's morning, ain't it?" David said matter-of-factly.

Before I knew it, he grabbed me by my hair and pulled me into him. My feet left the floor for a second or two.

"Look, let's get something straight right now and once and for all. Number one, I'm a grown man. Number two, this is *my* house. Not Destiny's. Not Honey's. Not anybody else's. And I have business to handle. Don't act like you don't know what I was into before you got with me. And just because you moved in here with me doesn't mean I'm going to stop doing anything I was doing before you got here!"

David's words were cold. His tone was angry and combative. His eyes were dilated, and he didn't blink, not even once. I could see the veins popping out of his neck when he spoke once again. When he was finished delivering his little sermon, he released the lock of my hair. I was too shocked to engage him further. My body stiffened. I dared not move. If I didn't know it any other time, I now knew David was truly an abusive man. This was the second strike and proof that there was more to come. I was beginning to think that moving in with David was a grave mistake.

Chapter 13

Bad Apples

AFTER SEVERAL MONTHS, THE new living arrangement was starting to take its toll on me. I wasn't too excited about coming home most days because home meant arguments, pushing and shoving, and plenty of biting of the tongue just to keep the peace. Running the streets on top of maintaining a nine-to-five kept David very busy and away from home some nights. He was paranoid and temperamental—always blowing up at the littlest things. He didn't engage in pillow talk like he used to, and his secret telephone calls became more frequent, causing him to always be on the defensive when I confronted him on it.

Although the sex was great, intimacy was lacking. Sleeping in the same bed that he once shared with his ex, Nettie, kept me up many of nights, wondering which side she slept on, the positions they had during sexual intercourse, the sounds she made, even down to how she satisfied the man that lay next to me. David never told me the story surrounding Nettie moving out, so for all I knew, she could have left him, making me the rebound chick. And who wants to write home about that? If I didn't know anything else, I knew I needed to be smart. One thing Honey taught me was how to do right by my money. And that's when I thought of a plan—I was going to save the majority of my paycheck. I brought my tithe over to Honey's on Saturdays, so she could put it in church the next day. Outside of paying my tithes, my car note, which David paid on occasion, and a few small credit card bills, I could really stash away my money while living with David. This was another one of the perks that came with dating a drug dealer. I promised myself that I would take advantage of this one thing, especially since I felt I was being shorted on so many other ends.

Sometimes, though, things were good between David and me. And when they were, David would surprise me with gifts like money or jewelry or even a quick getaway.

Although I had met David's brothers, Mitch, Devonte, and Hank, on several planned occasions, I met his mother, Claudia, by happenstance. Calling herself dropping off some mail addressed to David but delivered to her address, she was taken aback when I answered the door.

"Oh, God, not another one," she said, looking past me to see if she could spot David inside.

"Excuse me?" I said, challenging her to repeat the slight.

"Is David here?"

I recognized her from pictures I had seen of her. She looked the same, for the most part, except she was a bit shorter in person, maybe five foot even. She looked to be in her mid-to-late fifties. She had jet black long, wavy hair that she wore in a ponytail. Her makeup looked as though it had been professionally applied. Now I knew where David got his brown eyes from; his mother's eyes were a lighter shade of brown than David's were. Unlike David and his brothers, who were brown skinned, their mother was dark skinned. She had a large mole on the left side of her cheek near her ear. David always told me his mother was an identical twin, so I was sure the mole near her ear was a distinguishing trait from her twin sister.

After checking her out, I finally answered her question. "No, he's not here, Ms. Falls."

"No, don't do that. I'm not a Falls. Wasn't good enough for that family," she said in a curt manner.

"I apologize, Miss—"

She took a sip of whatever she had in her flask. "Well, will you tell him his mama is back from Seattle and I stopped by? And let him know I have something for him, too," she said, holding the envelopes up.

"I will," I said, reaching for the mail.

She snatched her hand back. "Nothing against you, sweetie. But you tell David he can come get this mail or I'll bring it back by another time. But there's no way I'm leaving it here with someone I just laid my eyes on for the first time."

I guess she had a point, so I didn't take it personal. "I will," I answered.

She turned to walk down the front steps but quickly turned back around. "By the way, I'm Claudia, David's mother."

"I'm Destiny." I was hesitant to say girlfriend because of the way she had greeted me only moments earlier.

"And *you are*?" she questioned.

"Destiny," I repeated.

"And you are?" Claudia questioned once again, expecting me to elaborate.

"I'm Destiny, David's girlfriend," I answered, finally figuring out what she was getting at.

She walked back up the stairs to engage me further. "Well, nice to meet you," she said, this time, extending her hand to greet me. "Let's hope and pray you get to stick around longer than those in the past have," she said matter-of-factly.

In front of me was the opportunity to snap back and make another enemy or befriend her, as cold as she was, and get answers to some of my unanswered questions—those that David either blatantly refused to answer or made up some haphazard story about.

"Would you like to come in and wait for David?"

"Is he coming back soon?" Miss Claudia said with seemingly a slight sense of hesitation in her voice.

"I believe so," I lied. I had no clue where David had gone this particular Saturday morning. David displayed very little accountability in the relationship, which was more apparent to me now that we were living together.

"Well, it is kind of chilly out here, and I can't promise I'm coming back out today, so I'll wait," she said, stepping into the house.

Although I was sure Miss Claudia had been inside David's house on several occasions and therefore knew her way around the house, I decided to play the role of an amicable hostess.

"Do you want anything to drink?" I asked.

"Oh, no, I'm good," she said, holding up her flask.

I didn't have to encourage her to take a seat; she grabbed the remote off the entertainment center and plopped down on the chaise section of the sectional sofa. I took a seat on the opposite end.

David didn't talk about his mom all that much, and whenever I asked him about her, he'd either get agitated or say, "You might not want to know the answer to that question, so squash it." So I made a habit of asking very few questions about his family and family life. But Miss Claudia was sitting just feet away from me. I knew I had a better chance of getting at least some of my long-held questions answered. Before I could ask the first question, Miss Claudia engaged me.

"Destiny, huh?"

"Yes, ma'am."

"That title is for old folk. I ain't old. Call me Claudia," she said, taking what appeared to be a final gulp of whatever she was drinking in the flask.

"How about Miss Claudia?" I suggested, a bit uncomfortable with calling someone twice my age by their first name.

"That'll do," she said, placing the flask on the coffee table.

"How long have you been dating my boy?" Miss Claudia asked, looking me directly in the eye.

"We've been on and off for about two and a half years now."

"Hmm ..." was all she said.

"Can you tell me what that means?"

"What 'hmm' means?"

"Yes."

"I think you know what it means," she said, reaching into her purse.

"No, I'm sorry, I don't," I replied, trying to seem naïve. I wanted her to spill the beans, and the only way she was going to do it was if I convinced her that I was clueless, like a blonde-black chick, so to speak.

Retrieving another flask from her purse, she responded, "Ever wonder why David has never brought you to meet his mama? I mean, doesn't that seem strange that you date a guy and he never brings you around his mama?"

"Well, he told me you were living in Seattle for a while, so I didn't think anything of it."

"What else did he tell you?" she asked in an interrogation style.

I hesitated.

"Come on, baby. Don't hold back. What else did he tell you?"

"He told me y'all's relationship is kinda shaky."

Miss Claudia burst into laughter. It took a good minute or two for her to regain her composure. I just sat and watched her enjoy the humor of her inside joke. And after she regained her composure, she continued. "Darling, shaky ain't the word for us. David is a lot like his father, very moody and temperamental. And in case you don't already know, which I think you do, he can be abusive, with his mouth and his hands."

She wasn't telling me anything I didn't know. But for some reason, hearing it from his mother's lips made it seem even more real.

"Yes, I know," I whispered.

"Look, I think I like you. So I'mma let you in on some

information, so you have an idea of what you're dealing with. But …" Miss Claudia paused.

"But, what?" I asked.

"But this is between you and me. You can never say a word about this to anyone. I mean, some of this you'll find out if you stay around long enough," she said before pausing to open the flask and take a sip of her good juice. "I had my oldest son when I was fifteen. I ran the streets as a young woman. All of my boyfriends, including David's father, ran the streets. So David running these here streets doesn't bother me in the least bit. It's second nature to him. We were one big happy family until somebody reported that they heard me and David's father fighting. The police, child protective services, and a whole bunch of other white folk got in our business and tore us apart."

"What does this have to do with you and David having a bad relationship?" I asked.

"Let me finish; I'm not done. Things weren't the same after David's father and I broke up. We went from having everything to not having enough of anything, so I did what I knew how to do. I went to the streets again. I sold drugs and lots of it. Been to jail and the whole nine."

I was beginning to understand why David never went into details about his family, especially his mother. Miss Claudia had just unloaded some heavy drama. I was stuck for a few minutes. I literally did not know what to say. And for those few minutes, neither one of us said anything. We both acted like we were engrossed in the show on Animal Planet, which was the channel Miss Claudia had stopped on.

"Did he tell you about Chantel?"

"Not really. He just said his sister Chantel passed away suddenly."

"That's it?" Miss Claudia said, seemingly shocked that I didn't have more tea to offer on the subject. But talking about Chantel was something David veered away from. His eyes would water, and his lips stammered whenever her name came up.

"That's all he ever said," I reassured her.

"Humph …" was her final comment on the subject. "You smoke?" she said as she reached inside her purse and retrieved a pack of Camel cigarettes.

I didn't think people even smoked Camel cigarettes anymore, let alone black people. But I answered, "No."

"Do you mind?" she said as she pulled a cigarette from the carton.

"No, I don't mind. This ain't a smoke-free home."

Miss Claudia chuckled. "I think I like you," she said once again, as she lit her cigarette and took the first pull.

That was all I needed. If I needed a cue giving me permission to pry, she had just given it to me. I decided to test the waters first and ask a not-so-prying question, like why she greeted me the way she did when she came to the door. I wanted to find a way that would make her bring Nettie's name up. Then I would go for the gusto.

"Can I ask you a question, Miss Claudia?"

"Ask me anything, honey," she said, reaching for the ashtray on the end table next to her.

"I'm curious as to why you greeted me the way you did."

"Oh, honey, that's just Claudia. I'm raw and real. You know how many times I've met the so-called one? And the last one, David just could not get rid of."

"Nettie?" I asked, wanting confirmation.

"Yes, her. I couldn't stand her. That woman had some kind of spell on David. And because of his guilt, he just let her do whatever, say whatever. And to top it all off, she kept a nasty house. Matter of fact, this is the cleanest I've ever seen this place. Kudos to you."

"His guilt? What do you mean by that?" I said.

"Never mind. Forget I even said that. That's opening up a different can of worms, and I don't think you can handle it."

What does she mean by David's guilt? I waited for a few seconds to see if Miss Claudia was going to follow up with further details, but she didn't. The rest of the conversation was filled with idle chatter about work, hobbies, and extended family backgrounds. I didn't fill her in on much about my family, because explaining my family dynamics was complicated. I gave her the generic version, which basically entailed where and when I was born, being raised by Honey, and being raised in the church. You know, the good version. When I was finished, Miss Claudia crushed the butt of the cigarette in the ashtray, and began to gather her belongings, including the mail she had brought over for David.

"I thought you said David would be back soon?"

"I thought he went to the gym."

"No telling where he's at. But I have to go. Got a hair appointment," she said, standing up.

"You sure you don't want to leave that here with me?" I offered one last time.

"Nothing against you. I said I like you. But I'll take the mail back with me. It'll give David a reason to come to my house to get it. Just tell him it's important."

"Okay. I will," I said, standing up as well.

I walked Miss Claudia to the front door.

"Oh, hey, this is for emergencies," Miss Claudia said, handing me what looked like a business card.

"Emergencies?" I said as I took the card. The back of the card had handwritten telephone numbers on it.

Miss Claudia walked over to the front door, turned back to me, and winked before letting herself out.

Chapter 14

Blast from the Past

A FEW MONTHS LATER, I stopped by Honey's to pick up *my* mail after running some errands one Saturday morning. I expected her to be engaged in her usual Saturday routine, cleaning the house while listening to a Myles Munroe sermon. But to my surprise, she was sitting down at the kitchen table, drinking a cup of tea when I walked into the kitchen.

"Hey, Honey. No cleaning today?" I said, walking toward the table.

"Nah, not today, chile. Not feeling the best," she said as she sipped her tea.

"What's wrong?" I asked, taking a seat at the table across from her.

"Dunno. Not feeling well in my stomach."

"That doesn't smell like green tea. What are you drinking?"

"Not my regular. This is peppermint and chamomile. Supposed to be good for the stomach."

"Have you been throwing up?"

"Nah, baby, but I'm plenty nauseous. I wish I could."

"Do you need to go to the doctor or the ER?"

"Don't think so. It's just a bug. It'll pass," Honey said, gulping down the last of the tea.

"You sure?" I said, reaching over to take the empty cup out of her hands.

"Yeah, Honey's gonna be just fine. Don't worry about me."

I washed Honey's cup and the remaining dishes in the sink, making small talk with her as I completed the task. But an awkward moment of silence fell as though both Honey and I drifted off somewhere with our own preoccupying thoughts. When I turned around, Honey was staring at me intently.

"What?" I jokingly asked.

"You ain't pregnant, are you?"

"No, Honey," I answered but suddenly realized my cycle was a few days late.

"You sure?"

"Umm … not that I know of," I said. With all the hell I had been going through with David, having a child would not have been good for either of us, although David had said on many occasions that he wanted a son.

"Well, you know how I feel about you playing house. I just hope you're smart enough to swallow some pills and keep yourself from repeating the mistakes women in your family have made."

Honey was clearly referring to Shannon, my auntie Roz, and a slew of other women in our family. The thought of being pregnant hadn't even crossed my mind until Honey brought the subject up. There was no way I was going to let her even think I might be pregnant, so I just gave her the ole fake confident spiel.

"Honey, now you know, I ain't got time for no baby. I don't even have the patience for one."

"I take it you gon' get your own place then, right?"

"Yeah … soon," I lied. I could sense I was being led into a trap by Honey. She was good at it. By my age, I knew better, although I didn't always see it coming and would sometimes fall right into it.

"And it wouldn't hurt you to come to church, either. You know how I raised you."

"Yeah, I know, Honey. I will," I lied again. I had no intentions on going to church. The guilt about my current lifestyle ran deep. There was no way I was going to visit New Zion without having a ring on my finger.

"The saints ask about you all the time," Honey continued.

"Yeah, I ran into Deacon Bronner the other day in Helman's."

"Oh, yeah?" Honey said with excitement.

"Yes," I confirmed.

"What did he say?"

"He just asked me how I was doing and said he hadn't seen me in a long time."

"Did he tell you about Lecrecia?"

"Of course," I said. Lecrecia was Deacon Bronner's daughter. There was always this competition thing between the two of us, which was fueled by Lecrecia's mother, Sister Jan, and Honey, for that matter. From the length of our hair to our apparel, down to our grades, we were in competition with one another. Quite naturally, it caused us to not like one another. The so-called good news about Lecrecia was that she was taking over Sister Jan's hair salon in Southfield. Deacon Bronner didn't forget to also brag about her engagement to some big-time executive from Connecticut. But the purpose of sharing this news with me, someone who wasn't even friends with his daughter, seemed questionable. The only thing I could assume was that Deacon Bronner had taken up where Sister Jan left off years ago. I hadn't seen that family in years. And frankly, I didn't care to know anything about any of the Bronners. I was living my own life. It wasn't perfect, but I was finally doing some of the things Destiny wanted to do.

"What do you think about it?" Honey asked.

"I don't think anything. I mean, it's good for her, Honey. I really have my own life to live at this point. I don't even know if I truly dislike her because of something she's done of her own will or if it's because of some twisted game or competition you and Sister Jan had going on for years."

Honey looked away for a quick second as if she was shocked

that I had called her out. She didn't say anything and neither did I. I quickly changed the subject to kill the awkward feeling that had begun to creep in.

"Well, Honey, I have to get going today. Hattie invited me to a get-together at her house. So I told her I'd stop by. But if you need me to go pick you up some soup and ginger ale, I'll stop by the store, so you don't have to go out."

"I'm fine, baby. This ain't nothing but a little ole twenty-four-hour stomach bug. I'mma drink some more tea and go lie down. Vera's gonna bring over some homemade vegetable soup."

Vera was Honey's middle sister and probably the best cook in the family. I knew Honey would be in good care if Aunt Vera was coming by to look after her. Like Honey, Aunt Vera was a widow. But unlike Honey, Aunt Vera's husband left her well off. They never had any children of their own, but they adopted a boy named Roland. Growing up, we called him Rolly for short. He was about four years older than me. Together, Aunt Vera and Uncle Charlie gave Rolly a good life. Rolly went into the Air Force after high school and became some high-ranking officer. I couldn't remember the last time I had seen him, though.

Also unlike Honey, who didn't date much at all after Albert Sr. passed away, Aunt Vera had many boyfriends after Uncle Charlie passed. We referred to her as the "Blanche" of the family, the character from *The Golden Girls* sitcom, as Aunt Vera was sassy but still classy. It was a surprise to many that she cooked as well as she did because she didn't look like the typical Susie Homemaker kind of woman. The men in the family made bets on how long they guessed she'd be with her latest beau. Aunt Vera knew about the running jokes in the family, but she was cool as all getup, oftentimes, chiming in on guessing how long the newest beau would be around. The last time I saw Aunt Vera was at Brewster's Bank when I went to cash my check, which was some months back. She was at the bank with her new boyfriend, Stewart, and I introduced the two of them to David.

Before I knew it, I had been at Honey's for more than an hour. I was surprised David hadn't paged me. When he wasn't tracking me down, it generally meant he was out dealing or involved in something else that I had no knowledge of. Yeah, I suspected he might have been cheating, but I had no proof, and David had already showed me on many occasions that he couldn't control his temper. So needless to say, I was careful to pick and choose my battles. Until I had proof, or my suspicion got the best of me, I deliberately chose to ignore the late-night calls and pages, the late-night runs, and the private conversations he held outside or in other rooms of the house.

I helped Honey get back in bed, kissed her on the forehead, and let myself out. I stopped by the gas station on Seven Mile and Hayes to get gas. As I pumped my gas, I heard a horn blow, but I didn't pay it any mind. The horn blew again, but this time, I heard my name called. The voice sounded familiar, but I wasn't sure who it was. When I turned around, I didn't recognize the car, so I turned back around and focused my attention back on my task. The horn blew again. This time, when I turned around, the driver side door opened, and emerging from the car was a familiar face—Ziek Wallace!

"Let me get that for you," Ziek said as he approached and took the pump from my grasp.

"Oh, my goodness! Ziek!"

"Yep. It's me in the flesh," he said, revealing his perfect set of teeth.

"Where have you been?" I said, looking him over from head to toe. He was still good looking.

"I moved to Tennessee for a little while. But I've been back for a minute now."

"What's in Tennessee?" I asked, leaning back on my car, facing him.

"The fam. But that's boring stuff. Let's talk about you. How have you been?" Ziek said, quickly changing the subject.

"I'm doing good. Just working."

"I know you're lying to me. You're too fine to just be working. You tryna tell me you ain't got no man?" Ziek said, as he took the pump out of the gas tank and placed it back on the fuel tank.

"Well ... yeah, I have a guy," I answered, almost wishing I didn't.

"Are you happy?"

"What do you mean 'happy'?"

"Happy. Like is he treating you good? Is he buying you everything you want? Is he taking care of you in the bedroom?"

"Of course!" I lied. David was failing at most of it, but at this point, I couldn't go back home with egg on my face, so I had to stay to make it work.

"You sure?"

I hesitated. I wanted to tell Ziek the truth, but since the chemistry between us had been so electrifying in the past, I didn't want to set myself up, especially with things being as rocky as they were between David and me.

"I know he ain't treating you right."

I shifted my weight to one side as if Ziek had it twisted. Something was still there. What this "something" was, I couldn't explain. Ziek looked me up and down from head to toe. "Girl, you still fine. That dude is lucky you even looked his way."

I was feeling like a geeky teenager all over again. I was sure that if I had a lighter skin complexion, my checks would have been rosy red. I hadn't heard charming words in quite some time, and it felt good.

"You still got the same pager number?"

"Yes," I said. "But I have a cell phone, too." David had recently bought us both cell phones. I kept my pager just in case he decided to repossess the cell phone on one of the many days he was in one of his funky moods.

"Cool. Give me your cell. It's just easier."

"Just page me. I return all pages."

Ziek chuckled.

"What's funny?" I said.

"Nothing."

"No, seriously, what's funny?" I repeated.

"He got you on lock like that?"

"Look, Ziek, I just don't want no trouble. I live with the man."

"I get it. I get it. Just give me your pager number again. I don't see your number in my directory," he said, fumbling through his cell phone.

"You erased my number for your chicks, I see," I joked.

"Nah, nah. When I changed from my pager to my cell, not all numbers ported over. So just gimme your pager number right quick, and I'll plug it in my cell phone."

"Let me get *your* new number," I said as I leaned into the car to retrieve my cell phone from my purse, so I could lock in his number. When I turned back around, Ziek was standing directly in front of me. Our eyes met. I couldn't move. I knew I needed to, but I didn't want to. Butterflies danced in my belly. I swallowed hard. As if we were statues, we stood in the same position for a good thirty seconds, not saying a word, just staring into each other's eyes.

"I want you," Ziek said, planting a soft kiss on my lips.

"Ziek, please," I begged. But before I knew it, we were engaged in a full-fledged tongue down right there at Getty's Gas Station. After some time, I managed to break away.

"Don't stop," he said, trying to pull me closer.

"I can't, Ziek. I can't."

"Why not?" he said, successfully pulling me close.

"Because I have a man."

"So. You already told me that."

"Yeah, but we live together."

"But me and you belong together."

"I got a man," I repeated. My lips said one thing, but my heart said something else. I turned my head away, but correctly interpreting the nonverbal cue, Ziek turned my head back around so we were facing each other once again. He pressed his body into mine, leaning me against my car. I closed my eyes and allowed his lips to meet mine, and we enjoyed another passionate tongue down.

With the thought of David or any of his associates witnessing Ziek and me kissing, I gently pushed Ziek back. "Stop. Please don't do that," I said, trying to catch my breath.

"Why? You want it as bad as I do."

"I can't, Ziek. Please, I—"

"Shhh," Ziek whispered, holding his index finger up to his lips.

"I have to go," I said, trying to walk away.

"Look, I won't say I'm sorry because I'm not. I still love you, Destiny."

"Ziek, I can't."

"I don't think you love him, Destiny," Ziek said, grabbing my left arm.

"I do. I love him."

"What's his name?"

"Ziek, I really have to go," I said, trying to free my arm.

"Okay. Just do me one favor?"

"What is that?"

"Just go out with me one time."

I paused, looking past Ziek as if David was sure to drive up any second. "Okay. Okay. Just one time," I bargained.

Ziek released my arm and opened my car door for me. I got into the car and he closed the door for me. I waved goodbye to him. Ziek blew me a kiss then motioned for me to roll the window down.

"You never gave me your number," Ziek said, leaning his head in my car.

We exchanged numbers and I restarted my car and drove off slowly. From my rearview mirror, I could see Ziek still standing in the same spot, watching me as I drove away.

I rehearsed the encounter over and over as I drove. All sorts of thoughts ran through my mind. *How could I be falling for Ziek all over again? I'm in love with David. I'm in love with David. I'm in love with David … or am I?*

Chapter 15

A Double Life

AT BOTH HER REQUEST and insistence, I met up with Claudia at Olive Garden. I didn't know the woman, really, but it seemed as though we struck up some unique friendship when she stopped by the house the first time. She said she just wanted to get to know me. The last time I had heard that line, it was from a one-night stand with a guy named Kenny. It's a good thing he sucked in bed like The Dom, because while he thought he was "wham-bam-thank-you-ing" me, I was just as glad to kick him to the curb. Except, he had done me no favors. I didn't even orgasm.

While I was a bit cautious on one hand about meeting with Claudia, especially since David told me to stay away from his own mother, I was curious on the other. Plus, I had to admit, I had other questions that I was sure she'd be willing to answer. And if she just answered one of them, I was going to be in a better situation than if I didn't meet with her at all.

Rushing into the restaurant like a bat out of hell, an out of breath Claudia went into the spiel of why she was almost thirty minutes late. "Sorry I'm late. Had a late night and an early morning, so I'm a little off track here. Worked out this morning and then had to get a manicure and pedicure. You get it, don't you?" she said, opening her arms expecting a hug.

"Oh, that's okay," I lied, hugging her.

Claudia was wearing expensive perfume, and I could tell because I had smelled the fragrance before. David had bought me a sample of it in a miniature glass vial. Although she was not that refined in speech or mannerism, Claudia was a beautiful woman. She was dark skinned like Viola Davis and had high cheekbones, as if she were of Indian descent. "Come on. I'm starving. I already know what I'm ordering," she said, holding up her index and middle fingers to catch the attention of the restaurant host.

"Table for two?" a young black male who introduced himself as Wade said as he grabbed two menus.

"That's a nice name," Claudia said.

"Thanks," the young host said as he escorted us to our table then proceeded with his customary routine of sharing with us the specials of the day, handing us the menus simultaneously.

"Are you a junior, like as in Wade, Junior?" Claudia continued.

"Yes, ma'am, I am," the young man answered, seemingly shocked Claudia was able to guess.

"You wanna know how I know?"

"Yes, ma'am," the young man responded, curious to know.

"Not many young Wades around these days. That name is for men of my age, like your dad."

The young host chuckled, but I wasn't sure whether he was chuckling because he found Claudia's answer amusing or if it was because he was downright baffled by the response altogether. The two stared at one another.

"Tell your dad, Ms. Claudia said hello."

"Wait a minute. You know my dad?" the young host asked curiously.

"I sure do," Claudia said, handing the menu back to him.

"How do you know my dad?" the young man asked.

"We used to do business."

"Oh," the young host answered in an unenthusiastic tone.

"So just tell him Ms. Claudia said hello."

The young host nodded. "Your waiter will be over shortly to take your orders," he said before walking off briskly.

Claudia peeled off her coat and placed it next to her on the booth seat. She was smirking. Although I wanted to ask her about the weird encounter she'd just had with the young host, I refrained. Instead, I decided to open the conversation up with a question of my own, in an attempt to get Claudia to disclose the true purpose of the lunch meetup.

"So is this about David's upcoming birthday?" I asked.

"This, like in us meeting for lunch?"

"Yes."

"Oh no, I'm just meeting up with you because you seem a little naïve, and I like you and don't want you to get hurt."

"Get hurt?" I asked, a bit offended by her comment.

"Well, you're a good ole church girl. What do you know about the streets?"

"I know enough," I said, letting her know I wasn't the least bit intimidated by her.

"Do you?" she said, now directly challenging me.

Before I could answer, our waitress, a thin, tall black woman who looked to be in her early thirties walked up to our table to take our orders. And after we both placed our orders, I focused my attention back on Claudia to address her challenge.

"What makes you think I'm naïve?"

"Am I wrong?" Claudia said, sitting back.

"Yes, I think you're wrong."

"Okay. I could be wrong, but I don't think so. And let me show you why I know I'm not wrong." Claudia paused for a moment as if she needed to gather her thoughts on how to break it down to me. "You've known my son for how long now?"

"Going on three years now," I said, letting out a sigh afterward.

"And you've been living with him for how long now?"

"About eight months, going on nine."

Raising her eyebrows, she continued. "Have you ever wondered what happened to Nettie?"

"No, not really," I lied.

"Well, you should."

"Why is that?" I said with flair.

"Because it's only a matter of time before she'll be wreaking havoc on you and David's life."

"What do you mean by 'just a matter of time'?" I said, seeking clarity.

Just when we were getting into the details, we were interrupted by the waitress who had brought our drinks, a Blue Hawaiian for Claudia and a Long Island iced tea for me.

"Thank you, honey," Claudia said, inspecting her drink.

Claudia waited for our waitress to leave before resuming the conversation. "So now, where were we?" she said as she took the first sip of her drink.

"Nettie," I said matter-of-factly.

"Oh, yeah. Nettie. So you don't know, do you?"

I didn't respond; I just gave Claudia the *you know I don't know* look.

"Nettie's not gone forever. She's just gone for *now*."

"I'm not following you," I said, taking a sip of my drink. I was becoming more irritated playing this verbal back and forth game with Claudia.

"Nettie's in jail."

My jaw dropped. "Jail?" I reiterated.

"Yes, jail."

"For what?"

"What else? Taking a rap for David," Claudia said, rolling her eyes.

"For drugs?"

"Nope. Gun charges, this time."

I suddenly lost my appetite, but I had to think quick on my feet, at least so Claudia wouldn't think the news shook me so hard. "So what are you saying?" I said, trying to get Claudia to spill more tea.

"That said, you and I both know the only reason you're in that house is because Nettie's in jail. What excuse did David give you about Nettie no longer being there?"

"He just said she was gone."

"Normally, I wouldn't get involved in David's personal life. You're naïve like my Chantel was. But when you're dating somebody like my son, David, you've got to be smart."

Not sure of what her definition of smart was, I just nodded instead of divulging what I had interpreted the term to mean.

After she paused, she continued. "All I'm saying is that Nettie's been around for quite some time, and there's a reason David keeps her around, even though he's in denial about it. I won't go into details, but I'll just urge you to be smart."

Irritated by her play on words and her vagueness, I just came right out and asked Claudia, "So what do you really mean when you say, 'Be smart'?"

Our waitress walked up with our meals. "Shrimp scampi?"

"Right here," I said, raising my right index finger.

"And eggplant parmesan for you," she said, placing the dish in front of Claudia.

We both said thank you and immediately resumed the conversation before our waitress could even walk off.

"There are quite a few people in this world that I dislike. But there are only maybe a handful that I just downright hate, and Nettie is in that group," Claudia said, unfolding her napkin and placing it in her lap.

"So you're saying you hate her, and you've known her for quite some time, but you like me, a woman you've only known for a short period of time. Is it smart of me to believe that?"

"Destiny, this has nothing to do with time. It's a personality thing. She has a spell on my boy, and before it's all over, either he's gonna end up killing her or she's gonna end up killing him. I want her out of his life for good."

"Well, David is a grown man. If Nettie's around, it's because David wants her around," I said. I could only defend David up to a certain point.

"Look, Destiny, Nettie's from the streets. She's got street smarts, and she's been around the block a few times, if you know what I mean. No offense to you, but she can run circles around you when it comes to David. For one, she knows his weaknesses. Do you?"

I felt a surge of heat make its way from the nape of my neck to the lobes of both ears. Both embarrassed and angry, I responded. "A son … he wants a son."

"Ahh, you got it. You're not as slow as I thought you were."

By this time, I was no longer sipping on my drink, and I hadn't even tasted one morsel of the food in front of me. I wanted to get to David. Even though I knew confronting him would probably end in some type of physical altercation, I was angry at him for playing me for a fool.

"How are you feeling right now?" Claudia said between chews of her eggplant parmesan.

"I'm pissed. That's how I'm feeling."

Claudia let out a loud laugh. "Don't be pissed. Be smart like I told you."

"Ms. Claudia, what does being smart mean?"

"You know David wants a son, right?"

I didn't answer. I just looked Claudia straight in the eye.

"*Right?*" she repeated.

I nodded.

"So give the man what he wants."

"You're telling me to get pregnant?"

"That, or act like you are. That is, if you want to get Nettie out of the picture for good," Claudia said, taking the last sip of her drink.

My mind drifted for a few moments as I meditated on Claudia's suggestion.

"Any woman that's willing to take gun charges for a man is more than a ride-or-die chick. She's a ride-for-life kinda woman. And to battle with that type of woman, you gotta be smart. You have to get the chess board out and put your checkers away," Claudia added, her way of qualifying her statement.

And there it was. Claudia's definition of being smart meant scheming—getting pregnant on purpose or pretending to be pregnant. "And what all do I get out of it?" I asked, curious to learn what other tricks Claudia had up her sleeve.

"Glad you asked. My son is a lot like his father. Give him what he wants, and he'll give you what you want."

As I sat there with my plate of food now gone cold, I couldn't help but replay David's words of caution about his mother in my mind. What Claudia said made a lot of sense. But then again, David made occasional reference that his mother was notorious for scheming and scamming people. When it came to David's secrecy—the private conversations and disappearing acts—I really had no choice but to become allies with Claudia, at least for the time being. She hadn't asked much of me, only that I trust her and keep the conversation confidential. What really did I have to lose?

I sat with Claudia, watching her eat the rest of her food and down another glass of Blue Hawaiian as we made other small talk, mainly about her time in Seattle. I didn't get any real bad vibes about her, but I was still cautious. If I didn't benefit anything else, I at least knew what I was dealing with in terms of Nettie and David. While Claudia's definition of being smart was in reference to Nettie and David, I had my own definition, and it included having a ram in the bush—Mr. Ziek Wallace.

It didn't take a lot of convincing for me to agree to meet Ziek at Eight Mile Run to watch him play pool the following Friday evening. Yes, I was taking chances with being caught. But with Ed in the picture now, it was easy to get out of the house under the pretense that I was going over to Aunt Ann's to see him.

At the bar's entrance checking IDs was a dark-skinned, muscular guy with a full beard. He was wearing a shirt with the name Shane on it. "Need your ID," he said, holding out his hand.

I pulled out my driver's license and handed it to him.

After scanning my driver's license, he looked back at me, staring almost. "Don't I know you?" he said, his eyebrows raised.

"Nah, man, you don't know her," Ziek blurted out.

Without taking his eyes off me, the bouncer held my license out for me to take. Shoving a pass of some sort in front of the guy's face, Ziek snatched my license out of the bouncer's hand and gave it to me, all while not even taking his eyes off the guy. And that was the Italian mobster-like side of Ziek—not afraid of anyone or anything. The bouncer moved back and let us enter, all the while staring at me as if he had a bone to pick with me.

"You know him?" Ziek asked as we walked over to our reserved booth on the opposite side of the lounge.

"No, I don't know him. Never saw him a day in my life."

"You sure?" Ziek said, looking back at the bouncer.

"Yes, I'm sure."

"Well, never mind him then. Do you want something to drink?"

"Yeah, I'll take my usual, a Long Island iced tea," I said.

"All right. You go on over to the booth and I'll order our drinks at the bar."

Ziek was a regular at Eight Mile Run, especially because he played pool at the competition level. I had watched him play a few times back in the day, but it was at a bar that had since closed, Main Street Tavern. Eight Mile Run was a newer establishment, known for good food, good drinks, and good entertainment. It was always filled to capacity on Saturday evenings. At just a little past ten o'clock, the lounge was nearly packed this night. From where I was sitting, I could see the bar and the related activity happening at and near it. Coincidentally, I spotted Ziek engaged in conversation with a woman who looked like she was mixed, maybe black and white. I couldn't be too sure because the room was dim. Whoever she was, she seemed to be pretty cozy standing next to him, not afraid to rub his back as they talked. Ziek stepped backward, causing her hands to slip. His little tactic worked because she stopped rubbing his back, wrapped up the conversation, and walked over to the other side of the bar. If I was just being smart, as Claudia would call it, I shouldn't have gotten jealous by what I had just witnessed. But I did. *He's just a ram in the bush, Destiny.* I had to keep that in the forefront of my mind, no matter how fun and exciting things became. *A ram, Destiny,* is what I kept repeating in my head until my thoughts were interrupted.

"Here's your drink. Nice and strong, just the way you like it," Ziek said, placing my drink on the table in front of me and handing me a napkin at the same time.

"So you remembered I like it strong," I said, stirring the drink.

"I remember a lot of things you like," Ziek said, winking simultaneously.

I lowered my head, a bit embarrassed that I'd left myself open like that. Had it not been for Ziek's instability, there would have been no David. Even though both of them ran the streets, David had a little more potential than Ziek. David was more educated, having at least graduated from high school, came from more of a stable family, even though they had their own version of dysfunction going on, and he did hold a job. Ziek, on the other hand, wasn't as polished as David. He came from a very dysfunctional background, with his mother having been addicted to drugs and a father who cared more about pastoring a megachurch than he did taking care of his own family. Without selling drugs, Ziek would most likely have been homeless, because as long as I'd known him, he never held a job.

Despite all the reasons I told myself Ziek and I would never work, our chemistry, both in and out of the bedroom, was like no other I had experienced. And Ziek was a lot of fun as well. It took me a while to pinpoint what it was, besides his looks and our parallel familial backgrounds, that drew me to Ziek. Finally, one day it hit me—Ziek was charming and charismatic, sort of like a preacher that wows the congregation Sunday after Sunday. Ziek was that one for me.

"You look beautiful," Ziek said as he sat down next to me.

I smiled sheepishly. "Thank you," I said as I took the first sip of my drink.

"So tell me, what have you been up to?"

"Working and trying to stash my cash," I joked. That was one of Ziek's favorite sayings back in the day.

"Hey, ain't nothing wrong with that." An awkward moment of silence passed. "So tell me about this man of yours," he said, making eye contact with me.

"Come on, Ziek. That's not why I'm here, to talk about him."

"Then tell me, why *are* you here?"

I was speechless. I took another sip of my drink.

"Are you happy with that dude?"

"Ziek, I like him."

"You know I've always been crazy about you, don't you?"

"Ziek, you know you and I have this crazy chemistry thing, but we'd never make it."

"Why would you say that?"

"Because."

"Because what?" he said, taking my drink out of my hand.

"You like a lot of women, and I can't deal with that."

"Destiny, if I have a woman, I can settle down with that one woman. But you've never seen me claim one woman."

"Exactly. Now, can I have my drink back?" I said, reaching for my drink.

"You and I should give it another try."

Just as I was about to respond, a medium-sized guy with slick, greasy hair walked up to our table.

"Ready?" he said to Ziek.

"Yeah, man. I'll be right there," Ziek said to the guy. "Look, let me go take all these dudes' money," Ziek said, alluding to having an easy win over the other guys that were playing pool with him.

When I finished my drink, I watched the guys play pool, taking intermittent breaks to go to the bathroom, fix my makeup, or call David. I must have called him a good five to six times, but he never answered. By the time Ziek was finished playing his games, it was shortly after midnight.

"The night's still young. What do you want to do?" Ziek said.

"Guess I'll be heading home."

"Do you have to?" Ziek said, looking at me with disappointment.

"I mean, I don't have to," I said. The fact that David didn't answer my calls and hadn't called me back meant I would not find him at home. I did have some time on my hands, so I let Ziek know I was open. "What do you have in mind?"

"Nothing in particular. I mean, we can just go back to my place and hang out."

"Hang out, huh?" I said, skeptical of his definition of hanging out.

"Just come check my new place out. I bought a condo, and I hooked it up."

It was probably against my better judgment to take Ziek up on the offer, but I thought I'd just hang out for a little while longer just to kill some time. Truth be told, I hated going home to that empty house, especially on the nights when David would stay out until the wee hours of the morning.

"So?" Ziek said, anticipating my answer.

"Okay. But just for a little while."

I followed Ziek to his condo on Jefferson. I parked in a guest parking space in the parking lot and waited for Ziek to get out of his car. When he did, I turned off the engine and met him at the building's entrance.

We took the elevator to the eighteenth floor, the clubhouse floor, just one floor below the penthouse level. Taking in the interior décor of the building, I followed Ziek as we walked down the long corridor to his unit. When he opened the door to his condo unit, my eyes zeroed in on the spectacular view of Downtown Detroit. A large ceiling-to-floor-length window sat behind the sectional sofa. My eyes widened.

"Come on in," Ziek said, chuckling.

I was mesmerized by the view. I walked into the condo and headed straight for the window. Sparkling lights flashed from cars, streetlights, and Canada's casinos across the Detroit River. I lost track of time for a moment, still mesmerized by the lights, the action, and the busyness outside. I snapped back into the present when Ziek said something to me.

"Are you gonna stand in front of the window all night or come and join me on the sofa," Ziek said, giving me a brief flashback of the movie *Mahogany,* starring Diana Ross and Billy Dee Williams.

"Oh," I said, turning around to face Ziek. He was holding a bottle of wine in one hand and two wine glasses in the other. "I'm sorry. It's just so beautiful out there. It doesn't even look like Detroit," I said as I slid my hands across the plush gray suede sectional.

"Come on. Let's watch a movie," Ziek said, gesturing with his head.

"I guess I should take my boots off," I said, noticing he had removed his and was barefoot.

"I don't have any demands," Ziek said as he placed the wine bottle and wine glasses down on the coffee table.

I removed my boots anyway and placed them on the mat by the front door. I couldn't help but notice that the walls were pretty bare. With the exception of the flat screen that covered nearly the entire space on the wall facing the sectional and the two eight-by-ten pictures of his sons, there wasn't anything else on the walls.

"This place is gorgeous," I said, walking over to join him on the sofa.

"Thank you. But it could use a woman's touch," he said, holding his hand out for me.

"You think so?" I said as I slid down on the sofa next to him.

"Yes. That's what this place is missing, a woman's touch."

I didn't readily respond because I didn't know if Ziek was just saying it to try to woo me or if he really meant it. I was cautious at this point. Ziek was too fine to be single. I was certain there had to be a woman or two lurking somewhere near, just as I was in a complicated relationship with David. So, I wasn't going to hold Ziek's feet to the fire.

"Wine?" Ziek asked, holding up the bottle.

"Sure."

I watched as he popped the cork and began to pour wine in one of the wine glasses. "This enough?" he said, lifting the glass, which was filled a little past the halfway mark.

"Yes, that's enough. I have to drive home."

"Says who?" he said as he poured wine into the other wine glass.

"I really didn't plan on coming over here," I said, taking a sip of wine.

"Well, you're here. Sit back and let's enjoy the rest of the night together." Ziek reached for the remote and leaned back on the sofa. "What do you want to watch?"

"Anything. Just find something interesting, not boring," I said, taking another sip of wine.

Before I realized it, I had downed three glasses of wine and was sprawled out on the sofa with my head in Ziek's lap as he ran his hands through my hair, stroking my scalp intermittently.

Just like the old times, Ziek and I enjoyed watching our favorite comedies and black and white movies until we just zonked out.

I woke up to the muffled sound of a tea kettle. I sat up and cased my surrounding. That's when I remembered I was still at Ziek's … in his bedroom … in his bed. I threw the sheets off me. *Whew!* I was happy to discover I was fully clothed, with the exception of my socks, which were balled up on the nightstand next to the bed. The last thing I remembered was lying on the sectional sofa watching *Same Time Next Year*, one of my favorite black and white movies, starring Ellen Burnstyn and Alan Alda. Ironically, it was one of Ziek's favorite movies as well.

As I attempted to get out of bed, the bedroom door opened. It was Ziek, holding a plate of food and a glass of orange juice.

"I figured you'd be hungry, so I made you something to eat."

"Oh, my god, Ziek! What time is it? I gotta get home!" I said, panicked as I lifted my cell phone to see the time.

"It's a little after eight."

"I gotta go!" I said, reaching for the socks to put them on.

I hurriedly grabbed my boots, which were by the bedroom door now, and thrust my feet into them. "Sorry, I have to go, Ziek."

"If you don't want to eat, just drink the orange juice. Put something on your stomach," Ziek said, handing me the glass of orange juice.

I gulped it down. "Where's my coat?"

"It's in the front room."

I followed him to the front room, where he retrieved my coat from the closet and helped me put it on.

"Hold on a minute. I'm gonna walk you to your car."

I waited for Ziek to put on some clothes, so he could walk me to my car. Like a gentleman, he opened my car door. But before I got in, I turned to face him.

"Did you have a nice time?" he said.

"I think I did," I said, tempted to ask the burning question

I had, since I couldn't remember everything that transpired the previous night.

"You think? You don't know if you had a good time?"

"I don't remember everything," I confessed.

"Oh, no … no, Destiny. Nothing happened. You fell asleep, and I put you to bed. I can assure you nothing happened. The most I did was kiss you on your forehead last night. I would never take advantage of you like that."

I smiled. I stood on my toes and gave him a quick peck on the lips.

"Thank you," I said.

"You're welcome."

I got into my car and Ziek closed the car door for me.

During the entire drive home, I practiced my story—*I went to see Ed and fell asleep at Aunt Ann's, watching movies.*

And just like that, the saga of my double life began.

Chapter 16

Daddy Issues ~ Part II

MIDWAY THROUGH THE CONVERSATION, after gauging my disposition and trying to determine whether I was going to be semi-cordial or downright rude—as I had every right to be—Ed blurted out his request. "I have some paperwork I want you to sign. Think if I give it to you, you can mail it back to me after you sign it?"

"Paperwork?"

"Yeah, my policies and some paperwork from the military. You know I was in the Air Force for a short period, don't you?"

"No, I didn't know that, Ed. You weren't around, remember?" I was beyond curt; I was perturbed. Irritated. I had gotten a late start to my day, and to hear him trying to play victim just put me in a bad mood altogether.

After figuring out I wasn't going to jump at the opportunity to be his chosen beneficiary, he changed the subject. "So you still with the same company?"

"Yeah, I'm still there."

"How's it going?"

"It's going well," I said, looking around the screened-in porch.

After a few moments of silence passed, Ed continued. "Why don't you just think about it. It could be good for you."

"Claiming life insurance proceeds?" I said facetiously.

"I just want to do right by you, Destiny. And one of the ways I can do it is by leaving you something after I'm gone, something besides hurt."

"I'll think about it," I said, holding my hand out for Ed to hand me the paperwork. I saw the sincerity in his eyes, and I heard his sincerity with my own ears, but something on the inside wouldn't allow me to give into Ed. I took the paperwork and turned to leave.

"Not staying for a while?"

"I have other plans," I said. I didn't have other plans, but I wanted him to think so.

Ed managed to muster enough strength to get up from his chair to see me out. I got a good look at him. I could see myself in him, not just the gap between our two front teeth. When I turned around to say my final goodbye, our eyes met. Ed looked sad. Desperate. But I was numb. I didn't hate him, but I didn't feel the traditional love or bond that existed in a normal father-daughter relationship. I unlatched the lock on the screen door and let myself out. I could feel Ed's eyes staring at me as I walked to my car.

"Hey, you don't want to say hi to your aunties?" he yelled out from the doorway.

"I'm in a rush," I lied. I didn't have anything against my aunties; my issue was with Ed and Shannon. My aunts' desire to get to know me was noble, but they had no clue that deep down, an angry and hurt Destiny existed—and that Destiny was dangerous.

"Then I guess we'll all just see you tomorrow," Ed yelled out to me.

"Okay," I said as I unlocked my car door. Aunt Ann was hosting Sunday dinner at her house, as she did often. I promised Shalisa I would come to Sunday dinner this go around.

I thought about Ed's request nearly the entire drive to Starter's, a newly-opened sports bar and grill on the westside, where I was going to meet up with Toya. She and I were getting together just to hang out and catch up, since we hadn't seen each other in several months. She picked the establishment because she said they had the best wings, waffle fries, and their alcoholic beverages were cheap.

Toya was already seated and enjoying a drink at our table when I arrived. She stood up to hug me when I approached. "Look at you, stranger. Looks like I need to schedule appointments to catch up with you," Toya teased before sitting back down and taking another sip of her blackberry mojito. I knew that's what she was drinking because she never drank anything else. Never.

"Stop it. Just stop it. You know I'm just busy working and tryna make it happen for myself," I jokingly said.

"Want a drink?" Toya said, lifting her cup.

"Yeah," I answered, skimming the menu. "I think I'm going to order a cosmopolitan. Something basic."

Toya summoned the waiter to our table, a tall black guy with light brown eyes and sandy brown hair that was cut into a fade. "Boris, can you get my friend, Destiny, a cosmopolitan?"

"Sure thing," he said as he retrieved an order pad from his waist and scribbled my order onto it.

"Oh, and I'll take another blackberry mojito," Toya added.

"You sure?" the waiter asked with raised eyebrows.

"Yes, I'm sure."

"That's your third, you know."

Toya chuckled. "I handle my liquor very well."

"All right. All right, sistah. Just don't wanna see anything on the news tonight about a beautiful young lady getting into an accident on her way home."

Toya chuckled a little harder. "Is that what you do at work?"

"I … I'm not sure I'm following you. What do you mean, 'Is that what I do when I'm at work?'"

"Flirt. Flirt with women you wait on."

"Only if they're pretty," Boris chimed back.

Toya's cheeks flushed a rosy red. "Oh, all right. I can get with that."

I couldn't help but smile because this Boris guy and Toya seemed like they had a thing for each other.

"Be right back," Boris said, winking at Toya as he walked away.

"Girrlll ..." Toya said, fanning herself with her hands.

We both shared a light chuckle. When Boris was out of our sight, we immediately sparked up the "girl conversation."

"So what's going on with you in the man category?" Toya said between sips of the last of her mojito.

Keeping it general as I always did with Toya, I just said, "It's going. Ups and downs here and there, but pretty good."

Toya smiled.

"What?" I said, trying to gauge her thought process.

"Nothing. I was just thinking."

"About what?"

"About life ... you, me, and Shonte hanging out as besties. Now, we're all grown and doing our own thing."

"Tell me about it," I said. "I couldn't have imagined going through some of the things I've gone through in my adulthood. Couldn't have imagined the man who abandoned my mother and me would resurface."

"Yeah, so how's the relationship with your dad going?"

"You mean, Ed," I said, correcting her.

"Yeah, Ed."

"Well, if that's what you wanna call it—a relationship. I went by his sister's house to see him before I met up with you tonight. He claimed he had some important issues to discuss with me."

"Is he still sick?"

"I guess. But I didn't get into all of that tonight. He wants me to sign some papers making me the executor of his estate."

"Well, ain't nothing wrong with that!" Toya cheered.

"I feel it's just a way to buy my forgiveness, lure me in with money or promises of money."

"Who cares, Destiny? This is a rough world, and if the man

wants to make it up to you by throwing a little money your way, take it. Don't let the insurance company keep it."

Before I could respond, Boris walked up to our table with our drinks in his hand. "Here's a cosmopolitan for you and a blackberry mojito for the most beautiful lady in the room," he said, placing our respective drinks in front of us.

"Thank you," we said in unison.

Toya's face displayed a vibrant smile and Boris returned the gesture by blowing her a soft kiss. Her eyes followed Boris until he was no longer in sight.

"Going hard for him, aren't you?" I teased.

"Girl, that's how you have to do them. Make'em think you're smitten. He has no idea that I know who he is."

"Who he is?" I repeated, expecting her to elaborate.

"He's co-owner of this bar. One of the girls that works at the hotel with me told me. He owns this with two of his partners. He used to work as a hedge fund manager."

"Did you just say hedge fund?" I asked, stirring my drink with a thin red stirring straw.

"Yep, I sure did."

"Does he know you?"

"Not from a can of spray paint. I just liked what I saw and sat in a spot where he could see me. And it helps that I have this short skirt on. You know, putting a little flesh out on display never hurts," Toya joked.

I just shook my head. That was one thing about Toya; she had no fear. She didn't even know the definition of rejection. She had a way of looking at the positive sides of things, almost always. If things didn't seem to work out the way she expected, she'd just employ a new strategy. That was one of the traits I most admired about her.

"Don't shake your head at me. You gotta be strategic in the man game. You see Shonte done snagged her one and is getting married in a couple of months."

"You're right," I said, taking a sip of my drink.

Toya frowned.

"What's wrong," I asked.

"Nothing."

"Something's wrong. Why the long face?"

"Just thought about my mom. I really miss her. She'll never get to meet my husband or my children." I could see Toya was trying her best to keep her emotions intact.

Words escaped me. I just let Toya have her moment while I gently caressed her back, trying to soothe her pain, which I knew was impossible to do. The symbolic gesture was what counted. And after a few moments, Toya seemed to be able to pull herself together.

"So what do you have left to do for Shonte's wedding?" Toya said, in an effort to change the subject and the mood.

"There's plenty to do, so you know I'm gonna need your help."

"Just let me know what you need. Whatever I can do, I'm down to help."

"Cool." I paused. "So what are you going to do about Boris?" I said, diverting the subject once again.

"Get those digits and go hard for that brotha," Toya said, followed by a burst of laughter.

We spent the rest of the evening catching up on work problems, men problems, family issues, and a slew of other spontaneous topics.

I left Toya sitting at the table flirting with Boris and went home. I needed to get home at a decent hour, so I wouldn't have to lie to David … again.

I could hear faint chatter coming from the living room as I walked up the front steps to Aunt Ann's house the next day. Before

I could knock or ring the doorbell, the door flung open, and three children ran wildly past me and down the steps.

"Gee! Be careful," I cautioned. A little girl who looked to be about nine or ten years old turned around and nodded. The other two kept running without paying me any mind.

I walked through the screened-in porch area, where Ed and I had our pow-wow just the night before, and into the living room where most of the men were hanging out watching sports. I flashed a courtesy hand wave and proceeded into the main part of the house.

Expecting me, Shalisa was standing in the entry holding one of the twins in her arms.

"Oh, let me see him," I said, walking up to her. "He's so precious," I said as she positioned the baby to face me.

"Hey, dinner's almost ready, so come on and join us in the dining room," Aunt Ann said as she rushed past me with a dish of food in her hands.

"Okay. I just need to wash my hands," I said, acknowledging the announcement.

"Where's the other one?" I said to Shalisa, focusing my attention back on her and the baby.

"Oh, she's upstairs with my husband. We went to church this morning, so she's a little cranky today. And he's sleepy. So I'm going to bring him upstairs for a nap. I'll be right back. Save me a seat next to you."

I followed the shuffling crowd into the dining room and sat beside an unfamiliar woman who I later learned was Aunt Ann's best friend, Regina. I placed my purse on the chair to my right, saving it for Shalisa. The food smelled delicious, and I couldn't wait to dig in. Aunt Ann was a great cook, probably not as great as Honey, but notably great, nonetheless. I watched as guests continued to shuffle into the oversized dining room. Duncan, who was really my uncle because he was Aunt Ann's husband, and Ed's brother Ron, who was also my uncle, escorted Ed to his seat. Ron carried Ed's oxygen tank and Duncan held Ed's arm as he guided him to sit next to Aunt Ann. Our eyes met. Ed looked away quickly and focused his attention on the smorgasbord of food on display.

"You've really outdone yourself, sister," Ed said to Aunt Ann, squeezing her hand as he took his seat.

Aunt Ann smiled bashfully.

When it appeared as though everyone was seated, an older gentleman that I hadn't seen previously said grace. I later learned he was Aunt Ann's pastor, Reverend Anthony Blake. Afterward, you could see nothing but plates, cups, utensils, napkins, and pitchers being passed back and forth as everyone filled their plates and cups with their desired helpings.

I was pretty quiet during dinner, feeling a little awkward. Truth was, I didn't really know Ed or his people, and I was beginning to doubt everyone's motives for welcoming me into the family after all these years. And noticing that I wasn't too talkative, Aunt Ann raised concern.

"Everything all right, Destiny?"

"Yep," I said, barely making eye contact with her.

"You're kinda quiet over there."

"Um … just got a lot on my mind."

"She sure does. She's gonna be executor of my estate," Ed said between chews of macaroni and cheese.

"Sir, I didn't agree to that," I snapped back. "Just because you're tryna throw a few pennies my way, it doesn't mean I'm gonna be all excited and hold my hand open to catch them."

Ed looked around. I could tell he hadn't expected my response or demeanor. He focused his attention back on his plate of food. That is, whatever was left of it.

All eyes were now on me.

Trying to assert authority that he didn't have, he said, "I'm still your father, and you owe me some respect."

"Says who?" I said, dropping my fork.

"Ed …" Aunt Ann said, trying to diffuse the escalating exchange between Ed and me. "Not here. Not today. That's not a conversation for this occasion."

"No, Aunt Ann, let him go for it. He wants to leave this world with a guilt-free conscience by throwing money my way, even though he was never, ever there! To tell the truth, I don't trust his motives."

My entire face felt hot. My palms were sweaty, and I could feel pebbles form across my forehead. I used my paper napkin to wipe my hands and my forehead.

"Don't let your watermelon-sized ego cause you to miss out," Ed threatened.

"Miss out? I already missed out! I missed out at parent–teacher conferences, on my birthday, only God knows how many Christmases, daddy–daughter dances … should I go on?"

I had blocked out all the other people in the room. It was just the two of us—Ed Harrison and Destiny Monique Crawford. If I could have spit out fire and blew Ed away in a gust of flames, I would have done it that day. I was *that* angry. But the tug on my jeans made my stop.

"Wanna go outside? I'll go with you," Shalisa whispered.

"I'm good," I said, glancing at her. "But I'm gone," I added.

I pushed my seat back from the table and stood up. "I'm sorry, Aunt Ann. I can't sit at the same table with your brother today. I'm going through too many changes, dealing with him. And for all I know, he might not even be my father. He claims he's my dad, but he didn't even sign my birth certificate. What a coward! I'm sorry, Mr. Harrison, I don't quite understand your definition of a father," I added as I grabbed my purse to leave.

"Come on, baby. Don't say things like that. Ed's your father. You got too much of him in you not to be," Aunt Ann pleaded.

My lips quivered as I stared at Ed. "You guys have a nice dinner, but I'm leaving."

"Come on, Destiny. You don't have to leave. We understand

you're hurt. We do," Aunt Ann pleaded as she stood, hoping I would change my mind.

"Sorry, I can't. Not today. Plus, I have someone outside waiting for me."

Shalisa stood up alongside me.

"I didn't mean to snap like that. I guess there's a lot of anger still there," I said to Shalisa as we exited the dining room.

"Don't worry about it, girl. Just call me when you get yourself together. I get it."

Shalisa walked me to the front door and watched as I descended the front steps and made it to the car where David was waiting.

"Take me home. I hate the sight of that man," I said as I got in the car and slammed the door. A steady stream of warm tears cascaded down my cheeks.

Chapter 17

Knock, Knock—Who's There?

I HAD RECENTLY JOINED the gym and was working out regularly in preparation for Shonte's upcoming wedding. I knew I'd be in plenty of the pictures taken since I was her maid of honor. Shonte was marrying a guy named Kevin Maxwell whom she met in the service. I hadn't met Kevin in person but was looking forward to meeting him. Like any bride-to-be, Shonte was excited, and she recruited me to be both her maid of honor and wedding coordinator. So most of my days followed a pattern—work, wedding coordinating essentials, gym, home. I had a little more than two months to coordinate my best friend's wedding, lose ten pounds so I could look my best, help David with starting a property management company, and decide what I was going to do about starting college part-time.

Living with David for going on two and a half years now, I learned that I no longer had the time to keep track of his every move. Although he didn't spend as many nights away from home anymore, he did spend some, but so did I. I kept Ziek close by, not for sexual reasons, but as an outlet. Sometimes, we'd meet up just to chat over a cup of coffee, and at other times, it was for a shoulder to cry on. It might have been wrong, but it felt right.

Having taken off from work to take care of logistics for Shonte's wedding, I managed to squeeze in a good workout at the gym afterward. By the time I returned home, I was tired, hungry, and sleepy. I took a quick shower, heated up some leftovers and sat in the living room to eat my meal and wind down. It was still pretty early, maybe close to eight o'clock, and I wasn't expecting David anytime soon. Most days he came home somewhere between ten o'clock and eleven o'clock. So when I heard keys jingling in the door, I got a little excited. The doorknob turned, but the door didn't open. The keys jingled once again, and the same thing happened—the door didn't open.

I wasn't so sure it was David at the door, so I put my plate down on the coffee table and tiptoed to the door to peep through the peephole. But before I could get up to the door, there were two consecutive knocks.

"Who is it?" I asked.

"It's me," an unfamiliar voice announced.

"Me, who?"

"Me, Nettie."

Without contemplation, I turned on the front light, unlocked the door, and flung it open. Standing on the opposite side of the door was a medium-height, dark brown-skinned, voluptuous woman who had short, auburn, curly hair. She was wearing a pair of jeans and a white and black T-shirt that had the caption "Lady D" on it. There she stood in the flesh—the infamous Nettie Calloway. And I'd only recently learned her last name after stumbling across mail addressed to her, which was in David's office drawer.

"How can I help you?" I asked, anticipating a verbal spat.

"Where's David?" she said, trying to brush past me.

"Excuse me?" I said, trying to block her from entering.

"You heard me. Where's David?"

By this time, we were face to face, staring each other down like two heavyweight boxing components, only we weren't going for a belt but vying for the love and attention of the same man.

"He's not here. You don't see him, do you?" I snapped back.

She giggled sarcastically. "Oh, okay. Well, I'm sure you know there's no guarantee he's coming home tonight," she said as she managed to get past me, gallop over to the sofa, and plop down on it. "And who are you anyway?" she continued as she propped her feet up on the coffee table.

"Maybe I should be asking you that question."

"I told you my name before you opened the door."

"Well, what do you want, *Nettie*?" I said, closing the front door.

"Actually, I don't want anything from *you*. I don't even know you. I'm good. I'm home. But I am wondering who you are and why *you're* here."

"My name is Destiny, and I'm David's woman."

She let out a devilish laugh. "You can't be serious."

"I've been living with David for a while. Where have you been? Oh, no, don't tell me ... confined to a cage in the penitentiary," I said with added flare. I wanted to rub her jail stint in.

"Don't worry about where I've been. David knows where I've been, and that's all that matters," she said, crossing her legs at the ankle.

"Well, then he should have known you were going to bring your trifling behind back here."

"Trifling? *I'm* trifling?"

I stood in front of her on the opposite side of the coffee table, blocking her view of the television. "I didn't stutter, did I?"

"You know he has a woman, and you still move up in here while I'm gone, and you call *me* trifling?"

"He's been dating me for going on four years, and you wanna think you're his woman? Okay. If it makes you feel good."

"Actually, it makes me feel great. Look around this house. I decorated this place. This is all me," she said, gesturing at the décor in the living room. "And where's Rusty? Rusty! Rusty!" she called out for the cat before I could even answer.

"Girl, please. David said he doesn't want you. And you and I both know that the only reason he let you stay here as long as he did is because you lost that baby." I must've hit a nerve with that statement because she jumped up off the sofa and got in my face.

"You don't know what you're talking about. The reason I was up in this piece is because David wanted me up in here. David plays with women like you, but he comes home to a woman like me because I got his back. I know David much better than you'll ever know him."

"I think you should go now," I said, walking over to the door and opening it.

"You can close that door 'cause I ain't going nowhere. I'm home," she said, scooping up Rusty, who had crawled from under the sofa. "Hey, boy. I missed you," she said, cooing with the cat.

"Well, I ain't going nowhere, either," I said, calling her bluff. But I knew good and well I wasn't going to stay in that house with David's ex, or baby mama, whatever she was to him. I slammed the door, grabbed my salad off the table, and sat on the opposite side of the sofa. I had completely lost my appetite, but the last thing I was going to do was let her intimidate me. So I sat there and forced myself to eat, acting as if I was watching the CNN broadcast. Through my peripheral vision, I could see her searching for the remote control. When she finally got tired of searching, she asked for it.

"Do you have the remote to *my* TV?"

"Sure," I said, taking it off the end table closest to me and tossing it to her.

"Thank you, ma'am," she said, smirking.

"And I ain't nobody's ma'am, especially yours, okay?" I shot back.

She smirked again as she started flipping through television channels. At this point, I knew the best thing to do was ignore her.

So I sucked my teeth and focused my attention back on eating my food. When I had finished the last of it, I stood and headed for the kitchen. I could see the front lights of David's car pulling into the driveway as I walked past the living room window. *Now, the real drama is about to unfold.* Instead of going into the kitchen, I made a beeline for the front door. From where she was sitting, Nettie couldn't see outside, so she had no idea David had just pulled up. I stood by the door and waited for him to enter.

The color in David's face nearly disappeared when he walked in and saw Nettie sitting on the sofa. She, like me, couldn't wait to light into him. "So I do time for you, and you move another chick up in here to keep our bed warm?"

"Nettie, when did you—"

"Get out?" Nettie said, finishing his sentence. "When did I get out?"

"Yeah, I thought—"

"Yeah, you thought. You thought I wasn't getting out until September, huh? Yeah, that's when I was *supposed* to get out. But don't worry about me. Worry about that piece of trash standing there next to you."

David turned to me. I couldn't wait to hear the lies he'd form his mouth to speak. "Destiny."

"Destiny, what?!" I snapped.

"This ... this wasn't supposed to happen like this."

"Like what, David? Like what?!" I said, folding my arms across my chest.

Nettie stood and started walking toward David and me.

"Nettie, no," David said, fanning his hand at her.

"Oh, so you wanna protect this thang right here, I see," Nettie said, putting the cat down and pointing at me.

David stood in front of me. "Nettie, would you please go over to my mother's house tonight and let me work this out?"

"You've got to be kidding! I ain't going nowhere. Ask your side piece to go over to your mama's house. Your mama don't even like me. So why do you even think I would step foot in her house?"

"Yeah, his mama don't like you because you're a user and a manipulator," I blurted out. That's what Claudia said about her, among other things.

"You see, David. That sounds just like something your mother would say!" Nettie yelled.

With his eyebrows raised, David turned to me. "You've been talking to my mother? I told you how my mother gets down, and you're chattin' it up with her behind my back?"

I unfolded my arms. "Really, David? Really?"

"Really, what?" David said, trying to appear oblivious.

"You got two women up in here calling this place home, and you're worried about who's having a conversation with your mother?"

"Destiny, I keep telling you that I don't owe anybody anything. I'm grown. But I specifically told you not to get tangled up with my mama."

"Who said I was tangled up with her?" I stopped to think about the strategy Claudia and I had discussed. She told me this day would come sooner or later. It was sooner than I expected, but I was determined not to walk away without leaving some verbal and emotional damage behind.

"David, I've had a long day, and I'm going to bed right now," Nettie said, attempting to head for *our* bedroom.

David grabbed Nettie by her hand. "You can't go up there."

"Whatever, David," she said, snatching her hand away.

Strong arming her, David pushed Nettie back over to the sofa.

"She can go to bed as soon as I grab my stuff," I said, storming past the two of them and heading for the bedroom.

I grabbed my Coach suitcase that I'd won in a raffle on the job and threw as many clothes in it as I could. I went into the closet and retrieved the shoebox I was stashing some extra cash in and put it in my gym duffle bag. With one swipe on the bathroom vanity, I put all my makeup and toiletries in the matching Coach bookbag. I was sure I'd have to come back for my belongings, but I grabbed enough stuff to keep me away for at least a few weeks.

When I walked back into the living room, Nettie and David were engaged in a heated debate. I didn't bother to listen to exactly what they were arguing about. David stopped and looked over at me but made no attempt to stop me.

"Bye, trick," Nettie blurted out. Before I could respond, David slapped Nettie with the back of his hand.

"I got your trick all right," I said as I turned around and spit at her. I missed.

"Now, Destiny, don't do that," David, the coward, begged.

"So you're taking up for her, I see. Well, since the two of you want to be Bonnie and Clyde, just make sure you and the jailbird make enough money to help support the child you'll never see!"

There! I did it! The look on both their faces was priceless. Before David could get a word in, I stormed out, leaving David with as many questions as I had for him. Tears welled up in my eyes as I descended the front steps of the house, but I promised myself I wouldn't cry, at least not at that moment. I had to be strategic, just like Claudia said. This was war, and if I was gonna win in any form or fashion, a good strategy had to be a part of my game plan.

I put my suitcase and bags in the trunk, got into my car, and started it up. With no set place in mind of where I was headed, I put the gear in reverse and backed out of the driveway.

As I drove down Crane Street, I kept replaying the scenes back at the house—me and Nettie. Me and David. Me, Nettie, and David. I wiped my eyes while stopped at the red light at the intersection of East Grand Boulevard and Gratiot. *How could he let me leave and not even try to stop me?* I hit the steering wheel with both hands. I had nowhere to go. Call it my pride, and it most likely was my pride, but it prevented me from going back home on more than one occasion. I just couldn't step foot back into

Honey's house, especially not in this broken state. I had enough money to stay in a hotel for a few nights, and unfortunately, it seemed that's where I was headed—alone, depressed, and angry at the same time. That is, until my cell phone rang. I looked down at my phone. It was Ziek. I hesitated to answer, almost forcing the call to go to voicemail. But what did I have to lose, or gain, for that matter? I pressed the talk button.

"Hey," I answered, trying to disguise my true emotions.

"What's up?'

"Nothing. Just out."

"Just out?"

"Yeah, just out driving around."

"Babe, it's almost ten o'clock. Why are you out just driving around?"

I didn't respond. I could feel the tears welling up again.

"Destiny?"

"Yeah," I answered softly.

"Is everything all right?"

I paused.

"Destiny, is something wrong? Did that Negro put his hands on you?" Ziek said with raised anxiety in his voice.

"No."

"Then what's wrong?"

"We … we just broke up."

"Did he put you out?"

"No, I left."

"Where are you?"

"Just driving around."

"Are you headed somewhere?"

"No, I'm just trying to clear my head."

"Come over."

"Nah, I'll be okay. I don't want to intrude on anyone."

"That's the last thing you'd be doing. Look, it's getting late, and I don't want you out there."

"I have enough money to pay for a room," I said, wiping my tear-stained face.

"Are you kidding me? As long as I'm in your corner, you ain't never gotta pay for no room. Look, just come on over. I won't be able to sleep tonight knowing you're out there in this frame of mind. Plus, it's raining like crazy."

"I'll stop by, but I don't need to stay," I said.

"Okay. Good … good. Then I'll see you soon," Ziek said with a sense of ease in his voice.

I replayed the earlier events of the evening during the entire drive to Ziek's house. *How could I be so naïve?* I found myself even rehearsing some of my conversations with David about Nettie. "You're obsessed with Nettie, that's what you are," David would say, trying to play reverse psychology on me. He would always become agitated when her name came up. No, I wasn't obsessed with Nettie; I was obsessed with not wanting to be played.

David called when I was in the McDonald's parking lot. I let the call go to voicemail. He called right back. I turned the ringer off. I didn't want to hear the sorry excuses he'd had time to invent. I was sure he was calling to get information about the baby that didn't exist, but I was going to keep him in the dark just as he kept me in the dark about Nettie and the true nature of their relationship. The worst part of it all was coming to the realization that David would have never allowed me to move in with him if Nettie hadn't been in jail doing time. I could feel the tears welling back up.

To take my mind off David and Nettie, at least for the time being, I turned on the radio to 101.5 FM, the twenty-four-seven gospel station. I needed to clear my mind before I got to Ziek's. I was vulnerable, the kind of vulnerable that would cause me to end up in Ziek's arms … and his bed.

Ziek was standing outside sipping on a Corona when I pulled up to his place. The rain had eased up some by this time, and he walked over to meet me after I parked.

"Hey, baby girl," he said as he opened my door and leaned over to place a soft kiss on my left cheek.

"Hey," I said as I tossed my phone into my purse.

"Where's your bags?" Ziek asked, peering through the back window.

"In the trunk. But I'm not staying."

"Just pop the trunk. You might fall asleep."

"Um ... I feel funny about invading your privacy like this. I don't have to go upstairs. I can go to the hotel."

"Come on. Stay for a while. We can just play it by ear."

Knowing that Ziek was going to be unrelenting in his effort to get me to stay at his place, I handed him the key to open the trunk. "Just grab my Nike gym bag," I said. I always kept an extra outfit and some of David's extra-large T-shirts in it as well. I figured I could use one of them to sleep in, if needed.

Ziek put my bag in his room, where he automatically assumed I would be sleeping. But I knew I was too vulnerable to lie beside Ziek.

"I can sleep on the sofa, Ziek."

"If anybody's sleeping on the sofa, it's gonna be me," Ziek said.

I forced a smile, and Ziek winked.

After settling in, I plopped down on the sofa, and Ziek sat down next to me. I handed him the apple pie I had picked up at McDonald's. "Thank you, baby girl," he said as he opened the box and began to devour it.

Ziek was a big *Twilight Zone* fan, and I didn't bother to ask him to change the channel. So we watched episode after episode, my head in his lap as he ran his fingers through my hair, gently massaging my scalp and putting me to sleep.

We were awakened by a knock at the door. "Who's that?" I said, wondering whether David had tracked me down.

"I don't know," Ziek said, getting up.

He turned on the light before peering through the keyhole. "Dang!"

"Ziek, who is it?" I whispered.

"This chick I know."

"Look, I think I should leave," I said, getting up. That's the last thing I wanted—to be involved in some more drama with another woman in less than twenty-four hours.

"No, you're good. She ain't like that because she knows she ain't my girl. She's just a chick I mess with."

And then it hit me. Men have all kinds of categories for women. I wondered what my category was in David's book. Before I could utter another word, Ziek opened the door, and a petite Asian-looking woman walked in. She squinted her eyes, trying to zero in on me as I sat on the sofa.

"Maelin, this is Destiny. Destiny, this is Maelin," Ziek introduced.

I stood, but we didn't bother to do the hand shaking thing. We just acknowledged one another with nods.

"Did I interrupt something?" Maelin said in a broken English accent, confirming my suspicion about her ethnicity.

"This is why I told you not to come by unannounced," Ziek said, walking back over to the sofa. By this time, I had started gathering my belongings.

"No, you didn't interrupt anything. Ziek and I are very good friends. I broke up with my boyfriend tonight, and Ziek was giving me a place to stay," I said. I knew how the woman felt, despite what Ziek had said to her. I could definitely empathize with Maelin.

"You don't owe her an explanation," Ziek interjected.

"Why not?" Maelin challenged, shifting the weight of her body to one side.

"Because you're not my girl. And this ain't your house. I told you more than once not to stop by unannounced. You're lucky I opened the door."

"Look, I'm going to leave. Y'all work this out between the two of you," I said to Ziek, attempting to head to his room to retrieve my bag.

"Destiny, you don't have to leave."

"Yes, I do. This is all too complicated. I need to clear my head, Ziek. It's too much drama for one night."

"Please stay, Destiny."

"Another time, Ziek," I promised.

"Can I use the bathroom?" Maelin asked in a tender voice. She was very soft spoken.

"Is that what you came over here for? You don't have one at home?" Ziek said. His tone was cold. Poor Maelin stood by the door and dared not move. "In a minute," Ziek added with obvious agitation in his voice.

"I'll get your bag, Destiny," Ziek said, walking past me.

"I grabbed my purse and walked over to the front door, walking past Maelin without any further acknowledgment.

Ziek kept apologizing as he walked me to my car. That is, until I asked him to stop.

"Ziek, you don't have to keep apologizing. It's cool. You say she's not your girl, and neither am I. Apparently, she felt comfortable enough to knock on your door at four in the morning. I'm just a guest, and I don't want to get in the middle of any additional drama. I've had enough for one night."

"Yeah, I hear you, Destiny. But you know how I feel about you. We're not an item because you're the one holding back."

"No, Ziek. We're not an item because, although there's this strong chemistry between us, there's a myriad of things that are different about us. Things that would cause our relationship to not last."

Ziek stopped in his tracks. "You know, you're right, Destiny. You're right. But I'm not gonna give up on us. Someday… one day, things are gonna change. I've never met a woman like you. There's something about you that—"

"Not tonight, Ziek," I interjected. "I can't handle this kind of conversation tonight. I'm going to find a room tonight. You go on back upstairs and do what you need to do to patch things up with

Maelin. I'll be fine," I said, giving him a soft peck on his cheek. "Thanks for everything, though," I added.

I waved bye to Ziek as I drove off. The numbness from what occurred with David and Nettie had worn off earlier, and the rawness of the pain now engulfed me like a raging fire.

When I finally pulled into the Westin hotel parking lot, I stayed in the car and gave myself permission to cry ... to really let it all out.

All cried out, I checked into my room, took a hot bath, wrapped myself up in the complimentary terry cloth bathrobe, and crawled into the king-sized bed, sinking into the comfort of its plush mattress.

Chapter 18

Damsel in Distress

"SO I GOT YOU the Family and Friends rate of thirty-nine dollars per night," Toya said as she slid into the front passenger seat of my car.

"Cool. That'll work. Anything will beat the eighty-four-dollars-per-night rate I've been paying at the Westin," I said. Although Ziek offered to pay for a few nights, I declined. I liked Ziek, but I was entangled with David, and my emotional state of mind was too fragile to be dealing with them both. Allowing Ziek to pay for my room would mean I owed him something—even if not sex, I owed him my time, my loyalty, and my honesty, none of which I was willing to give.

Toya always kept a part-time job, so she could use the money to pay for luxuries such as getting manicures and pedicures, getting her hair done at the salon every week, when she wasn't wearing braids, and, of course, every woman's favorite pastime—shopping. Say what you want about Toya; she had her flaws, but she was that loyal friend that had your back no matter what.

"So now, tell me what went down, again."

"Drama, girl. Drama. Ole girl was apparently in jail because she took the rap for David."

"For what?" Toya said as she munched on a handful of Lays potato chips.

"Weapons, I think. But who cares? Ole girl must've gotten out a little early and called herself surprising David and just popped up at the house."

"Now, you got to give me the details," Toya said with mounting curiosity in her tone. She sat up straight and turned the radio volume down.

Although I didn't want to relive the scene again, I recounted the entire encounter. That is, minus mentioning the fake pregnancy. I had made up my mind that I wasn't going into that part of the fiasco, which was, of course, a hoax. That was because the eastside of Detroit was small; everybody knew everybody, and I didn't want anyone to know about the lie. Why? Because news in the streets spread fast.

When I was finished detailing the saga, a stunned Toya sat in silence. "What are you thinking?" I finally asked, breaking the silence.

"That's all a hot mess, girl. Now, do you see why I don't give relationships my all? That's why I'm taking it slow with Boris. I'm not moving out until I know I can afford to take care of myself. I don't have time for nobody to be kicking me out of their place."

"I hear you. But Honey kicked me out. What was I supposed to do?"

Toya let out a loud sigh. "But you know what? I told you about my cousin. He just ain't—" Toya stopped mid-sentence. Her mouth flew open and her eyes were as big as quarters.

"David's your cousin?"

"I'm sorry, Destiny. Yeah, he is ... on my dad's side. Our fathers are half-brothers."

"Why didn't you tell me this before?"

"I tried. Do you remember when you were telling me about your first date? I told you I knew who he was," Toya said, trying to jog my memory.

"Come on, Toya. That went in one ear and out the other. And

that's not telling me the two of you are cousins. That's a different ballgame."

An apologetic Toya followed with, "I didn't want to get in the middle of it. Our family has issues, especially the men, and I didn't want to sway your mind either way. But I did tell you to be careful," Toya said in her own defense.

"Okay, so now, tell me. What's the real deal with David?" I asked.

"He's all about them streets. He always has been."

"What do you mean he's about the streets, like ruthless?"

"He's all about David … he gets whatever he wants and when he wants, and that includes money, cars, houses, drugs, and women."

"So you're saying he's a habitual cheater?"

"Look, Destiny, this is why I didn't want to say anything to you in the first place. Uncle Bobby, David's father, had an affair on his second wife, Camille, with Claudia. Claudia got pregnant with David and didn't want to let Uncle Bobby loose. It was a known thing that Uncle Bobby had two families. David's brothers are his half-brothers by Camille, not Claudia. When we would all meet up at my grandparents' house, Uncle Bobby would bring all the boys, except David. Uncle Bobby finally left Claudia alone when she pulled a gun out on him on Christmas, 'cause he didn't get to her house until nighttime. She accused him of loving his other boys more than he loved David. She's crazy. Have you met her?"

I debated whether I should tell her that Claudia had befriended me, and that we had a few conversations by way of in-person visits. Instead, I just gave a generic response. "Yeah, we met."

"Is she crazy or what?"

"I don't know. We ain't get close or anything like that."

"She's wacko, and everyone knows it, including David. *He* even keeps his distance from her."

I listened to Toya go on and on about Uncle Bobby, Camille, and Claudia. That is, until I couldn't take it any longer. Finally, I defended Claudia by saying, "She was just protecting her son and her emotions like most women in her shoes would've done."

"Well, ain't nobody tell her to spread her legs for a married man. She knows the game. Wifey and wifey's kids come first. The side chick gets the leftovers," Toya said emphatically as she threw another handful of chips into her mouth.

I couldn't help but compare my own situation to that of Camille and Claudia, Nettie representing Camille, and me representing Claudia. Deep down, I knew I was too good to be played like this, not by some street hustler like David. It was then that I made up my mind to go on and be with Ziek. At least I knew he had a genuine love for me. I hated that he loved the streets, but what could anyone expect from a man who had lived in the streets since he was a young boy? His mother was an addict, causing him to be shuffled around from various family members' houses until he finally left on his own at age sixteen. I could have made a clean exit from David, but I had that lie about the pregnancy out there. Although David had a ton of flaws, walking away from unhandled business wasn't one of them. At some point, I was sure he would hunt me down and confront me about how we were going to handle the pregnancy. I knew I needed Claudia's help to get out of the lie. The one thing she had was game … and plenty of it. They could say what they wanted about Claudia, but she wasn't that wacko in my book.

My stomach churned, and suddenly, I wanted to end the conversation. "You wanna go grab something to eat before I head to work?" I said.

"Nah, girl. I gotta shed some weight before Shonte's wedding. I refuse to have to squeeze into my dress, looking like Humpty Dumpty," she joked.

"Girl, you look fine," I said. Toya was nowhere near being chunky or fat. She was a workout fanatic, working out at least six days a week. "Well, then I'm gonna head on out and grab a bite to eat before I go to work."

The night shift was beginning to take its toll on me. I wanted an administrative type of job, where I could sit in a cubicle and work on a computer all day. I was starting to regret not going to college. I knew I wasn't cut out for the military, so it wasn't even a consideration. Then the idea hit me like a lightbulb. *Maybe I could start taking some college courses.* It could only benefit me in both the short term and long term. In the short term, I could have something else to focus on instead of tumultuous relationships, and in the long term, I could have a career. *Yeah, that's what I'll do.*

I thanked Toya once again for the discounted hotel rate and headed for Luxley's Diner to grab something quick to eat. Luxley's had the best beef burgers in all of Michigan.

Hattie was smiling from ear to ear when I walked into the breakroom. She had just come back from a seven-day cruise with her husband and their grown children and their spouses.

"How was the trip?" I said, reaching into the refrigerator to retrieve my leftover burger and fries from Luxley's.

"It was awesome. You know, it was like old times," Hattie said, beaming with excitement. It was no secret around the company that she had been involved in an extramarital affair with a guy at the plant some time ago, before I even started working there. I had heard about it but never brought it up.

"So how was the Cayman Islands? I heard it was beautiful."

"It *was* beautiful. Everything was just so fabulous. It's just what the whole family needed," Hattie said, downing the last of her can of Mountain Dew.

"Well, I'm happy for you. But I'm glad you're back; we missed you around here."

"Chile, please. These people don't miss me; they miss the good work I do around here. There ain't but one Hattie B. Chestnut, and that's me," she bragged. "Now, enough about me. What's going on with you?"

"Same ole, same ole," I said, hoping she wouldn't pry any further.

"What's up with you and your guy?"

"Umm ... I think we're just going to take a little break," I said, trying to make the breakup sound more congenial than it was in reality.

"Men don't take breaks. Don't you know that?" Hattie was not one to sugar coat anything. She gave it to you raw, no matter how bad it hurt.

"Well, we just need to work out some issues," I said as I opened the microwave door.

"Let me tell you something, Destiny," Hattie said, pulling a chair out for me to join her at the corner table.

I set the microwave for forty-five seconds and joined Hattie at her table. "Okay, tell me," I said, taking a seat across from her.

"Relationships are what you make them. If you don't put anything in, you won't get anything out. And whatever issues you have in a relationship, you need to work them out *while* you're in it. You don't give a man space, because all he's gonna do is fill it up with the company of another woman."

I looked down. I hadn't been honest with her, and I was sure the look of guilt was plastered all over my face. But I trusted Hattie, and maybe, just maybe she could give me some sage advice to follow if I came clean. I swallowed hard. "His ex-girlfriend came back to the house, and I left."

"What did you do a stupid thing like that for?" Hattie said. She squinted. "So you walked and didn't put up a fight?"

"For what? Ever since I've known David, she's been in the background somewhere. And he lied. He told me she was out of the picture."

Hattie brushed back the strands of hair that fell into her face. "Now, I know you've heard the phrase, 'fight for your man,' before."

"Sure, I've heard of it," I said, reflecting on all the women in my family. They all had no-good men they stood by through thick and thin, including Honey.

"Well, are you gonna fight or retreat?"

"Hattie, he let me walk out the door, and he didn't stop me. Isn't that telling me he doesn't want me?"

"Not necessarily. But what I know is that he, like most men, don't always sever relationships completely. They tend to leave the door open, and if you have a determined woman, she's gonna show up and not just crack the door open, but she's gonna burst it wide open and claim her territory. You see, I hate that it's like this, but this is more about you fighting for what you want than it is about anything else. If you want the man, don't just let another woman have him because she showed up on his doorstep."

The microwave had long beeped; my burger was probably growing cold again, but I had lost my appetite anyway. I nodded in agreement.

"Make sense?" Hattie said as she rubbed my left arm in a seemingly, "*I feel so sorry for you*," manner.

"But I like this other guy, too," I said, trying to get her thoughts on my decision to be with Ziek.

"Do you really like him, or is he a rebound guy?"

Truth be told, he was both. I liked him, and he was a rebound. But I didn't answer her.

"Look, I can't tell you what to do, but one thing Hattie B. Chestnut knows is that whoever your heart beats for is who you should put your effort into. If you go run off with this other guy because you don't have to put in any work, then I'm here to tell you that you'll be bored with him by the end of next week."

I looked up. I wanted to ask Hattie why she had an affair but still professed a deep love for her husband all the while. Before I could even form the words in my mouth, Hattie's watch chimed.

"Gotta go. My break is over. We'll catch up another time. Just remember what I said," Hattie said as she stood up.

David. Ziek. Ziek. David. One, I vowed not to love, and the other, I just liked—I liked the way he looked at me, the way he expressed his feelings toward me, and most importantly, the way he treated me. But did I love him for who he was? I had to admit that I was being selfish; I only liked Ziek because he boosted my self-esteem, which was at an all-time low, if I had to be honest with myself. And because I witnessed a plethora of women around me hang on to men that treated them like ragdolls, I vowed not to be one of them. Unfortunately, that generational curse seemed hard to break; I was becoming one of them, and I despised it. I was going to go with my earlier decision to be with Ziek and see where it landed me. I mean, us.

I fell backward on the bed when I got to my hotel room. I closed my eyes. I was more certain than ever before that working nightshift was soon going to be a thing of the past. I was only going to be able to get five hours of sleep because I had another appointment with the wedding coordinator for Shonte's wedding. Being the maid of honor came with a huge price tag. It wasn't money; it was something far more treasured than that—sleep.

Shonte's wedding was less than a month away, and there was a lot of ground to cover. Whatever she couldn't take care of over the phone, she relied on me to do instead. She'd put the money in my account, and I'd use my debit card to make the necessary purchases. I hadn't been still enough to think about Shonte getting married and living all over the world and possibly never moving back to Michigan. She was doing something very different than I was, and for a split second, I was jealous of her. Jealous that she lived in a house with both parents who supported her in everything she did. Jealous that she had the courage to join the military, which was something that wasn't customary for black women. But I knew if the shoes were on the other feet, Shonte would be imminently happy for me, so I denounced the spirit of jealously trying to invade my heart. Shonte was my girl, and I was happy for her. *My life will come together soon enough ... hopefully.* And I went to sleep on that notion.

"Where have you been?" he asked.

"I've been staying at the Marriott," I confessed, having been intentionally dodging Ziek's calls and pages over the last couple of weeks.

"I've been worried sick about you, Destiny," Ziek said, with a hint of agitation in his voice.

"I'm sorry. I've just had a lot on my plate, Ziek. A lot."

"So what's your plan?"

"What do you mean?" I said as I swept the mascara brush across the bottom lashes of my right eye. Most women never even bothered to put mascara on their bottom lashes, but not me. My bottom lashes were thick and long, and the mascara enhanced them all the more. In fact, I received many compliments on the appearance of my bottom lashes.

"Did you hear me? What's your plan?" Ziek repeated.

"As far as what?" I asked.

"As far as where you plan on living."

"Ziek, I'll be all right. My girl got me a discounted hotel rate for thirty-nine dollars a night."

"You can't possibly plan on living in a hotel long term, Destiny."

"For now, yes. Where else am I gonna go? I can't go back to David's, and me going back to my grandmother's house is out of the question."

"Come live with me."

My heart nearly skipped a beat. Shacking. That's what the church called it. As a matter of fact, that's what conservative society termed it as well. I put the mascara brush back in the tube and closed it tight.

"Well ..." Ziek said, anticipating my response.

"Ziek, I don't know if I'm ready for that yet. Plus, when that girl came over the last time, I felt uneasy. I felt it was best if I left. So—"

"You didn't have to leave. You *chose* to leave. She's not my woman. Have I kicked it with her in the past? Yes, but she's not my woman. Any woman, who is not in a committed relationship with a man but comes by his house unannounced and uninvited is on some other stuff. I put her out that night, right after I gave her a good piece of my mind."

"I hear you, Ziek. But I've had some time to think, too. I just don't feel as though I should be hopping from one man to the next." Even though I had made up in my mind to be with Ziek, I had to play if off. The last thing I wanted him to think was that I wanted to be with him out of a desperate need and not because I truly desired to be with him.

"That's what you call it?"

I didn't answer. So Ziek continued. "Look, Destiny. Few things in life are black and white. More often than not, there are gray areas. There's always an exception. Look at me. I could waddle in misery about my childhood, my drug-addicted mother, serving time, and so forth and so on. But what's that gonna do for me? Nothing. Absolutely nothing. I went through that phase of blaming God, my mother, my no-good father, and a slew of other people under the sun about my crappy life. But did it get me anywhere? Nope. So, one day, I just said to myself, 'Ziek, if you wanna be happy or at least experience some measure of happiness in this thing called life, you gotta get up from the place of misery and do something.' Yeah, I got into selling, but I bet I ain't that helpless dude waiting for something to fall from the sky. When people offered to help me or show me the way, I was open and accepted it."

I was quiet. He had said a mouthful. At first, I was thinking, *Men always have explanations for their bad behavior.* But the more Ziek talked, the more he made sense. I had one main concern—other women. "I told you what I just went through with David. I don't want to get in another relationship that reminds me of that one. I can't. I just can't."

"Babe, you know I love you. I've told you that plenty of times. Whether you believe me or not, I'm telling you the truth. I'd put everything on the line to be with you."

"The drugs?" I said, challenging the depth of Ziek's loyalty and commitment.

"Almost everything. You know that's my bread and butter. I have a plan, though. I ain't gonna be doing this for the rest of my life. I want a normal life. A wife and kids, you know? I just haven't figured it out yet."

I had to decline Ziek's offer to move in with him. I wasn't ready to move in with another guy who was married to the streets. I'd heard too many stories about girlfriends going down with dudes when their spot got raided, and Nettie was a perfect example. I was made for many things, but jail wasn't one of them. I wasn't going down for anyone. "My plan is to stay at the Marriott until I can save up enough money to get my own place."

Ziek was silent. I could tell my response hurt his feelings, but I had to look out for Destiny. The last thing I wanted to do was place a call to Honey, telling her I was in jail because of my drug dealer boyfriend, fulfilling her foretold prophecy.

"Okay. I've got an idea," Ziek proposed.

I was all ears.

"Are you listening?"

"I'm here," I said, sitting up on the edge of the bed.

"How about I give you the money to get your own place?"

That seemed like a plan, but I didn't want to sound desperate, so I continued to go along with the apprehension game.

"Umm … I don't know about that. I mean, are you sure?"

"Of course."

"I'll pay you back as soon as—"

"Look, money comes and goes ... comes and goes," Ziek said, politely cutting me off. Continuing, he said, "You ain't gotta pay me back. Look at it this way, I just want to help you get up on your feet. That David dude is a punk. I want him to see you rockin' and rollin' without him."

I laughed. Enjoying a genuine laugh was something I hadn't done in quite some time. I couldn't remember the last time I had a good laugh. That was the thing about Ziek—he knew how to put a smile on my face. Plus, I knew he generally cared about my well-being.

"So?"

"So what?"

"You gonna take me up on my proposal or what?"

"I mean ... I guess."

"All right. The grocery stores have apartment guides. Go get one and start looking. Get the hottest spot you can find."

"I have to find what I can afford."

"You got me. You can have anything you want."

It was something about his last statement that struck something in me. The hurt and depression I had been carrying for the past couple of weeks seemed to lift. I felt lighter. The internal tug of war seemed to have dissipated. I liked Ziek because he liked me. If I had to tell the truth, I fell in love with the notion that I didn't have to be disrespected or trampled on to be with a man. Yes, I needed Ziek, but I also liked what he brought to the table, too, which was an insatiable appetite to please me. So yeah, I was moving in this new direction to see where it would take me. I had to look out for number one—Destiny Monique Thomas. Yeah, her.

Chapter 19

Déjà Vu

I SETTLED COMFORTABLY INTO my new place at Herrington Heights, a high-rise community on the eastside of Detroit. Ziek told me I should get a two-bedroom apartment, so I could have an office or use the extra room as a guest bedroom. But I went with my gut and got a one-bedroom, just in case things didn't work out between the two of us; I would be able to swing the rent on my own.

I hadn't heard from David since the night I left the house, other than the voicemail he left a week or so after I left, telling me he didn't mean for it to go down like it did. In that same voicemail, he let me know he had gone to the post office and had my mail forwarded back to Honey's house. *Who asked him?* I was perfectly capable of submitting my own change of address form at the post office. My assumption was that Nettie was behind it, with her insecure self.

The very next day, I went to the post office and filled out another change of address form to have my mail forwarded to my new address at Herrington Heights. Afterward, I got in a quick workout at the workout facility in my building at Herrington Heights.

Claudia called just as I'd finished my cardio session on the treadmill.

"Hi, Claudia," I said, still panting from the extensive workout.

"How are you doing?" she said with flat affect.

"I'm doing fine," I answered.

"Have you heard?"

For a moment, my heart stopped. Those were the words someone would say before breaking bad news. And just that quick, all sorts of catastrophic thoughts crossed my mind. "Heard what?" I said, dropping my workout towel on the gym floor.

"About David?"

"What about him?" I asked, my voice cracking. Although we weren't together, and he did me wrong, I cared about David's well-being. His behavior forced me to be with Ziek, someone I cared about but didn't love, no matter how strong his allegiance was to me. I held my breath as I waited for the details.

"He's locked up."

"Locked up, like in jail?"

"Yeah, I think they got him this time," Claudia said.

My stomach churned. I felt a wave of heat hover over my entire body. Claudia's comment simply implied that David had been caught in something that he couldn't get out of, even with the best attorney money could buy.

"What did they get him on?" I asked.

"Got caught up in a sting. Smuggling and trafficking. I told that fool to be careful!" Claudia said, taking a deep sigh afterward.

"When did this happen?"

"A little over a week ago."

I wanted to ask her why she was calling me when David had Nettie. I sure wasn't going to take my hard-earned money to bail him out or hire an attorney for him. But since Claudia was team Destiny, I decided to play the sympathetic role and show a little compassion. "Well, have you seen him?"

"Yes, I went to his arraignment."

"What happened?"

"He's in deep this time. I don't see how he's gonna get away without doing some time."

I could hear the sorrow in her voice. Even though she and David had a strained relationship, Claudia was still David's mother. And no mother wants to see their child behind bars. I knew this to be true even in Ed's case. It's one of the reasons his family supported his decision to leave Michigan when Honey threatened to call authorities on him after learning of Shannon's pregnancy and the ensuing fight. So I cut Claudia some slack. "What do you need me to do?"

"Go see my son, please."

"Claudia." I paused for a moment.

"What? You don't wanna go see my boy?"

"Under any other circumstances, I wouldn't have a problem going to see David. But he made it very clear to me who he wanted to be with. I don't want to go up there and run into Nettie and get into it with her."

"Ha!" Claudia yelled.

"Huh?" I responded, not sure how to interpret her last comment.

"Run into Nettie? Please, chile. That girl ain't nowhere to be found. She done took David's money and run off somewhere. I told you she doesn't want anything other than to make sure David's not happy. And now since he's locked up, *she's* happy. She doesn't love David—never have. But my son, bless his little heart, he allows himself to get tied up with the wrong people. They take advantage of him and bleed him dry. Then what? He has to hustle harder, trying to rebuild what he's lost. I told him to get out a long time ago. He has a job; he's made enough to establish himself. But it's just something about those streets he doesn't seem to be able to leave alone. Now look at him."

I heard Claudia's voice crack a few times as she delivered that mini-sermon. Even though there was a part of me that wanted to gloat in David's demise, a greater part of me felt sorry for him …

wanted to see him. "I don't think I can see him if I'm not on his visitors' list," I said.

"You're on the list. He put you on it."

"Me?" I questioned.

"Yeah, he put you on the list," Claudia repeated.

"How?" I asked. I was certain they needed personal information to put me on the list, like a driver's license number or a social security number, some form of personal identification.

"I don't know about how all of that works. Things are different from the way they used to be. All I know is that he asked me to call you and let you know he wants to see you."

I wanted to play hardball with Claudia, even though she had been nothing but transparent with me as far as David was concerned. For whatever reason, she liked me. So I swallowed my pride and agreed to go see David. "Okay, I'll go. I'll go."

"Thanks. He needs you."

Really? He needs me because Nettie's gone again, I wanted to say. *What if she comes back?* But like I said, I swallowed my pride and committed to going to visit David. "I can't go today, but I'll go over the weekend."

"Whew … thank you. I'll tell him when he calls. He calls me every other day, collect. He's trying not to run up my phone bill, so he doesn't call every day."

"Where is he?"

"Right now, he's at Jackson. You know where it's at, don't you?"

"Yeah, I know where it is," I said. I had taken several trips down to that prison with Honey to visit my cousin Marcus when he was locked up.

"All right, then. Call me after you go see him, and let me know how things go," Claudia said with apparent excitement in her voice. Her tone sounded happier than it did when I first answered her call.

"I will," I confirmed.

A barrage of transient thoughts raced through my mind after

I hung up with Claudia. *David ... in jail ... probably going to be doing time. Probably can't sleep ... can't eat. Scared. Lonely. He misses me.*

My head began to throb. Was I being stupid for going to see David? Should I give him a taste of his own medicine? Should I just leave David in the past and move full speed ahead with Ziek? This feeling was familiar; I had experienced this feeling before. Déjà vu? I closed my eyes as I rode in the elevator up to my floor, trying to focus on the remaining things I had to do for Shonte's wedding.

"Need your license and keys, if you have them, ma'am," a heavyset white woman said in between loud chews of the Snickers bar she was eating.

With my driver's license already in my hand, I slid it underneath the glass partition in the space provided. She picked it up and scanned a fluorescent light over it. She looked at me then back at my license, apparently verifying I matched the picture.

"She's good," she said to a male guard who then handed me a number tag, so I could retrieve my license and car keys at the end of visitation hours.

Like the other visitors, I shuffled into line to be escorted to Visiting Hall H, a large room with dull-colored cemented walls. Large digital clocks displayed on the front and back walls serving as constant reminders of the remaining time for visitation. A large group of visitors, mostly women, surrounded the three vending machines located near the visitors' entrance, buying up goodies for their incarcerated loved ones. Rows of chairs were situated in the front of the room, while tables and chairs were situated in the back. I took a third-row seat on the far right of the room and waited for David.

I spotted him as he was checking in. It felt awkward. I never imagined I'd be like "them"—those women whose ride-or-die loyalty included visits to jail, putting money on their dudes' books, accepting collect calls, and the list goes on. But there I was, sitting there, wishing I could rescue David from his impending fate.

"Thanks for coming," David said, leaning over and greeting me with a warm embrace.

"No touching," the guard warned, standing up from his post. He was tall, thick, and very muscular. With a slight nod, David acknowledged the warning-slash-reminder, which seemed to put the guard a little more at ease.

"You look good," I said, admiring David's fresh haircut and clean shave. I expected him to look a little disheveled.

"Thanks," David said, not making direct eye contact. I could tell he was embarrassed about what had gone down with Nettie. "You know I want to apologize for being weak that night," he said, fidgeting with a candy wrapper he held in his hand.

"Do you want some snacks?" I asked, pointing in the direction of the vending machines.

"Nah, I'm good," David said, reaching for my hand. "How are you?"

"I'm doing well."

David lowered his head.

"David?"

"Oh, hey. I'm good. I … umm. I just wanna say I'm sorry for not being there. When my mama told me you lost the baby, I couldn't sleep for nights. You wouldn't answer my calls or pages. I just—"

"Don't, David," I said, holding up my hand. Although David had done his share of wrongdoings, causing me to miscarry wasn't one of them. I wasn't ready to tell him the truth about the fake pregnancy, especially the fact that it was all Claudia's idea. In fact, I had no plans on telling him at all. I didn't think he would ever be able to trust me again if he knew I lied about something that serious. And besides, for all I knew, Claudia and I were all David had at the moment, and it felt good knowing the tables somehow had turned—he now needed *me*, and I was going to relish the moment.

David lowered his head again; he was embarrassed, and he should have been. He had chosen another woman over me more than once. And there I was, coming to his aid when he was in trouble. "Claudia said you wanted to see me," I added, changing the subject.

"I did. I missed you. I know I owe you more than an apology. It's just that … I felt obligated to her."

And "her" was Nettie—he felt obligated to Nettie, not me. "So what did you want?" I said, nonchalantly. My bluntness threw David off. He wasn't used to me giving him the cold shoulder. But what did I have to lose? Nothing.

"Look, I probably gotta do some time, and I know that. But I want us to be together when I get out … start over … start fresh, you know?"

I gave David a long, hard stare. "You do know that's what all guys say when they're locked up, don't you?"

"I promise, things will be different." David looked around, casing the room. "Look, my brother Hank has a package for you. I told him before any of this went down, if anything ever happened to me, to make sure he contacted you and gave it to you."

"I don't want no drug money, David," I lied. Drug money was paying most of my bills each month. Ziek was a drug dealer just like David. "Why didn't you give it to Claudia?" I continued, wondering why he would have Claudia contact me and not his brother.

"Because my mother doesn't have financial integrity. She'd spend it."

"Oh," I said. I didn't have much conversation in me. I was really there out of curiosity and loyalty to Claudia.

"So, do you think we can pick back up where we left off when I get out?"

"I'm seeing somebody else," I said. It felt good to say it, too. I watched as David's bottom lip quivered.

"Is it serious?" he asked as he crumpled the candy wrapper and threw it on the floor.

"Serious enough," I said, picking the crumpled candy wrapper off the floor. "Don't litter," I joked.

"Well, tell him to enjoy it while it lasts, because when I get outta here, I'm going after what's mine."

Even though I tried my hardest not to show it, a warm smile spread across my face. That was one of the things I loved about David; he had no fear—he went after what he wanted. Confidence. That's the word. He had a boatload of confidence, and it was alluring, almost like a drug. I still wanted to play hard, so I came back with, "I love him."

"I don't believe you," David said, shifting his body to one side of the folding chair he sat on.

I didn't respond. David knew me well. He knew me better than any other man I'd ever been involved with. The chemistry between us was intoxicating at times and blissful at others. And our lovemaking was electrifying.

"You have an attorney?" I asked, changing the subject.

"Of course. You know me."

"What is he or she saying?"

"It's a she. She's sharp. She told me to plead guilty, and I'd probably get anywhere from six months to three years."

"Three years? That's a long time," I said. I couldn't fathom putting my life on hold for three years. Some of my friends were in serious relationships and even marrying. David didn't deserve me waiting for him. His poor choice of staying in the streets until he got caught and had to do some time was unfair to me. Staying with Ziek, even though I didn't love him, was equally unfair.

"That's the worst-case scenario," David said, trying to console me.

"I can't promise you I'll be waiting for you. I have a man right now, and he really loves me."

"But do you love him?" David challenged.

"I—"

"Do you love him," David said, cutting me off.

"Fifteen minutes," the heavyset guard announced.

"What does that mean? Just fifteen minutes left?" I asked.

"That's for people who have more than two visitors. You can only have two visitors at a time. If there are other people in the waiting area, the time is split in half-hour increments. But you don't have to worry about that, since you're my only visitor."

"Oh," I said, looking around the room at other visitors shuffling back into line to exit the visitation room.

We spent the next twenty some-odd minutes talking about what happened the night of the raid, how David was coping in jail, his expectations for sentencing, and what he planned to do upon his release. Somewhere during the conversation, the hurt and pain David had caused during the duration of our relationship started to dissipate. I didn't want him to notice it, so I continued to play hard, acting nonchalant in my responses and disposition.

At the end of the visit, I stood and stretched my arms over my head.

"I wish I could make love to you," David whispered.

I giggled. It felt good to know that David was still physically attracted to me. I had lost a few pounds since he saw me last, and I smelled good because I was wearing Chanel no. 5, which was a gift David had given me. And most importantly, I looked good. I was wearing foundation, blush, eyeliner, mascara, and lipstick—all the things that enhanced my beauty and kept David captivated.

I was able to walk with David to the inmate exit area, where the inmates were shuffling into a line to go back to their cells. As he walked through the exit door, he mouthed, "I'm coming for you."

I read his lips, and I was certain it was what he said. I waved bye. I wanted to blow him a kiss, but I refrained from being a mush. I had to remind myself that I was playing hardball. I wanted to make David lament on his belly, begging for forgiveness. Begging for me.

By my fourth visit to see David, Ziek began to ask questions. Not only was I out of pocket for several hours, but I didn't answer his calls or pages during that timeframe. I tried to play it off as best as I could without leaving him with more questions.

"You've been unavailable on Saturday afternoons here lately. What's up?" Ziek said quizzically.

"Shonte's wedding is in a couple of weeks, so I'm doing a lot of running around, tryna get everything together. You know I'm her maid of honor, right? Plus, Honey ain't been feeling well lately, so I've been picking up fresh soup for her and dropping it by the house," I lied. I hoped he'd buy the lies because I was certain he had already heard in the streets that David got caught up in a sting.

"If I didn't know any better, I'd think you were the one getting married, as busy as you've been around here," he said, winking.

Whew! He bought it. I raked my hands through my hair in an attempt to give it some volume. All the while, I kept looking at Ziek out of the corner of my eyes.

"Then dinner tonight? Can we go out for dinner, just the two of us?"

"Sure. I should be home by six thirty or so," I said. I padded the time, so he wouldn't be able to put two and two together. Visiting hours were over at four, and it would take at least forty minutes to drive back to our side of town.

"All right, I'mma go handle some business, and I'll meet you back here at six thirty." Ziek leaned over and gave me a soft, wet kiss on the lips.

I stopped styling my hair and allowed my eyes to follow Ziek out of the bathroom. I was barricaded by admonishing thoughts. *You don't deserve him, Destiny. He's too good to you, and you're taking advantage of it. You seem to like guys who treat you like crap.* I closed my eyes and shook my head. I needed to clear my conscience. *I'm not cheating; I'm just going to visit my ex. Just visiting.* And with that, I reapplied my lipstick, coating it with a light stroke of sheer lip gloss. I stood back and examined myself in the mirror. I was falling out of touch with the person staring back at me. Who was she? Who had she become? She was really just a church girl gone wild. But the bigger question was, *How can I stop her before her life spirals out of control*? That's because dating a drug dealer usually came with a huge price tag. You had to constantly look over your shoulder, for the cops as well as rivalries. You were considered their property, since they housed you, bought you lavish gifts, and paid your bills. You were expected to be loyal to them at all costs. Being disloyal could cost you everything, including your life. But I was in too deep. I had so much vested with Ziek. Yes, he had set me up in a luxury apartment, doused me with lavish gifts, mostly jewelry, and helped me pay my bills, but the biggest expense was none of those tangible things; it was my time. I traded all those things for my time. Yes, technically, we did have our separate residences, but what man who is taking care of you, is going to do it just because? Ziek didn't leave too much room for me to even consider dating someone else right under his nose. I could get away with the one-day-a-week visits on Saturdays because it only covered a small window of time. At the end of the day, I was going to be as careful as I could because I was unwilling to suffer the cost of getting caught.

I sat in the visitors' waiting area awaiting David's arrival, casing my surroundings once again. I imagined that it wasn't too exciting around there. The bare brick walls were boring and offered no décor or atmospheric enticement. The digital clocks still displayed the time remaining for the visitation intervals.

We did the customary no-touch greeting when David finally came out. "What took you so long?" I asked. I'd been waiting nearly fifteen minutes.

"Some clowns up there got into a fight, so it delayed us from leaving our block," David said as he leaned back in his seat. "So this will be a short visit today," he added.

By this time, our conversations were customary—I'd talk about work, obtaining or not obtaining my workout goals, planning for Shonte's wedding, Ed, and sometimes, Shannon, and David would talk about prison life, what he was going to do differently when he got out, and how he imagined our lives would be once we got back together. Occasionally, his eyes would glance over at the digital clock on the back wall. "I hate it when you have to leave."

I didn't say anything; I just nodded. As much as I wanted to play hardball with David, I knew I kept coming back for a reason. Was it closure? I wasn't convinced that it was. There was a part of me that wanted to tell him to kick rocks. But then, there was an opposite feeling, an ego thing—to prove to myself that I was just as worthy as Nettie of being his number one woman—that made me want to ride this thing out. Of course, I had to question David's motives as well. What did he have to gain from these visits? Was it just a way to keep his options open so he could have someone to run back to, or did he have genuine remorse for how we ended? Did his reasons even matter?

I let David clutch my left hand in both of his as if he were holding a fragile little bird. "Your hands are so soft," he said as he began to stroke the top of it with his right hand.

I tried to play if off when I noticed one of the guards had witnessed David and me touching. He nodded, his way of letting us know it was okay. Although touching was prohibited, some guards were more lenient than others and would allow minimal physical contact.

I stood when the guard announced the end of the visitation session.

"You leaving?" David asked as I moved my hand away and stood up.

"Yes. I have to be somewhere this evening." I purposely made mention of my dinner engagement with Ziek to make him jealous.

"Oh, okay. Are you coming back next week?" he said as he stood up.

"I can't promise. I have a lot going on."

David nodded. "So I'll just see you next time you come, then," he said in a somber tone as he prepared to shuffle into the line with the other inmates. I waved goodbye and headed for the exit door. I didn't want to get sentimental. I wanted to be strong. I needed to be strong.

I zipped down I-94 to meet up with Ziek at his place, since Caper's was on his side of town. He wanted us to drive together, not in separate cars. He was old fashioned and driving together gave us our "we time" before we got to the restaurant.

My phone rang, and I picked it up from the front passenger seat. It was Auntie Lynn. I answered. "Hey, Auntie."

"Hey, girlie." She still had that nickname for me. "How's it going?"

"It's going good," I lied. And I was telling a lot of those lies lately. Auntie Lynn had no idea of what was going on in my life. And as close as I was with Auntie Donitra, I even kept certain things from her, not because she didn't deserve to know, but because I was ashamed. Auntie Donitra was dating a pilot, and a lot of her free time was spent flying back and forth to the Caribbean, which was his route. I only wished I could date a guy that I would be proud to bring home to Honey, show off to Shannon, and brag about to the rest of my family and my friends. The Dom was the most successful person I had dated. But I felt out of his league, working at a plant while he was in college getting all sorts of degrees and other accolades. The blue-collar worker and the drug dealer were the type of men I gravitated toward.

"I'll be up there this week. I need to check up on Honey. When was the last time you saw her?"

"I stop by a couple of times a week. If I'm extremely busy, I at least stop by on Sundays to make sure she has fresh food to eat."

"How does she look to you?"

"I … I…" I had to pause. Even though I knew Honey wasn't the same Honey, I didn't want to admit it, not even to myself.

"I get it," Auntie Lynn said, using my hesitation as the answer to her inquiry.

"Yeah," I said, my voice cracking.

"I'mma need you to pick me up from the airport."

"Sure. When?"

"Thursday. I'm gonna go ahead and book this six A.M. flight. I'll be there by eight thirty. I'll use Honey's car to get around once I get there. But I need to check up on her. I don't like the way she's sounding. We need to get her to her doctor. I hate to say it, but something's not right with Honey."

The truth of the matter was that Honey's health was declining. I could see it with my own eyes, but I was in denial.

I wiped the constant flow of tears that escaped their ducts after the call with Auntie Lynn. Honey was my world. I held nothing against her for putting me out. She was well within her rights to do so, being that I violated her three strikes rule.

All she needs is some good ole tea mixed with some potent herbs we can get from the holistic doctor who attends New Zion. She'll be all right. Honey will be just fine.

The funny thing is I don't quite think I believed what I was repeating in my head. But only time would tell whether Honey would indeed be all right.

Chapter 20

Jailhouse Pimpin'

WHEN I PULLED UP, Auntie Lynn was standing outside at Terminal 4, where United Airlines was located. I almost didn't recognize her; she was sporting a short hairdo and she had gained some weight, ten pounds or more, since I'd seen her last. The one thing that made her identifiable was her high-pitched, rambunctious laughter. She was engaged in conversation with a tall white guy, not sure what about, but he had apparently said something she found hilariously amusing. I could hear her, even though my window was rolled up. After recognizing me, she waved and cut her conversation with the gentleman short. She attempted to reach for her suitcase to bring it to the car, but the gentleman picked it up for her and brought it to the back of my car. I lifted the latch to open the trunk. He and Auntie Lynn engaged in other small talk at the rear of the car. It wasn't until then I noticed the gentleman had an accent. But whatever he was saying to Auntie Lynn, she still found it amusing. She let out that loud, rambunctious laugh a few more times. While I waited, I changed the radio station to WLLS, Smooth Jazz, Auntie Lynn's favorite station. I assumed their conversation would eventually come to an end, but when I noticed patrol making their way up to the parked cars, motioning for them to move, I got out of the car to advise Auntie Lynn and the gentleman.

"Patrol is coming. I gotta move before I get a ticket."

Auntie Lynn giggled softly, and the tall gentleman walked her over to the front passenger side of the car, opened her door, and closed it after she got in. I put the car in drive and pulled off, unaware of whether they had even said their final goodbyes.

"So you're picking men up at the airports now, huh?" I joked as I veered into the exit lane.

"Girl, he asked this old white man if he could switch seats with him on the plane, and he's talked my ear off since we left Atlanta."

We both laughed.

Remembering her telling me about another love interest, I said, "Well, what happened with Patrick?"

"White Patrick?"

"Is there a black one?" I teased.

"Oh, yeah. Patrick ... I don't know about him. Dating outside of your race is not all that intriguing. Basically, there's another whole dynamic that's pretty much cultural, and you have to both acknowledge and respect it. I have Detroit in my genes, no matter where I live in this country. Patrick is from the other side of the tracks. He believes in this cookie-cutter type of life that's just not realistic."

"Give me an example," I said.

"It's sort of hard to explain, but when you're living it day in, day out, it becomes an issue. One thing I do like about Patrick is that he knows what he wants. And that's me! Oh, and the sex is amazing." She let out that rambunctious laugh again.

"I heard they're not that endowed down there," I said, hoping she'd confirm whether it was an old myth or the truth.

"He satisfies me. That's all I can say. It's not like I've been around the block a few times and can say I've been with X number of white guys. And plus, who's comparing anyway?"

Auntie Lynn paused.

"What?" I said, trying to guess what was on her mind.

"I can't believe I'm having this conversation with my niece."

"You're just ten years older than me, and I'm an adult, in case you didn't remember," I joked, hoping she would agree and resume the conversation.

"Yeah, I know, but I'm still your aunt. Seems weird talking to you about grown stuff."

"We're going to Honey's now, right?" I said, changing the subject.

"Yep. Her appointment is at eleven. We need to make sure she's on time. You didn't mention that I was coming in town, did you?"

"Of course not. Honey has no idea."

"Good," Auntie Lynn said as she checked her freshly manicured nails for chips and cracks. "Dang!" she said, noticing a chip on her left pinky finger. "I'm gonna have to get this fixed today," she said, holding the finger up.

"We can go by my nail shop later on," I suggested.

"Cool," she said, still examining the chipped fingernail. "Hey, I didn't ask. What's going on with you?" she asked, now focusing her attention on me.

If she only knew the drama going on in my life. But I decided to keep my answer generic. "It's going all right. Working and thinking about taking some classes."

"Still dating that guy … what's his name?"

"David?"

"Yeah, the David guy, the one Honey doesn't like."

"David," I confirmed.

"What's the deal with him?"

"Well, we actually broke up. I'm seeing a different guy. A guy named Ziek. Ziek Wallace."

"Does he have an older brother named Chad?" she asked as she adjusted her seat, pushing it forward.

"Yeah, he does. But I've only seen him once."

"I know them … that family. Chad and I went to high school together. So Ziek must be the one with the funny-colored eyes."

"They're hazel," I said, correcting her.

"I could never tell whether they were green, hazel, or gray, so I just called them funny colored. But that Chad ..." Auntie Lynn paused.

"What?" I said, urging her to complete her train of thought.

"We used to kick it back in the day."

"Really?" I said, shocked that Auntie Lynn would even be associated with any of the "Wallace boys," the name they were known by in the streets. "What happened with you guys?"

"Honey happened, that's what, after I came home with a hickey and black eye on the same night. She shut that down real quick. And she told Chad she'd put him and his crack-addicted mama in their graves if he did so much as look my way again."

We both laughed. Her, of course, with wild laughter. Honey was a Christian, no doubt. But she didn't take no stuff. And because she was widowed with young children, she had to play both mother and father roles. I guess she was in the father role when she hemmed up Ziek's older brother, Chad.

"He hit you?" I said, shocked by the news. Ziek was a gentle giant who barely raised his voice, let alone his hands.

"Hit ain't the word. He pummeled me," she said, her right hand tracing a faint scar on the left side of her face, near her ear.

"Are you kidding?"

"No."

"But I thought you got bit by Sparky?" I said, recounting what apparently was a lie they had all told about the scar. Sparky was a Doberman pinscher that belonged to one of our neighbors on Fischer Street. Since many years had passed, the scar wasn't so pronounced anymore. But back in the day, the scar was quite visible.

"That was a lie I made up. I was embarrassed. No one in the family knew, except for Honey. Not even your mama."

"Shannon," I said, correcting her. "I had no idea that's where that scar came from."

"Yeah, that's what people said when I finally told them the truth about the scar."

I was shocked that Auntie Lynn had endured physical abuse as a teenager. In reflection, it appears that us Crawford women attracted abusive men. And I was no different. I had seen David's violent side quite a few times, but I always made some form of an excuse for his behavior. After all, addressing it only made matters worse.

"His brother, Ziek, isn't violent, is he?"

"Nah, nah. He's the total opposite. He's as gentle as a dove, at least with me. But I ain't gonna lie, he deals."

"Be careful with that, Destiny. You don't want to get caught up with that."

"Caught up how?"

"Like being with him when a bust or raid is going down or when somebody wants to settle the score with him. Those Wallace boys have a shady reputation."

"He never carries stuff on him when we're together. He promised he wouldn't."

"Now, I could go on and on and give you a speech about it, but I'm not. I'm just gonna tell you to be careful." She paused for a moment then continued. "You know, I know Donitra is your girl—your favorite auntie—and that's cool, but believe it or not, you're more like me than Auntie Don."

"You think?" I said, getting off the expressway exit for Honey's house.

"Of course. Like you, I wanted to obey Honey's rules, and I tried. But I'm sorry, they were too rigid, and there were no exceptions. The three strikes rule? Impossible to abide by. I knew I wasn't coming home on prom night, so I saved my strikes up. But Honey had a surprise for me. She gave me two strikes for that one incident, one for missing curfew and the other for not coming home at all."

Auntie Lynn burst into laughter, recounting the days of her

youth. But within moments, her laughter was drowned out by an eerie moment of silence. We had to be thinking the same thing. I wasn't brave enough to bring the conversation up, so she did. "I think there's something seriously wrong with Honey."

"What makes you think that?" I said, trying to play it off.

"She hasn't been herself."

"I mean, she's been a little under the weather here lately. But I just think it's because she's worn out," I said, trying to *sound* optimistic.

"Nah, that ain't it. I think it's something else."

And that something else we never spoke of; we drove the rest of the way to Honey's house in silence, both of us thinking but neither of us speaking.

We always said Honey had a keen sixth sense. We told her the HVAC tech was coming to the house to check the furnace, since it had been shutting on and off for the past week and a half. But Honey didn't look like she was expecting the HVAC tech when we arrived; she was completely dressed in one of her favorite ultra-suede outfits, a top and skirt. Sitting at the kitchen table, where we knew we'd find her, Honey was enjoying a cup of her favorite green tea.

"I sho' knew something was fishy," she said, looking up with wide eyes when Auntie Lynn walked toward her.

"Hey, Mama," Auntie Lynn greeted with open arms and a soft kiss on the left cheek.

I stood back and savored the mama-and-daughter moment. For the first time in probably my entire life, I felt like Honey's granddaughter and not her daughter. Attempting to embrace Auntie Lynn just as warmly, Honey tried to stand up but nearly lost her balance. Both Auntie Lynn and I were able to grab her before she fell. Our eyes met as we lifted Honey back to her feet.

Neither one of us said anything; our silence and facial expressions conveyed both our thoughts and emotions.

"Got up too fast," Honey said as she tried to balance herself against Auntie Lynn.

"Yeah, Mama, you probably did. But let's go by Dr. Randall's so he can run some bloodwork on you and make sure that daggone diabetes ain't tryna creep up on you again," Auntie Lynn said. It was her way of trying to make it less obvious that her declining health was the reason for her visit.

"Lynn, I had you. You didn't have me. You'll never be able to outslick me."

"What are you talkin' about, Mama?" Auntie Lynn said, helping Honey back into her chair.

"You've sure been talking about Dr. Randall here lately. I know that's the reason you're here," Honey said, looking Auntie Lynn up and down.

"Nah, Mama. I came in town to check on my property," Auntie Lynn lied. "You know I'm thinking about selling it. So I'm meeting with the realtor to go over upgrades that might be needed."

Dang! Auntie Lynn was good with the lies. She didn't blink or stutter; she was just off the cuff with her lies. She winked at me when Honey wasn't looking. I cracked a half-smile. Honey's loss of balance had me worried.

"Well, that sounds reasonable. But I still don't know if I believe you," Honey said, taking what appeared to be her last sip of tea. "Now, that was good."

We didn't have to bribe Honey to go see the doctor that day, even though she typically hated going to doctors. She felt they were negligent in diagnosing Albert Sr., which caused him to die young, at forty-two years old. Ever since I could remember, Honey's long-held saying was, "Stay away from doctors."

Honey's longstanding doctor, Dr. Aaron Randall, was short in stature, about five-foot-five, with salt and pepper hair and smooth dark skin. I hadn't seen him in years, but he remembered me the moment he walked into Exam Room 1, where we were waiting.

"Well, hello, ladies. Nice to see you. Don't tell me this is Destiny," he said, peering over the rim of his glasses.

"It's me," I said, extending my hand.

"Well, well, well. Haven't you grown up to be a beautiful young woman." His eyes alternated between looking at Honey and me. "And you must be one of Honey's daughters because you have her eyes, nose, and smile," he said to Auntie Lynn.

"Yes, I'm Lynn, the middle daughter," Auntie Lynn said, extending her hand to Dr. Randall.

Dr. Randall focused his attention back to Honey. "So, Ms. Crawford, we haven't seen each other in a long time. Been almost three years since your last visit. Where have you been?"

"Has it been that long?" Honey said as if she were unaware of her intentional medical neglect.

"Sure has."

"Well, you know I sometimes go to the local clinic up my way when I have a little cold or something. You know me, I try to stay away from doctor offices. Y'all always tend to find something wrong with people," Honey joked, trying to further make light of her inconsistency with medical follow up.

"Oh, come on, Ms. Crawford. You know me better than that," Dr. Randall responded, chuckling. "So what brings you in today?"

Honey didn't say anything. Instead, she looked at Auntie Lynn. "Go ahead, you're the one who thought I needed to be here."

Auntie Lynn swallowed hard. I could tell she didn't want to utter the words necessary, but she managed to do so. "She hasn't been feeling herself lately."

"Like what? Is she fatigued? Nauseated?"

"Umm … yeah, but it's more so that she's weak, with no energy. She's not really eating like she normally does. She—"

"It's probably diabetes tryna come up on me," Honey interrupted.

"Well, this is a medical practice, and we don't guess around here," Dr. Randall said, finishing up his notetaking. "Come sit," he said, motioning for Honey to sit on the examination table. He did a onceover after she sat and started asking Honey a barrage of other questions, questions whose answers were a bit troubling. Although Honey had never told us, she had a fainting spell in the house.

"How come we didn't know that you fainted in the house recently? Do I need to take a leave of absence from my job to come stay with you until you get better?" Auntie Lynn said, her eyebrows raised.

"Don't be silly. You have a life of your own to live. I just need to get tested for diabetes and take some supplements. I'll be just fine."

Dr. Randall performed a physical examination on Honey, rechecking her vitals, feeling for lymph nodes in her neck, and checking her eyes, ears, and mouth. He asked her to lie back on the exam table and pressed on her stomach. Honey almost leaped off the table.

"Ouch!" she squealed.

"Okay. Okay," Dr. Randall said, trying to disguise his concern. "Do you think you can walk to that door for me?"

Honey slid off the side of the exam table onto the floor, and it happened again—she lost her balance. This time, she fell to her knees because no one caught her in time. Dr. Randall helped Honey get to her feet and over to the chair where I had been sitting until Honey fell.

"Okay, Ms. Crawford, this is what we're gonna do. I'm going to set you up for some bloodwork and some other tests. Based on the results of these initial tests, we'll know how to proceed," Dr. Randall said as calmly as he could, trying not to alarm Honey.

My heart sank as I watched Dr. Randall fill out medical order after medical order for Honey. Make no mistake about it, Honey was sick. Something was wrong with her, and whatever it was, she could no longer disguise it.

It rained the day of Shonte's wedding, but it didn't stop the show at all. Having planned a lot of the activities around her wedding, including her bridal shower and bachelorette party, I couldn't wait until everything was over because I was exhausted. Shonte, as she said, was marrying her best friend. Her fiancé, turned husband, Kevin, seemed as though he was really into Shonte—a Ziek type of man—except Kevin was no drug dealer but an upstanding military officer.

Throughout the wedding ceremony, my eyes scanned the sanctuary in search of Ziek. He said he would meet me there, since I stayed at the hotel with the bridal party the night before and drove with them in the limo to the church for the ceremony that morning.

The reception started and ended, and there was still no sign of Ziek. I tried to mask my disappointment as best as I could by dancing until my feet hurt, but my heart was breaking on the inside. My best friend was enjoying what was probably the best day of her life, and there I was, fighting back tears from disappointment in Ziek, the residue from the painful breakup with David, and the fear of not knowing Honey's true health condition, which I believed in my heart of hearts was serious in nature.

I woke up to the sound of my house phone ringing. Almost instinctively, I reached for the receiver and answered. There was a familiar voice recording. *Must be David.*

"Yes," I said, accepting the collect call charges and waiting for the call to connect.

"Hey, baby," his voice whispered.

It wasn't David; it was Ziek. "Ziek?" I said, making sure I'd correctly detected his voice.

"Baby, I'm sorry I missed the wedding. They got me."

I was smart enough to know that "they" meant the police. Ziek was in jail. "Where are you?" I asked, even though I already knew the answer.

"County lockup."

"What happened?" I asked, even though I was certain he had met up with the same fate as David.

"Can't talk over the phone. I'mma beat it, though. Don't worry."

I knew Ziek. I knew he didn't want me to worry. He was street and could handle county lockup; I was the one who was a nervous wreck.

"Oh my, gosh, Ziek. I can't believe it," I said. I paused. "So do you need me to get in touch with an attorney for you?"

"Already did that. He's on it. I'll be all right, even if it does go to trial. He thinks I can beat it," Ziek tried to assure me.

My mind went blank. I can't even recall the remainder of the conversation. It was all beginning to resemble a nightmare. My world felt as though it was falling apart.

Auntie Lynn ended up extending her visit, so she could accompany Honey to her follow-up appointment. And having taken the day off myself, I accompanied Honey as well.

Doctor Randall had us meet him in his office this time. This was clue enough for me that it was indeed serious, and a discussion surrounding Honey's health was needed. Auntie Lynn and I sat on either side of Honey, with Auntie Lynn on her right and me on her left. Honey fumbled with the straps on her purse as her eyes watched Dr. Randall flip through her medical chart.

"How have you been feeling, Ms. Crawford?" Dr. Randall said, glancing up at Honey for a quick second.

"Better," Honey said, not looking at him directly.

"Well, the results of all your tests are in. Your bloodwork shows that your hemoglobin is low. You will need iron supplements. Your A1C looks good, so no diabetes."

"Thank the Lord, no diabetes!" Honey said, clapping her hands for added emphasis.

"But—"

There was that "but" factor. My shirt raised and lowered, matching the palpitations I was experiencing.

"But, what?" Auntie Lynn interjected.

Dr. Randall directed his attention to Auntie Lynn. "Your mother's liver function tests are abnormal. Her liver enzymes are very high, extremely high. And the CT scan of her abdomen shows gross inflammation and thickening of the colon."

"So what does that mean?" Auntie Lynn said.

"It usually means there's something wrong with the colon." After answering Auntie Lynn's question, he immediately diverted his attention back to Honey's medical chart.

"Are you saying I have colon cancer?" Honey said with all manner of calmness in her voice. Her disposition never changed, either.

"Well, that's what it usually indicates. Most of the time, it's cancer. But we won't know for sure without a colonoscopy and a CEA test," Dr. Randall said, looking up from Honey's chart.

"What's a CEA test?" Auntie Lynn and I said in unison.

"It's a test that looks for and measures cancer antibodies."

"So you really think it's cancer?" I said, wanting Dr. Randall to make his suspicion crystal clear.

He nodded then lowered his head, now pretending to be

sorting out papers in Honey's medical chart. Honey looked past Dr. Randall to the plaque hanging on the wall behind him.

"So you went to Yale for medical school. I never knew that. As a matter of fact, I've never been in your office before, and I've been seeing you for nearly twenty years now."

"Yes, I did attend Yale School of Medicine."

"I need to excuse myself," I announced as I stood to leave. I needed some fresh air. I don't even remember the walk through the lobby of Dr. Randall's office. Outside, I leaned against the brick wall that separated the two office buildings, the doctors' offices and the imaging and radiology center. I kept replaying Dr. Randall's words in my mind—cancer ... thickening … colon … cancer. *Honey has cancer!* My legs felt weak. My world felt as though it was caving in on me. I let out a loud scream as I fell to the floor.

With Ziek now in jail and the jail's policy of a visitor being on one inmate's visitation list at a time, I had a decision to make. Was I going to be team Ziek or team David? My heart leaned toward David, but my loyalty was to Ziek. Why? It was simple. Ziek had always been there for me. So I had my name removed from David's visitation list and placed on Ziek's. I know I should have told David I was removing my name from his visitor's list, but I didn't.

For the next several months, I drove back and forth almost every weekend to see Ziek. And every weekend, there was the same group of women who had apparently driven up to see their love interests as well. I was them and they were me. We were all down for our men. That is, until one visit sort of changed the trajectory of my relationship with Ziek.

"Falls, right?" the guard said as he looked up from the paperwork on the clipboard he was holding. He was being facetious, knowing he had checked me in several times previously, but when I was visiting David.

"No, I'm here to see Ziek Wallace … W-A-L-L-A-C-E," I said, rolling my eyes.

The guard smirked. "I've been on vacation and just assumed you were visiting Mr. Falls. Unless you have a twin, it's you who's been visiting David Falls, right?"

"Mister … guard. Johnson. That's your name, right?" I said, glancing at his name tag.

"That's me, young lady."

"I had my name taken off Mr. Fall's list and added to Ziek Wallace's visitor list. That's who I'm here to see," I said, handing him my driver's license.

"I gotcha, I gotcha," he said, peering over the rim of his glasses as if he were scrutinizing my ID. He looked up at me then down at my driver's license. "That's you all right," he said as he put a checkmark next to Ziek's name. "Wallace, Z, has a visitor," he announced to the white female guard sitting next to him.

It didn't take long for Ziek to come out. He looked frazzled. His eyes were red and puffy. He seemed as though he hadn't shaved in a few days, and the curls in his hair looked dry. He snuck in a peck on my right cheek.

"Hey, baby," he said, taking a seat.

"Ziek," was the only word I could utter.

He took a deep breath. "Sup?"

"What's going on?"

"What do you mean?" he said, rubbing his temples.

"You don't look like yourself. What's going on?"

"It's my mama."

Was he talking about the drug-addicted mama he'd always talked about? I didn't say anything. I waited for him to expound.

"She's not doing well."

"What's wrong with her?"

Ziek just gave me "the look," so I knew it had to be serious. "Oh, sorry to hear that," I said, trying to console him.

"Yeah, pulmonary hypertension. Life done caught up to her, I guess. She's in hospice now."

"Is she?"

"Yeah, and they don't expect her to leave."

"So what do you want me to do?" I volunteered.

"I'mma need you to make sure my mama's funeral arrangements get taken care of. She still needs to be buried with some sense of dignity."

"I hear you," I said, validating his feelings.

"So I'mma need you to go to my cousin Dexter's house and tell him to give you my black Nike bag. It's got my stash in it. Take about fifteen grand out, and when my mama passes, go over to Garrett & Sons Funeral Home and tell'em Z sent you there."

"Whoa, whoa, Ziek. You're talking as though your mama is already dead," I said, reaching instinctively for his hands to hold them. I quickly dropped them in my lap when I remembered the no-touch policy.

"Destiny, my mama's lived a hard life. She's dying, and that's the hard truth. Say what you want. Yeah, she was an addict, but she's still my mama, and I want her to leave this world with some dignity."

I was silent for a moment. I understood where Ziek was coming from. Yeah, I wanted to be down for my guy, but I didn't have that type of relationship with his mother nor his family. And putting me in charge of funeral arrangements for a woman I barely even saw made me uncomfortable. The last thing I wanted was to get into a fight with the family over that fifteen thousand dollars as if it were fifty grand.

"So?" he said, realizing I hadn't verbally agreed to fulfill his request.

"I'm thinking," I replied.

"What's there to think about?"

"So you mean to tell me I can just walk up in there and tell your sister and your brothers—your whole family, for that matter—that I'm going to be handling the arrangements for your mother's funeral, and they ain't gonna look at me like I lost my mind?"

"They'll know I sent you. My sister will spend the money on clothes. She might even go as far as to upgrade her car. My brothers and I aren't even that close, so I don't trust them with money. Who else is there?"

I nodded. "Okay. Okay. I got you. I'll do it," I agreed.

Even though I knew Ziek was indisputably saddened by his mother's terminal condition as well as the predicament he found himself in, he managed to crack a smile. I returned the sentiment by winking at him twice and blowing him a gentle kiss.

Chapter 21

I Do, But I Don't

Two Years Later

I WAS FINALLY ABLE to kiss plant life goodbye when I got hired at Consumers Energy, a local electric company in Michigan. In addition to working first shift, some of the other benefits included great health benefits, a pension, a matching 401k plan, and generous paid time off. Working in the billing department allowed me to meet a lot of people, both in the office and over the telephone. The best thing about the new job was getting off at four o'clock, which allowed me to check on Honey more frequently, now that she had to retire early because of her declining health. And of course, it helped that I passed Honey's driving to and from work.

As I would normally do when I lived with Honey, I grabbed the mail out of the mailbox on my way in. With the volume of mail in the mailbox, it was my guess that Honey hadn't checked the mailbox in several days. I scanned the pile of mail in my left hand as I walked up the driveway to the back door.

Honey was standing at the stove, stirring a pot of what appeared to be beef stew when I walked into the kitchen.

"Hey, Honey. How are you feeling?" I asked as I placed the pile of mail on the kitchen table.

"Baby, I feel good. I told y'all I was gonna be all right."

"Honey, you have cancer. That's not all right."

"Destiny, you must don't know the God I serve," Honey said as she turned the heat down on the pot of soup she was stirring.

"Honey, I know God is a healer, but until the doctors give you a clean bill of health, you have to take it easy."

"Chile, Honey don't know what that phrase means. I've been working hard nearly my entire life. That's all I know, pretty much."

A forced smile spread across her face. I smiled back. This was the first time since her diagnosis that I felt ready to take on that deadly disease. *Honey can beat this. We can beat this.*

"You want some?" Honey said, holding up the large spoon she used to stir the soup.

"Sure," I said as I walked over to the cabinet to retrieve two bowls.

"It sure is delicious," Honey said, swiping her right index finger across the spoon's tip to taste the soup. "Vera dropped it off."

"Oh, did she?"

"Yeah … her and that new fella she's done picked up. I don't know about her. Thinks she always has to have a man in her bed," Honey said, shaking her head.

I was beginning to regret having agreed to have soup with Honey. Once she got on a roll about Vera's love life, I knew a barrage of questions regarding mine was soon to follow. But it was too late. Honey was now motioning for me to bring the bowls over to her, so she could dump loads of the tasty stew into them.

I waited for Honey to fill both bowls then sat them on the table. I paid close attention to Honey as she walked over to the table from the stove. Her balance seemed fine, and she didn't have a problem sitting down.

"So how's that new job going?" Honey asked after taking a few spoonfuls of soup.

"It's going good, Honey. Real good."

"I take it you like your department, too?"

"For the most part, I do," I responded.

"Good. That's good," Honey said, pushing her bowl of soup away.

"You don't like the soup?"

"I do. I love it. I'm just full," Honey answered, after which, she began to excessively belch.

I moved my chair closer to Honey and began to pat her on the back until the belching finally subsided. "Does this happen often, Honey?"

"What? This burping?"

"Yeah," I said with mounting nervousness.

"It happens quite a bit. I just wish it'll go away for good. Reminds me of pregnancy. I burped a lot with my girls but not with Albert Jr."

"Well, I wouldn't know anything about burping while pregnant," I joked, figuring we both could use the laugh.

Honey and I both chuckled. It did my soul some good to see Honey laugh and maintain a good disposition. Whether it was genuine in nature was questionable. Nevertheless, I had to take Honey at her word—that she felt well.

"Why don't you try to eat just a little bit more, Honey."

"Baby, I'm full. Just put it in the fridge. I can always eat more if I get hungry later."

"Just a little bit more, Honey. You didn't eat enough."

I managed to persuade her to eat a little more of the beef stew. As she ate, I cleaned the kitchen and we chatted some more.

Before heading out, I helped Honey get dressed for bed. Then it happened again—Honey lost her balance. This time, she fell forward onto her bed, which, as unfortunate as it was for Honey, was fortunate for me—there was no way I could have picked her up by myself.

After some clever maneuvering, I was able to get Honey in bed comfortably. I stood back and watched her until she closed her eyes. *Is this what it's gonna be like when she closes her eyes for good?*

As much as I didn't want to face it, losing Honey was going to be a reality one day, especially with her refusal to take chemotherapy. Her motto was, "If God doesn't heal me, then it's meant for me to go on home. And that's what I'm gonna do."

I planted a soft kiss on Honey's forehead, turned the volume on the television down, and headed for the front door but did a beeline to take one last look at the stove to make sure Honey had indeed turned it off. As I descended the front steps, I couldn't help but notice the black Mustang with tinted windows parked behind my car. The park lights were on, but the car's engine was not running. The first thing that crossed my mind was Ziek. *Had he left business undone in the streets and someone was now coming for me?*

The passenger window rolled down. "I've been looking for you," a familiar voice uttered.

I stopped in my tracks. "David? Is that you?" I said, squinting my eyes, trying to zoom in on the figure inside the car.

"Yes," the voice answered.

My jaw dropped as the driver side door opened and David emerged. I took a step back. For a quick minute, I thought about whether I should run back into the house. I'd cut ties with David once I became team Ziek when Ziek went to jail. *Is he coming back for revenge?*

"You look like you just saw a ghost," David said, walking around the car toward me.

"What are you doing out? I mean, how did you get out?" I asked. David had a three-year sentence, which was longer than Ziek's sentence. So logically, I had to wonder how David had gotten released before Ziek.

"Overcrowding and good behavior," David said with a sheepish grin as he approached me.

"So you're out for good?" I said, still stunned by his surprise visit.

"Out for good," David emphasized as he threw his arms around me and lifted me off my feet.

In that moment, my attraction to David was overpowering. I felt like a little girl with her first playground crush. "How did you know I was going to be here today?"

"You want the truth?" David said, putting me down.

"No, I want you to lie to me," I said facetiously.

"I took a chance. I went by the plant and nobody wanted to give up your whereabouts like you're some celebrity there," David joked.

"I don't work there anymore," I admitted.

"I know that much now. I figured your grandmother's house would be my best bet. I'd drive by here often, hoping to catch your car outside at some point or another."

I was flattered. After all the drama I had been through with David, especially as far as Nettie was concerned, he was finally pursuing me. I was smitten all over again. And as if we had never skipped a beat, I wanted to be with David. In that moment, Ziek wasn't even a consideration. How long was I supposed to wait for him anyway? After all, both David and Ziek had put me in vulnerable situations by going to jail.

Like a car sliding across an icy road on a cold winter night, I slid my way into David's bed and back into his life. Not at all considering the consequences of my actions, we were back at it. Just like that, I had fallen back under David's spell. Without notice to Ziek, I cut off all ties with him, which included submitting a written request to the prison to have my name removed from his visitor list and blocking his collect calls. I knew he would be getting out of jail soon enough, but I figured I'd cross that bridge when I came to it.

Unlike Ziek, David was never the type of guy to plan romantic dates. He was more spontaneous—a go-with-the-flow type of guy. That's why I was surprised when he suggested we go ring shopping one day.

"Let's go to Jared's."

"Jared's?" I said quizzically.

"Yes," David said, chuckling.

"Like, as in the jewelry store, Jared's?"

"Yep, like as in the jewelry store, Jared's."

"Like, as in wedding rings?" I said with increased excitement.

"Yep, like wedding rings," David said, grinning.

I froze. Although it's every girl's dream to get married, I had long stopped dreaming about it; it seemed like more of a fairytale than reality for me. I seemed to only attract men who didn't have integrity or those who just exhibited too many red flags early in the relationship.

"So, let me get this right. You want to get married?" I said, searching for clarity. I needed David to be crystal clear. No more figures of speech and insinuations.

"Yes, I'm ready to get married and start a family."

"And you want to marry *me*?" I said, holding up my left ring finger.

"Yes, I want to marry you," David said as he got up from the lounge chair he was sitting on.

"Where's Nettie?" I said.

"I have no idea," David said, rolling his eyes.

"Well, I have to ask. I need to make sure you want me for me and not because you are out of options or think I'm desperate."

"Destiny, why are you going there? You know I've never thought you were a desperate woman. If anything, I'm a little worried about your answer. I don't deserve you, and I know that. I realize I was stupid in the past. I could have lost you for good."

"You're right about that. I had moved on."

"Well, it looks like you're going to have to break some bad news to him," David said, confident that I would accept his proposal.

"Oh, really?"

"Really," David emphasized, his dark eyes and piercing gaze hypnotizing me.

Against my better judgment, I agreed to marry him. At the time, I felt like my options *were* limited. I loved David, but I obviously wasn't thinking clearly.

I lay in bed that evening thinking about the proposal. Although it wasn't the proposal I'd fantasized about as a little girl, it was a marriage proposal, nonetheless. I knew Honey wasn't going to be too happy about the news, and I had reservations about whether I should tell her. But my loyalty to Honey required that I bite the bullet and tell her that I had accepted David's proposal. So I stopped by Honey's on my way home from work a few days later to share the news with her.

Sure I'd find her watching her soaps, I headed straight for her room, holding another pile of mail in my hands.

"Hey, Honey. I brought your mail in," I said as placed the pile of mail on her dresser.

"I didn't hear you come in," Honey said, adjusting her eyeglasses.

"You look good, Honey," I said, looking her over.

"Yes, baby, I'm doing fine. I'm doing a heck of a lot better than I was a few weeks ago."

I was happy to hear those words coming out of Honey's mouth. I sat down at the foot of the bed and pretended to be just as intrigued with the soap operas she was watching, but in reality, my eyes were just fixed on the television as I rehearsed in my head how I was going to tell her about the proposal.

When the last soap opera went off, I turned to face her. "What do you think about me getting married?"

"If that's something you want to do, go for it. But make sure you marry the right man." I lowered my head. "Some guy done asked you to marry him?" Honey said, looking at me intently.

"Y—yes," I confessed as I ran my fingers across the stitched pattern in her comforter.

"That David character?" Honey said, not even batting an eye.

"Honey, he's not a character. He's not perfect, but he's trying." Honey hunched her shoulders. "What does that mean?" I asked.

"Do what you want. But if you want my opinion, I'd say that marrying that guy would be the worst mistake of your life."

"Why would you say that, Honey?"

"I've been around bad apples all my life, and I can spot one a hundred miles away. Say what you want, but that guy is a bad apple, and he's full of worms."

"Come on, Honey. That's a strange analogy. What do you mean by that?" I asked, adjusting my position on the bed.

"You'll see," Honey said as she turned the television off and reached for her Bible.

Needless to say, I didn't get Honey's blessings. I thought about Honey's words up until the day of the wedding. *Has she seen something in a prophetic vision?* Only time would tell because Honey sure wouldn't reveal the vision to me if she did have one. Growing up, one of her favorite sayings was, "A hard head makes a soft behind."

Our wedding day was like a clip from a *Twilight* movie. David and I didn't wear anything elegant or super flashy. Instead, I wore a royal blue strapless cocktail dress that Hattie gave me a few years back, and David wore a black suit that he paired with a white dress shirt and a black tie. David's brother, Hank, walked me down the aisle as I held a dozen white roses purchased from the local supermarket. Although it was chilly in the church, small, round pebbles adorned David's forehead and temples profusely. They popped out faster than he could wipe them.

A man named Pastor Carl, who was a distant relative of

Claudia, performed the ceremony. And just like that, David and I were married.

I said, "I do," but somewhere deep down, I knew I didn't—I wasn't fully committed to David or the marriage, and I was fully aware of it going in.

Chapter 22

Merry Go 'Round

BY THE END OF the second year of our marriage, I had seen several sides of David—the charming side that made me love him in my own way, the charismatic side that was alluring and made me want to ride with him no matter what, the dark side that scared me, the hood side that was intriguing, and even the unpredictable side of him that kept me on my toes. I was overly skeptical, highly suspicious, and very guarded.

Now living in a new house, not an apartment, we had more space. But that space kept us in separate rooms most of the time. One of the things that kept us on common ground, however, was the quest to build his business, something he had started before his most recent incarceration. David was determined to put the money he made in the streets to good use and make it work for him. With his past, including the multiple convictions, David wasn't going to get a job in Corporate America and work his way up to a corner office. So, outside of work and attending classes, I did what I could to help him build the business. Sometimes that meant cleaning properties that he wanted to flip, going to view properties he wanted to buy, and performing basic business due diligence. We hired Traci, David's godsister, to handle administrative tasks. She was reliable initially, but her on-again-off-again relationship with her guy seemed to get in the way later on.

Emerging from his office, David said, "Are you expecting anyone?" He was referring to the incessant banging on the front door.

"Nope. Not banging on the door like that," I replied as I arose from my lying position on the sofa.

The banging continued, and David walked over to the front door and peered through the peephole. "It's Traci," he said as he unlocked the door to let her in. A bloody-faced Traci fell into his arms and burst into tears the moment David opened the door.

"He tried to kill me," she mumbled as she sobbed uncontrollably.

"Who?" David asked, pulling Traci back so her voice would no longer be muffled.

"Donovan," Traci answered.

"I'mma kill him!" David said, prepared to retrieve his gun from his office.

"David, just hold on. Don't you go gettin' involved. You're on parole," I cautioned, trying to get David to think rationally.

"Destiny, I don't need you to remind me of my incarceration record! Don't no man have no business beating a woman to a pulp like this!" he barked.

I stood there, shocked, reminiscing about the times David, himself, had slapped or choked me. I wanted to call him a hypocrite to his face, but I knew all too well what would ensue next. Instead, I just played the compassionate wife-slash-play-sister-in-law role. "I'll get some paper towel and an icepack," I said, heading for the kitchen.

"And while you're at it, grab that throw off the chaise in my office so Traci can wrap up in it," David yelled out, closing the front door and ushering Traci over to the sofa.

Did he just tell me to get his all-time favorite throw for Traci to wrap up in? He won't even let me touch that throw, as if Jesus Himself bought it for him.

To avoid any mounting disagreement with David, reluctantly, I unraveled some paper towels, folded them neatly and grabbed an icepack from the freezer. I went into David's office and snatched the throw off the chaise and went back into the living room where the two of them were.

David was whispering something into Traci's ear but stopped as soon as I entered the room.

"Here," I said, handing him the items.

David took the items out of my hand without so much as saying thank you. I gave him the *ain't you forgetting to say something* look.

"Oh … thanks," he said.

I strutted off without saying anything.

"Where are you going?" David asked.

"I'm getting ready to take my shower. I gotta work in the morning, remember? It's only Thursday," I said with a hint of sarcasm.

"So you're not gonna help?"

"You look like you got it," I said as I proceeded upstairs.

He sucked his teeth. I could hear him speaking in a soft tone to Traci. The way he was catering to her made my stomach ball up in knots. I didn't totally buy the godsister story. I guess because my intuition just wouldn't let me. Like any woman would do; I sized up the other woman, comparing her traits, both physical and intellectual, to my own. Traci was four years younger than me, which made her eight years younger than David. She was tall and thin, sported a short hairdo, sort of like the old Halle Berry look, and she didn't wear stylish attire. From what my limited investigation revealed, Traci grew up dirt poor. Her mother suffered from schizophrenia and had a total of nine children, of which Traci was number seven. Her father, she never knew. From what Claudia had told me, Traci's mother wasn't even sure who Traci's biological father was, as she was taken advantage of by men who lived in her building due to her mental incapacity. At some point, Traci and six of her siblings were placed in foster care. That's when Claudia's neighbors, the Richardsons, took Traci and her younger sister, Debra, in. Living next door to the Falls family, Traci became best friends with Chantel, David's now deceased sister. So this is supposedly how the "play-sister-slash-godsister" relationship came into play. But in my opinion, the fact that Traci wasn't a blood relative of David's, made her fair game, and her naivety meant she could be easily manipulated, especially by David, who was a master manipulator.

I wiped the fog from the bathroom mirror, prepared to inspect my nakedness after taking a hot shower.

"Why did you treat that girl like that?" David said, startling me.

"Like what?" I said, reaching for my towel.

"Rude, Destiny. You were rude!"

"I wasn't rude. I was just shocked that you were nearly cradling the girl like a newborn baby," I said, drying off.

"Well, maybe if someone could get pregnant again around here, I'd have a real newborn to cradle," David said, retaliating.

"That was a cheap shot, David. Real cheap. You can really be a creep sometimes," I said, snatching my robe off the bathroom door.

"There you go with the name calling."

"I call it like I see it," I hurled back at him.

"Yeah, you think so?" David said, his eyes narrowing as he spoke.

"Yes, I do. You won't even let Baby Jesus touch that throw in your office. But now, you wanted me to fetch it, so you could wrap Traci up in it? *I'm* your wife, not her! If I didn't know any better—"

"Don't even go there, Destiny. You're out of order."

"Really? Me, out of order?" I said, throwing the bath towel onto the floor.

"You know, what?"

"What?! What, David?" I snapped as I put my robe on and tied its belt tightly.

"This is my house, don't forget it."

"No, this is *our* house. You might have fronted the money for the down payment, but don't you forget that if it wasn't for my credit, we wouldn't be here," I shot back.

"Like I said, it's my house, and Traci's gonna be here," David said, turning to leave.

"For how long?" I challenged, following him into our bedroom.

"For as long as she needs to be here," he said, turning back around to face me.

"You think?"

David didn't readily respond; he rolled his eyes and kicked the bench at the foot of our bed. I didn't take my eyes off him, either. I fought back tears as I stood paralyzed in that moment, watching the man I said "I do" to defend another woman over his own wife. On top of that, he had just launched the ultimate verbal attack on me by criticizing me about my inability to get pregnant.

"I don't think, Destiny. I know," David responded, almost daring me to challenge him.

I followed David and watched him descend the stairs to go back to catering to Traci, I assumed. The thought of it enraged me. I went back into the bedroom and slammed the door behind me.

I didn't bother to put on a fancy nightgown because I didn't want David to touch me. As a matter of fact, it would have suited me just fine if he would have spent the night in his office on the chaise, as he would do some nights. But I knew that wasn't going to happen. David had too much pride. He was about image, and there was no way he was going to let Traci even think he had gotten kicked out of the bedroom.

As I laid my head on the pillow, my mind kept rehearsing the hurtful words David had said to me earlier—*Well, maybe if someone could get pregnant again around here, I'd have a real newborn to cradle.* I licked my lips. The savor of salt permeated my taste buds. I used the flat bedsheet to wipe my eyes. And even though David's words felt like a scalpel ripping through my flesh, they woke something up in me. It was time to see a specialist. I hadn't always practiced safe sex over the years, and I never missed even one menstrual cycle. Something was wrong.

I woke up a little after five o'clock the next morning. David had slid into bed at some point throughout the course of the night, but I didn't even hear him. Although I was still fuming over what had transpired the night before, I decided to do something different. Instead of being angry and seeking vengeance by not performing my wifely duties, I got up, curled my hair, applied some makeup, put on my cute red and white house dress, slid on my slippers, and went downstairs to cook breakfast.

I could see the kitchen light was on as I walked downstairs. To my surprise, Traci was in the kitchen, sitting at the table sipping on a cup of coffee when I entered. "I hope you don't mind," she said, as she blew over the top of her coffee trying to cool it.

"Mind?" I asked.

"Yeah, mind that I made a cup of coffee."

"No, I don't mind," I said as I opened the refrigerator door to retrieve the carton of eggs and a stick of butter.

"Thanks. I'll make sure I buy a bag when I'm at the grocery store. Do you like any other flavors besides hazelnut?"

"Hazelnut is fine," I responded, making brief eye contact with her.

"I'll pick up coconut from Dunkin Donuts, because I know David likes coconut."

"Um hm," I mumbled back, trying to focus on my task. An awkward moment of silence ensued. I began humming one of my favorite hymns, "The Waterway."

"Wow, Destiny. I didn't know you could sing," Traci said as her eyes lit up.

How could you? You don't even know me, I wanted to say. Instead, I said, "A little bit." I used to sing in the choir at church and lead a few solos here and there. But I never told people much about my singing.

"Well, you truly have a beautiful voice."

"Thanks," I said as I continued my task of making breakfast.

After some time passed, Traci followed with, "Hey, I just want to say thank you for letting me stay here. I know it caused some beef between you and David last night. And the last thing I want to do is cause trouble for you guys."

"It's okay. We'll all work it out," I said. I really wanted to find an indiscreet way to ask her how long she anticipated staying with us. But I didn't trust her well enough to not repeat my inquiry to David. I needed to find a way to bring peace in our home … and in our marriage.

"How's your eye feeling?" I said, changing the subject.

"Sore. Still sore."

"Thinking about filing a police report?" I asked, turning around to look at the now black and blue eye.

"No. I'll let David'em handle him. If I file a report, he'll go to jail, lose his job, and then he'll really be after me."

"He's hit on you before, I take it."

"Yes," Traci said as she rigorously stirred her coffee, almost nervously it seemed.

"And you think street justice is gonna make him stop?"

"I'm leaving for good this time."

I guessed that meant she was anticipating staying with us until she could save enough money to afford her own place, which was obviously disappointing news for me. "Well, let me know if you need me to help you find a place," I said. Offering to help her find a place was probably the only way she'd get out sooner rather than later. I just hoped my desire for her to get out was disguised well enough.

"Thanks, Destiny. I appreciate it."

"The grocery stores have apartment guides. I'll pick one up for you today if you like."

"Pick what up?" David said, entering the kitchen.

"Oh, an apartment guide," Traci blurted out.

"What do you need that for?" David said, looking at Traci then at me.

"A place," Traci said.

"Don't be ridiculous, Traci. Christmas is right around the corner. You ain't going nowhere before then. This is not the time for you to be alone."

"I don't want to invade you guys' space, David. I can always go to Mama Claudia's house, you know."

"Here, is fine. Plus, it'll be more convenient now that you're working for me."

"Us," I chimed in.

David rolled his eyes. "Yeah, us," he said.

"Breakfast will be ready in a minute," I said, urging David to eat at the table with me ... us.

"Not hungry," David said, grabbing a slice of bacon off the plate before heading toward the back door.

"David, your wife just cooked this amazing breakfast. You're gonna sit down and eat it," Traci chided.

To my amazement, David stopped in his tracks. He put his briefcase down by the back door and made a beeline for the kitchen table. "Guess I can spare a few minutes," he said, pulling out a chair to sit.

I wanted to throw the hot bacon grease on him. He had just said he wasn't hungry, but when Traci told him to stay, he acted like some programmed robot and obliged her. I was furious! But I couldn't let Traci know. I fixed David's plate and sat it down in front of him like he was a king.

"Thanks, babe," he said, his response almost knocking me off my feet.

"You're welcome," I said. I guess he expected us to play this little game as long as Traci was around. If she only knew how he'd disrespected me the night before.

"Not going to work today?" he said, gazing at the casual way I was dressed.

"No, I actually took off today. I forgot that I have to take Honey to an appointment," I lied. I took off, so I could watch the hussy he had invited into our home.

"Oh," he said, focusing his attention back to the plate of food before him.

"Traci, come help yourself to a plate," I offered, handing her a plate.

I was able to successfully play the devoted wife and sister-in-law roles this particular morning. It was killing me on the inside, but I was determined not to be defeated by Traci nor David. I took the day off, so I could stay around the house in an attempt to foil any plan Traci might have had to get cozy with David because he only worked four to five hours a day outside of the home.

I smiled intermittently at both David and Traci as we all broke bread at the kitchen table. I had won this round, and I knew it.

Chapter 23

Baby, I'm Back

BECAUSE HER HEALTH WAS seriously declining, we didn't leave Honey alone much anymore. I was now taking her to church on Sundays whenever she felt well enough to attend. Her refusal to take chemotherapy or radiation meant the cancer would continue to progress, spread, and eventually take her life. Honey said either way it turned out, it was a win–win situation for her—either God could heal her or take her to heaven with Him.

Although most of the family didn't agree with Honey's decision, we had to accept it. Auntie Lynn and Auntie Donitra took turns coming to visit, giving Auntie Roz and me a break. Sometimes, when I needed some space from David or any ensuing chaos, I'd spend the night on Saturday evenings and return home on Sunday after getting Honey settled in. Nicole, Roz's daughter, used to spend the night a few times throughout the week. But when Honey said Nicole's kids got on her nerves with all the whining and crying, surprisingly, Shannon, of all people, hired a young woman named Yasenia to stay with Honey, replacing Nicole.

With Traci still living with David and me, I tried to be as unpredictable as I could with my comings and goings. I limited the times I stayed at Honey's and split the cost with Shannon to hire Yasenia for a weekend night. I almost never announced my days off, just in case the two of them had any "household" plans, if you know what I mean.

Without announcing my intended destination, I put my gym clothes in a duffle bag along with my toiletries and an extra set of clothes.

"I'll see ya," I announced to David as I stood in the doorway of his office.

"Yep," he said, swirling around in his chair to give me a once over. He noticed I had my duffle bag, but he didn't comment. It was a known fact that I would be spending the night at Honey's if I had my duffle bag packed. But little did he know, I was meeting up with Claudia at the mall to do some Christmas shopping. Traci was out getting her hair and nails done, so I didn't have to see or speak to her.

Claudia met me outside of JCPenney in Fairlane Mall on the other side of the city. I didn't want to chance running into anyone David knew. Although he preferred that I didn't get too close to Claudia, he was a little more relaxed about us having some contact, especially with Traci being there.

"Let's hurry up and get this shopping out of the way. This place is super crowded. I know I'mma need a drink after this," Claudia said, holding out her arms to embrace me.

"I know, right? I haven't even put a dent into my gift list," I said as I kissed Claudia on the cheek.

"David tells me Traci's staying with you guys for a little while. Is that right?" she blurted out as she released her embrace and we walked into the store.

"I guess. No one has ever discussed time frames. But yes, she's staying with us."

"She's lazy, isn't she?" Claudia said, inspecting a black and gold blouse that caught her eye.

Not wanting to get into a gossip session with Claudia, I lied. "She helps out around the house some."

"Well, she didn't do crap at mine. I love Traci like a daughter, but she was nothing like my Chantel. To tell the truth, I dunno how they remained friends all those years."

Claudia was going into territory I had no knowledge of, so I tried to change the subject. "What do you think I should get David for Christmas?"

"Not a bad gal, just had some unfortunate events take place in her life," Claudia continued, not even considering my question.

"Yeah, she seems cool," I said. Telling Claudia how I really felt about Traci staying with us wasn't worth the risk. Claudia was in it for whatever she could get out of it. She befriended me, not because she liked me so much, but because I was the link to David, her financial support system.

"How do you think this goes with my complexion?" Claudia said, holding the blouse up to the side of her face.

"Umm ... it's nice," I said.

"You don't like her, do you?" Claudia said, reading the expression on my face.

"She's cool," I reiterated. I wanted to leave it at that and see if Claudia would expound.

"Don't trust her around David?"

"Claudia, I don't know. I don't think it's good for anyone to come live with newlyweds, especially a young, attractive woman who is not a blood relative." There. I'd said it, and Claudia could take it back to David if she wanted.

She hung the blouse back on the rack. "Well, you know the remedy for that, don't you?"

"What is it?" I said, urging Claudia to be direct with her line of thinking.

"Make love to him every morning and every night. Wear him out, so he won't have energy for anyone else. Empty everything in him."

"So I can't simply trust him to honor his vows?"

"Come on, Destiny. You're not that naïve, are you? Don't be silly. Every woman has to use her womanly wiles when dealing with her man. For a man, the desire to step out on his wife doesn't start in his head or heart. It starts with his eyes and ends with his penis. It's as simple as that. That's nothing new. Go ask your grandmother. She'll tell you the same thing."

Claudia had said a mouthful. I loved making love to David, but our issues outside of the bedroom were beginning to spill over into the bedroom. I wanted to follow Claudia's advice, but there was one thing standing in my way—my pride.

"I'll see," I said to Claudia.

"Come on, let's go over to Marshall Field's. I have a hot date tonight, and I need some lingerie."

"A date?" I said, raising my eyebrows.

"Yes. Mama still got it. He's a doctor. Met him when I went to visit my friend Carmen at the rehab center. Had a knee replacement about a month ago."

"Yeah, I think I remember David mentioning that to me."

"That's where I met Mitch. He's an orthopedic surgeon. Drives a really nice Mercedes Benz, S Class."

"Nothing wrong with that. Good luck with him," I said, trying to sound cheerful.

We spent the remainder of our time at Marshall Field's buying perfume, clothes, and other gifts for Christmas before heading to Antonio's Bar and Grill to have a couple of drinks, which was more like a ritual for Claudia.

Somewhere between my second raspberry martini and Claudia's third gin and tonic, I felt a pull on the back of my sweater. When I turned around, I was staring into his sexy hazel eyes.

"Oh, my goodness! Ziek?" Without thinking, I wrapped my arms around his broad shoulders as I stood on my toes.

Ziek just smiled. I had no idea he had been released. "Where have you been?" Ziek whispered in my ear as he hugged me tightly.

Releasing my embrace, I replied, "Here. I've been here." I stepped back to get a good look at him. He looked good, like he had never been to prison. He was cleanly shaven, nicely dressed, and smelled good, as he always did, with the exception of the time I saw him looking disheveled when he was locked up.

"Who's your friend?" he said, pointing at Claudia, who was meticulously eyeing him.

"Oh, sorry. Ziek, this is Claudia, my—"

"Her mother-in-law," Claudia interrupted.

"Nice to meet you," Ziek said, reaching his hand out to shake Claudia's. He played it off well.

"Likewise," Claudia said, proudly extending her hand.

If I didn't know any better, I would have thought Claudia was making sure Ziek knew I was a married woman. And not only that, but one who was married to *her* son. I was taken aback for a moment, especially after our earlier conversation. This was a prime example of why I couldn't tell Claudia everything; her loyalty was to her son, not me.

"You look good," Ziek said, now ignoring Claudia.

"Thank you," I said, trying to be as congenial as I could. In actuality, I wanted to jump into Ziek's arms.

"How've things been?" he asked, checking me out from head to toe.

"Good. Real good."

"So where are you working now? I know you don't work at the plant anymore."

"No, I don't. I'm at Consumer's Energy now. And I'm in school, too."

"Oh, I see you're really tryna move on up in the corporate world. And I ain't mad at'cha," Ziek said, licking his lips.

I turned to see if Claudia was looking, but she was too busy eavesdropping on the conversation with an older man and a much younger woman sitting to her left.

"So you take care of yourself," Ziek said as he slowly backed away. He had gotten the hint with my formality. But when he was sure Claudia wasn't looking, he slipped me a piece of paper and mouthed, "Call me."

I nodded then quickly turned my attention back to Claudia.

"What's the deal with him?" Claudia said, turning her attention from the couple to me.

"Oh, just an old friend of mine," I said, taking a sip of my now room-temperature martini.

"I saw the way he was looking at you."

"Oh, Claudia, where are you going with this? He's an old friend of mine that I haven't seen in years."

"Why are you getting defensive? I just said I saw the way he was looking at you."

"It's not that type of ballgame, and he knows that."

"Are you sure? 'Cause he sure seemed shocked to learn that you're a married woman."

"That's because I haven't seen him in years. How would he have known?" I said, stirring my drink, trying to disguise my nervousness.

"Look, sweetie, let's table this topic for another time. It's getting late, and I have to get home to get ready," Claudia said, downing the last of her drink as she stood to leave.

We did the separation hug thing, and I helped Claudia collect her shopping bags. "Talk to you later," Claudia said as she left a modest tip for the bartender and scurried out of the restaurant.

I watched Claudia until she was no longer in sight. When I was certain she wasn't coming back, I slowly unfolded the piece of paper Ziek handed me, which read:

I've been looking for you. Give me a call.
Ziek
555-337-2811

I was certain David had the impression I was spending the night at Honey's when he saw me holding my duffle bag earlier. But unbeknownst to him, this was one of those weekends Yasenia was staying with Honey and not me.

I parked up the street, a few houses away from ours, and walked toward the house. I kept the keyring with the house key on it in my hand, so I wouldn't have to fumble through my purse to search for it. Traci's car was in the driveway. I guessed she thought I didn't need my parking space, as she was familiar with the routine of my staying at Honey's some Saturdays. I crept up the stairs as inconspicuously as I could. I could hear the television as I approached the front door. Discreetly, I slid my key into the lock and turned it, unlocking it. With full force, I pushed the door open. The room was dark, except for the flash of light coming from the television. I could see the faint shadows of the two of them abruptly moving around on the sofa. Traci's feet flung off the sofa onto the floor, and David sat straight up.

"I thought you were spending the night at Honey's?" David said, clearing his throat.

"Is that why the two of you are so cozy up here on *my* sofa?" I said as I flipped the light switch to the on position.

They both looked like deer in headlights. "Destiny, it's not like that. It's not what you think," Traci said, pulling David's throw over her feet.

"Let me get this straight. I catch your feet in my husband's lap and you want me to believe, '*it's not like that*?'"

"He was just rubbing my feet, Destiny. You know I have

problems with my feet," Traci said, lifting the throw and revealing large keloids on the toes of both feet.

"That's what they have podiatrists for," I snapped back, focusing my eyes on David. "So what do you have to say for yourself? You want to act like I'm trippin', and the minute I step out, you got your fake sister's feet in your lap. What was she doing, rubbing them against your john?"

"Go 'head, Destiny. It was harmless," David said as she slowly stood. I tried to see if he had an erection. He didn't appear to have one, but that didn't mean he didn't have one previously, before I caught him in the act.

"So where are you going? You don't think you owe me an explanation? Where are you going?" I said, confronting him.

"Back to my office. I was working and was taking a short break."

"Yeah, a break all right," I said, slamming the front door.

David rolled his eyes and walked out of the living room. I turned my attention back to Traci.

"I'm sorry, Destiny. I know what it looks like, but I would never do anything in your house. David is my—"

"Did I hear you say you found a place?" I asked, cutting Traci off.

"Uhh … I've been looking, but—"

"How about we go looking for a place tomorrow," I suggested. I think I found one *for* you."

"But I got bad credit. I would have been out of here, but I'm having a problem finding a place that will accept my credit."

"I'll put the apartment in my name. But you have to be able to afford it."

"You'll do that for me?" Traci said, trying to act sincerely grateful.

"Absolutely," I said as I walked out of the room and headed for David's office.

David was sorting through some mail when I reached his

office. He looked up at me then resumed his task. He was one bold man. I had just caught him with another woman's feet in his lap, and he was acting as though he hadn't done anything remotely wrong.

"Can I help you?" he said, tossing a piece of junk mail into the trash bin.

"I'm going to put Traci's apartment in my name, but just temporarily, until she can get her credit together."

"I asked you to do that in the beginning," David said, not looking up at me.

"And at the time, I didn't want to do that. I didn't know Traci from a hole in the wall. And besides, I don't want jacked-up credit. I work hard to protect my credit."

"Just don't put her in the 'hood or nowhere near that fool she was with."

I ignored David's comment. Traci was going to end up living in an apartment that *she*, not *we* could afford, wherever it happened to be. "I have to stop by Honey's. I'll be back in a couple of hours," I lied.

David finally looked up from his task. He nodded, and I walked away. Traci had retreated to her room by the time I walked back into the living room. The decorative pillows were thrown to the floor on the side of the sofa near the sliding door to the deck. I shook my head and walked out. I thought about Claudia's advice as I walked to my car. The last thing I wanted to do was make love to a man who was on the verge of defying my trust right under my nose in my own home.

I couldn't get out of our neighborhood good before I was reaching for my cell phone. I pulled the car over at the nearest gas station and retrieved the neatly folded piece of paper Ziek had slipped me. He answered on the second ring. "Hey, it's me," I announced.

"What's up?" Ziek said.

"I need to talk."

"So do I," he said.

"Where do you want to meet?"

"Come to my place."

"Uh … I don't think that's a good idea."

"Destiny, you know me. I know you're a married woman. Have I ever disrespected you?"

I hesitated before answering. "No."

"I live in the same complex, just in the Berkeley building, eighteen-A."

I logged Ziek's phone number in my phone under the pseudo title, Counselor, and ripped up the piece of paper he had written his number on. I had leverage over David, and I couldn't afford to let him catch me with anything that looked remotely suspicious.

Ziek met me in the lobby of his building. He had changed his clothes from what he was wearing when I saw him at Antonio's Bar and Grill. He was now wearing a pair of gray sweatpants and a blue and gold University of Michigan hoodie.

"You look mighty comfy, don't you?" I said as I walked up to him.

"Hey, I'm chilling in my pad. I ordered some Chinese food. I'm waiting for them to deliver it."

"Oh, so you weren't down here waiting for me like the perfect gentleman?" I teased.

"Baby, yes I was," Ziek said, chuckling as he grabbed me and pulled me into him.

"Ziek … I'm married," I said, looking around, particularly at the front desk attendant.

"That's Mr. Murray. He's my dude. He ain't paying us no mind."

"Not out here, Ziek. I don't want to get caught."

"Okay. Okay," Ziek said, releasing his hold.

I followed Ziek to the elevator after he received the food that was just delivered. I pressed the button for the eighteenth floor. With his free hand, Ziek pulled me into him once again. "Ain't nobody but me and you, Destiny. Just me and you."

Before I knew it, we were engaged in a passionate kiss. With my eyes closed, I could see David's face, as if he were standing in the elevator with us. "I can't, Ziek. That's not what I came over here for," I said, backing away.

Being the gentleman he'd always been, Ziek obliged. "Okay. I hear you," he said as he held the elevator door open for me upon reaching our destination floor.

Ziek made my plate, poured me a glass of red wine, and placed both on the table in front of me. But just that quick, I was no longer hungry. My appetite had completely vanished. So I nibbled on the shrimp fried rice while Ziek devoured the food on his plate. Noticing I had barely touched my food, he inquired. "What's wrong?"

"Nothing. I'm good. Just wondering if I made a mistake by coming here."

"Nope. You made a mistake by marrying that fool you married," Ziek said with a sly grin.

"What makes you think that?" I asked, curious to know what he had to say.

"Come on, Destiny. David is from the streets just like me. He'll never totally leave the streets alone because he's been in the game too long. No matter how hard he tries, the streets will always be calling his name. And guess what? He'll go back every time, even if he strikes it rich one day."

"Well, he's working on that," I said defensively.

"Oh, really?"

"Yes. We're launching a real estate company together," I boasted. Although there was some time between Ziek and me; Ziek still knew me. Almost as well as David.

"Okay, I just have one question for you."

"Shoot," I said, taking a sip of red wine.

"Have you seen the business documents, like the incorporation files?"

"Well, uh—"

"I'm not tryna rain on your parade. Hey, I was locked up, so what did I expect you or any other woman to do? You had to do what you had to do. I'm not knocking you for going on with your life. But I am cautioning you to wise up. Know what's going on under your roof. Don't be taken by surprise after the you-know-what hits the fan."

I lowered my head. Ziek was on to something. I had not seen any of the business documents outside of the loan applications for properties we were contemplating purchasing, using my credit, of course.

"Look, Destiny. You got a good head on your shoulders; use it. Don't let that thing in your chest confuse you. That's one thing dudes like me and David love about you—you're not just gorgeous, you're smart, too. That's why I wanted you to take care of the arrangements for my mother's funeral when I was locked up."

I managed to muster a half-smile.

"And by the way, I was expecting you to be at the funeral, but now I know why you didn't show up."

"I wasn't married at that time. I didn't come because I would have felt out of place. Your family didn't know me, and I didn't know them. I just did what I needed to do and left you guys to grieve in peace."

"Well, I would have loved it if you were there. You should have known they were gonna let me out for my mama's funeral."

I didn't answer. I mean, I didn't want to go into a full-length discussion about should've, could've, would'ves. The fact remained that I didn't know Ziek's mother like that, nor his extended family, for that matter. I felt obligated to return the favor to Ziek for helping me out during my time of need. Therefore, I handled his mother's funeral arrangements as he requested.

Filling the awkward silence, Ziek added, "But hey, Destiny. It's all good. I'm the same ole Ziek who's been crazy about you from day one. Ain't nothing changed."

I smiled. The atmosphere was a little lighter, and the heaviness that I felt moments earlier had dissipated. I was no longer focused on David, Traci, or her ugly feet in his lap. In that moment, I was enjoying the attention Ziek was giving me. "I'm sorry. I thought I was doing the right thing."

"It's all good … it's all good," Ziek said, forcing a smile.

And in kind, I forced a smile as well.

"Come on, let's go watch a movie," Ziek said, grabbing the wine bottle and our now empty wine glasses.

Like David and Traci, Ziek and I sat cozied up on his sectional sofa watching one of his all-time favorite actors, Humphrey Bogart, in the movie, *Sabrina*. It was a first for me, but Ziek said he couldn't count the times he'd seen the flick. And with my head in Ziek's lap, he ran his long fingers through the strands of my hair, gently massaging my scalp between strokes. I closed my eyes and imagined my head was in David's lap, and it was *his* hands running through my hair, caressing and stroking my neck and shoulders. When his hands moved into my shirt, I didn't stop him. And when his hands unhooked my bra, I didn't stop him. Before I realized it, I was totally naked … and I still didn't stop Ziek. We made passionate love right there on his sofa, with the movie and soft music playing in the background. And when our lovemaking session was over, I jumped up as though David had walked in on us.

"What's wrong?" Ziek asked, trying to maintain his balance, as I had just pushed him off me.

"I can't believe I just did this!"

"Did what? Make love to me?"

"Yes," I said sorrowfully. "I'm a married woman, Ziek."

"You're an unhappily married woman, Destiny. There's a difference."

"Not in the sight of God."

"Destiny, don't do that."

"Do what?" I said, looking for my undergarments, which were strewn across the floor.

"Bring God into this. This is about you and me. We were meant to be. I know I was gone, but baby, I'm back."

"And you came back to a married woman."

"You can get a divorce."

"It's not that easy."

"I never said it was easy. But we can work on it."

"I'm sorry, Ziek."

"Sorry for what?"

"That I lured you into my mess. I'm confused. I don't know what I want. I love David, and I want my marriage to work."

Still naked, Ziek sat up on the sofa. "Why would you feel guilty about being with a man who loves you … who adores you … who would give his life for you?"

"Because I said, 'I do' to someone else," I said as I put my underwear and bra back on.

Ziek became silent. His eyes alternated between watching me put my clothes back on and his favorite actor on the television screen. Feeling guilty, I sat on the sofa next to him when I finished getting dressed.

"I didn't mean for this to happen tonight."

"Destiny, you can't fight this thing forever. You're fighting what you feel because I'm not the polished guy who goes to church. You're fighting me because I'm from the streets and might not fit in with your uppity family."

"Now wait a minute, Ziek. My family is not uppity. We have issues just like any other family."

"Okay. Okay. I won't go there. Look, I'm sort of messed up

right now. Let's just end the night on a good note," Ziek said, his voice cracking.

"Yeah, let's do that," I said, leaning over and giving Ziek a soft peck on the cheek. I could see him fighting back tears. "I'll let myself out," I said as I stood to leave.

I didn't get home until one o'clock in the morning. I took a quick shower, put on my nightgown, and slid into bed on the far left, opposite David. He let out a loud sigh. I pulled the covers up over me. He turned over and slowly moved toward me, placing his muscular arm over me as he pressed himself against my buttocks. I froze.

Chapter 24

Pendulums

SHE WORE CHEAP PERFUME, the kind you purchase from CVS or Walgreens. And she must have bathed in it this particular day. The smell invaded my nostrils and made me want to vomit. This was the third time we had gone looking for an apartment for Traci. Christmas was a little more than a week away, and I was determined that she wasn't going to spend Christmas with us … in our home, that is. I wanted her out of our house so badly that I stomached the unpleasant odor of her cheap perfume, her hoodrat vocabulary, and a volume of lies about her so-called brother-sister relationship with my husband as the three of us drove around the outskirts of Detroit, looking for Traci a place to live.

"Is this the address?" I said, looking up from the notepad I had scribbled the address on. The apartment accepted low-income residents, for which Traci qualified. Although it was a fairly new complex, I could tell Traci wasn't too fond of it—probably because of its distance. But I was making sure she was a good distance from our home.

"Yep. I know this area. This is it," David said, pointing to the sign that read Merigold Gardens.

"This is too far out," Traci blurted out from the back seat.

"What do you mean 'too far out'?" David said, looking at Traci through the rearview mirror.

"You know, from you guys," she responded with all manner of boldness.

"Why do you need to be close to us?" I said, looking at David.

"Well, I'm gonna be working with you guys, so it only makes sense that I live sort of close to where I work. Know what I mean?"

"Traci, this is not that far from us," David said, reading my nonverbal cue.

"Let's just go in and see the place, Traci. You might like it," I suggested.

Reluctantly, Traci agreed. David let us out in front of the leasing office and circled the lot until he found a parking spot. Finally taking her eyes off David, Traci opened the door to the leasing office, and we went in.

"Good afternoon, ladies," an older white woman said, greeting us. Seated, she reminded me of Ms. Garrett from the television show, *The Facts of Life*. Her reddish-brown hair was neatly pinned up, forming a thick mushroom-type ball.

"Good afternoon," Traci and I said in unison.

Still seated, the woman replied, "I'm Maureen. Maureen McGuire. But people, including my family and close friends, call me M&M for short."

"Oh, how cute. Like the candy?" Traci said, finding the parallelism quite amusing.

"Yes, like the candy," Maureen confirmed. "So how can I help you two ladies?"

"Um, we're looking for a one-bedroom," I said, holding up the magazine posting of the apartment layout I had ripped from the apartment guide.

"I need a two-bedroom. I need an office," Traci said.

"You can't afford a two-bedroom," I said, rolling my eyes.

Just then, David walked in.

"Well, how many people are going to be living in the unit?" Maureen said, a little confused by David's presence, as if we had the *Three's Company* type of thing going on.

"One. Just me," Traci said.

"Yes, just my little sister here," I said, pointing to Traci.

"Oh, okay. Well, we have two one-bedrooms available now, and one will be available in February. That one is nine-hundred and twelve square feet."

"Well, how many square feet are the apartments that are available now?" David asked.

"They're only eight-hundred and sixty square feet. But even though they're smaller, they have a little cove area that you can use for an office. The main difference between the two floor plans is that the larger one has an eat-in and dining room area and a walk-in closet. The smaller ones actually have better features, including stainless steel appliances," Maureen said, reaching into a folder on her desk to retrieve brochures for us.

"Can we have a tour?" David asked.

"Sure," Maureen said, finally getting up from her seat.

We took the tour of the apartment, and although it took some convincing, David and I were finally able to persuade Traci into going with the apartment at Merigold Gardens. I completed the residential application, received approval, signed the documents, and David left the security deposit and partial rent for the month, because Traci was moving in after the fifteenth of the month.

We moved Traci into her apartment four days before Christmas. With my job being done, as far as Traci was concerned, I could now focus on myself, my marriage, and finding a way to get rid of Ziek. He was beginning to exhibit signs of control and obsession, calling me throughout the day, paging me in the middle of the night, and showing up at my job unannounced. He was not the Ziek I used to know. In fact, his new bizarre behavior frightened me and was the reason I decided to call it quits with him, although I knew I had to disguise the breakaway under some other pretense.

I planned on stopping by Ziek's on my way back from the corporate Christmas party to deliver the news to him. But my plan was foiled by David's impromptu decision to attend the corporate function with me. Pretending I was out of sanitary napkins and needed to run to Walgreen's to get some, I drove over to Walgreen's and called Ziek on my cell phone.

"I can't stop by tonight," I said.

"Why not?" he inquired.

"Because David wants to come to the party with me."

"Tell him you need to stop by to see your aunt. You know, your father's sister. That way, you can drive separate cars," Ziek suggested.

"He's not gonna fall for it."

Ziek was silent.

"What's on your mind?" I made the mistake of asking.

"Do you really want to know, Destiny? Do you really want to know what's on my mind?"

I didn't respond.

"Well, I'mma tell you anyway. You got me looking like a fool. That's what's on my mind! You run over here when your husband's treating you like crap, then the minute you think you see some changed behavior, you go crawling back just to get the same treatment all over again. Then what do you do? Come running back to me, expecting me to help you heal. But guess what, Destiny ... I'm not gonna be your fool anymore."

"Ziek ..."

"Don't 'Ziek' me."

"But I told you from the jump I was married."

"And you acted like you were gonna leave that fool!"

"I never said I was going to leave my husband, Ziek. I always said that I wanted my marriage to work," I said, turning on the AC because, ironically, the heated conversation was making me hot.

"Marriage? Is that what you call it?" I didn't respond. "Let me ask you something, Destiny," he continued.

"What?" I said sarcastically.

"Are you the only one that believes you're in a marriage?

Your husband is out here in the streets doing his thing. He has businesses with other women, including his mama, and you don't know nothing about it. Are you *that* naïve to think you have a two-way street marriage?"

"Okay. I get it, Ziek. I get it! But that doesn't mean I can just abandon my vows and go tiptoeing through the tulips with you."

Ziek chuckled. "But you know what? It's my fault. Don't worry about it. I had a nice evening planned for us. I knew you'd have to go home at some point. But don't worry about me. You go on and enjoy your night."

Ziek hung up before I could respond. Although I knew I needed to end the affair with Ziek, I was taken aback by him actually dumping *me*. I slowly put the gear in drive and headed back to the house, without the sanitary napkins or my self-confidence.

Throughout the evening, I watched Dr. Jekyll mingle with my coworkers as if he were the perfect husband. He told his share of jokes, had his share of food and drinks, and thoroughly enjoyed the exquisite business discourse he engaged in with the CFO of the company. Heck, I even encouraged him to have a few more drinks, a deliberate attempt to stave off Mr. Hyde from appearing and taking center stage both at the function as well as at home. He was playing his role so well that I wanted to join him and parade around the banquet hall as the lucky Mrs. David Falls. But I couldn't. I kept replaying the earlier conversation between Ziek and me; his words stung.

Although I managed to fake a few laughs and smiles throughout the night, I spent the majority of the time thinking about how I was going to make changes in my life in the new year, which was quickly approaching.

Chapter 25

Family Reunion

NO DOUBT ABOUT IT, Honey was the glue that kept us all together. As she was transitioning, I knew things were getting ready to unravel. I could feel it in my spirit. Honey held on as long as she could, waiting for Albert Jr. to return home. He should have been ashamed of himself for showing up at the hospital smelling as though he had bathed in alcohol. But there he was, just as bold as ever, at Honey's hospital bedside, having returned home to Michigan after nearly eighteen years. The friction in the air between him and Roz was as thick as a brick. Roz, standing by Cliff, couldn't roll her eyes any harder when she saw him leaning over Honey's hospital bed, nearly about to fall over in it with her. When Roz had enough of the emotional show Albert Jr. was putting on, she let him have it.

"Maybe if you had brought your raggedy butt home over the years, you wouldn't be up in here crying crocodile tears over Mama."

"Oh, Roz, just shut up. Don't try to act like you were the perfect daughter because you weren't, not by far," Albert Jr. shot back.

"Nobody said anything about being perfect. But one thing I was, is present, something you can't say you were!"

Their back and forth was rather embarrassing, especially when hospital staff had to come in and intervene.

"Umm, excuse me, but this is the intensive care unit, and we ask family members to keep their voices to a minimum. Although the patients can't respond to you, they can hear you," a nurse said after overhearing the verbal spat between Auntie Roz and Albert Jr.

"Okay, we apologize," Cliff said, apologizing on Roz's behalf.

"We understand. We'll keep our voices down," Auntie Roz echoed.

When Albert Jr. left the room, I leaned over Honey's bed and laid my head next to hers, holding her hand as warm, salty tears ran down my face. We all knew for some time Honey didn't have long to live, but this was the moment *I* wasn't prepared to face, watching and waiting fearfully, shockingly, and with profound sadness as Honey's breathing became even more labored. And then, Honey took her last breath, ushering me into the worst day of my life—Honey was gone … gone forever.

"No, Mama! No, Mama! Don't leave me!" Roz begged, falling to her knees beside Honey's bed.

As they normally do when the alarm goes off, hospital staff came running into the room. I lifted my head and stood back so they could follow standard procedures. We all watched as they did their routine check—no pulse, no heartbeat, no other signs of life. After doing so, the doctor on call, Dr. Pinder, looked up at the clock on the wall and made the final call.

"Time of death is thirteen hundred-thirty-three."

The sound of his voice was penetrating, as if someone had driven a stake through my chest. I fell to the floor, landing on my knees. I began to wail, until I could feel the strain on my vocal cords.

"It's gonna be all right, Destiny," Auntie Donitra said as she rubbed my back in a circular motion.

I knew I wasn't the angel that Honey hoped I would be, but it had nothing to do with the love I had for Honey. Wiping my tears,

I glanced over at Shannon, wondering if, now, she would finally be the mother to me she had never been. But if her buried head in Craig's chest was any indication of how things would transpire in the future, I knew I would be on my own. And to add insult to injury, David was nowhere to be found during the most difficult time of my life.

After we said our individual farewells to Honey, we left the hospital for Honey's house. I decided to make a pit stop by my house first to see if I could catch up with David.

David's car wasn't in the driveway when I pulled up. I called him on my cell once again, but he still didn't answer. So as quickly as I pulled into the driveway, I pulled back out and headed for Honey's house.

I parked on the street in front of Honey's, buttoned up my coat, and prepared myself to brace the frigid temperature of a typical winter day in Michigan. I pulled my hood over my head, put on my leather gloves, and positioned my scarf over the lower half of my face before I got out of the car.

The tension between Albert Jr. and Roz had spilled over from the hospital to Honey's, as they were already arguing over who would get what when I walked in. The action stopped me in my tracks. I mean, after all, it wasn't like Honey had much, but it seemed insensitive and selfish for the two of them to be fighting over some outdated furniture and a few pennies, as Honey would have said if she could have witnessed.

"You're a thief, Roz!" Albert Jr. yelled right before guzzling down Hennessy straight from the bottle.

"And you're a murderer! How dare you think you can come up in here making demands!" Roz yelled as she stood toe to toe with him.

Cliff jumped up from the sofa and stood between Roz and

Albert Jr., protecting his wife, of course, but also giving Albert Jr. the look as though he'd peel his skull cap back if he so much as touched Roz. Frustrated, Albert Jr. threw the bottle of Hennessy across the room, hitting the bay window and shattering glass everywhere.

"Would you two just stop it," Aunt Vera pleaded as she paced back and forth. "Honey's pastor and members from her church are going to be here any minute, and that should be the last thing you want them to see ... y'all arguing just hours after Honey's closed her eyes."

We might have teased Aunt Vera and called her Blanche, but one thing was for certain, we did respect her. Albert Jr. and Aunt Roz didn't say another word. Poor Serita, Albert Jr.'s wife, got down on her hands and knees and started picking up the broken glass from the Hennessy bottle. She was as homely looking in person as she was in pictures. Although Albert Jr. stayed away for years, it didn't keep them from occasionally sending family pictures to Honey.

Serita was wearing a worn-out pair of jeans and a faded Hampton University sweatshirt. She wore almost no makeup, with the exception of a funny shade of pink lipstick and some lip gloss. Most of her hair was pinned up, except for a curly bang that covered most of her forehead. Their sons, Albert III and Jonathan, stood nearby, seemingly incensed by their father's behavior and embarrassed by their mother's. And detecting his sons' emotions, Albert Jr. stormed out of the house.

As I knew it would, the unraveling had begun. Our true family dynamics were shaky. As I'd always known, Honey kept our family together. Sure, we had problems, and lots of them, but we were still a family. I knew things were going to change, and they'd already begun to do so.

I left the quarreling family members to themselves and made my way to Honey's room, something I knew I'd have to do sooner or later. My eyes cased the room, looking at things Honey once used or even touched. Her lavender slippers were neatly placed on the side of the bed she slept on. Her Bible always stayed within her reach, on top of her bed as if it were her husband. The remote control was neatly placed on her nightstand. Her bed was neatly made, the way she had made it the day she collapsed and had to be rushed to the hospital. I took off my coat, threw it across the bed, and sat at the foot of it.

I still hadn't heard from David since I'd left him a message telling him I was heading to the hospital. I lay back and closed my eyes, my mind racing, thinking about a myriad of things, from my tumultuous marriage with David, a job that was becoming increasingly demanding, the desire to have a child, my estranged relationships with both my parents, and now, Honey's death. At some point, I dozed off. That is, until I felt someone shaking me.

A blurry figure stood over me. "Come on, let's go. It's almost ten o'clock," the voice said. It was David standing there, holding my coat.

Almost immediately, my sorrow turned into anger. "David, I've been calling you all day. Where have you been?"

"Destiny, don't question me. I told you a thousand times that if I don't answer your calls, it's because I'm busy," he said in an agitated tone.

"David, I'm tired. I have a splitting headache, and I don't feel like driving," I said, getting up.

"Then leave your car here. You can get it tomorrow."

"I'm not leaving my car here," I said, snatching my coat out of his hand.

He snatched the coat back from me. "What's your problem?"

"David, give me my coat. I'm not in the mood to argue with you. You know Honey just died, so give me a break," I said, holding my hands out for my coat.

"I'll be waiting outside," he said, throwing my coat at me and kicking my boots on his way out of the room.

As David exited, Shannon entered. "You know we have other guests out there, so—"

"Why aren't you more concerned about how I might be feeling right now, rather than being concerned about what the so-called guests can or cannot hear?" I said, cutting her off.

"Look, Destiny, whatever the two of you got going on, just know that issues between husband and wife should be handled behind closed doors, not in the company of others."

"I didn't ask for your unsolicited marital advice. Funny thing, you want to tell me how to be a wife, but you never knew how to be my mother," I said as I slipped my feet into my boots and walked past her. I wanted my comment to cut deep and wound her like she'd wounded me all my life.

On my way out, I said my goodbyes to Aunt Vera, Auntie Donitra and Auntie Lynn, leaving my car keys with Auntie Lynn, who could've used my car to get around anyhow. I also greeted some of the guests, mostly church members who I hadn't seen in what seemed like eons, as I made my way from Honey's room to the living room.

His attempt at an apology fell way too short. I didn't bother to respond. And then he followed with, "Look, I'm sorry about Honey and all, but, Destiny, you get to the point where you disrespect me, and it ain't cool."

"*I* disrespect *you*?" I said in astonishment.

"Yes, Destiny. You have a habit of disrespecting me."

"Okay. Okay, David. I disrespect you."

I saw the look in his eyes again, the same look he gave me right before he grabbed my hair when I first moved in with him. And before I could say another word, David swung on me, hitting me dead in the eye. The force of the blow was so hard that I let out a loud yelp. "Ouch! Oh, my goodness, you hit me, David!" I yelled.

"Yeah, 'cause you don't know how to close your mouth," he said, looking at me then back at the road.

"Claudia told me a long time ago to watch out for you, 'cause you beat women!"

"What?! What did you say?!" David demanded, now driving down the interstate like a maniac. I didn't respond. "See, I told you running your mouth with my mother was gonna get you in trouble."

The pain from the hit was beginning to intensify. I put my hand over my left eye and remained quiet for the remainder of the ride home.

I took a shower and went straight to bed when we got home. I assumed David was doing his usual nightly routine, counting his money in his office then catching up on the sports highlights on ESPN before going to bed. I prayed that it was one of the nights he fell asleep on the chaise in his office.

Some time in the wee hours of the morning, I felt David's body brush up against mine. I kept still, trying to appear sound asleep. But that didn't stop him. He pulled up my nightgown and tried to spread my legs apart with one hand. "Spread your legs."

I took a deep sigh, trying to pretend I was oblivious to what was going on.

"I said, spread your legs," he said, this time, with a little bass in his voice.

His hands moved from rubbing my inner thighs up to my groin area. I could feel the hairs on my arms and at the nape of my neck rise. I held my breath. Although I could stomach David feeling me up, I was in no mood to have sex with him. So when he began inserting his fingers inside me, I grabbed his hand. "David, please."

"Please, what?" he snapped, yanking his hand from my grasp.

"I'm not in the mood," I said, scooting over to the edge of the bed away from him.

"Look, Destiny, I'm your husband, and I ain't gonna beg you for no sex."

I didn't respond. I was hoping his ego would take over and he would just roll over, refusing to beg for sex, like he'd done on an occasion or two previously. But it was wishful thinking. David pulled me close to him by tugging on my nightgown, ripping it in the process. He forcefully rolled me over onto my back and lifted my gown, preparing to climb on top of me.

"You like it rough, I see," he said, spreading my legs open with his.

"David, please," I said, trying to pull away from him.

"You gonna give me what belongs to me, Destiny, and I don't care about how you feel. Now, come on," he said as he forced himself inside me with one push.

"David, please," I begged.

He didn't pay me any mind. He thrust his body back and forth, from side to side, and back and forth repeatedly. Finally, I just stopped resisting. I lay still and let him have his way with me, feeling like a rape victim as he stroked up and down for what seemed like an eternity. *How can he be enjoying this?*

Finally, David collapsed on top of me, having orgasmed, his body tremoring. His breathing was heavy and the weight from his body felt as though someone had dumped a pile of bricks on top of me. In that moment, he was *not* my husband; he was nothing more than an unknown rapist who had violated me in the most humiliating manner. I dared not move for fear of upsetting him, so I just lay there until he finally rolled off.

My eyes saw the clock hit five o'clock. I had not gotten an ounce of sleep. Between grieving over the loss of Honey and being struck and then raped by David, I was numb, void of any real emotion. I glanced over at him. He was still in a deep sleep. The thought of going into the kitchen, grabbing the sharpest butcher knife I could find, and stabbing him to death was not inconceivable. In that moment, I could clearly understand just how people committed crimes in the heat of passion—I was *that* angry with David.

Chapter 26

Goodbye, Honey

PULLING UP TO NEW Zion stirred up memories. I grew up going to this church. Living with Honey, going to church on Sundays was an absolute must. After I turned eighteen, Honey let up on the mandatory Sunday requirement. She did, however, continue to enforce the holy house rules she had established. These included curfews, no opposite-sex visits and overnight restrictions, secular music prohibition, no card games, and no alcohol consumption, just to name a few.

I focused my attention on the entrance and could see separate groups of people waiting to enter the church. A great cloud of witnesses, as they say. I leaned my head on Auntie Donitra's arm and watched as groups of people made their way through the church entrance and disappeared behind the closed doors. A steady stream of tears rolled down my cheeks and fell into my lap, onto my black lace dress. And as if she was in the limousine waiting with us, I could smell Honey, wearing her favorite perfume, Beautiful, by Lancome. I inhaled deeply, trying to breathe in more of the familiar scent, just a little more of Honey. I closed my eyes, and I could feel her around me, hearing her tell me everything was going to be all right.

"Come on, Destiny. It's time for us to go in," Auntie Donitra said, handing me Kleenex at the same time.

I sat up straight and wiped my eyes with the Kleenex I had taken from Auntie Donitra. A frigid wind crept into the limo when the driver opened the back door. From there, everything seemed to go in slow motion—exiting the limo, greeting guests, and walking into the sanctuary during the processional. I remembered seeing a lot of familiar faces, some giving me the *I feel your pain* stare, while others tried their best to comfort me with scriptures or other fancy sayings about death. But I was in a very dark place, slowly sinking and wondering, *Who would care if I died?* Would David? Shannon? Ed? Taking my life would have probably only best served my own selfish needs. I didn't want to go through the grieving process; the pain from the loss seemed insurmountable. Honey was my world. The easy way out would be to just die.

I managed to keep putting one foot in front of the other, making my way down the center isle to the casket, squeezing Toya's hand with each step. She'd met us in the vestibule area and walked in with the family.

"You can do this, Destiny. You can do it," Toya whispered in my ear.

I swallowed hard before taking the last two steps forward. There she was, lying there as though she was just enjoying another peaceful Saturday afternoon nap. She looked beautiful. Honey. My Honey. I walked up closer, examining her total appearance—from her rosy cheekbones down to the purple velvet shoes that matched the purple velvet dress she was wearing. The beautiful gold necklace I had bought Honey the previous Christmas hung around her neck. I managed to crack a smile. I leaned over and planted a soft, wet kiss on Honey's lips. "Goodbye, Honey, my new guardian angel. I'll always love you," I whispered.

As I turned to take my seat, I recognized the faces of two people I was not expecting to attend—Ed and Aunt Ann. Our eyes met. Aunt Ann waved, and Ed blew a kiss. I acknowledged their presence with a slight nod and took my seat on the second pew between Toya and Auntie Donitra.

Mr. I-Don't-Do-Funerals, also known as David Falls, was nowhere to be found. Throughout Honey's homegoing service, my mind raced with thoughts about leaving him. But leaving him meant leaving hopes and dreams of making a life with the man I fell in love with behind … at least temporarily. It also meant leaving a world of secrets, lies, pain, and abuse behind.

My thoughts were interrupted when the choir began to sing John P. Kee's, "He'll Welcome Me," one of Honey's all-time favorite songs. And strangely enough, instead of releasing a well of tears, a peace surrounded me, enveloping me like a newborn in a blanket. It was when I knew that, despite my grief, I would somehow make it. I had Honey's blood in me. I was a strong woman who, despite all odds, would overcome them all. I stood up and began to sing and clap along with the choir.

If Ed would have never showed his face, Honey's funeral would have gone off without a hitch. As the family was gathered in the vestibule of the church at the end of the service, Ed attempted to extend his condolences to Shannon.

"Why are you here?" Shannon snapped.

Embarrassed, Ed withdrew his extended hand and attempted to extend it to Craig instead.

"Don't try to shake his hand," Shannon barked at Ed.

"Shannon, I'm just trying to extend condolences to you," Ed said, speaking in a calm, even tone.

"We don't need your condolences. And neither does your daughter. *Your* daughter, Ed. Yeah, the one you left behind."

"Shannon, come on, this ain't the place for this," Auntie Lynn said, trying to diffuse the situation.

"Oh no? So just where is the place to confront the man who beat and abandoned me while I was carrying his child? A man who went on about his business without a care in the world!"

Shannon shouted, trying to move around Auntie Lynn to get in Ed's face.

By now, a crowd of spectators started to gather around, while groups of other spectators, watched from afar. Craig tried to lead Shannon out of the vestibule by grabbing her by the arm, but he wasn't quick enough—Shannon was able to maneuver her way around Auntie Lynn and land a hard slap on Ed's face.

Don't ask me how Ed was able to restrain himself. Perhaps it was his guilt, but whatever it was, it allowed him to take that slap without flinching.

"Come on, let's go," Auntie Donitra said, trying to usher the family out of the church.

I was headed to the limousine when Shannon yelled out to me, "So you had nothing to say to the man, huh, Destiny?"

"Don't answer," Auntie Donitra said, walking on the opposite side of me to shield me from Shannon, who was now trying to run up on me.

"No, let her come here so she can get what's coming to her, too," I said, now trying to move Auntie Donitra out of the way.

"Destiny, think about Honey. We just gave her a beautiful service, don't ruin it with arguing and fighting. This is Honey's day," Auntie Donitra pleaded. And it was the only thing that stopped me—Honey. I was ready to confront both people who had abandoned me. But since it was Honey's day, as Auntie Donitra had reminded, I just turned back around and continued to walk toward the limousine.

We buried Honey in Forest Lawn Cemetery. Although it was a clear, sunny day that first Saturday in March, it was barely twenty-five degrees outside. Behind the sunglasses I wore were red-stained eyes from crying, but also behind them was a disguised week-and-a-half-old black eye I'd received from the hands of the man I called "husband."

Chapter 27

It's Over

I COULDN'T BELIEVE HOW fast time had flown by. It was now going on six months since Honey's passing, and the heavy grief was just beginning to lessen. Things hadn't changed all that much between David and me. Sex for me was more out of obligation rather than enjoyment. I knew it and he knew it, too. Communication had become sparse between the two of us. Yes, we were growing apart, but neither of us knew just how to let go of our egos in order to fully commit to our marriage. I wasn't perfect, but, for the most part, I responded to the way I was being treated. David was cold, and I was tired of being rejected during the day but wanted at night. We essentially just played it by ear, day in, day out.

Awkward was our normal. That's why I didn't pay it any mind at first when I noticed David standing in the doorway of our bedroom one Friday morning. Slipping into my navy and white pin-striped pants suit, I pretended as though I didn't see him. But in my peripheral vision, I could see him as he stood watching—watching as though he had X-ray vision and could see right through me.

"What?" I finally said, turning to David.

He didn't flinch. Instead, he just changed his posture, shifting his weight onto his right side as he leaned against the doorway molding. In the middle of buttoning my jacket, I stopped, getting a good look at him. His eyes were dilated, a look I was all too familiar with. It was the look I saw right before he'd hit, slap, punch, or strangle me.

"What?" I repeated, trying to hide my trembling hands.

After waiting a few more moments, David asked me the one question I hoped I never had to answer. "Did you cheat on me?"

"Huh?" I said, trying to play dumb. *Cheat?* My stomach did a series of Olympic-styled summersaults.

"You heard me, Destiny. Did. You. Cheat. On. Me?"

"David, don't be ridiculous," I said, turning my back to him to resume my task. My entire body broke out in a cold sweat. I played it off by pretending I was hot. I started unbuttoning the jacket, and with one swipe, I wiped the sweat from my forehead.

"The streets talk, Destiny. Didn't I tell you that years ago?"

I didn't say anything. *Has Ziek sought revenge on me?* But even with trembling hands and legs, I was able to maintain my composure. "What did the streets tell you, David?" I challenged, looking back at David.

"Destiny, I ain't tryna play tit for tat with you. Did you sleep with Z?"

I was caught. Z was Ziek's street name. I let my nonverbal cues admit my guilt. A single tear escaped the crevice of my left eye. I looked away.

"Just what I thought," David said. And before I realized it, David slipped off one of his Nike slides and hurled it at me.

"I'm sorry," I said, ducking. "I'm so sorry, David," I pleaded. In that moment, I was unsure whether I was indeed sorry for the indiscretion or terrified of impending doom that David might exact on me.

"Yeah, you're sorry after you get caught! But were you sorry when you were lying up there with your legs spread open for another man?!"

"David, I'm sorry," I pleaded. "It just happened. I was hurt over a lot of stuff … the Traci situation. It just happened," I said, backing up as he slowly walked toward me.

Before I could say another word, he grabbed a lock of my hair and pulled it hard. "You got me out here looking like a straight fool in these streets!" he said, tightening his grip after uttering each word.

"David, please. Please. Let go of my hair," I begged as my knees folded, bringing me to the floor.

"Get up!"

"I can't," I said, trying to free the lock of my hair from his hold.

He pulled tighter. And just when I thought he was loosening his hold, I tried to make a run for it. But David was too quick. He grabbed my bra strap and pulled me backward. When I fell into him, he grabbed me around my neck and began choking me, hard. Staring into his eyes, I saw evil, hate, and bitterness, all while the breath of life was leaving my body.

"I should choke the life outta you right now!" he said, tightening his grip around my neck as he led me over to the bed. Unable to breathe or speak, I closed my eyes. *Am I going to die right here … right in the bedroom I've shared intimate moments with David?* Better yet, was I going to die at the hands of the man that vowed to protect me?

"Please, David. Please, stop," I begged as I tried to get away from his grip.

"No, you seem to like being on the bed, I see. You stay right there," he said as he pushed me onto the bed and sat on top of me.

"Please, David. Please. It was a mistake," I pleaded once again.

God must have heard my prayer because after enduring the grueling hate-laced speech of his, David got up. Looking down at me, he said, "Don't worry about packing your bags. I'm leaving this time."

"Oh, you can leave now, after we've spent all of my grandmother's money on your business ventures," I accused as I tried to sit up.

"Destiny, please. Look around this house. Half the money went on renovations to this house," David said as he made his way over to the armoire and flung its doors open.

"And the other half went into your business. You and Traci's business," I said.

David turned around and looked at me. He had that surprised look on his face. But he was way to bold to admit his guilt, so he just sucked his teeth as if he didn't care.

"Yeah. You didn't think I knew that you two opened a business together, did you?" I said, looking him dead in the eye.

"So what! She's like my sister," he said matter-of-factly. Even though he was trying to act as though he didn't care he'd been caught, I could tell he was shocked that I knew of his shiesty business dealings, evident by the rapid movements of his Adam's apple.

"That you sleep with," I blurted out. I was angry that David was using this one offense against me to bail out on our marriage, even though he had committed countless offenses. And I was angry at myself for creating the opportunity for him to do so.

David sucked his teeth again, turned back around, and began to grab his belongings out of the armoires.

After gaining a little strength and composure, I crawled to the head of the bed and watched David fling, sling, toss, and throw his clothes and other items into suitcases and duffle bags. I licked the salty taste from my lips. I didn't know if the stream of tears were the result of nearly being choked to death just moments earlier or from watching the man I called "husband" pack his life up right before me with the intention of leaving me for whatever or whoever. Was I wrong for the affair with Ziek? Oh, absolutely. Was I a physically and emotionally neglected wife? Oh, absolutely. But as sure as my name was Destiny Monique Thomas-Falls, my husband was leaving me, and the suitcases lined up by the bedroom door were proof.

I listened to the sound of David tussling with the suitcases and bags as he headed downstairs. I could hear the faint noise of him rumbling around in his office, gathering important papers, I assumed. He made a few trips back and forth to his jeep, packing it up. Finally, I heard the jeep's engine rev up. Slowly, I eased my sore body off the bed and tiptoed to the side window and peered out of it, watching David back out of the driveway and drive off. I fell to my knees.

"He left," I uttered between sobs.

"Who left?" the voice on the other end asked.

"D … Da …" I tried to get the words out, but they were unintelligible.

"I can't understand you, Destiny. Are you talking about David?"

"Yes," I said, now sobbing uncontrollably.

"Well, what happened?"

I paused as I attempted to get my emotions in check. Auntie Donitra waited patiently on the other end. I reached over and grabbed the box of Kleenex David always kept on his side of the bed and wiped my tears. When I was somewhat composed, I recounted the events that led up to David leaving.

"So what's your next move? Are you filing for divorce or are you fighting for your marriage?" Aunt Donitra said. She sounded like Hattie.

"What's there to fight for? He said he doesn't want to be with me."

"Did he say those exact words? 'Cause you know it's all about his ego at this point. Yeah, he's fuming over your infidelity, but his ego in the streets is what's really got his blood boiling. So again, did he say he wanted a divorce?"

My thoughts raced. I began to recount the entire exchange between David and me, trying to remember whether he did indeed say he wanted a divorce, even though I didn't think it mattered. The fact that he said he was leaving was devasting enough. In my mind, leaving me meant divorce was sure to follow.

With the cordless phone up to my ear, I ventured into the master bathroom. I looked in the large mirror that hung on the wall above the dual sink. A frazzled woman stared back at me. She was worn. She was tired. She was wounded. She was grieving. She was lost. She was lonely and isolated and had been for quite some time, even in her marriage. *Maybe this is what she needs.* And as strange as it seemed, I inhaled.

"Did you hear me?" Auntie Donitra asked. I had zoned out and hadn't heard what she said to me, causing her to repeat herself.

"Yeah, I heard you," I lied.

"Are you gonna be all right?"

"Yeah … I think."

"Well, I'll check on you later," Auntie Donitra said.

"I'll be fine, Auntie Don … just fine," I said. Yes, I know the words came out of my mouth, but did I truly believe what I'd said. That is a resounding no, as Honey would say.

Chapter 28

Till Death Do Us Part

THE DAY JASPER CUNNINGHAM came to Consumer Energy was the day when things turned around at the company. J.C., as he preferred to be called, was my direct manager. I enjoyed my work and truly began to see myself as a professional. Known as a no-nonsense type of guy, he was what they called a "numbers man," meaning, he was all about increasing revenue and profits while lowering costs and managing risks. Not to mention, he was also good looking. But I was moving past the era of hooking up with every man that looked my way. Besides, J.C. was a married man with three beautiful children.

J.C.'s voice resonated with power and authority, which made him well respected throughout the organization. Then there were times when you couldn't read the expression on his face, like the day Jerry McDonald was fired. No one knew it was coming until Jerry came storming out of J.C.'s office threatening to sue the company for age discrimination. There was no telling what J.C. was calling you into his office for, which is why my heart almost skipped a few beats when I received an email from him summoning me to his office for a three o'clock meeting one Friday afternoon.

Perfect. Just before the end of the day and the end of the week. Now, I know I'm gone. What could I have done wrong?

I nearly went blind watching the clock tick-tock away all

afternoon. Three o'clock was fast approaching, and I was growing increasingly nervous by the second. I tried to pass the time by listening to music as I rehearsed my parting speech in my head. But that's when I heard those familiar words from none other than my sweet Honey—*Don't be ridiculous, Destiny. Don't expect the worst; expect the best.* A gentle breeze hovered over me. There Honey was again. She was watching over me, no doubt. I took in a deep breath as I reflected on the past eight months. I had spent them working on myself, focusing my attention on work and school. It kept me from thinking about David and our failed marriage. It also kept me from thinking about Honey so much. If the best revenge was truly success, I was more determined than ever to see for myself.

I went to the restroom to freshen up and reapply my makeup before my meeting with J.C. I stepped back to get a look at myself in the full-length mirror. This time, the woman staring back at me had gained some strength. She didn't look frazzled and defeated as she had previously. This woman was rebuilding herself, and I was eminently proud of her. I winked at her and walked out of the restroom.

J.C. was leaning back in his chair when I walked into his office. "Come on in and have a seat," he said, pointing at the chairs directly in front of his desk.

"Close the door?" I asked.

"Yep. Close the door."

I closed the door and took a seat in the chair to the left of his desk.

"How's it going out there?" J.C. asked.

"It's going well," I said, tapping my fingers on my hips.

"Well, you know me. I'm gonna cut straight to the chase. As you know, I'm relatively new here, but I'm not new to the business nor to recognizing my people for their hard work."

I exhaled. This was going to be good. I could feel it.

"I recognize you've been putting extra time in. And you've

played a key role in helping the team reach its goals over the last few months. I want to personally commend you."

"Thank you," I said graciously, straightening my posture. Although I was flattered by the compliments, what J.C. and the team didn't know was that, yes, I was staying at the office late, but it was because, since David had left, I wanted to spend as much time as possible out of the house. I hated going to the quiet, empty house. Going home meant revisiting the torture and abuse that occurred there. And I couldn't go over to Honey's anymore because she was no longer living. We had cleaned the house out, and it sold right away. What I didn't know, however, was that after a while, I would grow accustomed to the silence and would welcome it. By the time I'd get home from work at nine or ten o'clock in the evening, there was nothing left for me to do but run a hot bath, light a candle, and meditate while my body soaked in the lathering suds and my troubles washed away.

"Did you hear me?"

"Excuse me?" I said, having zoned out momentarily.

"I'm promoting you to supervisor of Special Events."

"Me?" I said, pointing my finger inward.

"Yes, you. You deserve it."

"So what does this mean for me in terms of duties and responsibilities?"

"You'll still be reporting to me, but in more of a direct fashion. You'll have the three coordinators under you, who *you* will supervise. We have a few big events lined up for the remainder of the year, and I have confidence that you'll help us exceed client expectations."

"Thank you," I managed to utter. "Thank you. You don't know what this means to me."

"Well, you earned it. Congratulations," J.C. said, extending both of his hands, one to shake mine and the other to hand me a new name plaque for my desk—Destiny M. Crawford-Falls, Supervisor, Special Events.

I stood and extended my hands. "I don't know how to say thank you, J.C.," I said, inspecting the name plaque.

"Well, you just did."

"I'm ready. I'm ready for this."

"I have no doubt you are."

I had done it. I had achieved something on my own. I owned the promotion, and the feeling of pride that came with it belonged to me. For a moment, I had forgotten about my husband leaving me. And to be brutally honest, in that moment of exhilaration, I didn't even feel its sting. Something was happening on the inside, and it felt good ... real good.

I started not to answer my cell when it rang, but a phone call at two-thirty in the morning typically signified an emergency of some sort. So I reached over and answered my cell.

"Hello?" I answered in a groggy tone.

"Destiny?" the voice on the other end uttered. I immediately recognized the voice. It was Claudia. "Destiny, have you heard from David?" she continued, panting between breaths.

Didn't she get the memo? David and I are no longer together. He left me over some trash he heard in the streets. "David?" I asked, after I had composed myself a bit.

"Yes, girl. Your husband."

So she apparently didn't receive the memo. If her son didn't tell her, I wasn't going to. I played it off. "I haven't heard from him tonight."

"Well, I did. He's in the hospital!" Claudia said frantically.

"What hospital?"

"St. John, I think ... wait ... yeah, St. John," Claudia confirmed.

"Well, what's wrong with him?" I said, sitting up in the bed, fearing that he had met some unfortunate end in the streets.

"He's in excruciating pain. Gonna need emergency surgery

for stones, they say. I'm on my way over there now. Can you meet me there?"

"I ... I don't think I should go."

"Why? You're his wife, aren't you? You meet me up there, so you can call the shots. Don't you let no other woman decide what's best for your husband. David can act crazy, but he ain't no fool. Now, get on up and get yourself together, and I'll see you in a little while."

Claudia hung up before I could even respond. I knew the "other woman" she was referring to was Traci. I flung the covers off me and sprang into action. I was dressed in no time and on my way to the hospital.

My mind raced with panicked thoughts as I headed to the hospital. *What if he asks me to leave? What if he ignores me? What if Traci is pregnant and that's the real reason that he left?* I know they say fight for your man and your relationship, but the thought of encountering any of those scenarios was too frightening. I had thick skin, but it wasn't *that* thick. And when my cell phone rang again, my stomach churned. I hoped it wasn't Claudia following up with even more bad news.

Barely looking at the caller ID, I pressed talk and accepted the call. "Hello," I answered with slight trepidation.

"Des ..." he mumbled.

I paused. My breathing stopped for a moment. I hadn't heard his voice in months, not since he asked me to go into the basement and locate the title to his 1969 convertible Camaro. And that was only about a month and a half after he left. He was apparently selling the classic car to raise capital for the real estate company *we* were no longer building together. I remember holding the title in my hands, contemplating burning it in the fire pit out in the backyard. Just like our marriage went up in smoke, I wanted everything he attempted to do to go up in smoke as well. But I was no longer in that state. It was something about the sound of his voice that didn't make my stomach churn with disgust. I finally responded. "Yes."

"Hey … you sleep?"

"I was but not anymore," I said, intentionally leaving out the fact that I had already climbed out of my bed and was on my way to his rescue.

"Sorry to wake you. I'll make it quick," he uttered in a voice barely above a whisper.

"Okay. Go ahead," I said, putting my phone on mute to block out the sound of my car's engine.

"I'm in the hospital."

"Why? What's wrong?" I asked, trying to act oblivious.

"I'm in excruciating pain."

I was quiet. Of course, I cared about David. After all, he was still my husband. But he had done some disrespectful things to me. The thought of cursing him out and turning the car around in NASCAR fashion to head back home did cross my mind. But something was pulling and tugging at me. *Do I still love this man?*

David undoubtedly interpreted my nonresponse to mean I didn't care. "Well, I can see you don't really care. Sorry to be a bother."

Before I could respond, he hung up.

I spotted Claudia's car parked in a parking space for the disabled when I pulled into the Emergency Room parking lot. I paused before reaching for my purse and opening the car door. Within moments I would face whatever and whoever were behind the sliding glass doors of the hospital, and there was no going back. With one foot at a time, I stepped out of the car and onto the pavement. *You can do it, Destiny*, I repeated to myself as I walked toward the emergency room entrance. The cool breeze swept through my jogging suit. I could feel my ponytail swinging in the wind. Confidence was building with each stride I took, until finally, I stepped onto the entry mat and the double doors opened wide. And there she was, huddled up in a corner talking to someone on her cell phone. Traci—the pretend wife.

"There she is," Claudia's voice rang out. When I looked up, she was talking to the person I assumed was David's doctor and pointing at me.

"Are you Mrs. Falls?" the doctor asked as I approached.

"Um … yes," I said, somewhat hesitant.

"Are you sure?" the woman dressed in green scrubs asked with raised eyebrows.

"Yes, I'm sure. I am Mrs. David Falls."

"Well, I'm Dr. Brady. Do you mind following me to the consultation room?"

It sounded bad. *Consultation room? Why? For what?* But I didn't ask any questions, at least not out there. As Claudia and I followed Dr. Brady into a nearby room, I could see Traci slowly walking behind out of my peripheral vision. I didn't say a word, but I was already prepared for what I was about to do to her.

Dr. Brady opened the door to a small, quaint room. In it was a mini-sofa, a desk, and two chairs. An X-ray display machine hung on the wall behind the small desk. "Have a seat anywhere you like," Dr. Brady said. She attempted to close the door, but a hard pull from the outside swung the door wide open. "Excuse me. Can I help you?" Dr. Brady said with a surprised look on her face.

It was Traci standing on the opposite side of the door with all manner of boldness. "Is she with you?" Dr. Brady said, looking back at Claudia and me.

"No, she's not with us," I said as I leaned over to get a good look at Traci. Our eyes met.

"I'm his current girlfriend," Traci said, pulling on the doorknob a little harder.

Dr. Brady stood in front of the door to block Traci from entering the consultation room. "Excuse me, but that's the wife and that's the mother, and in the eyes of the law, they are considered next of kin before any girlfriend."

"But I came in with him," Traci yelled.

"You may have, but that doesn't give you any legal authority over his wife or his mother. Now, if you don't leave, I'm going to have to call security."

Before she released her hold on the doorknob and stormed off, Traci made sure to call me every expletive she could think of. But one thing for sure was that the cat was now out of the bag; Traci had admitted to being David's girlfriend. I wasn't sure when the godsister-slash-godbrother role turned into a sexual relationship, but it had. And I was sure it was long before she showed up at our house after being beaten by her so-called boyfriend. Perhaps he had found out that Traci and David had something going on, and he flipped out on Traci. Who knows? It was all one twisted mess, and I was certain that Claudia knew Traci and David's relationship was sexual in nature.

"Bye," I said, smiling and waving, purposely adding insult to injury.

"Whew! You wouldn't believe how many times this happens around here," Dr. Brady said as she closed the door and locked it.

"We're sorry about that," Claudia said. I could tell she felt sorry for Traci, but I didn't. She'd played the fake-godsister-slash-play-sister act, lived in my home, and was sleeping with my husband right under my nose. I had no sympathy for her. As a matter of fact, I was beginning to question why I'd gotten out of my comfortable bed to see about David. But my thoughts were interrupted when Dr. Brady closed the door and started speaking.

"Okay, now. Mr. Falls came in earlier tonight complaining of severe abdominal pains. Upon examination, he was found to have tenderness in both the left and right upper quadrant areas. He was taken for a CT scan and ultrasound, which revealed that he does have gallstones. And for that, he will need emergency surgery." She paused.

"What else?" I asked nervously.

"The CT scan also showed inflammation in his pancreas."

"Oh, my god! He doesn't have cancer, does he?" Claudia said, jumping up out of her seat. She was being extra, and I wasn't sure if the act was for me or the doctor.

"The scans didn't show any lesions, but inflammation of the pancreas is what we call pancreatitis, and he appears to have a severe case of it."

"So what does this all mean?" I asked.

"Well, we've paged a surgeon to come remove the gallbladder and stones, but he will have to be treated for the pancreatitis, and that's usually done in the ICU."

"ICU?" I asked as I rubbed my sodden palms back and forth along my thighs.

"Yes, but maybe only for a day or so. Afterward, he can move to a regular floor."

"What does this mean in the long term?" I asked.

"A few things. First, we're going to need to put a central line in."

"What's that?" Claudia said as she nervously rocked back and forth in her seat.

"It's just like an IV, but it's placed in a larger vein, either in the neck, chest, or groin area, so a patient can receive a larger amount of medication. And in Mr. Fall's case, with the amount of fluid and medication that he needs, we need a bigger vein. The veins in his arms are just not big enough. And for this procedure, we'll need you to provide informed consent, Mrs. Falls," she said, as she directed her attention to me.

I nodded. This was the first time I felt different about our dynamic—David's life was in *my* hands, not Claudia or Traci's. And if it came down to it, I had the decision to keep him on life support or take him off life support.

Dr. Brady continued. "Second, if Mr. Falls drinks alcohol, he's gonna have to stop. Immediately. I'm afraid this isn't going to be something that Mr. Falls is going to be able to recover from in a week or two. It's going to take him several weeks to get back on his feet. He will definitely need ongoing care after he's released," she added.

I was beginning to think I shouldn't have come to the hospital and should have let Traci continue to play the wife role. *Ongoing care?* Had I just set myself up to be on the hook for taking care of a sick man who had no previous loyalty to me? One thing I didn't want to be growing up was just like most of the women I grew up around. Honey. Shannon. Roz. Mrs. Deneen. And Deneen was one of our neighbors when we lived on McKinley Street. From our house, we could hear her husband cursing her out and whipping on her at all hours of the night. Sure he'd killed her the night before, we would always be surprised to see her emerge from the house the next day with black eyes, busted lips, and knots spread across her forehead. But Mrs. Deneen never left Kirk. Perhaps it was his smooth skin, curly hair, or his magic wand—his penis. Whatever it was, something kept Deneen there, and it wasn't children because they didn't have any. Then I thought about the old white lady I'd stumbled upon when I worked at Hudson's. She was taking care of her ailing husband who didn't treat her well in their marriage, either. I'm sure this wasn't God's intended design—for women to get dogged out but have to remain loyal to their abusers, rapists, unloving, and unfaithful husbands. *Couldn't have been.*

"For how long?" Claudia asked.

"As long as it takes him to get back on his feet. Maybe four to six weeks? Could be longer. Could be shorter."

Claudia looked over at me, but I kept my focus on Dr. Brady. I'm sure she wanted me to play the devoted wife and play loving caretaker after his mistress, who couldn't cook, fed him a bunch of garbage, brought him up to the hospital sick as a dog, and called me all kinds of F and B words because I wouldn't let her come into the consultation room with us. And Claudia didn't say a word. I was fuming on the inside, and Claudia had no clue. When she didn't hear the response she'd expected from me, Claudia sucked her teeth and left the room, slamming the door behind her.

"What's that about? Did I say something wrong?" Dr. Brady asked with a confused look on her face.

"Oh, never mind her. She gets worked up about everything. She'll be all right," I said, trying to downplay things.

"Well, I'm sort of glad she left. I wanted to ask you some other rather personal questions.

I swallowed hard. "Personal questions?" I asked, leaning forward.

Dr. Brady flipped through the chart and traced her fingers down the page until she apparently found what she was looking for. "Well, yes, sort of."

"Oh, okay," I said hesitantly.

"I'm concerned about some of your husband's other lab results."

"What do you mean?"

"Umm ... how do I say this? Has your husband, Mr. Falls, ever used IV drugs?"

"No ... no. Not to the best of my knowledge. I mean, I'm going to be honest with you, he used to sell drugs when he was younger, but I've never known him to *use* drugs. I've never even seen any paraphernalia in our home," I lied.

"Are you sure?"

"Doctor, whatever those lab tests show have to be from something else, not drug use."

"Oh, okay ... I asked you because oftentimes, patients are too embarrassed to admit it. But it's my strong suggestion, not now, but after Mr. Falls gets well, that you two sit down and have a frank discussion about his health."

"Is he dying?"

"No ... no," she said, shaking her head. "He's not dying, but he needs to stay on top of his health."

I buried my head in my hands. My head began to throb. The pressure of it all had finally caught up to me—Nettie, Ziek, Traci, David going to jail, Ziek going to jail, Honey's death, the affair with Ziek, David leaving me, Shannon and Ed's abandonment, all of it.

"Mrs. Falls." She paused. "Come on, Mrs. Falls. Your husband needs you. You have to get yourself together and be strong for him right now." She paused.

"I'm sorry. It's just a lot. I've been going through a lot," I said, gently massaging my temples.

"I understand. I understand," she said as she stood. "Come on, let's go see your husband."

"Okay," I said as I stood and attempted to compose myself before leaving the room. I readjusted my shirt and followed Dr. Brady out of the room.

"Let me warn you, though. He's heavily medicated, so I doubt he will be able to respond to you," Dr. Brady said as she turned the light off and closed the door as we exited.

Claudia was just walking back into the waiting area, apparently after having gone outside to smoke a cigarette. Together, we followed Dr. Brady to David's assigned examination room.

I wasn't prepared for what I saw when she pulled the curtain back. David was hooked up to every type of machine known to man it seemed. Both his blood pressure and heart rate were elevated. IVs were hanging everywhere. Slowly, I made my way over to the head of the bed. "David," I said in a somber tone. He moaned. "Shh ... don't try to talk. I'm here."

"Need you to provide consent, Mrs. Falls," Dr. Brady said, handing me a form to sign.

I skimmed over the form, signed it, and focused my attention back to David. "I'm here, babe," I said as I caressed his hands. That's when I noticed that he was still wearing his wedding band.

I spent the next two weeks going back and forth between work and the hospital until David was finally released. The ride home was a little awkward. Silence filled the air until finally, David spoke. "I want to apologize."

I kept driving. I wanted a full-fledged apology. I knew the circumstances weren't right to have that discussion right then, so I tried to change the subject. "What pharmacy do we need to stop by to get your prescriptions filled?"

"Walgreens on Main Street." He paused. "Destiny, I need to get this out. I—"

"How about we just get you feeling better and back on your feet," I said, cutting him off.

"I want us to start over," David said, ignoring my comment.

"I want you to mean it, David. Before you can be honest with me, you have to be honest with yourself."

"What are you tryna say?"

"Would you be coming home if you hadn't gotten sick?"

"Destiny, I missed you like crazy. There were so many nights I just wanted to come home. I missed you. Your smell. Your laugh. Your smile. I always told you there was something different about you. But you cheating on me was a hard blow. I never thought you could do it."

"Neither did I. But I was vulnerable."

"Look, I don't want to go down memory lane. Can we just start over?" David said.

"How about we just take it one day at a time, David? How does that sound?"

"Okay. I can get with that. One day at a time," David agreed.

And that was our agreement. One day at a time. No promises. No expectations.

Chapter 29

The Precursor

PERHAPS DAVID MEANT WHAT he said when we drove home from the hospital that day. Be it his incapacitation from the surgery or recovery from pancreatitis, I saw an immediate change in him. He wasn't coldhearted as he had been previously. Once he'd gotten up on his feet, there was no telling what I'd walk into when I'd come home from work. From the flowers, candy, and exquisite dinners, to the spontaneous weekend trips, David had become the husband I'd always imagined. The insecurity in me had me anticipating a slip up. But David was consistent. He was a changed man. He did more and wanted more. In fact, he stumped me for six one Saturday morning over breakfast when he said he wanted to start a family.

"Let's have a baby," he said between chews of bacon.

"Whoa! Where did that come from?" I replied, shocked by the suggestion, which came out of nowhere.

"Me. It's pretty quiet around here, wouldn't you say so?"

"David, I have school and work. When would I have time to take care of a baby?"

"You can quit your job. We have plenty of money, especially with the real estate business taking off. We're good. It's my job to take care of you and our child."

This certainly wasn't the David I had lived with previously. He was more like the David I met in the very beginning. Sensing my reservation, he lowered his head then shoved the rest of the bacon in his mouth. When I didn't readily respond, he followed up on his suggestion. "Look, Destiny, I know we've had a rocky road, but I'm ready for us to really settle down and be a family. You know?"

"I hear you, David. So what does that mean for Traci and Nettie and whoever else has been lurking in the background?"

"Done. I'm done. They're gone."

"You sure?"

"Are you sure *you're* ready? I mean, I ain't the only one who's stepped out."

"I'm not trying to make an excuse for myself, but when you step out on a person time and time again, it leaves them vulnerable."

"So that's all it was with Ziek, vulnerability?"

"Yes," I responded, taking a sip of orange juice without taking my eyes off David.

"Okay. Okay. Why don't we do this. Let's not bring the past up anymore. You forgive me, and I forgive you. Let's move on and start our family. It'll be different. We'll have something that will keep us connected forever."

There was that word "forever," again. I knew there was no such thing, but I played along. I wanted a baby, actually. But there was just one thing that seemed to be standing in our way—my infertility.

After some finagling, I was finally able to get an appointment with Dr. Parker, the infertility specialist my OB/GYN, Dr. Dorinda, had referred. I'd been seeing Dr. Dorinda since forever, so long that I no longer called her by her last name, which was Gunn. I called her by her first name, with her doctorate credentials, of course. And for the first time ever, David accompanied me to a doctor's visit.

"You're nervous, aren't you?" David asked as we walked into the office hand in hand.

"How did you know?"

"I can tell. Don't be nervous."

I knew my medical history was going to be discussed in front of David. I'd previously told him about the scarring from the chlamydia, which was part of the reason I had difficulty getting pregnant. But what made me nervous that day was the possibility that Dr. Parker could say there was no hope for me to get pregnant and have a baby.

"Dr. Chelsea Parker," a tall, fair-skinned African-American woman greeted as she extended her right hand. She was stunningly beautiful. In fact, if I saw her out in public, I would have thought her to be a model not a doctor. She was a cross between Iman, height wise, and Tyra Banks, complexion wise. Her long, thick eyelashes batted with every syllable she uttered.

"Destiny Falls, and this is my husband, David Falls."

"Nice to meet you two."

She looked us over in a mini-second then quickly focused her attention down at the new patient paperwork I had just completed. David and I sat down in the chairs that were directly in front of her glossy cherry wood desk.

"So you want to have a baby?"

"Yes, we do," David answered.

"And how about you, Mrs. Falls?" she said, noticing that David answered for us.

"Oh, yes, I do."

"Just making sure, 'cause your husband answered so quickly," she said, chuckling. "So now that we have that settled, we can go into a little history. Is that okay?"

"Sure," I said. David nodded this time.

"All right. This part helps me gather pertinent information that I use to create a treatment plan, if that's what it boils down to."

Before I took a few preliminary tests, which included extensive bloodwork drawing, we answered what seemed like a thousand questions. Based on Dr. Parker's initial assessment, I was likely the person suffering from infertility, because if what Claudia told me was true, David had gotten Nettie pregnant, even though she had lost the baby. When I completed the new patient paperwork, I didn't indicate that I had been pregnant before, and I was praying the subject didn't come up in the meeting with Dr. Parker. I already had one strike against me—Ziek—and having David now discover that I lied about being pregnant, would put a monkey wrench in our current plans to repair the marriage and start a family.

Even though I believed deep down that I was infertile, just hearing the confirmation from the specialist made me feel some kind of way for a moment. But with David by my side and being under the care of one of the best fertility doctors in the Midwest, I felt a little at ease for the first time in a very long time. Maybe, just maybe, some of my dreams were going to come to fruition after all.

Chapter 30

Lord, Help Me!

I WAITED ANXIOUSLY FOR the next three weeks for the results. Not only would I have some answers, but Dr. Parker would have a treatment plan for us to begin.

That morning, I didn't eat breakfast with David because I had to fast just in case Dr. Parker wanted to take another ultrasound or some other tests that required me to be in a fasted state. So I made David breakfast and sat at the table with him.

"You're kinda quiet this morning. Are you nervous again?" David asked before taking a sip of coffee.

"Umm … I don't know if nervous is the right word. I just wish you were coming with me," I said as I ran my fingers back and forth along the edge of the table.

"Me, too. But you know if I could get out of seeing these people, I would. One missed appointment and back to jail I go."

"I know. I know … you gotta do what you gotta do."

"I'll be at the next one, though. I promise. Do you want my mother to meet you there?"

"No. I'm good. She doesn't have to come. I'll be all right," I assured him. I had mixed feelings about Claudia. Her loyalty seemed questionable when it came to David and his women. And besides, her knowing my sensitive medical history was something I wasn't comfortable with.

"Go on and get yourself together. I'll clean up," he volunteered.

"Are you sure?" I had to ask. David had never volunteered to clean the kitchen.

"Yes, I got it. You go get ready."

I leaned over and gave David a quick peck on the lips. He pulled me toward him and we enjoyed a passionate kiss that led from me leaning over the table to lying on the table.

"You just had some last night," I said, my words muffled from the tongue down David was giving me.

"Yeah, but I want some more," David said as he spread my legs and stood between them.

There was no stopping David once he got started. So we made love right there in the kitchen, on the kitchen table, just minutes before I left for my doctor's appointment and he left for his parole check-in.

"Destiny Falls," a young male assistant announced.

I placed the magazine I was skimming through down on the coffee table in front of me. The young assistant, who had a feminine demeanor, anxiously waited for me in the doorway.

"Well, don't you look phenomenal in that black dress," he said as I approached.

"Thank you," I said.

"It's nice out today, ain't it?" the medical tech said, making light conversation.

"It is," I agreed.

"Just follow me to the back. Dr. Parker wants to meet with you in her office again today."

As we neared Dr. Parker's office, the young assistant stopped in his tracks. "Oh, excuse me. I didn't introduce myself. I'm Trey Jennings. I'm the newest tech here," he said enthusiastically.

"Nice to meet you, Trey," I said as I eased around him and entered Dr. Parker's office.

"She'll be right with you. There's coffee and water to your right, if you desire any."

"No, I'm fine," I said, taking a seat.

"And if you need anything else, just press that little silver button on the table right there, and someone will be right with you," he said, pointing at the wooden accent table in the corner.

I sat in Dr. Parker's office alone, admiring the office décor, including her framed degrees, awards, and featured articles on her practice, not to forget to mention, framed holiday pictures as well as pictures of her and her family at outings and on vacations. After nearly twenty minutes, Dr. Parker came scurrying into her office.

"Sorry about that. I just had one of my patients admitted to the hospital, and I was on the phone with the staff over there," Dr. Parker said, a bit out of breath and a little frazzled. "So how have you been?" she said as she plopped down in her cherry red leather office chair and began to flip through the charts and folders until she had finally located mine.

"It's been a cross between being anxious and being nervous, and sometimes, even being scared," I admitted.

Dr. Parker exhaled. "Well, you know when a couple is concerned about infertility, the first thing we do is try to confirm the diagnosis. And as you know from your last visit, it starts with a series of tests and multiple follow-up tests. If we can't confirm a cause, we can't confirm a true diagnosis. Sometimes, couples have a problem conceiving due to external factors, like stress, medication interference, or even certain medical problems like hypertension. In your case, however, we have determined that you have significant uterine scarring from what most likely came from an STD. Now, we can do something about that today, a procedure called a D & C, where we essentially scrape the scarring away. You would need some months to heal, but you could try to conceive afterward, and you'd probably have a good chance of conceiving right away. But that's under normal circumstances."

I wanted to leap out of my seat. While it was embarrassing to learn that an STD from years ago was ruining my chances of becoming a mother, there was still hope. But then her last statement resonated. "Normal circumstances? What do you mean, *normal* circumstances?" I said, clutching my purse.

"Well, that's if there's nothing else going on." She took a deep breath.

My ears felt hot. "So?"

Dr. Parker took another deep breath. "One of the tests we took, the test for the human immunodeficiency virus, or HIV, came back positive," she said, not looking directly at me but past me.

"Excuse me? It came back what?"

"It came back positive. I had it tested and retested, and it came back positive all three times. I'm sorry. I'm so sorry."

Asking about pregnancy was no longer my concern. I was worried about my life at this point. Tears began to flow. "So … So … Dr. Parker, you're telling me I have HIV?"

Dr. Parker nodded. She lowered her head and flipped through some more papers in the folders. "But everything else looks good. Now, I know the natural response is shock and fear, but there are a lot of advancements in HIV treatment, and it's no longer the death sentence it used to be."

"Oh, my god! Oh, my god!" I bellowed between sobs. "I hate my life. All my life, I've had nothing but pain. I just … I just wanna die," I said as I slid off the chair and onto the floor.

"Mrs. Falls, let me help you up," Dr. Parker said, having made her way over to me.

"I just want to die," I said, now sobbing uncontrollably.

"No, you don't. You have more to live for. You can still become a mother. I'll refer you to an excellent infectious disease specialist who will take good care of you. Once we know where you are in the disease progression, we can customize a treatment plan for you. You can still have a baby. I have a few patients that are HIV positive and are either pregnant now or have already delivered."

I heard what Dr. Parker was saying, but having a baby wasn't on my mind. Determining who had given me the deadly disease was. "Can I just be left alone for a while?" I said, looking up at her.

"No problem," she said as she leaned over and retrieved a box of Kleenex from her desk and sat it on the floor next to me. "You can take all the time you need. I'll be in the front. Just push the button over there on the wooden table when you're ready, and I'll come back in, so we can finish up."

After I heard the office door close, I buried my head in my hands and wept some more. *This has got to be a nightmare. This can't be my life. It's literally going from bad to worse.*

How I made it home without getting into an accident was because of nothing but the grace of God. I don't even remember stoplights, stop signs, street signs, or even other drivers, for that matter. All I could think about was how close my dream was to becoming a reality. I had a good job. Check. I was working toward my degree. Check. David and I were working on our marriage, and it looked hopeful. Check. We owned a home. Check. The only thing that was missing, it seemed, was a child. Neither of us were parents, so it would have been a joyous occasion for both of us. Now, with one positive test result, my world had literally turned upside down in what seemed like thirty seconds. Never in a million years did I think HIV would come knocking on my door.

David's truck wasn't in the driveway when I pulled up, and I was relieved. I wasn't ready to tell him that he needed to go get tested for HIV, when he would have been expecting me to tell him we had the greenlight to have a baby. The bitter taste of backwash made me make a mad rush for the bathroom as soon as I unlocked the front door.

As I sat on the bathroom floor with my back resting on the tub, my knees touching my chest, and my bare feet firmly planted on the cold ceramic tiles, the agonizing thought of dying and losing what I tried so hard to fight for flooded my mind like an endless river flowing from the Peruvian Andes through Brazil. Trying to make sense of my current situation, I reached for the roll of toilet paper I had placed on the floor next to me, wiping incessantly, trying to stop the steady stream. The pounding in my head brought me back to my knees, onto the folded bath towel I had placed on the floor. The pain felt emotionally gut wrenching, as though I was literally dying, my organs failing one by one. And then I could feel it coming up again. I rushed over to the toilet and let it all out again—yellow bile coming from my empty intestines as well as my liver. I opened my mouth wide, trying to release the yellowish-green poison that churned on the inside.

This cannot be happening. What am I going to do? Suddenly, I could hear Honey's voice. *When you don't know what else to do, just pray.* Well, I guess her words came in handy at a time like this, because I surely didn't know what else to do. I covered my face with the palms of my hands and tried to compose myself. I needed God to take away the throbbing in my chest that felt as though it was literally taking my breath away. Then I could see their faces again—Chris. Tommy. The Dom. Ziek. David. But which one? *Which one had infected me with this deadly disease?* More embarrassing was that I knew I had to deliver this devastating news to David, who I just couldn't face. There was no way he was staying with me, risking his health. So a baby and my marriage had gone out the window in the same moment and on the same day. I felt as though there was really nothing else for me to live for. I grasped the bottle of pills I had retrieved from the medicine cabinet only moments earlier.

"Oh, Lord, please help me!" I yelled out as I maintained a tight grip on the almost-full bottle of David's Oxycontin pills. Other than the sounds of my occasional sniffling and my recent outburst, the house seemed eerily quiet. I was all alone in the empty house, just me and the bottle of pills. I squeezed down on the cap, twisted it counter clockwise, and it popped off with relative ease. Slowly, I began to pour the little, oval-shaped white pills into the palm of my hand, leaving just a few in the bottle. And in that very moment, my life was literally in the palm of my hands. I tightly closed my hand, balling a tight fist. Then I slowly scooted up a little, so I could reach the full glass of water I had placed on the side of the double sink. With the pills still clenched in my left hand and the glass of water in my right hand, I closed my eyes and let out a deep sigh. A cool breeze swept across my face, like a light wind on a late August day. And one by one, the little white oval pills escaped through cracks and crevices in my semi-clutched hand and fell to the tiled floor. Somehow, my grip on the glass of water loosened, and it, too, fell onto the cold floor, glass shattering and water splashing all around me.

I sat in the same position, not moving, seemingly emotionally paralyzed. I recalled events that had transpired throughout the course of my life. And as far back as I could remember, I had looked for love in all the wrong places … and in all the wrong people. And that's when it hit me. None of the men I had been involved with could ever really give me the love I was craving on the inside. And as much as Honey loved me, even she couldn't satisfy my internal hunger for love. It was agape love, not eros love, I longed. It was unconditional love that required nothing from me, except submission. It was the love I was running from when I stopped praying and going to church. It was my first love—the love that comes only from God.

"God, I can't take it anymore," I sobbed. "I can't do this anymore by myself. I need you!"

As I had been taught as a child, I recited the Sinner's Prayer, repenting of my sins and giving my life back to Christ where it belonged. Afterward, I took a deep breath. Things just *had* to get better.

Blood oozed from the palm of my hand, and a burning and stinging sensation followed. My hand had slipped off the edge of the tub and onto a large piece of glass. Trying to control the blood flow, I grabbed a handful of tissue and balled my hand into a fist, making it serve as a makeshift tourniquet. I'd seen the technique applied on the many medical television programs I'd watched with Honey growing up. But this was real life, and the blood just soaked right through the tissue. I grabbed another handful of tissue and repeated the attempt. I was growing desperate, fearful I had created a bigger problem than anticipated. So with all my might, I placed my injured hand back on the edge of the tub and my left hand on the corner of the sink and lifted myself up. Carefully and with focused precision, I tiptoed through the glass but inadvertently stepped on a few pieces, cutting the soles on both feet. I hopped over to the linen closet and retrieved a large beach towel and spread it out on the floor.

With meticulous effort, I began to remove the particles of glass from the bottom of my feet, one by one, until I heard the faint sound of David rumbling around in our bedroom. I surveyed my surroundings; it was a mess. Glass, blood, water, and my fallen tears were all over the bathroom floor.

"Destiny," David called out.

"Wait. I'll be out in a second," I answered, trying to disguise my anxiety.

"Hey, babe. Gotta tell you something."

"Okay. In a minute. I'll be out in a minute," I answered.

"Well, hurry—" David stopped mid-sentence as he opened the bathroom door and surveyed the horrific scene. And as in slow motion, our eyes met. There was little, if anything, to be said. It looked like the typical *I'm trying to kill myself* scene—glass and blood everywhere. "Destiny! Destiny, what's wrong?! What's going on here?!" he yelled, looking at my wounds then at the mess I had made all over the floor.

"I wanted to die," I whispered.

"No. No. No, Destiny. Oh, my goodness!" David said as he tried to lift me off the floor.

My body was limp. My arms slumped over his back as he pulled me up from the floor and scooped me up like a newborn.

"Just put me down. I don't want to live like this," I said between sobs.

"Live like what?" David said as he carried me into our room and pulled back the comforter on the bed and laid me on it.

I didn't answer.

"Destiny, what's going on?" he continued, inspecting the cuts on my hands and feet.

"My life is a mess," I said, my eyes focused on the ceiling fan lights above.

"Okay, Destiny, you're scaring me. What's going on? You went to the doctor today. What did they say?" He paused. "We can't have a baby? Is that what they said?"

"No," I said, trying to sit up.

"Then, what?"

"She said … she said. She—"

"She said what?" David said, cutting me off.

"She said I have HIV."

"You got what?" David said, releasing his hold on my foot.

"HIV," I repeated.

"No way!"

I nodded. "I have the paperwork in my purse," I said, pointing to my purse, which I had laid on the chaise in our bedroom.

"Can't be," David said as he nervously combed his fingers through his hair. He paused for a moment before following up with, "You sure this ain't some kind of joke you're playing on me, Destiny?"

"You think I'd do all of this to play a joke?" I said, holding my hand up and pointing down at my feet.

"You got to get to a hospital, Destiny. Look at all this blood," he said as he tried to put pressure on my hand. "Wait. Hold your hand here while I go get a towel," David said, guiding my left hand over the cut on my right palm before going to retrieve a towel from the linen closet.

We did as much as we could to stop the blood and clean the wounds, removing visible glass from my soles and putting pressure on the cut on my right palm.

"Destiny, this doesn't look too good. I'm not convinced we did a good enough job," David said, inspecting the wounds.

"I don't feel the burning and stinging in my soles anymore. I think we did."

"Let's just go to the E.R. to be sure."

Although I didn't want to go to the hospital, I knew it was probably the safest thing to do. So with David's help, I changed my clothes, slid my feet into a pair of black flip-flops, and rode in David's vehicle to Saint John Hospital.

The sun's rays beamed between the openings in the blinds. Highlights from the previous night's sports were showing on ESPN, David's favorite channel. The moment my feet hit the floor, I was reminded of what had transpired the previous day. The soles of my feet were sore. I looked down at my bandaged feet. My mind rehearsed the conversation with Dr. Parker. *Don't cry, Destiny.* I fought back tears as I tiptoed over to the window and closed the blinds tighter, barricading darkness in the room. I was careful not to use my injured hand, which now had nineteen stiches in it.

I could hear the tingling sounds of silverware approaching. The bedroom door opened slowly. "I made you some breakfast," David said, walking toward me with the tray of food.

"I'm not hungry," I said as I got back into the bed.

"Destiny, you're gonna eat. You're not gonna lay here and go into depression."

"David, I'm just not hungry."

"Can you just at least eat a little? For me?" When I didn't respond, he added, "Please?"

I acquiesced, scooping a spoonful of scrambled eggs on a piece of toast and folding the bread in half. I took a few bites and washed it down with the glass of cranberry juice David had poured. "Here, I'm done," I said to David, so he could take the tray. He took the tray but didn't say anything. There was awkward silence. "Don't you have some questions?" I asked. It was as if we were both avoiding the difficult conversation that loomed over our heads for the last almost twenty-four hours.

"I mean, what do you want me to say? I'm leaving you?" David said, placing the tray on the dresser.

"Why not? What's keeping you with a person who has a deadly disease?"

"My vows," David responded.

His vows? I wanted to believe David, but he had showed me time and time again that his vows meant nothing to him. That he could bail out on me whenever. Only time would tell whether his word was indeed his bond. "But I don't want you to stay here because you feel sorry for me," I said.

"Of course, I feel some way and hate you have that diagnosis, but I'm not staying because I feel sorry for you; I'm staying because I *do* love you."

As much as I hated to utter the next sentence, I knew I had to; there was no getting around it. I took a deep breath and let it out. "You're gonna have to get tested."

"I mean, I guess. But let's cross that bridge when we get to it."

"We're there now, David," I said, forcing him to come to terms with reality.

David lowered his head. Then he walked over to me and

planted a soft kiss on my lips. Neither of us said a word; the look in our eyes spoke for us. We were both sorry for what we had done to each other and to ourselves. David picked the tray up from the dresser and carried it downstairs to the kitchen. I called out of work and slid back under the covers.

Chapter 31

The Help

I FILED FOR SHORT-TERM disability, under the guise of a severe asthma flare up. Truthfully, I hadn't had an asthma flare up since I was a teenager, but it was the excuse I gave J.C. Only Tribeca Healthcare, the administrator of our short-term disability benefits, knew the real reason—mental anguish.

Being on short-term disability allowed me to receive one hundred percent of my salary for the first twenty-six weeks. That was one of the best things about Consumer's Energy; they had great benefits. I had my share of lying in the bed crying, drowning myself in my sorrow. But that saga was beginning to wear me out, quite frankly. Neither excessive crying nor all the hugs and kisses David gave me could make the HIV go away. I missed working and was bored to death sitting at home watching paint chip away on the walls. At the same time, I knew I would be doing myself a disservice by trying to hide my pain through hard work. I realized it was time to do something—something different. I pulled out the business card of the psychiatrist Dr. Parker had referred. I dialed the number but hung up before someone could answer.

Call back. Something on the inside wouldn't let me walk away from the phone without calling back and making an appointment with Dr. Fleming. I redialed the number. This time, I waited for someone to answer and made the appointment for my first counseling session with Dr. Fleming.

It didn't take that long for me to become comfortable with Dr. Fleming. Unsuspecting of her race, because she looked white, I was surprised to learn that she was actually from South Africa, Kimberley, to be exact. We spent the first session introducing ourselves. But it would take several sessions to begin peeling back the layers of trauma that spanned over the course of my thirty-five years of living on this earth.

I made sure to lay my workout clothes out on the chaise the night before my sessions with Dr. Fleming, which was twice a week, Tuesdays and Fridays. It was my way of reminding David that I had an appointment. I could sense that we weren't really working on our marriage anymore. In fact, living together seemed like more of a convenience type of thing. Neither one of us really had the courage to admit it. Our days were spent building the real estate business, and our nights were spent doing the same thing—looking over invoices and researching business development opportunities and funding. I almost always went to sleep before David, except for the nights he wanted to have sex. We'd do our thing and David would go back downstairs into his office until the wee hours of the morning. Sometimes, he'd fall asleep on the chaise in his office. And whenever there was a social function to attend, I stayed home. I couldn't chance being seen out in public having fun while on disability. Being bound by these types of stipulations was driving me crazy. On the inside, I was craving my independence, my freedom.

I used David's truck to go to therapy this particular Tuesday because he had a business meeting and didn't want to appear too flashy driving his new BMW truck. By this time, Dr. Fleming had begun to delve into the history of my dysfunction. Next to Shonte, she was the only person who knew how to get me to fully open up. According to Dr. Fleming, my trauma stemmed from the moment Ed's sperm united with Shannon's egg.

"You didn't know that, did you?" Dr. Fleming said as she leaned forward.

"No, I didn't," I said.

"You were conceived by two young people who didn't quite know who they were at the time. Then you were nurtured in an environment of shame, blame, and abandonment. There was no way that type of toxic environment couldn't have had an effect on you."

"Well, I'm stuck on why Shannon gave me away. Why didn't she keep me? She went as far as to have me. So the deed was done."

"You were a constant reminder of her shame, Destiny."

"What about Ed? What was his excuse?"

"Well, from what you've shared, he ran away out of sheer fear."

"But what about me? Didn't I matter?"

"Men don't carry the seed or their children in their bellies; they carry their children on their backs and shoulders. For them, the critical bond takes place once the child is out of the womb."

I began to bawl, because for the first time ever, I recognized Honey's part in the absence of my father in my life. But there was no sense in getting angry with Honey. She was dead and gone. Be it her ignorance that kept Ed away, she tried her best to take good care of me, nonetheless.

Dr. Fleming was beginning to look like a blurry figure sitting across from me. I grabbed Kleenex from the box sitting on the middle of the round table where we sat during our sessions.

"Do you see how it works? None of us came here to be perfect; we came here to learn and grow. And we can't do either without pain. Pain begets love."

And that's when all the bible verses started coming to my remembrance. John 3:16—"For God so loved the world that He gave his only begotten son." Psalms 34:186—"The Lord is close to the brokenhearted; He rescues those whose spirits are crushed." Romans 8:18—"For I consider that the sufferings of this present time are not worth comparing with the glory that is to be revealed to us." And my all-time favorite—Hebrews 12:11—"For the moment all discipline seems painful rather than pleasant, but later it yields the peaceful fruit of righteousness to those who have been trained by it."

By the time the session was over, I knew what I needed to do about my relationships with Shannon, Ed, and David. I was also beginning to have a different perspective about my HIV status. I kept rehearsing Dr. Fleming's words as I drove home. *Destiny, you're cheating yourself out of your own freedom. Your name is Destiny for a reason—you have a great destiny!*

I listened to the gospel station as I drove home. It brought back memories of my youth. I found myself singing along with each and every song. I had found my voice, both literally and physically.

Chapter 32

All For My Good

A BEAUTIFUL BOUQUET OF colorful flowers greeted me when I walked into my office. I leaned over to smell them. The aroma traveled up my nostrils, and I closed my eyes, trying to savor the freshness. Being happy to be back at work was an understatement. Six weeks had passed quickly. I was still seeing Dr. Fleming, but only once every two weeks, on Fridays.

I powered up my computer, anticipating a gazillion emails to sort and voicemails to listen to. I didn't realize J.C. was in his office until he walked up on me.

"Welcome back," he said with a gigantic smile.

"Thank you. And thanks for the beautiful flowers," I said.

"We're just glad to have you back. I know you have a ton of stuff to go through, but before you get into that, I'd like to speak with you in my office."

"Sure," I said as I reached for the pile of mail that was neatly tucked into the cubby space and placed it on my desk.

J.C. turned to head for his office and I followed, closing the door behind us.

"Before we get into what I want to talk to you about, I need to ask some rather personal questions, and I hope you don't think I'm probing," J.C. said as he walked over to his desk and sat down.

I unfolded my hands and rubbed them on the sides of the

chair I was sitting in. *What personal questions does he want to ask me?* "Oh sure," I said, trying to disguise my nervousness.

"Before you went on leave, I think I remember you mentioning that you and your husband had a brief separation but were back together, am I correct?"

I exhaled. Whew! That was an easy enough question to answer. "Yeah, but that was then." Without going into details, I added clarification. "I think we're going to be going our separate ways," I said.

"As in divorcing?"

I nodded.

"As much as I'm sorry to hear that, I'm also happy to hear it. And please don't take it the wrong way," J.C. said, chuckling. Sensing the puzzled look on my face, he continued. "Consumer's Energy is currently working on a major international deal. We need a team of about three people to go to Dubai and stay until this deal is finalized."

"So what do you need from me?" I said, straightening my posture in the chair.

"This is where you come in. This project needs your skills. You have the organization and coordination skills to get this project off the ground."

"Me?" I said, pointing at myself.

"Yes, you."

"I mean, I've always wanted to visit Dubai. It's on my bucket list. I—"

"Whoa, Destiny. Wait," J.C. said, interrupting the whole spiel I was about to dive into. "This won't be just a visit, like a four-or-five-day trip. It won't even be a two-or-three-week type of thing. We need this team to be there for a minimum of eighteen months."

"A year and a half?" I asked, making sure I'd heard him correctly.

"Now, I understand if you're unable. I know you're just coming back from sick leave. But I think this opportunity will be good for you. You know, good for your career."

"Say no more. I'm in," I said. Something on the inside just felt right. Perfect timing. It would make my upcoming conversation with David much easier. I now had a way out, other than going into the real reasons why.

"Are you sure?"

"I'm positive." Before I realized it, I had uttered the word. Positive. And it didn't hurt anymore. Hearing or saying the word "positive" no longer stung.

"Okay. Then it's a wrap. I'll get the logistics worked out."

"How soon is this all supposed to take place?" I asked, prepared to start jotting down dates on the notepad in my lap.

J.C. bit his bottom lip. "You don't have much time, just under two weeks. Thirteen days to be exact. I know it's a narrow deadline, but I purposely held off assigning someone to the project, with the hope that you'd come back. So do you think the deadline is feasible?"

"I can make it happen," I said, even though I knew preparing to go away for eighteen months wasn't going to be smooth.

"Now, I'll be going over there with you guys initially. But I'll only be over there for three weeks. We'll get the project off the ground good, then me and some of the other executives will head back to the States. I'll probably come over once every quarter, but you guys will be in charge of the day-to-day workings of the project."

J.C. spent time going over the project and giving me the opportunity to ask questions. With less than two weeks to prepare for the big move, J.C. agreed to let me work half days up until my departure for Dubai, so I could handle the necessary essentials.

"What do you think?"

"Sounds good to me," I said as I stood to leave. "Thanks for thinking about me, J.C. I needed this," I added as I opened his office door.

"No, thank you, Destiny. I'm happy you are in a position to take advantage of this wonderful opportunity. Oh, I don't mean I'm happy about your marriage not—"

"Don't worry about it. It was a long time coming," I assured. It sounded awkward, but I knew what he meant.

I almost leaped to the ceiling when I left J.C.'s office. The only thing that kept me from breaking out in a dance was Lilly, the plant lady, who had stopped by to water the plants in J.C.'s office.

Surprisingly, David was home when I got home that afternoon. I had picked up dinner from Peking Kitchen—sesame chicken, vegetable fried rice, and spring rolls. There was no use in setting up a so-called perfect environment to tell David the news I was about to drop on him. I put my briefcase by the dining room table, where we sometimes ate, and I went into the kitchen to make our plates.

"I have the fundraiser at the Hyatt tonight, remember?" David said when he saw me making his plate.

"Oh, yeah, I forgot," I said, putting the food on his plate back into respective containers.

"I don't want to eat now because I won't be hungry later. But that chicken sure smells good," David said, inhaling the savory smell of the food.

"No problem," I said nonchalantly.

"You okay, Destiny?" David said quizzically.

"I'm fine," I said without looking at him.

"Are you sure?"

"I'm fine, David."

"So how was your first day back at work?"

"Fantastic. It was fantastic. I got put on a special assignment."

"Well, come on. I want to hear all about it," David said, taking my plate out of my hand. I followed him into the dining room and sat down in front of the space where he'd placed my plate. "So tell me all about it," he said.

"Well, the project is not here," I said, unfolding my napkin and placing it in my lap.

"So where is it?"

"In Dubai."

"That's great. That's on your bucket list, right?"

"Yes, it is." I paused.

"Finish. Finish telling me about the project, Destiny."

I leaned over, opened my briefcase, and retrieved the black folder and placed it on the table in front of David.

"What's this?" David said, examining the folder. The words Law Offices of Wilson & James were displayed in gold lettering on the front of the folder.

"Open it," I said as I picked up my fork and dug into the rice to begin to enjoy my meal. I looked at David out of the corner of my eyes as he opened the folder and meticulously read over the documents.

"You want a divorce?" David said as he slumped back in his seat.

"No, David, *you* want a divorce."

Large pebbles formed on David's forehead. He wiped them off with his left hand. "Where did you get that from? I never said that!"

"Remember the day you let me use your truck a few weeks back?" David nodded. "Well, you left some paperwork behind."

David scratched is head. "Paperwork? What paperwork?"

"When were you planning on telling me about the condo downtown? And of course, I don't have to guess who's living in it," I said, dropping my fork.

The color in David's face disappeared. He looked like he'd seen a ghost. I could have bought him for a quarter. "Destiny. It was already in the works before we got back together."

"No need to explain. You now have your freedom to do as you please. I won't be around. I'll be in Dubai for the next year and a half. Who knows? I just might stay if I like it there." I felt a burden lift off me as I uttered the last word of that sentence. I felt a shift in the atmosphere.

When Aunt Ann learned I was moving to Dubai, she volunteered to throw me a going away party at her house. Everyone seemed to be happy for me, even Shannon, which was surprising. The set up and décor were flashy, complementary to Aunt Ann's taste. Tents and tables and chairs were set up in the back yard, with each table decorated with peach and white ornaments. A fancy centerpiece sat in the middle of each table.

When it was time to give my speech, I stood. I felt light and free. I thanked everyone for attending, the lovely gifts that were given, as well as everyone's sincere well wishes. To my amazement, Ed and Shannon were able to be in the same space without spewing words of hate or exchanging hateful facial expressions. Shonte, Auntie Lynn, and Auntie Donitra all surprised me and traveled to attend my going away party.

In the days that followed, I made it my business to personally say my goodbyes to a few folks. I left Shannon with a special phone, so she could make international calls to me free of charge. Toya and Boris were engaged and expecting their first child, a girl. Toya promised to name her Destiny, after me. I knew I wouldn't be there for their baby's birth, so I gave Toya my gift before I left.

"I'm gonna miss you like crazy, girl," Toya said between sobs as we embraced in the living room of Toya and Boris's new townhome.

"Me, too," I said. "But please stop crying. I gotta go see other people tonight, and you're gonna have me walking around looking like a zombie with my makeup smeared all over my face."

"Okay," Toya said, trying to compose herself.

We embraced one last time before I headed to Claudia's. I

knew she felt some way about me giving divorce papers to David. But she still wanted to see me before I left for Dubai.

I spotted David's car in Claudia's driveway as I slowly drove up the street. *Is this a setup?*

Loud sirens coming from behind grew closer and closer. As I glanced in my rearview mirror, I could see flashing lights of police cars approaching, so I pulled over. One. Two. Three. Four. Five. Six. Six police cars and a fire rescue truck sped past me. My stomach turned flips when I realized they were stopping in front of Claudia's house. I put the gear in drive and sped up to the house.

I jumped out of the car so fast after I'd pulled up to Claudia's that I barely remember putting the gear in park and turning the ignition off. I ran past a few police officers, who unsuccessfully tried to block me from entering the house. But I shot past them and bolted into the house. And that's where I found David, sprawled out, face down on the living room floor. Blood oozed from his body onto the plush gray carpet. "David!" I screamed.

A stocky police officer pushed me back. "Sorry, ma'am, you can't go near him. This is a crime scene."

"David! David! David!" I yelled frantically. But his limp body didn't move. I caught a glimpse of Claudia standing over in the corner, near the kitchen, in a daze. "What happened?! What happened to him?!" I screamed.

"She shot him," Claudia said in a low voice.

"Who? Who shot him?!" I screamed, frantically looking around.

Before Claudia could answer, two police officers descended the staircase, escorting a handcuffed Traci out of the house. As she was being led out, she repeatedly yelled, "He gave me AIDS! He gave me AIDS!"

My legs buckled. My mind immediately went back to the conversation I'd had with Dr. Brady when David was in the hospital. And that's when I realized that David knew all along that he had HIV.

I fell to my knees, watching as the medics tried desperately to save David's life. In that moment, I had to decide whether David needed my forgiveness or my prayers. I did the only thing I knew to do—pray. *Oh, Lord, spare his life. I'm begging you. Give him another chance!*

Chapter 33

Clear Blue Skies

AS THE 737 ASCENDED above the clouds, and the busyness of Downtown Detroit disappeared, I exhaled. Symbolically, I was leaving my shame, blame, hurt, anger, and disappointment behind as well. I owed no more explanations or apologies, not even about my HIV status. My numbers were intact, and Dr. Boyd, my infectious disease specialist, bet his life that if I followed the regimen he'd put me on, I would remain healthy and undetectable.

I was off to Dubai, on a new journey of life and discovery. Flying at 33,000 feet, the skies opened. They were expansive, clear, and blue just like the possibilities in my future. The sun beamed through the window where I sat. I smiled and closed my eyes. After recommitting my life to God, I finally understood the true meaning of love. Yeah, things were going to be fine, just fine. *My life belongs to Him.*

Thank you for reading
From Pain to Love: My Heart Belongs to Him
If you enjoyed this book, please leave an
online review to help spread the word.

CONNECT WITH KEA SIMONE

Website: www.keasimone.com
Instagram: @author.kea.simone
Facebook: facebook.com/mskeasimone
YouTube: Kea Simone

CPSIA information can be obtained
at www.ICGtesting.com
Printed in the USA
LVHW042357170920
666435LV00001B/214

9 780578 670232